Echoes From The Swamp

by

Max R. Ibach

Double Dragon Press

An Imprint of
Double Dragon Publishing
PO Box 54016
1-5762 Highway 7 East
Markham, Ontario L3P 7Y4 Canada
http://www.double-dragon-ebooks.com
http://www.double-dragon-publishing.com

ISBN-13: 978-1973770947
ISBN-10: 1973770946

A DDP First Edition July 19th, 2017
Book Layout and
Cover Art by Deron Douglas

PROLOGUE

Two men sit facing each other across a short expanse of dark oak desk in a secondary office of an East Texas funeral home. The older of the two is an attorney, Gordon Beaudreau. He is bespectacled and wears a three-piece, charcoal gray suit with a faint blue pin stripe. The suit accents his eyes that seem the color of new steel.

Sitting across the desk is Neal Marston, the 28-year-old heir to the estate being settled. His clothing is less formal: faded jeans, a short sleeved mint-green collared T-shirt with a dog-tag chain peeking from beneath. The attorney pushes a stack of documents across the table to the younger man who signs where indicated without really inspecting them.

The lawyer views the signature and asks for some form of identification. His voice carries a faintly French accent that hints of Cajun country. Neal produces a military ID card. Beaudreau compares the card signature block to the signed documents. He then checks the photo before he nods.

Gordon Boudreaux separates the client copies before he shuffles the remaining papers into their original folder. The folder then goes into a slim-line briefcase. From a lid pocket of the briefcase, he produces a sealed #10 envelope. He slides both the duplicate documents and the envelope across the desk to the client.

"These are yours," he offers. "I have the balance of your inheritance in my car. We have been holding certain items since the woman entrusted with their keeping became ill and transferred them into our custody." The two men leave the room through an outer door that emerges into the parking lot. "I gather you were not in close contact with your mother?"

"No, I was given up for adoption at a very young age. I never knew her."

"Too bad," the lawyer offers. "She was quite a woman. Do you know anything about her?"

"Only her name and that only recently," Marston informs. "Your secretary told me that she was ill and in a hospice. I left immediately to go to her, but by the time I arrived, she had died."

The attorney stops behind a white Lincoln Town Car with a beige interior. He opens the trunk. They stand looking down at an unfinished oak chest. The container is impressively bound with hammered brass straps and round head rivets. Two massive hammered brass hinges hold the curved lid is held in place. A padlock secures a matching hasp. Emblazoned across the top of the serpentine shaped lid, deeply carved into the wood in Old English letter style, is the solitary word *Mannheim*. The chest appears to be quite old. The exterior bears scattered dark spots, the result of moisture contact with unfinished oak. Here and there, the scars of heavy use track irregularly across its surface.

Boudreaux announces, "This chest is yours. Where is your car?"

Neal indicates the red and white pick up truck with a white camper shell parked two spaces to their left. Each man grasps an ornate brass handle at opposite ends of the chest. They proceed to lift the sturdy container from the trunk. The attorney sags forward under the unaccustomed weight; it is amazingly heavy for its size. Once out of the trunk, they move in rapid short steps to the rear of the truck. Neal unlocks the camper shell, and with the tailgate lowered, they lift the chest into the truck-bed. The brass lock securing the hasp displays the initials U.S. deeply etched in the side.

"The key is in the other chest in my car." Boudreaux offers, as he returns to the Lincoln.

Neal places his hands on the oaken chest. A sense of great loss courses through his body as he stands in contact with the only family legacy he has ever known. Tears stream down both cheeks to be wiped away on a naked forearm. It is one thing to not know who your parents are, but quite another to never know any of your own people. The absence of relatives makes the world seem hollow.

Perhaps now I can fill in some of the blanks.

Boudreaux returns with a miniature chest the size of a shoebox, identical in shape and structure to the larger chest. The attorney also carries a bronze urn in an open topped cardboard box. A wide blue rubber band secures the lid of the small chest although there is an empty hasp for a padlock. The attorney hands both items to Neal.

"I believe that concludes our business," the lawyer offers. "If later there are further questions, you may reach me here." He hands the young man a simple cream-colored business card engraved with the name Gordon Boudreaux and a phone number. The attorney extends his right hand. "I was privileged to know both your parents. I regret that you did not."

They shake hands before Boudreaux climbs into his car, slides it in gear and glides out of the parking lot. Neal places the cardboard box containing the bronze canister bearing the cremains of his mother in the cab before he returns to the rear of the truck. He removes a bone-handled pocketknife from a front pants pocket before sitting on the tailgate.

Using the knife, he slits the end of the envelope the attorney gave him. Inside is a certified check in the amount of $236,000.26. He stares at the cashier's check, much larger than any he's ever seen, bearing his name. He glances around to see who might be coming to claim it from him. When nobody appears, he returns the check to the envelope, folds it in half and places it in his shirt pocket.

He picks up the smaller chest, places it across his lap, removes the rubber band and opens the curved lid. Inside is a brass key in a red plastic holder and a lock of golden hair in a zip-lock plastic bag. Underneath rests a bundle of envelopes tied both ways with a pink ribbon. Another solitary envelope lies atop the pile, the flap secured by a glob of red sealing wax impressed with the letter 'S'.

Neal slits the sealed envelop at the end before blowing into the opening to expand the cavity. Within is a single sheet of rich looking, cream-colored bond paper. He unfolds the document and stares at a letter inscribed by an incredibly delicate hand using an ink pen, the kind rarely seen anymore. The letter reads:

> My beloved son,
> I have lived with the knowledge that I gave you up for adoption at the age of two months and that you will not remember me. For this act, I remain eternally regretful; I beg

your forgiveness. That action was extremely difficult for me. Please do not take that statement lightly. I gave you up for the very best of reasons: your health and well-being.

You are my only heir. I have but one request of you. I ask that you take my ashes and scatter them on the Hundred-&-Forty-Foot-Hill above Oliver Marsh near where the town of Amerada once stood. There will be a stone tablet there to mark my final resting place. You will recognize the place by the inscription on the last page of the last entry in my journal.

Your inheritance will accompany this letter in the form of money and a chest containing a manuscript that tells the story of your father and some other very special people. I hope you enjoy reading about our lives as much as we enjoyed living them.

~Mom's name or initial? S or Sarah

The tears arrive again as he removes the key from its container. He opens the lock securing the large chest. Inside are thin cardboard boxes stacked one atop the other. Each is of a size to contain a ream of paper. He opens the top box and stares numbly at the first page.

The writing is calligraphy, with each letter precisely drawn and legible. He thumbs through an inch of paper. The ornate writing continues throughout the entire box. His senses blur at the hours of concentration required to draw each letter of each word on each page. The effort expended to write in this fashion would demand the devotion of the medieval monks who created the first books ever written. The first page is an introduction:

As I write this letter, I am leaning against the base of a very large red oak tree. Over the years, I have come to regard this place as mine. From somewhere in the distance comes the insistent cawing of a crow. Below me in the tall marsh grass are mysterious trails that twist and turn like some elusive living thing to vanish in the distance. To the east, Canadian Geese wheel and honk in a bronze sunrise as they return to the marsh from a night spent in a rice field somewhere. Your father loved this place at this time of day when everything is fresh and clean and ready for a new beginning.

The first unaccustomed chill of fall arrived last night. The air here at dawn is cool enough to raise gosling bumps. I waded through frost-covered grass by flashlight in order to be here before sunrise. Today will be my last journey here. My health is in serious decline. I have come to this place every day for the past few months when my strength and the weather permitted. This is an inspiring place for me. My idea has been to finish the last few pages of the story here where everything began and ended.

Amerada no longer exists. When the fires of revenge finally finished with it, one of God's cleansing hurricanes arrived to complete the job. Thankfully, your father wrote everything in diary form. I have transposed from his many journals in an effort to put the story into readable form. In the *Manheim* chest, you will find recorded the significant moments that formed our lives. Some of those recollections are insinuated in my memory like open sores.

The morning has turned from chill to this delicious hour. The sun and the wonderful embrace of an old sweater now warm me. Time grows short for me. Perhaps today I will finish writing the last few pages that tell of your father's many adventures that shaped his life. Perhaps you will come to understand something of who and what we were. This accounting is written in his words but in a sense, the first story is ours together because we shared the entire occurrence. The following quote is from the beginning of your father's first journal:

> 'In the beginning, my family was lost in a joyless sort of fog while we marveled at the huge sum of money we could earn merely by gathering information. The amount offered by the Ironstone Group for our participation in this project far exceeded any other opportunity in my parent's lifetime.'

The final entry in his first journal recorded on his last day in Amerada, is as follows:

> 'The Amerada Project has cost us dearly. I consider our entry into the proceedings to be a very subtle and perhaps little understood form of insanity.'

May God hold you in the palm of his hand.

Love,

Sarah Grace Woodling-Graves

Neal Marston removes a stack of pages from the first container. He begins to read in a parking lot in a small town in Texas, *The Song of Mannheim.*

Chapter One

The man stalks his first victim for two weeks. The 16-year-old girl is the only daughter of a family living on the outskirts of Shidler. The neighborhood has been carefully selected. The site is far enough removed from his hideaway to belay suspicion.

Pam Drabber works five nights a week in an ice cream parlor four blocks from her home. The place closes at 9:30 on weeknights. On those nights, she walks the four blocks alone. At the mid-point of her journey, a 6-foot-tall untrimmed privet hedge parallels the sidewalk. The hedge is dimly illuminated by a pair of streetlights, one at each end of the block.

The man decides that an entryway through the hedge will be his waiting place. The hedge formerly surrounded a lot where a house was destroyed by fire several months ago. What remains is a blackened hulk awaiting demolition. The houses on either side of the decaying mass were removed several years ago. Only the foundations remain of the former structures. On the abandoned lots are tall trees and shrubs whose shade once covered manicured lawns. The overgrown shrubbery of suburbia is all that remains of someone's dream.

A streetlight provides too much radiance for the stalker. On the night before he abducts the woman, he breaks the nearest street lamp with three shots from a pellet gun. Thursday night arrives with an intermittent light rain falling. Nobody travels this seldom-used street on this particular night.

Overhead, a partial moon rides the night sky like a small segment of an orange rind. Broken clouds obscure the sky. They offer additional concealment. The man kneels behind the hedge where he can see through a break in the foliage.

The girl hurries home with an umbrella carried low above her head. The canopy is slanted downward in her direction of travel. As she passes the opening in the hedge, the man lances outward to encircle her neck with a chokehold. The umbrella tumbles to the ground springing away from the captive as she struggles.

As they pass through the opening in the hedge, he *thunks* her on the head with a homemade sap. The blow produces instant unconsciousness that causes her to sag in his grasp. The man drags her through the opening. The umbrella remains on the sidewalk against the hedge. When he is hidden from view by the darkness of the foliage, he binds her arms behind her back with duct tape. He moves her deeper into the overgrown lawn so that she is closer to his truck.

Her skirt rides up past her waist as he drags her by the ankles. He lays her in the deep shadow of a sumac clump near one side of the foundation. He removes her underwear before he completes the binding of her arms. When he finishes with her arms, he turns her onto her back. He stuffs her panties into her mouth before he seals her lips with a double-cross of tape. A double turn of tape around her legs above the knees completes her capture.

He looks warily around. When he is satisfied with her bindings, he retrieves the umbrella from the hedge. After minor difficulty, he manages to collapse the canopy before thrusting it into the snarl of privet limbs on the house side of the barrier. He scans the area again, seeing that the partially lit thoroughfare remains deserted. Insects revolve around the remaining streetlight half a block away, providing the only movement in the dark night. He slings the girl across his shoulder, then moves in the dark shadows past what remains of the burned house.

Behind the blackened skeleton, a partially incinerated garage offers sanctuary to his vehicle. A seared grape arbor and a thoroughly scorched pecan tree near the garage provide a further screen to mask his movements. The kidnapper's elderly pickup with its dome light removed is parked inside the abandoned garage facing outward toward the alley.

The girl probably doesn't weigh 100 pounds. She is slim and shapely, just the way he likes them. He opens the door of the old truck and dumps her heavily on the floorboard. Her head bangs off the transmission cover. She groans softly.

He folds her knees up against her chest as he closes the door quietly. At this point, he notices that one of her sandals is missing. The man is very nervous. He does not want to return to the hedge to look for the missing shoe, so he makes one circuit of the truck while feeling with his feet for the missing footwear. The sandal is apparently not near the vehicle. He gives a snort of exasperation before firing up the engine.

The old truck starts on the first crank. He leaves the lights off until he clears the neighborhood. Two blocks from the hedge, he throws on the light switch and dims the headlights. One lighted street corner later, he turns onto the highway headed out of town.

A county sheriff's cruiser passes him headed in the opposite direction. He watches the taillights fade in the rearview mirror before consulting his pocket watch. The luminous dial indicates 10:30.

An hour later, he turns off the highway onto a dirt road. Near the first curve in the road, beneath a tree overhang, he kills the engine and headlights. He waits for a while until the bugs begin to keen in the woods again. He watches for a following vehicle. When none shows, he is satisfied that he is safe. He moves further along the road and turns aside into a small meadow.

He drives through foot-tall grass to the far tree line where he parks facing back the way he had come. He sits listening until the night noises begin anew. Finally, he lifts the girl from the floor onto the seat beside him. She is less limp than when he dropped her there. He senses that she is awake.

He makes one last look around before he opens the driver's door and moves to the passenger side of the cab. The girl remains propped up on the seat with her head lolling forward. He opens the door and pulls her legs toward him before he begins cut away her clothing with his pocketknife. He feels her tremble as the back of the knife slides across her skin. The sharp edge of the keen blade slices through the cotton fabric of her blouse like a hot knife through butter.

When her blouse and brassiere lie on the floor he turns his attention to her skirt. He cuts the waistband before he rips the cloth down through the hem. Next, he slices the tape above her knees. She makes muffled screams against the gag.

Her movements are groggy and uncoordinated, but her eyes are open. She looks up at him in horror. She turns onto her side facing the dashboard as she battles her bindings.

"It's all right, little missy. I'm gonna take good care of you," he says, as he pats her bare hip.

She flinches from his touch. He chuckles in the darkness, and slices the ankle binding before he turns her onto her back.

The girl's naked body gleams white in the intermittent moonlight that leaks between the clouds. She fights the restraints again as she makes urgent whimpering sounds. When he leans back from her to ready himself, she kicks him in the chest with both feet. The man grunts in surprise, then grips her ankles and pulls her to the edge of the seat.

She shakes her head as she screams against the tape. Her sounds are barely audible through the gag. Her struggles slow his advances until he administers an open-handed slap to the side of her head. The blow stuns her. While she recovers, he pulls her to the edge of the seat again. He holds the pocketknife in his right hand as he presses the largest of the well-honed blades against her throat. She shrinks from the bite of the cutting edge.

"Hold still, little missy. Don't make me cut ya."

When she is subdued, he holds her by the waist with both hands while he has his way with her. When he is finished, he again tapes her legs, rolls her back onto the floor, and returns to the driver's seat. The girl lies on the floorboard sobbing. Before he arrives at the hideaway, there are more muted screams against the gag and more frantic efforts to free her arms.

Her frenzied movements finally end. She settles onto her side where she curls into a fetal position. He parks at the end of the road. There, he lifts her across his right shoulder and enters the shack to deliver his prize naked, bound and helpless. The sight of her nearly scares the others to death when he lays her across the rough-hewn wooden table in the main room. She lies face up where she stares in wide-eyed terror at her captors.

"She shore is a perty little thang," one says, as he strokes her thigh.

The girl screams anew. One of the others takes a knife from his pocket and cuts the tape securing her arms. Another removes a length of cotton rope from a nail protruding from the wall. Together, the four of them spread her out on the table. They tie her wrists to individual table legs before removing the tape and panties from her mouth. Now, they can listen to her scream while they take their turns. She threatens to tell what they have done. After listening to her threat, they realize that she can't leave, not alive anyway.

Pam Drabber is the first young woman to disappear. She lasts nearly a year before her body reveals her condition. When that happens, they make the-keeper-of-women dispose of her. The insatiable appetite of the monsters within them dictates that they find a replacement.

This time, two of them conduct the search. While they scour the countryside for the next pretty girl of their choosing, they are careful not to be noticed. They stalk Beverly Watson for a week. Then, on a Friday night, they stop her car on a backcountry road several miles from her family's farm.

They hit her on the head with the thunker. They tie her up and gag her before they dump her on the floor of the ratty old truck. She is placed on her on her stomach with her legs folded back toward her shoulders and her ankles tied to her neck. She can't rise up to attract attention from that position. Her car is driven to an out-of-town truck stop where it is parked with the keys in the ignition. The abduction is easier than a falcon snatching a house finch off a bird feeder.

Her captors take her to the shack where they have their way with her. When they are finished, they turn her over to The-keeper-of-women-of-Women. He will be her master, her trainer, and eventually her killer.

The girl is chained by an ankle to a metal ring in the wall of the root cellar near a bed. From there, she will provide sexual service until it is her turn to be slaughtered. Beverly Watson lasts nearly seven months before her condition becomes apparent. She is then disposed of in the usual fashion.

The disappearance of women in lower Texas along the Gulf coast continues for six more years at the rate of about one girl a year. All the women are listed as missing persons, because no bodies are ever found. None call home to indicate otherwise.

Chapter Two

A tall bearded man sits in the bleachers of the Shidler football field while the Shidler Warriors get their butts stomped by a visiting team. The man pays little attention to the game. Instead, he watches the women in the audience from beneath the bill of a black baseball cap. Several pretty girls catch his eye, but none are prettier than the head cheerleader for the Shidler Warriors. Her name is Charlotte Mayhew.

The man watches her for the duration of the game. Near the end of the contest, a man of smaller stature joins him. They both wear overalls that cover pale blue work shirts. Their apparel is the standard work uniform of most men in the area.

When the game is over, the men follow the cheerleader as she rides home with two of her brothers in a farm truck. The rest of the Mayhew family follows in a brown four-door sedan. The family lives on a farm 16 miles west of Amerada in the blind-section-line-country where the roads are no longer maintained as they were during the oil boom of the early 1920s.

The men watch the Mayhew farm through the night. They mentally record all family activities. They take special note of the fact that the house does not have the modern conveniences of running water or electricity. There is a privy located some 10 yards from the back of the dwelling. The men take turns watching the farmhouse from a thicket 20 yards from the back door.

Three nights after their initial contact, they capture Charlotte when she goes to the privy alone in the early morning hours wearing a thin cotton bathrobe and carrying a flashlight. They *thunk* her on the head when she leaves the outhouse on her way back to the house. She is the prettiest girl they've captured. The anticipation of how good she will be has been more fun than a carnival ride.

The men are careful not to abduct women too near their home, because a victim found missing nearby might draw attention to them. Every time they snatch a new girl, there is the usual search by people in the county. They all storm around looking for the missing woman, but fail to find her.

In the case of the very popular Charlotte Mayhew, they search the woods, the creek bottoms and even drag the Gravel Pit Lakes looking for a body. Eventually, the sheriff releases a statement indicating that the missing girl is believed to be a runaway. The sheriff's department finds a trucker who claims to have given a woman matching her description a ride from Amerada to Houston where he let her out on an obscure street corner.

The search stops and everyone decides that she has fled for a better life elsewhere. Everyone, except the Mayhew family. They know better and never stop looking.

Mark Mayhew Jr. is the eldest son and the most woods-wise member of the family. The light brown-colored soil of the family ranch dries quickly following a rain and develops a thin crust. Tracking deer, Javalina and the like is easy for Mark Jr.

The morning following his sister's disappearance, Mark trails her abductors to a point about a half-mile east of the farm. The trail vanishes near the tire imprints of a vehicle. Additional spoor in the area indicates three men occupied the site several times before the abduction. Further information is impossible to determine because rain the day before the kidnapping obscured many of the older signs.

There are indistinct footprints indicating as many as three men were at the site of a small fire pit deeply dug into the ground. Their tracks indicate that they took turns watching the house from atop a knoll about 20 yards from the dwelling.

Two sets of man-sized footprints lead to the outhouse. From the privy door, the tracks move east in a line to the tire imprints. One set of tracks leading away from the outhouse is deeper than the arrival prints. The man was obviously carrying Charlotte.

Lee tires made the imprints at the fire pit. The imprints are identical to those of the family truck: Lee Road Master. The brand with its aggressive tread pattern is the most popular tire sold by the tire store in Shidler. The depth of the tread indicates the tires are practically new and of a width corresponding to the size of a light truck tire. Mark is able to measure the wheelbase of the vehicle. It is that of a half-ton pickup truck.

Mark makes a mold box of one-inch thick wood, three inches deep. He places the open frame around the best set of tracks. He then sprays the prints with a light coat of clear lacquer. He makes a plaster-of-Paris mold four feet long that is reinforced with small gauge chicken wire fencing. He discovers that the tire on the left rear wheel has a tire plug.

The plug is to repair small punctures in tubeless tires without removing the tire from the rim. The method uses a piece of heavy gauge loosely woven fiber-cord threaded through the eye of a large awl with an indented-groove along one side. The item that caused the puncture is removed from the tire. The fiber cord is then coated with rubber cement, and the needle is pushed through the puncture into the tubeless tire. After insertion, the needle is partially withdrawn, rotated to form a bulky knotted mass inside the tire. The needle is then withdrawn. The surplus is trimmed flush with the top edge of the tire tread. What remains in the tire hardens and forms a seal to prevent air loss. The rubber cement turns the outside cord into a firm object that will leave an impression in soft soil.

In this instance, the tire plug is within an outside valley of the left hand rear tire, two lands in from the outer edge. Mark Jr. spends a lot of time in Shidler and Amerada checking left rear tires on pickup trucks in a dedicated quest for a repair plug. He finds several, but they are never in the correct location in the tire tread.

On December 15, 1948, Mark discovers a match. The tire is on a truck at Karl's Burger Heaven in Amerada. He parks near the rear of the lot, well away from the target vehicle to await the return of the driver. Half an hour later, a tall heavily bearded man wearing faded blue overalls returns to climb into the truck. The man turns south on the highway as he heads out of town.

Mark follows the truck to where it turns onto the refinery road and then later onto a dirt road. The refinery road crosses a set of railroad tracks. Beyond the railroad tracks, the truck turns right onto an unmaintained road leading into the river bottom. Mark follows.

When the trail forks, tracks in the road indicate the man took the right fork. Mark's heart is racing. He stays well back so as not to be noticed. The dirt trail enters an area of dense trees, past a series of 'No Trespassing' signs. The trail bears in the general direction of West Clear Creek. Mark has long since lost sight of the truck but continues to follow the two-wheeled trace.

As he rounds a sharp hairpin turn skirting a marshy area about a half mile along the trail, he finds the truck blocking his way. The tall man stands nearby as he awaits the vehicle that follows him. The man trains a shotgun at the boy's head while instructing him to get out of his vehicle.

Mark climbs through the open door. The man strikes his head from behind with a butt stroke that renders him unconscious. Mark Mayhew Jr. is not heard from again. He becomes another missing person for everyone to wonder about.

Chapter Three

By a quirk of geography, and the manner in which school districts are defined, the Mayhew farm falls within the boundaries of the Shidler school district. The Mayhews are a large family with six boys ranging in age from 12 to 20. Sandwiched within the pack of male heirs is Charlotte Elaine Mayhew. She is an energetic, pretty, little thing with long blond hair and blue eyes. She has excelled academically from the time she entered grade school. At the beginning of her junior year of high school, she becomes the captain of the varsity cheerleader squad for Shidler High School. The same year, she is also elected as the homecoming queen of the Warrior football team.

Four of the male Mayhews have distinguished themselves athletically in the Shidler school system. The Mayhew boys have always been good athletes and so their abilities are dually noted, but they are considered nothing exceptional within the family history. When Charlotte makes the honor roll for academic achievement, the cheerleading squad and also becomes homecoming queen in the same year, the entire family is ecstatic. All the aunts, uncles, nieces and nephews in the area attend every high school athletic event to watch the pride of the Mayhew family perform.

Until Charlotte arrived, Mark Mayhew Sr.'s elder brother Melvin had been the scholar of the family. The brothers grew up in Iowa on a farm where Melvin learned at an early age that he did not want to be a farmer. With a small amount of help from his father, Melvin put himself through college and then through an eastern business school. He was enormously interested in the field of finance. He was recruited as an understudy in one of the more successful brokerage houses at Wall Street and Broad in New York City.

By age 33, Melvin had become wealthy. His source of wealth first came from stock market and later from real-estate investment. Eventually, his wealth permitted him to enter the investment banking business. At age 53, Melvin retired to a family estate on the Maine coastline. Being retired with very little else to occupy his mind, Melvin begins to closely monitor the academic achievements of the Mayhew children. Any found with above average academic abilities are encouraged to do better. When the time comes for college Uncle Melvin sponsors the brightest.

At age 13, Charlotte becomes the light in Uncle Melvin's eyes. Her transcripts indicate an academic ability far in excess of any of the other Mayhew children. Charlotte's class pictures that year reveal an exceptionally beautiful young woman with intelligence beyond her years. Every summer, as soon as school is out, Charlotte rides the train from San Antonio to New York City under the very close supervision of Melvin's head butler.

In New York City, she absorbs culture from the wealthy side of the family. From those yearly experiences, she gains further knowledge that will help her to do well in life. When she returns from New York in August of 1948, she has just one week remaining before commencing her junior year of high school. She brought with her a new wardrobe and a desire to follow in her uncle's footsteps in the investment banking business.

When football season began, Uncle Melvin received a photo of Charlotte in her long, white formal dress; the one he had helped her pick out during her visit. She wears a crown and a purple ribbon across her chest that reads, 'Warrior, Homecoming Queen, 1948'. Uncle Melvin responds by sending Charlotte a $300 check and a long letter telling her how proud he is of her accomplishments.

The night of November 9, 1948, Melvin Mayhew receives a telegram from his brother's family. Charlotte has disappeared without a trace from the family farm. Melvin Mayhew flies to Houston, Texas where he rents a car and races to the farm. After several hours of listening to the desperate mumblings of family members, Melvin pieces together the story as it is known. It is apparent that Charlotte has been kidnapped.

Mark Mayhew's family is middle class and without the financial resources to pay a ransom. It is obvious to Melvin that the motivation for the kidnapping cannot be financial gain. The local sheriff's department has accepted a missing persons report after Charlotte was missing for 24 hours.

Melvin discovers that other young women have disappeared in that portion of the state under similar circumstances; the alternative possibilities for the abduction are too horrible to contemplate. Melvin calls the Amerada County sheriff's department where he speaks with Sheriff Harvey Kraven. The sheriff hangs up and quickly drives to the Mayhew farm. The bumpkin sheriff and his chief investigator profess to being totally baffled by the disappearances of Charlotte and the other young women. They offer little more than cold cases and missing person reports from the other disappearances.

Melvin resolves to do what he can to find the abductor of his beautiful niece on his own. Over the years, Melvin Mayhew's business interests have flourished because of his ability to size up people. After a single conversation with Sheriff Kraven, Melvin is convinced that the man is a fraud as a law enforcement officer.

Shortly after the meeting, Melvin makes a discreet inquiry through a U.S. senator who is an old college chum and a long time personal friend. He receives the name of a man who heads a team of 'elite maniacs', as the senator described them. They are people who can be retained for a price to expose or otherwise locate elusive criminals and then discreetly dispose of them.

On November 15, 1948, armed with a name and a method of locating a mysterious Mr. Jonathan Black, Melvin flies to Rapid City, South Dakota. There he places a phone call to an unlisted phone number. Later, he is picked up by a windowless van and transported to meet Mr. Black. During their meeting, Melvin pledges a half-million dollars for the identity and prosecution, legal or otherwise, of his niece's abductors. As additional incentive, half of the money is paid up front.

Melvin asks to be advised weekly of the progress of the investigation. He suggests that the Amerada County sheriff's department not be informed of the investigation being conducted within their jurisdiction. Following the meeting, Melvin is driven in the same windowless van to the Rapid City central business district where he is discharged on an obscure street corner.

Ralph Pine is dispatched on November 22, 1948 to Amerada County. He will work undercover while posing as an oilfield worker. His job is to seek information concerning the disappearances of young women in the area. Agent Pine works days in the oilpatch. He spends nights and weekends where men gather.

During the course of his travels, he does a lot of bar hopping, pool playing and domino shuffling. He becomes a familiar face in the entertainment parlors. By the end of a month, he has become friendly with the fathers of two of the missing girls.

On December 16, 1949, Melvin Mayhew receives a telegram from his brother. Mark Jr. has also disappeared. The family car has turned up in another small town 15 miles from Shidler.

Melvin makes another frantic trip to his brother's home where he remains for a week. While he is there, he consoles the family and helps search for clues. On his way back to Maine, Melvin stops by Rapid City where he has another conversation with Mr. Black. He is informed that an agent is on the scene and will deliver frequent reports of his progress.

During the three months Agent Pine is on assignment, his reports indicate that the Amerada sheriff's department is as incompetent and corrupt as any he has ever heard about. His inquisitive nature comes to the attention of the local criminal element. On March 5, 1949, Agent Pine is found dead by gunshot wound floating face down in an irrigation canal near Shidler. At this point, the investigation takes another twist.

Chapter Four

Sixteen-year-old Axle Marston and his father depart home in the dark of morning, heading east in an 8-year-old, light-blue, '41 Pontiac. The boy sits in the passenger seat periodically nodding off, lulled by the early hour and the hypnotic effect of the tires humming over blacktop. The boy awakens briefly just after daylight. Beyond the vehicle windows, he sees moist, black earth peeking at the sun through pinto-patches of melting snow. He dozes again. An hour later, he comes awake.

"How much further?"

In the low areas along the highway, the sullen earth displays world-class mud, where the fresh green shoots of early grass are visible. Unusually warm weather for the spring of '49 has broken the hold of winter. Clusters of grape locust, yellow crocuses and tulips adorn passing yards along the highway. The three and a half hour trip from Gillette, Wyoming to Rapid City has been a monotonous affair.

'Big Mike' Marston has spoken little, which makes his son wonder what is bothering him. The boy stops trying to create conversation. He entertains himself by counting the frequent antelope that dot the rolling green, beige and white-spotted prairie.

Near the edge of Rapid City, they stop for gas. Big Mike refers to a portion of a city map he carries in a large Kraft envelope. Thirty minutes later, they are back on the highway revitalized by a root beer and a bag of salted peanuts apiece. Mike consults the map as he navigates along obscure side streets on the outskirts of the older part of the business district. The streets are lined by narrow, two story, redbrick storefronts. Mike stares obliquely through the freshly wiped windshield.

"We're looking for a sign that reads, *Madam Gluba, your future told in revealing detail.*"

"We got up at four in the morning, and drove all this distance to have our fortunes told?"

"Not exactly," Mike answers, as he concentrates on the traffic.

"There," the boy offers, "near the corner."

He points to a sign across the street. The faded advertisement projects from a brick wall near a street corner. The sidewalks are unusually wide for this section of town where the streets are narrow and paved with brick. A row of flowering crabapple trees stand in a row along the edge of the sidewalk about three feet in from the curb. The trees are cloaked in a burst of early blossoms sponsored by the warm weather that still carries an edge of winter.

The fortuneteller's sign is made of metal and shaped like a cloud. The border is outlined in small, frosted-white light bulbs. The paint scheme is a thoroughly oxidized and faded red, white, black and blue affair. The boy and his father scrutinize the storefront as they pass by on the opposite side of the street.

Beneath the marquee is a stairway leading up. Morning sunlight illuminates a portion of the well used unpainted wooden steps that climb the stairwell to vanish beyond the top of the door frame. The boy views the ominous looking doorway with a certain amount of dread. The shadowy opening looks like a place he wouldn't want to enter.

On the face of the building, an expanding-steel security screen dangles in scissors-like regimented rows, from a track above the door. The mass of metal strips resemble an accordion as they hang against the left-hand doorjamb where they are secured as a bundle by a length of old chain with a new padlock. Beyond the security-screen, an indecipherable, dark blob obscures the first few steps of the stairwell.

Mike drives past the sign to make a U-turn in the middle of the next block. He returns to parallel park at the curb a quarter-block from the stairway. He turns off the engine and drops the car keys into his left coat pocket. Leaning forward against the steering wheel, Mike surveys the neighborhood. His eyes sweep the street bit by bit, burning with more than normal intensity. He misses little while remembering everything.

Without looking down, he retrieves a pack of cigarettes from his right-side coat pocket. He lights one with the dashboard lighter and inhales deeply. He savors the pleasurable moment as he rolls down the driver's side window. His dark eyes continue to survey the sparse flow of foot traffic as pedestrians mill along the sidewalk.

Madam Gluba's parlor is on the second floor. The street level storefront at the corner is vacant with a hand drawn sign advertising 'This Space for Rent', followed by a phone number.

The upstairs portion of the building front features a round, almost turret-like, buttress projecting out above the sidewalk at the corner. The overhang commands a view of both side streets. Three white wood-framed windows encircle the redbrick cylinder. The view from within is screened by Venetian blinds backed by drawn beige-colored window sheers. Block lettering in gold leaf and outlined in black are displayed on all three windows. The motif advertises 'Madam Gluba' more elegantly than the metal sign projecting from the building.

"You know, we're missing some pretty good fishing back home," the boy offers, with a slight note of sarcasm.

The younger Marston is an avid fisherman. He is also a miniature version of his father. They both stand over six-foot tall, are muscular, with black hair and dark eyes. Axle is still growing and weighs around 190 pounds, while his father depresses the scales at 230. The elder Marston is tapered downward like a rail splitting wedge.

A noticeable difference is the father's nose, which was broken at some point in the past. The repair job was accomplished with less detail than was necessary. As it looks, his nose has little hope of repair and no other expectation beyond mere use and survival. Above his left eyebrow, a thin scar tracks across his eye to end a half-inch below the eye socket. Whatever caused the wound narrowly missed damaging the eye in passing. Big Mike Marston is 36 and looks every inch a military man who has endured his share of battles. Axle's features lack the crows-feet of time around his father's eyes, or the deformed nose and facial scar. Otherwise, he looks much as his father did at age 16.

Mike removes a thin, gold pocket-watch from his vest and turns his head sideways to exhale a stream of smoke out the window. The watch is attached to an ornate chain with a watch fob on the opposite end. The fob resides in a vest pocket on the other side of the button line. He toys with the watch.

"Don't ever start smokin'."

Axle doesn't bother responding to the comment since he has no intention of smoking and has heard the admonishment before. Mike glances at the timepiece before he returns it to the vest pocket. His medium-gray herringbone tweed suit is new. He wears a light gray felt hat with a snap-brim perched on the back of his head.

In deep contrast, the boy has the burr haircut of a jock. His dark hair is less than a quarter inch long. He wears jeans from the denim graveyard in the back of his closet. The jeans hang to his ankle bones where they reveal fuzzy white, athletic socks that sprout from brown penny-loafers. Above his empty belt loops he wears a white cotton T-shirt with an open weave; a horizontal, multi-colored, band of stripes stretches in a gossamer web across his muscular chest. Over the T-shirt, he wears his prize possession: a high school letter jacket. The red and gray affair has leather sleeves and a large 'G' with three metal bars and four metal devises.

Too much wrist shows below the knit cuffs. The sleeve-shortage indicates that the boy is busy outgrowing his favorite item of wearing apparel. The jacket hangs open in front. The leather elbows display the barely noticeable surface cracks of daily use.

"You want to tell me what we're doing here?" Axle asks, in mild exasperation, "Besides watching trees bloom?"

"We're here to get a job. I've questioned my sanity for seeking an undertaking that might bring danger to my family…" The boy stares at him for a second with his mouth slightly agape. "Never mind, just thinking out loud." Then he adds, as an afterthought, "It's time you learn about what I did during the war. Perhaps that will help explain what we're doing here." Mike leans back in the seat; gestures toward the sign with his cigarette hand. "My job, and that sign are going to directly affect the rest of your life."

While he talks, he stares through the windshield. His eyes continually sweep the street. Axle nods hesitantly. He is transfixed. In the past, his dad has always side-stepped any and all questions regarding his military service.

"During the war, I was an Army officer assigned to the Office of Strategic Services. After the war, the OSS sort of disappeared into the military sub-structure. Last week my unit was disbanded altogether. A selected group of people will be employed by a civilian contractor known as the Ironstone Group. They will perform a specific peacetime function, whatever the hell that means. Specifically, they will perform sensitive investigations. The job offers will be a pay for hire, sort of soldier of fortune. They will involve all of us as a family unit," Mike growls, while he continues to scan the street. "That means our entire family will be in the line of fire."

"If we're really all in it together," the boy says, "then why isn't Mom here?"

Axle watches a hot dog vender tend his wares from a pushcart on the corner near the subject doorway. It is mid-morning. In spite of an earlier doughnut, followed by the root beer and peanuts, he is so hungry he is willing to risk food poisoning in a public place to have something more to eat.

"Your mom is coming by separate car," Mike continues, as he flicks a column of spent cigarette ash out through the open window. "We were instructed to travel separately. Our cover story for the day, in case anybody in Gillette asks, is that I've lost my job and we have come here to find employment. Your mom is supposed to be on a shopping trip with a lady friend."

"Sounds weird," Axle responds.

Mike takes a deep puff, expels the smoke and watches it curl around the top of the steering wheel before continuing with the story. Axle rolls down his window. A gentle breeze carries the smoke out the driver's side window.

"During the war," Mike resumes, "I did a lot of things. Most of those assignments involved working behind enemy lines. I'm not going to recite all of them to you, only one for emphasis. One night, eight months before D-day, I parachuted into Nazi occupied northern France. My mission was to organize guerrilla units in that area so we could disrupt the German war machine. My mission was in support of the D-day invasion."

Axle looks at his dad. "Is that why Mom didn't hear from you for long periods of time?"

"Yeah, and the letters she received were written before I departed on the mission. They were mailed at random intervals while I was gone. I went in alone, because I preferred to work alone. One man operating as a guerrilla can be a formidable adversary, because he can travel faster than a group and he leaves fewer traces of his presence. And of course, a single individual does not attract attention in a rural setting."

Mike glances at his son, whose full attention seems riveted on the gearshift knob.

"You mean like the French Resistance?" the boy says.

Mike agrees. "Actually, I worked with two different cells. They supplied men when I needed them. They helped me move supplies and hide from the Germans. I communicated with my contacts in England by keyed short-wave radio. I had to vary my location, frequencies and the times of my next transmission. I used a telegraph key to send encrypted messages that had to be decoded. Those days were really a frightening time in my life. I had several really close calls."

Mike absentmindedly feels the scar across his eye. The boy stares at his father in rapt adoration.

"Periodically, my superiors would send in a low level Mosquito bomber at night to drop supplies. French contacts and I blew up railroad bridges and performed other guerrilla warfare missions until the American army overran our position. I remained the employee of a super-secret government agency after the war. Times are changing. That type organization is no longer needed. I will become a civilian contractor. I'll be doing the same thing I did in service, but this new operation will involve my entire family. A few of us are about to be interviewed for a specific job." Mike smiles. "The organization now deals in explicit investigations that sometimes involve customized mischief to achieve a goal. Instead of being paid as a major in an armed service, I will perform as a civilian for a monetary consideration. We are about to undertake a task of covert surveillance for which we will be generously paid."

"What does covert mean?" the boy asks.

"It means secret," his father answers. "We will gather information in a small town without anyone knowing what we are doing."

"Did you have to kill anybody during the war?" Axle asks, as he studies his father's face.

"Yeah," Mike says, as he looks at his son. "That's what soldiers do in war, they kill people. It doesn't take a lot of brains to pull a trigger or use a knife." Michael Marston glances out the side window as he pauses before staring at his son. "Being a good man is a far greater accomplishment than killing someone in combat. There's nothing to be proud of in killing another person. If there had been a way not to have killed someone, I wouldn't have." Mike looks away again as he takes another drag from his cigarette. "It's difficult to wake up one morning and discover that you are middle-aged, undereducated and economically challenged. During the war, all of us were busy sailing through life as though we didn't have a future. The war is long past. Now, it's time to find gainful employment. It's like playing football in college and discovering after graduation that there aren't any opportunities in the civilian economy for running off tackle. The desire to earn a living is the only reason I've even considered involving my family in this thing." Mike pauses again. "You, your mom, and I have the opportunity to make a lot of money in a short time, courtesy of the Ironstone Group." Their eyes lock. "We will move as a family to a small town in Texas. While we are there, we can't even hint that we are involved in anything, but working for an oil company. We can't go slinking around suspiciously like Agent X-33 in some Grade B imitation spy movie. We don't need to go in there dressed like flood victims either, but we have to act as though we're only a shade above impoverished. We have to live absolutely normal, while not drawing attention to ourselves."

"Being evasive while trying to act normal is one of my worst things," Axle says. "Every time I try something sneaky, or do anything I know I'm not supposed to do, I always get caught. What happens if we're discovered in Texas?"

"It could get real exciting. The organization hasn't told me the degree of risk involved. That's mostly what this meeting today is about, but I have a feeling I'm not fond of." Mike takes another drag, glances at the short butt. "Because there is a lot of money offered for the assignment, I suspect that it's probably really dangerous. There will probably be life-threatening situations involved. Some night we might have to pull out and run for it." Mike hesitates momentarily. "I have a suspicion that there is something about this contract that has already gone sour. If there wasn't, then they'd send in just one man. There wouldn't be a need to use an entire family unless they know a single operative won't work. In this business, decisions are based on facts. Our problem is that we don't yet know the facts. We also don't know if the spooks will give us the truth beforehand."

Mike drums the fingers of his left hand on the steering wheel. He stops talking for several seconds, before commenting, "Hello," in a low voice. Up the street, a wino staggers out of Madam Gluba's doorway. He looks drunkenly around then returns to his stairwell.

"Somebody's gettin' itchy," Mike suggests. "They're beginning to wonder if we're gonna show. Before we go see the madam, I want you to know that we don't have to do this, but $50,000 might come in handy somewhere down the road."

"Fifty-thousand dollars?" the boy gasps, as he forsakes the hot dog vender to look at his father. "Wow, the fortune telling business must be a lot better than I thought."

"Fifty-thousand sounds like a lot of money, but it might take us a long time to discover what we need to know. It might take a year or more. If you think about three people working on the same project for a year, it doesn't seem like such a large amount. If we get lucky and discover what is needed in a month, then we can move on to the next assignment with a lot of money in our pocket." Axle nods thoughtfully. "Don't get carried away with the Madam Gluba thing; the sign is just a front. There's going to be some important super-spooks from the organization up there. They will evaluate the three of us. They'll be the brains of the outfit. The ones who sit around daydreaming about the extraordinary skills of the people they'd like to employ. They do the recruiting, but they are generally the ones who've never served a tour in the field where they might get their hands dirty. Field agents try to avoid them as much as possible, that way their flow of insane ideas is dramatically slowed."

A couple hot-dogs would be really good right now, maybe with a cream soda on the side.

"Are you going to take the job?" Axle asks.

"Maybe," Mike says, "but then with these folks, you don't know if they've given you everything they know, or if they're pounding sand up your ass."

Axle smiles at the comment, he can count on one hand the times he's heard his father use what his mother would call a 'dirty word'. Above the Gluba sign, one of the window curtains twitches.

Axle observes, "Somebody's watchin' out the upstairs window. The curtain facing us has moved twice while we've been here."

"I wondered if you'd notice," Big Mike says. "If we take this job, you'll be doing things that'll require you to grow up really fast. Noticing what goes on around you is one of them. It usually takes someone who's more than newly minted to notice things like the curtain move. The security of the organization seems to be slipping. What do you think of the hot dog vender?"

"Seems kind of odd," the boy says. "Since we've been here, two people have approached him and been turned away. It's as though he doesn't have anything to sell."

"The vender's one of the security guys, same as those two fellows sweepin' the gutter at the corner," Big Mike says, as he wishes he had another cigarette. "They've got the guard-spooks out. Somebody important is in residence. Lock up, and let's go have a talk with whoever's up there." Mike reaches across the front seat to pat his son's left knee. "People in this business tend to be strange. We'll be talking to a couple of the strangest you'll probably ever meet." He rolls up his window before opening the door. "It's best not to contribute to the conversation unless spoken to directly. These people don't like conversationalists, so when you don't say anything it makes them think you're smarter than you are." Mike gives a little chuckle. "They won't even use their real names. They may seem as strange as snow in July, but remember, they're evaluating us for the job. Your mom will be going through the same ordeal with several other agents. In her case, the agents will probably be women."

Father and son open their respective doors, lock the car and head for the stairway. When they turn into the stairwell, they are confronted by a filthy wino sitting slumped against the wall. He clutches a paper-sack wrapped bottle to his chest. The bum's face is partially obscured by a floppy brimmed hat. He smells of booze. Father and son step around the bum as they climb upward. The steps above are littered with scattered newspapers and food wrappers long past their prime.

The wino mutters, "Hi, Major, long time no see," without shifting out of his imitation stupor.

"Hi, Harry," Big Mike mumbles, as the two Marstons ascend the steps.

At the top, they turn left. Two doors later, Mike opens the entry labeled 'Madam Gluba'. An enormous woman sits behind a large desk, wearing pendant-style, crescent-shaped earrings and an off-white turban. A purple colored velvet cloth drapes the piece of furniture before her. The edges of the covering are gold fringed and hang to within an inch of the floor. In the middle of the velvet covering sits a large crystal ball on an ornate gold-colored metal base.

The woman wears a flowing, sky-blue dress the size of a small circus tent. The dress material is liberally sprinkled with crescent-moons, stars and constellations in various sizes. Her left hand lies on the velvet where it appears to be the size of a baked ham. Her thick wrist wears a chain-link charm bracelet with a lot of ornaments. The other hand remains out of sight below the tabletop. The fat lady's hair is dyed a strange shade of reddish-purple that reminds the boy of raspberry Jell-O. In a shallow drawer to her left stands all the paraphernalia necessary to manicure a woman's nails. She closes the drawer.

"Welcome back, Mike," the behemoth says, after the door is closed. She gestures to the curtain behind her. "Mr. Black is expecting you."

"Hi, Francis," Big Mike responds. "How's business?"

"Can't complain," the woman answers, as the new arrivals move past her. "I expect a really big day. Go right in."

Father and son enter through a purple curtain screening a wall behind her. Axle glances at the fat lady as they pass. Her right hand grips the butt of a pistol in a holster attached to the right side of her leg compartment. Beyond the curtain is a metal door with a small red light on the upper door jam. Through that door is another made of metal with a brass-enshrouded peephole. Axle notices they are within a cage made of metal bars.

An electric door-lock buzzes before the two Marston's enter into an indirectly lit room with deep pile beige-colored carpet. On the far side of the chamber, a portly man in a black three-piece suit sits behind an expansive dark-wood desk. The suit bears a faint, cream-colored pin stripe with a matching cream shirt. A broad lavender necktie vanishes beneath his vest, and a decorative handkerchief peeks out of the suit coat pocket. A nameplate aligned with the forward edge of the desk bares the name 'Jonathan Black'.

Mr. Black does not appear to be into long-term weight control, as he resembles an overweight gerbil. He wears wire framed bifocal glasses beneath a generous forehead. The bald pate terminates in a thin band of dark hair fringing the rear of his near-naked skull above his shirt collar. Mr. Black waddles around the end of the desk, extending a hand.

"Glad you could make it, Mike. We weren't certain the pay for hire business would be acceptable to you." Black turns to Axle. "I'm Jonathan Black, and you must be Axle, the young man I've heard so much about."

Mr. Black shakes the boy's hand with both of his.

"Pleased to meet you," Axle responds.

Jonathan Black reminds the boy of an undertaker. Axle has to suppress a desire to wipe his hand on his jeans when Black returns it to him. Axle shifts his stance a little so that he stands to the right of his father where he tries not to look too young. Mr. Black turns his attention to Big Mike.

"Have you told your family what this is all about?"

"Not in fine detail," Michael answers. "I thought I'd leave that up to you, since I don't have all the facts."

Black nods as he presses an obscure button beneath the top edge of his desk.

"We'll get right to it then. How was the trip?"

"Nearly four hours long and boring," Mike responds, as he surveys the room. "That damned prairie makes a person pray for a tree or something to look at besides grass, snow, antelope and rolling hills."

Several seconds later, two men enter through a side door. They saunter to a couch on the far side of a coffee table. Across from the couch sits a pair of armchairs separated by an end table supporting a brass lamp. Behind the couch, an immense mirror in an ornate gold frame covers most of the wall.

One of the new arrivals is dressed in a dark blue suit, the other in dark brown. The man in blue reminds Axle of an insurance salesman. The one in brown wears the look of a salt-cod left out in the sun too long. Brown suit's posture is rigid, as though he's forgotten to take the hanger out of his coat.

Mr. Black utters, "Meet Mr. Blue and Mr. Brown."

Neither man extends a hand. Axle follows his father's lead as he nods curtly at the new arrivals. Both men closely scrutinize the father and son.

Black strolls to the couch, his belly preceding him like the cow-catcher on a locomotive. He ushers the Marstons into the armchairs with a wave of his hand. Black alights on the couch with his cohorts. A dark leather briefcase lies atop the coffee table in front of Mr. Black.

An attractive blond with the complexion of a fresh peach enters the room from behind the couch. She stands with her feet together near the end of the coffee table and asks if anyone would like something to drink. The four men request coffee, Axle asks for a soda. Everybody stares at one another until she returns with the refreshments.

The coffee arrives in a silver pot on a pewter-colored metal tray accompanied by four massive white porcelain mugs. A white porcelain creamer and matching sugar bowl without design are clustered around the soda in its tall glass bottle. The tray also contains four ornate silver spoons and a short stack of small green napkins. The woman places the tray in the center of the coffee table and leaves. Black lifts the silver service coffee pot and pours coffee into the mugs. He concentrates on the stream of dark liquid.

"Axle, I am told you are quite an accomplished athlete."

"Only fair," Axle answers, as he swallows nervously.

"Come, come." Black returns the pot to the tray. His hands move to unlock the briefcase. He lifts the hinged lid. "No need to be modest young man; you're among friends."

From the case, he produces three Manila folders, which he shuffles into order and places on the table. With his other hand he moves the briefcase to stand on its edge on the floor. Finished, he arranges the folders so their hinged side is aligned with the edge of the table. Black snares a coffee mug, adds cream and sugar, and stirs the contents with a spoon. He moves to sit on the edge of the couch cushion. Everyone samples the coffee while the boy nervously downs his soda. Black leans forward with his elbows on his knees, opens a folder and peers down through his bifocals.

"We know all about your father," Black mutters. "So, we will devote most of this interview to become acquainted with you." Black busies himself by reading silently from the top folder, then looks up. "It says here that you've lettered three years in wrestling, football, baseball, and basketball in a very large school." He turns a page. "Tell me in as much detail as you can remember, anything about the woman who just entered and left the room. You may use assumptions as well as facts."

Startled, the boy begins sweating. He looks at his father, clears his throat and then glances momentarily at the mirror before responding.

"Sure," he begins, as he closes his eyes. Thin frown lines form across his forehead. He begins his recital as though reading from a script. "She is about 5 feet 4 inches tall with a nice figure. She has great looking ankles, so she is probably about a 120 pounds."

Mike smiles at his son's description, as he thinks, *That's my boy.*

"Hair dark-blond, eyes green, full lips, frosty pink lipstick with nails to match. She wears glasses, but wasn't wearing them when she was in here. Most men would describe her as pretty. There is a small mole about the diameter of a wooden matchstick near her left temple, an inch from her ear lobe and an inch below the eye-support of where her eyeglass frames would be. There were small indentations on either side of her nose where the glasses would ride. The glasses are probably for reading, not general wear. Her complexion appears flawless. She's wearing a beige, cotton blouse with a large pointed collar, like a man's dress shirt. The blouse has some sort of endless-chain Indian-design embroidered around the collar and both sleeve cuffs. Her skirt is full and dense with small pleats. Because it hangs limply and holds the creases well, it is probably made of something other than cotton. The skirt is the same color as her blouse and extends to about an inch below her knees. Identical decorations encircle the hemline of the skirt. They are the same shade of brown as on the blouse. She's wearing a wide leather belt woven from dark brown leather strips. The belt is composed of silver conches and has a matching silver buckle. The buckle has an irregular shaped piece of turquoise about the size of a quarter inlayed into its center. The oval conches touch each other and are embossed with Indian designs. She wears hose with a small run on the left leg, probably originating from her big toenail. Her earrings are silver and dangly. They feature the Indian folklore symbol of Ko-Ka-Pelli, the god of fertility playing a flute. She's also wearing dark leather platform sandals about the same color as the belt. They have open toes and cork heels. Her hair hangs nearly to her waist in the back and is drawn into a pony-tail secured by some sort of brown colored clasp." Axle sits quietly for an instant with his eyes still closed. "Oh, and she wears Channel #5 perfume. My mom wears the same thing. That's all I can remember."

The boy opens his eyes and takes a nervous sip of soda from the bottle.

Black asks his father, "Major, did you tell him to be unusually alert while he's in here?"

"No, I told him to speak only when spoken to. He has a photographic memory."

"If the subject had been a man, would you have remembered as much detail?"

"Probably not," the boy answers. "I'm more into women than men."

Everyone except Brown laughs. Blue turns to Mr. Black.

"That was a very impressive description. The only thing he didn't give us was the color of her undergarments and any birthmarks. Could you have done what he just did at age 16?"

"I probably could have at 25, but not 16," Black answers, as he smiles at the boy. "Pleasing figure, huh?" Black smiles, as he tilts the folder for a better reading angle. "According to our file, you have a very good memory that is either photographic or nearly so. We've just had a demonstration of that. You maintain an 'A' average in school, and you skipped the sixth grade. Your father has given you a passable knowledge of weight lifting, boxing, judo and other forms of martial arts. You've never lost a bout on the wrestling team. You were the captain of last year's baseball team. We consider these attributes, for someone so young, to be no small achievement."

Axle colors slightly, while he stares at the three men on the couch. He nervously rubs both hands on the legs of his jeans. Black continues.

"You've attended two different schools since junior high and you seem to have had only one reported altercation at each institution for which you received two-day suspensions. Your ability to defend yourself and others seems to have adequately discouraged additional confrontations by your classmates. Our report states an opinion, *'Subject possesses an urge to defend the underdog and to come to the rescue of distressed damsels'.*

The three heads on the couch swivel to Axle.

"As a teenager you are the weakest link in this assignment," Black observes. While he speaks, he alternates his gaze between Axle and the folder. "Your defense of other people may cause a problem in our line of work." Black locks eyes with him. "Those two personal traits, while commendable attributes in every day life, can cause a serious problem in undercover work." He pauses while he gazes toward the door to the next room. "Are these tendencies something you can control, or do they control you?"

"Controllable," Axle replies, returning the stare of his accuser. He wonders where the personal information came from. Black ponders the boy, before nodding his head and closing the folder. He turns his attention to Mike.

"We need a family," Black offers. "Preferably one with an older teenage boy. The fact that your family has no other children is a plus for the assignment." Black addresses Axle. "The reason for this requirement is obvious. *Too many lips sink ships.* A tough teenage boy is the desired persona we need. You'll have access to certain areas of information that adults are never privy too. It is commonly known that teenagers generally know what is going on in a community long before their parents have a clue. That is the main reason we want a family with a smart teenager for this assignment. Do you have any questions, son?"

"No, sir," the boy answers, in a stronger voice than before.

Black nods. He sits back and crosses his arms on his chest. He then speaks almost absently to his accomplices.

"Do either of you gentlemen have any questions for the youngest recruit in the history of this organization?"

Brown opens his mouth for the first time, as he offers, "If someone asked you to shoot your dog, could you do so?"

His voice is harsh, like two pieces of sandpaper rubbing together. The boy has to strain to understand him.

"I don't have a dog," Axle answers. Everyone except Axle and Brown laugh.

"Merely a hypothetical question," Brown continues in his nearly overpowering rasp. "If you had a dog and one of us told you to shoot the animal, could you follow orders?"

"That depends on the reason for the shooting," Axle responds, as he becomes aware of an intense dislike for Brown. "If the animal is incurably ill or injured to the point recovery is not likely, then I could reluctantly kill the animal. If the dog is healthy, then you'll have to find yourself someone else to perform your repulsive and senseless order."

The men chuckle, however Brown never cracks a smile.

"Am I to understand," Brown retorts, "that you have trouble following orders?"

"My parents are not in the habit of issuing orders that go beyond human decency," Axle answers, as he glances at his father. His father looks straight ahead. The boy straightens in his chair. "Let me re-state the answer, Mr. Brown. I could probably be coerced into slashing the tires on your car or pouring sugar into your gas tank. I might even be persuaded to set your car on fire and feel no remorse, but I wouldn't kill your dog."

"I sense you don't like Mr. Brown," Black offers. "Is there a reason for that?"

"Excuse me, but he seems like sort of an asshole, at least he asks asshole questions."

Everybody but Brown again chuckles.

"Any more questions, Mr. Brown?" Black asks, without looking at his colleague.

"None," Brown answers. "As you're already aware, I disagree with the idea of using a teenager for undercover work. I reluctantly agree that he seems qualified, unless he lets his mouth runaway when it shouldn't. If that happens, then he might be 16 going on dead."

Black questions, "How about your wife, Mike? Has she agreed to undertake this assignment?"

"She's all right with the idea, but she doesn't have any real concept of the danger involved," Mike answers. "Most people wouldn't. She should be here shortly. One of the female agents is driving her here so you can ask her without any speculation." Mike pauses. "I want my family to have your best briefing on this assignment before we place ourselves in harm's way."

"Then we should adjourn to the briefing room," Black offers. "We can proceed with the final details of the assignment there."

Everybody passes through a door into a conference room with a roll-down movie screen in position across one end. A podium stands near the screen, and plush theater seats are arranged in elevations that rise upward toward the rear of the room. The back wall contains several projection ports. A dark lens extends through the middle opening.

Maggie Marston rises from a front seat to give her son and husband a quick peck and a hug. The three alight in the front row with Maggie in the middle. Mr. Blue positions himself behind the podium, the room lights dim, and a projector flashes a colored photo onto the screen. The slide is the bust of a middle-aged man with a bullet hole in the center of his forehead. Powder burns radiate outward from the ragged hole. His face is ashen with dark circles of settled blood beneath the skin of his face, neck and chest. The body is lying on a metal gurney with his lower half covered by a green sheet. All three members of the family intake air. They all swallow as they sit a little straighter. Axle has never seen a dead body before. He shudders.

Blue begins, "Agent Ralph Pine was inserted into the Amerada, Texas area as a roustabout with an oil company. He was in place for three months before being found dead on March 5th of this year. His body was discovered floating face down in an irrigation ditch near Shidler, Texas by a farmer three days after Agent Pine failed to report for work. His hands and torso indicate that he had been tortured. A sharp instrument, possibly pruning shears or a chisel, amputated several of his finger digits. The cause of death was a low-velocity, copper-jacketed, pistol round fired point-blank from a .25 caliber handgun. The bullet was recovered from the cranial cavity. We have no knowledge of what information the perpetrator was seeking, or if Agent Pine revealed the information they sought.

"Agent Pine was a single man. We feel this fact may have brought attention to him. His contacts with our office came by phone from towns outside the mission area. We have no reason to believe that his calls were monitored, or that Agent Pine had gained more information than his reports indicated. His reports were filed at pre-determined times from different pay phones in adjacent towns, because the local phone system consists of party lines. Additionally, the phone company channels all calls through a common switchboard, so phone calls could be easily monitored. Agent Pine was a highly trained, motivated and experienced agent who would not compromise his mission."

Big Mike Marston extends a hand up into the light beam of the slide projector.

"Yes, Mike," Black says. "Do you have a question?"

"Before we get too far down the road of the people who have lost their lives in this effort, I'd like to make a couple comments before we're told what information you want us to gather."

"That's reasonable enough," Black responds.

The projector is turned off. The lights in the room are turned on.

"Have you lost more than one agent in the target area?

Mr. Black quickly responds, "Agent Pine is the only agent we have used to this point."

"Will there be other operatives working the area that we should know about?"

"We do not intend to use any additional agents while you're there."

"My son and I noticed that your organization has become sloppy at surveillance," Mike contends. "Although my son is an amateur, he spotted the hot dog vender outside as a phony." Mike gives a chuckle. "Small wonder, the guy doesn't have anything to sell. When you decide to cut costs on an operation, don't do it with the props you're using." Mr. Black opens his mouth to reply, but merely compresses his lips. Being admonished is not something he is used to experiencing. "Furthermore, my son also detected someone peering from behind the curtains of the upstairs window. The two goons sweeping the street were obvious plants. They remained in a group and kept sweeping the same spot over and over again. In view of these factors, the loss of Agent Pine may have been caused by the nonprofessional nature of this organization. From all outward appearances, this outfit has more leaks than a colander in an Italian restaurant."

"The plants outside were there to see if you would detect them, Major Marston," Black replies. "We wanted to know how observant you and your son would be. I planned to debrief you separately, but since we are pressed for time today, I elected not to. Did you by any chance pickup the tail that followed you from Gillette?"

"Do you mean the yellow Packard sedan that passed us several times with the blond woman driving?" Mike answers. "The same blond that came into the room awhile ago bearing refreshments?"

"You appear to not have missed much." Black has an air of annoyance about him. "Mr. Blue, will you please skip over the history of the case and get directly to the details of what our client is asking us to do."

"Just a minute," Mike barks, with annoyance in his voice. "I've had a taste of you free-form thinkers before. You seem capable of losing an anvil in a locked room."

"That comment is uncalled for, major," Black retorts. The exasperation in his voice is noticeable. "I ask you now, are you at all interested in this assignment?"

"I'm interested from the aspect of the amount of money involved, which now seems insubstantial," Mike answers. "You've already lost one agent and that makes me skeptical of your ability to perform this operation. I'm interested only if several initiatives are satisfied."

"And what are those?" Black asks, skeptically.

"First, that we have no personal contact with any of you home-office types while we're on assignment. Secondly, the money involved will be a $100,000 for each person involved, not the $50,000 you've offered. The total sum is to be paid in advance. Third, you describe Agent Pine as being one of your better agents. I'm more objective than that. I look at him and wonder if perhaps he failed to do the one thing that might have saved his life; he didn't think."

"Your requirements make it impossible for us to supervise the operation," Black answers. "We can't operate under your conditions."

"You've made at least one glaring error from the onset, Black," Big Mike thunders. "You assume that you are going to supervise me while I'm involved in a dangerous situation where somebody's already been killed. Furthermore, if something happens to me I want whoever survives to have a trust fund of another $100,000 to help them get on with life. There will be three of us involved and we will all be at great risk."

Black stares piercingly at Mike. "I need to speak with my associates in private. Let's take a short break. You ought to know by now that should anything happen to any of you, the survivors will be adequately provided for by the organization."

"No, Black, I don't know that at all. In fact, I've wondered more than once how you people propose to compensate anyone for the loss of a family member. What exactly will our lives be worth to the organization?"

"I cannot answer your question convincingly, but your background and abilities are worth more to us than you can even imagine."

With the last comment, the three suits march out of the room with Black in the lead. Mike moves to the roll-up movie screen hanging across the end of the room. He moves the edge of the item away from the wall for a look at the reverse side. Maggie watches her husband for a short while.

"You don't like this situation, do you?"

"No, I don't. I've been involved in several of their cute little wartime operations. For that reason, I've learned to cover my backside when I'm in the field. You know, of course, that the room is bugged and they are somewhere in the building listening to us."

Maggie's face flushes as she glances around. Axle remains in his seat and scours the room. He searches for some indication that what his father says is true. The boy doesn't see anything suspicious, but nobody contributes further conversation, at least verbally.

Mike Marston's mother, Belinda, had been severely injured in an automobile accident when Mike was eight years old. The injury left her unable to hear, so Mike and his parents learned Sign Language. Later, when his father died of a stroke and Mike's mother came to live with his family, both Axle and Maggie learned to sign. The elderly woman died two years ago, but the Marstons continued to practice sign language so they didn't lose their ability. Mike signs to his wife and son.

"Mic behind screen and probably another in light fixture overhead. Watch what you say."

Approximately 10 minutes pass before Mr. Black and Mr. Blue return to the room. Black has an irritated manner about him.

"We reluctantly agree to your terms. How do you propose that we communicate with each other during the project?"

"I'll have an answer for you when this briefing is finished," Mike mutters, as he drops onto a seat beside his wife. "Oh, and one other thing," Mike growls, as he leans forward toward Mr. Black. "You didn't mention the money. I need payment well enough in advance so it can be placed in trust before we begin training. Day after tomorrow will be fine."

Mr. Black nods, as he makes a noise that sounds like a snort.

"Will a cashier's check be sufficient or do you desire cash?"

"Cash should work nicely," Mike answers, as he turns to face the front of the room with a slight smile on his face.

Maggie squeezes his hand. Mr. Black moves to stand before his newest recruits where he extends a hand individually to the three Marstons in turn.

"Welcome to the Ironstone Group. We will train you to perform every future mission. We expect you to follow orders as they are given. If you do not, you will be dismissed immediately. Our guidelines are very stringent for any assignments you might undertake. You may terminate your employment with us at any time following the first year. The first year's employment is mandatory because of the type of training you will receive. Most of your assignments will involve some degree of risk; therefore, you will be paid by individual assignment as it is performed. Do you understand the terms of employment as I have explained them?"

Mr. Black looks at each member of the Marston family individually as he receives their individual responses. A chorus of, "Yes, sirs," fill the room.

"Very well," Black mutters, as he looks at Blue. "You may continue the briefing."

As the room lights dim, Blue turns on a small hooded light above the podium. He clears his throat as he leafs through a sheaf of notes. He begins the briefing anew.

"This is an information-for-hire project, as most of your assignments will be. In all cases and for your future guidance, the name Ironstone Group is not for public dissemination outside the organization. This project involves missing women in the general area of Amerada, Texas. Our client is a very wealthy, vengeful man living on the east coast, and has absolutely no faith in the Amerada County sheriff's department. He is concerned with the disappearance of his niece. He is convinced that she was kidnapped, although no ransom note or any form of communication has been received. The girl disappeared five months ago from a farm in an outlying area of Amerada County. The family has given up all hope of finding her alive. They are concerned only with the discovery and punishment of her abductors."

A photo of a very pretty blond teenager flashes onto the screen. The photo is a school picture, the kind every kid comes home with and the parents buy a dozen or so to mail to relatives. Blue continues.

"The nearest multiple habitation to the farm where she lived is Shidler. Shidler is a small community with a population of about 3,200 people. It is located 38 miles inland from the Gulf coast and 86 miles from Houston. People concerned with the production of oil, small working ranches and family owned farms sparsely populate the remainder of the county. The petroleum industry constitutes most of the economy. Commercial fishing is also a minor factor.

"A total of eight young women and one young man have disappeared in similar fashion during the past nine years. None of these people have been recovered either dead or alive. None of them have been heard from following their disappearance. Agent Pine is the first person to have been killed in connection with this investigation. He is also the first of our agents lost during any peacetime mission.

"The sheriff's department is a rather primitive and largely untrained organization run by an elected official. The sheriff has been in office over 10 years."

A photo of the sheriff appears on the screen. The photo is grainy and has been taken with a long lens. He wears a light brown western style suit along with a Stetson hat. He wears cowboy boots, a brown striped white shirt with a matching string tie.

"This is Sheriff Harvey Kraven," Blue offers, as he glances at the screen. "He is 42 years old and prior to becoming sheriff, he lived on the edge of a large marsh south of Amerada. He is unmarried and from a rural mountain area of Arkansas. He has a seventh grade education and no apparent family history prior to his arrival in town. This has caused us to wonder if Kraven is his real family name. Sheriff Kraven is quite popular within the community, as he continues to be reelected and has had very little political competition. We had a government agency solicit information from the sheriff in the matter of the missing persons. The agency was stonewalled. The sheriff and his establishment have proven to be both inefficient as well as incompetent in this matter. Thus, we have been hired to resolve the issue. The sheriff's summation of the disappearances has been the same in every instance. He infers that the young people merely ran away for a better life elsewhere.

"The sheriff's most recent investigation located two alleged witnesses. One was a trucker who claimed to have given a young girl a ride from Shidler to Houston at about the time of the woman's disappearance. The description of the girl matched those of the missing person and seems to support the instance of a runaway. The Houston police were informed, but there has been no discovery. The case has gone cold.

"The second witness was an attendant at the Shidler bus station who identified the photograph of the missing girl as being a person who bought a bus ticket for Houston about the time she vanished. The fact the investigation provides two methods of leaving town makes it seem suspicious. Additionally, both of these witnesses have since disappeared. No follow-up has been performed that we are aware of."

Blue pauses for a drink of water before continuing.

"With the single exception of the young man, all the other missing persons have been women of high school age. The oldest we know about was 19. They have uniformly been young and pretty. They all vanished on a Friday night. None of them told a friend that they were leaving. All but one of the missing women was from Amerada County, although none lived within the town limits of Amerada."

Blue pauses for another drink of water.

"I wish to emphasize that kids who run away generally tell a close friend they are leaving and where they are going. In every instance, these victims disappeared without leaving a clue. The young man involved vanished while searching for his missing sister. The family car turned up in the small town of Bailey some 40 miles away. The keys were in the ignition and the car had been wiped clean of all fingerprints.

"Since all the victims are women, the crimes are presumed to be of a sexual nature. Apparently, what we are looking for is a new species of criminal that some law enforcement agencies are referring to as a *serial killer.*

"Whoever we are seeking operates from the vicinity of either

Shidler or Amerada. Pins posted on a map representing missing people place Amerada near the center of a circle of abduction. We elected to insert Agent Pine into Amerada as a starting point. The fact that he was killed while conducting his investigation seems to verify our assumption.

"Your job will be to collect information that will help identify the person involved in these abductions. We believe this information will also include the Pine murder case. Once the culprit has been identified, the Ironstone Group will deal with them in our usual fashion. You are to report every scrap of information uncovered no matter how incidental it may seem. We will determine its relevance."

Mr. Blue looks up from his notes.

"That, in essence, Major Marston, is the issue we are dealing with. You now know the substance of the case. I will not try to minimize the risk involved. We feel that Agent Pine must have stumbled onto something. Whatever he discovered, the information cost him his life. When we learned of his death, we sent a team to his quarters. They found nothing. The place had been thoroughly searched and his car torched. We checked his drop points, but there was nothing at either of them. We were checking his drop points every day. There had been only an acknowledgment that he was visiting them. On other assignments, he had posted code words that let us know he was alright. On this one, he did not. That concludes my portion of the briefing. Are there any questions?"

Big Mike looks at Maggie. "What do you think, sugar?"

Maggie murmurs, "I'm game."

Mike turns to Axle, who offers, "Me too, Pop."

"We're in," Mike says to Mr. Black, "but I want some form of communication that doesn't include phone calls from distant places and drop points that can be discovered by tailing us. My understanding of our cover is that we are supposed to live on the income I make as a field mechanic for an oil company. In a small community, everybody seems to know how well off everyone else is. You have confirmed that the telephone system consists of party lines. People tend to eavesdrop. Frequent travel out of town by anyone who is not required to travel will attract attention after only a few trips.

I'd like to use a keyed shortwave radio system of the type we used during the war. We can transmit in Morse code on pre-determined frequencies using coded messages. Not many people use shortwave these days. Hardly anyone can read a keyed message for that reason."

"Do any members of your family besides yourself have telegraphy experience?" Mr. Black asks.

Axle offers, "We have a HAM radio station at home, so I have some ability, but I need a lot more to be really proficient. If I attend a school, then I can probably pick it up in a hurry."

"What do you think?" Black asks everyone in the room.

"Sounds better than phone calls on party lines or drop points," Blue answers. "If we change the times of transmission and the frequencies every time you transmit, then your communications should be relatively difficult to detect. The set can be hidden in the house. Nobody outside the federal government has direction finding equipment, so you should be able to communicate undetected for an unlimited period of time. I personally like the idea."

"Okay, Mr. Blue, you may continue with the dissemination of information in private. We have a 'Go', so we will begin making arrangements for your training and departure. I have selected August 12th as the target date for your arrival in Amerada. I've also selected a jumping off point in central Oklahoma. I'll leave the method of movement for your household goods to you. My opinion is that a moving company would be too extravagant for your income and also too traceable. That mode of movement is therefore out of the question. Anybody got any problems with that?"

Axle asks, "Do I get to take my car?"

"That's up to your parents," Black answers. "What kind of car is it?"

"I just got it licensed," Axle offers, with enthusiasm. "It's a '36 Ford coupe with a 47-Mercury engine, an Auburn clutch and a rumble seat."

"Sounds normal to me," Black answers, as he smiles.

"He can take the car," Mike mutters. "For the move we'll need a large enclosed stock trailer with a two-inch ball-hitch. I wouldn't think that the organization would have any trouble supplying that?"

Black nods. "That won't be a problem."

Mike continues, "School will be out during our move, so Axle can make the first trip during a weekday as though I am working. Then he can return for the final load on a weekend."

"Fair enough," Black comments. "We will arrange for the type of trailer you request to be on-site in Oklahoma on a date you specify."

The briefing is followed by a question and answer period lasting six hours. Every aspect of the mission is discussed. Over the next few weeks, a fake identity for the family is established. They will have lived near Seminole, Oklahoma. The family is to have lived in a small, six-house, oil-field camp that has been recently razed because of oil depletion in the area. Two of the six families who occupied the camp were killed in separate automobile accidents after they settled elsewhere.

The Fitzpatrick family was killed near New Orleans. Two of the remaining four families were young, childless couples, two of which gravitated into other occupations. The remaining two were lured to Arabia and South America with two different oil companies. School records are altered to reflect Axle's participation in two different schools in two years. The remainder of his schooling finds its way into the files of three defunct school systems that consolidated with other districts in three different states.

Michael and Maggie Marston are given family background identities originating from Eldora, Iowa and Minneapolis, Minnesota, respectively. New identities become an easy task, because neither has any living relatives. Backgrounds are established that will withstand everything but an intense FBI investigation. Everybody keeps his first and middle names and the family name becomes Mannheim.

Chapter Five

The kidnappers eventually tire of every captive, or she becomes pregnant. At that point, the captive is marked for death. When her time arrives, the-keeper-of-women is the one to dispose of her. Getting rid of the women is more fun than using them.

This one is pregnant and beginning to show, as they all do. He decides that the next day, August 12, 1949, will be the day. He awakens her and tells her what is about to happen. It is after midnight.

"Today's your day, girlie. We're goin' to visit Old Lucifer and he's gonna love ya ta death."

He enjoys the look of naked terror on her face. He always takes them to see Old Lucifer when they first arrive. The trip is part of his training program. He shows them where they'll end up if they don't cooperate. With them watching, he feeds Lucifer something. If the critter is big like a deer, Lucifer grabs it by the head and begins rolling as he tries to tear off a piece. If he can't tear it up or swallow it whole, he takes it to the bottom of his pool. There, he wedges the body beneath a waterlogged tree. A day later, when the body is good and ripe, Lucifer sinks to the bottom of his hole where he tears up the remains and devours the entire carcass in big chunks.

After one session of watching the creature savage his prey, the comment of, "Going to see Old Lucifer," produces the desired results in every woman. Lucifer scares them so bad they'll do anything to get another chance to perform in the desired fashion. The-keeper maintains the horror by describing in detail what is about to happen. While he talks, he jabs her in the ribs with his index finger.

"He's going to grab you there, and there, and there, and there."

He performs as though he is tickling a child. She becomes hysterical before he stops. That's when he makes her perform a sexual favor for him. When she finishes pleasuring him, he pulls her up off her knees. He tells her that they will leave to go see Old Lucifer at 3:00 in the afternoon. She gnaws the knuckles of her left hand while she stares at the wind-up clock on the shelf above the fireplace.

At 2:45 that afternoon, he wrestles her onto her stomach. He sits astride her while he ties her hands behind her back. He removes the dog chain from her ankle before he ties her legs together above the knees. Her hysteria gives way to loud piercing screams of terror when she realizes that he actually intends to do what he threatened.

"Ye might as well be quiet, girlie," the-keeper mutters. "Ain't nobody gonna hear ya way out here."

He kneels with one knee in the middle of her back. When he finishes binding her, he slings her across his shoulder before he carries her to the creek. There, he drops her between the two middle seats of the boat and places a dog collar around her neck. The collar is attached to both oarlocks by dog chains so she can't jump overboard. He starts the outboard, and backs away from the wharf before he turns downstream toward the saw grass flats.

The endless dance of water and sand has carved leisurely channels through the tall grass. Somewhere beyond vision, the rich broth of the stream mixes with the saltwater of the Gulf. When he enters the marsh, herring gulls begin to follow the boat. The woman alternately sobs and pleads for mercy during the trip. By the time they arrive at Lucifer's gator hole, her voice is so ragged she can barely speak.

He carries her on his shoulder to the top of the knoll above the gator hole. Near the top of the rise, he stops to scan the area. When he is certain that Lucifer is not atop the bank searching for a meal, he drops her on a steep clay bank. He arranges her upright on her knees so she is facing the marsh.

He holds her in place, resting against his right thigh, using her long hair as a handle. She kneels there with her eyes closed. The entire time, she shakes her head.

He looks down at her snarled blond hair. If he leans a little further forward, he can see her cute upturned nose. He directs his attention to the dark muddy water below the bank. The pool is nearly round, and 40 feet across. Tall marsh grass and reeds define the edges. Large lily pads decorate the water further into the pool. A large dead tree lays angled downward into the pool.

The-keeper-of-women examines the boundaries of the gator

hole. Before him in the saw grass are channels and potholes too numerous to know them all. Swarms of water birds swirl above the flats as they work the marsh for their livelihood.

The naked girl is crisscrossed with the white strands of rope that secures her arms. She presses hard back against him. Her eyes are wide with terror. He pulls the chain on the old bronze school bell bolted to the trunk of a big water oak tree atop the rise. The bell clangs three times. A cloud of ducks, gulls, rails and coots burst into the air. The birds scatter into segmented flocks to land farther out.

Across the pond, a snout appears from the grass followed by two wide spaced yellow eyes near the spiked crown of a long dark gray-green back. A long thick tail undulates as the apparition moves across the pool to the bottom of the bank where it lies motionless, looking up. The girl screams.

"No, oh, God no!" repeats her scalded voice, while shaking her head and trying to back away from the edge of the bank.

The man laughs as he speaks to the creature below him.

"Look what I brung you fer supper, old one!"

Lucifer has arrived in the form of a giant alligator 16-feet long and 50 years old. The animal weighs more than 500 pounds. Its compound jaw crushes bones, sounding like a hammer snapping a bundle of wooden matchsticks.

The man gives a shudder when he considers how the women never last very long when Old Lucifer takes 'em home for supper. The gator always comes to the bottom of the bank when the bell rings.

Lucifer floats motionless in the water griping the bank with his front feet as he awaits the treat that follows the sound of the bell. The reptile eats whatever he is given: deer, coon, chicken, or teenage girl, it doesn't matter. Lucifer is neat too. There is never anything left over to indicate that a girl was fed to the animal in the muddy pool. The-keeper cackles again in the heavy still air of the marsh.

He rants, "Ye be vanished without a trace, girlie. Lucifer be th' greatest garbage disposal ever invented."

The girl cringes before her tormentor as she gazes downward in horror. She tries to back away from the inevitable slide down the bank as she pleads for her life. Her words jumble together in a continuous sentence uttered as fast as she can draw breath.

The-keeper listens to her some more before bending forward to cut off a lock of her hair. He places the hair coil inside a glycine envelope from his overall bib pocket. The envelope contains a piece of foil-backed white paper from a cigarette pack with the girl's name scrawled across the back. Later, the envelope will go into the box with his other trophies. Next, he removes the collar from her neck.

When he tires of listening to her, he places a foot in the middle of her back and shoves. Charlotte Mayhew's final scream echoes across the marsh. She continues to scream during the time she has left.

Chapter Six

Axle crosses the Red River Bridge before dawn. He looks down at the sullen red muddy water. *Well, here we are, sentenced to Texas. I sure hope this assignment is not some form of extended misery.* The macadam road stretches before him like a dark gray serpent with a white stripe down its back. The drive has turned into a punishing program engineered by circumstance to cause tooth decay coupled with emotional damage. WHAT?

Axle is so eager to finish the drive that he has stopped only for gas. He has surpassed the sappiness of upscale teenage dining. During the next 11 hours, he consumes eight double colas and a stupendous bag of lard fried potato chips. The lingering taste of the cheap chips makes chugging colas a necessity.

The last 100 miles has involved a hallucination featuring the world's largest hamburger accompanied by a front-end-loader quantity of butter-colored fries. The imagined beverage is a frosted glass of pineapple milkshake thin enough to be vacuumed up through a straw. Maintaining vigilance while listening to the tires drone on the highway is difficult.

Axle hangs his head out the window where the windblast helps him stay awake. His head changes the airflow within the car and chip crumbs are scattered everywhere. He grabs the bag and crumples it against his thigh before tossing it out the window. The residue from the bag will undoubtedly create a bald spot on the grass-covered roadside shoulder.

The boy is developing new dimensions of boredom when he rounds a curve and sees in the distance a mound of startling greenness. Amerada materializes. He hopes there is an eatery ahead that features something more than rice, beans, and tortillas.

The end of the summer vacation of '49 arrives. In most communities, kids are reporting for football practice. Instead of an anticipated practice, Axle is moving the family possessions with all the dynamics of an over-the-road-trucker.

He rehearses the new family history for the hundredth time. His family has lived for the past 16 years in a remote oil field camp. He is the son of Michael and Maggie Mannheim of central Oklahoma. Amerada will be his first hometown of a lifetime. He was born in a house that formerly stood in a vanished oil field camp.

Gone is his favorite red and gray letter-jacket with its red chenille 'G' for Gillette. In its place is a glossy red warm up model with red, white and black knit cuffs. This creation came from a pawnshop in Shawnee, Oklahoma. The disgusting jacket with its flannel lining hangs from a bar suspended above the backseat of the car with other items of the family's wardrobe.

Three months ago, the Homestead Oil Company announced that the Waynesboro camp would be razed and the leased land returned to private ownership. The action was the result of reduced oil production from a rapidly depleting oil reservoir at the 5,800-foot level. Diminished oil production has diverted the local employees' attention to pressing issues like the price of the next meal. Other camps owned by other companies met the same fate. Poverty swooped down on the oil patch like some ethereal bat out of the night. People scramble for jobs in other parts of the country before money becomes too scarce to travel.

Disruption in the region made it easy to insert the Mannheim family into the general flow of people out of the area. Enter Axle Reed Mannheim with most of the family possessions in a four-horse trailer provided by Mr. Jonathan Black. Axle has made the trip with a swiftness and boldness that astonishes even him. Luckily, he hasn't made a wrong turn, because at age 16, he is hormonally incapable of asking for directions. His father has the same problem. Once in South Dakota on a pheasant-hunting trip, Big Mike made a wrong turn and lost his way.

Maggie muttered, "Do you know why the Jews wandered in the desert for 40 years?" Mike knew better than to respond to his wife's question. "Because Moses wouldn't ask anyone for directions."

The current trip is Axle's first solo journey since he acquired a driver's license. He is so elated with the open road and his success at finding the town, that his mind hums like the soft burr of a radio slightly off-frequency.

His parents came to Amerada once before the move. They remained four days while supposedly cleaning before returning to their imaginary home in Oklahoma. Two workmen from the organization came late at night to install a shortwave radio.

The unit is masterfully hidden with the transmitter encased in a tin enclosure attached to the side of a floor furnace in the crawl space. The installation matches the galvanized enclosure of the furnace and blends perfectly with the rest of the heating system. The shortwave is slaved to a Hallicrafters radio installed on a table in Axle's bedroom. An antenna wire runs up the inside of the wall from the table radio to vanish beyond the ceiling where it engages a heavy-duty wire to an outside antenna. The lightning arrester on the tall transformer pole near the house becomes a shortwave radio antenna.

The dial for the Hallicrafters is the remote tuner for the shortwave unit beneath the house. An obscure switch labeled 'mute' transfers the radio function from ordinary AM to shortwave. The transmitter key and earphones plug into individual phone jacks in the center of dual rubber footpads on the forward bottom of the radio housing. A counter-sunk brass screw serves to hide the female phone jacks contained in the center of each foot cushion. The male jacks for the key and earphones are inserted into the footpads. When not in use the transmitter key and earphones are hidden within the inner door-facing of the bedroom closet door-jam in Axle's bedroom.

The door-facing is hinged with blind hinges so that it swings outward to reveal the equipment, but only when the closet door is closed. The person removing the gear must be inside the closet with the door closed before the door-facing will open to allow entry. A single light bulb dangles at the end of a two-strand wire from a porcelain light fixture in the ceiling inside the closet. A 60-watt bulb provides light to open the concealed compartment within the closet.

To open the compartment, a 16-penny nail is inserted into a hole in the inner edge of the door-facing. The nail trips an inner lock and then functions as a handle to rotate the facing board on its hinges. The nail has its own hole in the wall of the closet where it appears to function as a clothes-hanging peg. An item of apparel will always be dangling from the nail.

For their telegraphy training, all three Mannheims are turned over to Rick Morresy. Morresy is a master telegrapher who is retired from the Army Signal Corps. The family becomes proficient on the transmitter key within the five weeks of allotted time.

Axle has a natural aptitude for telegraphy and is more proficient than either his mom or dad. He can send and receive at 40 characters a minute. Rick Morresy is a HAM Radio freak. This has cost him three marriages. He maintains his own radio station in his home. His nightly efforts allow him to increase the range of his transmissions through the oddity of night-effect. Night-effect involves a portion of the ionosphere. The ionosphere exists between about 31 miles and 250 miles above the earth. Charged particles refract radio waves back to the earth. This quirk of the atmosphere permits radio signals to skip off the ionized particles to be beamed around the world. The degree of success depends on the time of day or night, the season and the solar cycle. During nighttime, radio waves bounce off the ionosphere to be received in distant places that could not normally receive communication during daylight hours.

Rick Morresy's HAM colleagues refer to him as 'Night Owl'. He is addressed as such on the 60-meter wave band around the world. Morresy became very fond of Axle because of his quick learning. He nicknames him 'Singer'. Night Owl claims that Axle plays the keys the way a musician plays a musical instrument. Axle can hardly wait to arrive at his new home, so he can contact Night Owl by keyed message.

Chapter Seven

The new house is a two-story dwelling constructed of native stone and is situated in the southwest corner of town. They had anticipated that Axle's arrival in town would be at night. Street signs are scarce in Amerada so Big Mike drew a map to help his son find the address. Axle's mission is to locate the house, unload the trailer and then return as quickly as possible for the final load of family possessions. The transfer must be completed by Friday. Axle's parents have a great deal of faith in their son's ability to function as more than a normal teenager. During the trip, he has considered the enormous responsibility that has been entrusted in him. He hopes to perform his duties without the slightest hitch.

The highway into town leads down a gentle slope, around a curve and across a wooden bridge. The span is restricted to one-lane of traffic, so a flagman has been posted at each end of the bridge. A cavity in the middle of the northbound lane gives testimony to the fact that something very large dropped through the lane. A sign near the approach end of the bridge reads West Clear Creek, while another illustration indicates 'One Way Traffic'. An old man performs the mechanical function of a traffic signal. He maintains the vacant stare of an empty billboard as he flashes the reversible STOP/SLOW placard clutched in his left hand.

There is another stolid elder at the reverse end of the structure performing the same function from the opposite direction. *There's a job to aspire to. Grow up and become a flagman at the town bridge.* Axle waits in a line of traffic for safe passage into his new hometown. When his turn arrives to travel the bridge, he crosses looking down at the water.

"Oh boy, look at that," he mutters, when he sees a fish break water downstream.

The creek is substantial, deep and looks to be teaming with fish. He speculates about all the fun to be had there. There will swimming plus fishing by trotline for giant catfish and bass by the score. He imagines days with his skin puckered from hours of being immersed in the clear tempting water. The water is moving in two slow braids across a riffle 50 yards downstream. His last glimpse of the creek bottom features a bittern flying downstream. The bird skims low over the water as it flashes beneath the bridge.

A patch of incredible greenness serves to identify Amerada. Entry is made between two rows of tall sycamore trees. As the copse of trees arrives, so does a sign stating "Amerada, Pop 1,801". He passes the city limit sign and is cast into a world he never before imagined.

From the sign to the first stoplight, he travels within a tunnel created by the huge trees. The trees were planted more than 40 years ago. The limbs have been trimmed by passing truck trailers so that the initial feature of entering town is to travel through a square green tunnel. The three blocks of emerald beauty is enchanting. The splendor of the tunnel gives his tired mind an emotional lift. The day is fine and the importance of arriving in his new hometown is indelibly etched in his mind. Axel specially notices that several of the tree trunks have been scared by vehicle impact.

Have to watch that; sudden stoppage against a large tree trunk would not be in the best interest of one's health.

He catches glimpses of the town through the trees. All the houses seem to be of the same style. They are all made of wood and one story tall. The only significant difference seems to be the color of paint. His dad referred to that style of construction as a shotgun house: you could shoot in the back door and the shot would pass out the front door without touching anything else.

What kind of town is this without at least one elevator to ride? The town's most major structure seems to be the condemned bridge at the north edge of town. According to his father's map, the creek circles the outskirts of town to cross the highway a second time further south. Probably another less than functional bridge out there as well.

He speculates, "The Gulf coast lies about eight miles to the south. There will be fish there as big as this car." During the summer, huge tropical storms will come roaring ashore. He remembers seeing the after effects of a typhoon in the orient on a Movie-Tone newsreel at a Gillette theater. The position of the creek might mean they'll all be washed out to sea when the first hurricane arrives. That is his first hint of possible trouble in paradise.

Near the end of the enchanting tunnel, the macadam road surface becomes a series of potholes linked by an occasional strip of ancient asphalt. He clutches the steering wheel as he jams on the brakes. His speed drops to about two miles an hour, but even that seems too fast.

The next obstacle is a road grader with its ripping-claw extended. The machine is gnawing the asphalt off the roadbed ahead of him. Two red dump trucks follow the grader gathering refuse. A piece of asphalt the size of a slice of key lime pie flips off the dump box of the nearest truck to land with a thump on the hood of the Pontiac. The chunk adheres squarely in the middle of the new paint job.

He passes the grader and the trucks before he stops for a traffic signal. While waiting for the light to change, he glances at the gas gauge. The needle is bouncing on empty. Unless he finds a service station soon, he will be viewing the scenery from afoot.

He turns left onto Main Street at the stoplight. The first building is a gas station with an adjoining grocery store. Two rows of red gas pumps stand sentinel-like on elevated concrete islands in front of a small blond-brick building with white trim. The roof is a steep green gabled affair with flaking paint that towers over two service bays.

A car on a hydraulic lift in the first stall is in the throws of a brake job. Naked brake shoes dangle at chest height from their respective axle back-up plates. The entrance to the remaining bay is clogged by a row of new tires standing on edge as they lean against each other. The tires create a long black caterpillar like presence that blocks the doorway as they await storage.

An extended roof exactly a car width wide covers the area beyond the first row of pumps. An old dog lies in the shade of the roof. The animal's basic lineage is so lost in past generations that it has degenerated into basic brown dog.

In the shade of the overhang sits a long wooden bench. At the end of the bench stands a square metal drum with a hand crank pump that sprouts through the center of the top. The body of the drum is painted red and labeled 'Kerosene'. Someone has added a white hand-painted scrawl that reads 'No Smoking'.

An old man wearing faded blue overalls and a pale blue work shirt with the sleeves rolled up sits on the bench near the drum. The man is puffing a corncob pipe. Atop his head is a finely striped herringbone gray billed cap of the type favored by railroad engineers. The old man is as dressed up as he is ever likely to be. The scene is so countrified that all that's needed is banjo music and someone playing a jug with a juice harp twanging in the background.

Axle parks next to the outside row of pumps and exits the vehicle. He walks around the car as he checks the tires. The old man nods as the boy passes by on his way inside the station. Axle nods in return.

Attached to the City Service brand service station is a small grocery store with a sign above the front door that announces 'Vaughan's Grocery'. The screen door to the establishment displays three, finger sized holes in the screen wire mesh. A metal sign on the door advertises Sunshine Crackers.

A narrow, black rubber hose lies across the concrete apron. One end vanishes beneath the brick veneer of the station wall. The other end disappears into the ground beyond the far pump island. As car wheels passed over the hose, a bong sounds within the station office to summon the attendant.

A stern looking, middle-aged man wearing khakis with the name 'Bob' embroidered above his left shirt pocket ambles out. Bob's face bears the scars of an ancient case of near terminal acne from when he was a youngster. Axle lifts the engine hood.

Bob offers, "Howdy, need some gas?"

"Fill 'er up," the boy answers, as he ducks beneath the hood.

The gas pumps are transparent round glass tubes standing atop a red pump body. The tube is a foot in diameter and a yard tall. The metal index within the glass cylinder displays six gallons of amber colored gasoline. The clear glass column is filled using a hand pump. The long pump handle is mounted to a round-keyed metal shaft protruding from the side of the pump housing. A decorative blown-glass globe atop the crest of the pump displays the trade name of the gasoline company servicing the station. This one wears a large white crown with red trim. The circumference of the bottom edge of the globe bears the inscription Crown Oil Company.

Bob inserts the nozzle and begins draining gas into the tank. While he works the nozzle, he inspects the vehicle. He leans back as he looks slant-wise at the youngster beneath the hood.

"Boy, you don't see cars this old around here that ain't all rusted out. Is this a '41 Pontiac?" The boy nods, while pulling the dipstick to check the oil. Bob tosses him a rag from his hip pocket to wipe the gauge-stick with. "Thought it was. Brother-in-law had one. They ain't worth shit."

About like you Bob-o, Axle mentally informs himself.

"Depends on how well you take care of it," Axle answers. "This one's never given any trouble."

"Are you from around here? I haven't seen you before."

"Nope," Axle offers. "I'm from up north, just arrived in town."

"Stayin' long?" Bob asks, as he prepares to fill the glass column again.

"Hopefully, forever," Axle mumbles, with a thin smile.

He considers that Bob has just given the car six gallons and counting. Bob wipes the windshield with a damp sponge before he removes a couple of the more persistent bug splatters with a single edge razor blade scraper. He dries the glass with another rag. Bob completes the windshield as Axle finishes with the engine before he slams the hood closed.

Bob holds out his hand, as he says, "I'm Bob Harrison. Welcome to Amerada."

"Axle Mannheim," the boy answers, as they pump hands.

Bob has a firm grip and a big smile that displays a mouth full of tobacco stained yellow teeth. He pulls a plug of Browns Mule from a shirt pocket. He bites off a fresh chaw before offering it to Axle, who declines. Bob returns the plug to a shirt pocket. Bob turns to spit downwind before wiping his mouth with the back of a hand.

"You're a big kid," Bob says. "How old are you?"

"Sixteen," Axle answers. "I'll be 17 in September."

Bob has a thirst for information. He inhales, working the fresh chaw around in his mouth.

"What's your daddy do?"

"Field-mechanic for the Barnwell Oil Company," Axle answers.

Bob nods vigorously as he turns back to the pump.

"Have to wait before I pump the top full again," Bob announces, as he fills the sight gauge again then drains another 10 gallons before the tank is full. "I make that 18 gallons."

"More like 16," Axle offers. "The tank only holds 18 and it wasn't completely empty.

Bob nods his head as he returns the nozzle to its hook.

"Forget about the other two," Bob mutters. "My memory ain't what it used to be." They adjourn to the office to settle the bill. Bob begins writing with a pencil in a ticket booklet. Shortly he looks up from the receipt book. "You still in school?"

"Yes, sir."

"I hope you play football."

"Yep, every chance I get," the boy answers.

"Thought so," Bob says, "you got the look. I'll bet you lift weights?"

"Yeah, six days a week."

"Are ya any good at football?" Bob asks.

"Respectable."

"We generally have a really good team. Practice starts in a couple days. High school sports are just about our only entertainment, so the people hereabouts can hardly wait for the next season to start." Axle nods as he watches Bob finish the ticket.

"Took second in the state last year," Bob mutters admiringly. "Our school is small but the local boys are real tough. You be sure an' sign up afore practice starts, ya hear?"

Well, that clears up one question. Until now, Axle had figured that the local sport might be sweating.

"Where's the school?"

"One block north and four blocks west," Bob says, as he gestures with a hand. "Ya can't miss it."

"Thanks for the information."

Axle sprints out the door before Bob can launch into a new topic. He moves around the dog in passing. The animal thumps his tail on the concrete without even moving his head. The old man is now asleep with the pipe in his mouth. He is slumped over against the 'No

Smoking' sign on the kerosene drum.

This place will surely go up in flame one of these days. When it does, it will singe hell out of the dog and startle the hell out of the old man.

His thoughts are diverted as he considers buying the makings for a couple sandwiches instead of finding a restaurant. He moves the car and the trailer to the side of the concrete apron away from the potential fire hazard of the old man and the fuel drum. He heads for the front door of the grocery store.

The screen door slaps the jam behind him as he pauses to allow his eyes to adjust to the dim light. A candy display case sits near the entrance. Across the aisle is a free standing pop cooler. The cooler is filled with ice, water and soda bottles. The glass top of the cooler has two horizontal sliding metal lids that overlap each other in the middle. One side is three inches open. The cooler is red with a white *Love Cola* seal on the side. Axle's attention span makes it only as far as the candy display. Behind the counter, a matronly looking woman sells him five Jolly-Jack candy bars at a penny apiece from a tear-away strip.

Past the pop cooler stands a meat case with a slanted glass front. A meat scale sits atop the counter in a position so everybody can see the weight registered on the dial. The walls of the store are lined from floor to ceiling with canned goods. A shallow, wooden, multi-stalled fresh vegetable bin hangs near the meat counter. Skeins of chili peppers hang tied to cords along with red onions in ventilated sacks. The items add aroma to the scene as they dangle from open ceiling rafters.

Axle peels the first candy bar and drops the wrapper into a tall trashcan near the end of a wooden counter. The counter features a cash register along with a roll of white wrapping paper in a black cast iron holder with a tear away blade on one side. A spool of twine sits atop the highest shelf behind the counter. The string runs through a series of screw eyes in the rafters to dangle near the end of the paper roll. A grimy-looking oscillating fan in a far corner periodically blows the string to and fro.

Hanging from the ceiling in each corner of the room are strips of opaque yellow flypaper. The surface of each strip is generously anointed with dark victims in various stages of decay. Across the room are shelves with bolts of cotton cloth along with other dress making accommodations. A glass case holds thread, needles and crochet hooks. The floor is divided into sections by three-tier wooden shelves containing canned goods. Wheat flour and cornmeal in cloth bags lean against the counter face.

A hairy-armed man dressed in a white blood-streaked apron stands behind the meat counter. He is feeding meat scraps into a motorized meat grinder. One gander at the butcher makes Axle envision hair in the hamburger. He finds his shopping experience in Amerada to be less than desirable. He decides that he doesn't want to purchase anything further from Vaughan's Grocery. He passes back through the screen door on his way out.

The woman says, "Ya'll come back, ya hear."

Axle smiles at her, while making a vow to die of starvation before buying anything from the meat counter. The light of midday reveals fly specks on the candy bar wrappers. He approaches the car where he discovers a blond teenager standing on the rear bumper of the trailer. He is rummaging through the cartons inside. His attention has settled on one of the smaller boxes that won't quite fit through the space between the top of the tailgate and the roof. He tries pulling it through the gap without success.

Axle speaks from very close behind the kid, in loud voice, "Lose something?"

The voice startles the thief so badly that he flinches upward, ramming the top of his head into the overhead cross bar. The kid releases the box before he bends forward at the waist cradling his head.

"I was just bein' neighborly," the blond haired criminal offers. "I was tryin' to straighten one of your boxes that seemed about to fall out."

The kid is about 14. He is about 5 foot 4 with the gangly look of early youth. His facial skin has the approximate texture of a cinder block. His height makes him 10 inches shorter than Axle and approximately three years younger. The youngster has the features of a ferret. He probably lies every time his lips move.

."Thanks for the help," Axle answers. "Don't do it again."

The kid stares up into the face of his proposed victim, his mouth half open. He seems about to reply before deciding that Axle is a little too large to run his smart mouth further.

"Carry your ass outta here," Axle offers. "I never could stand a thief. What's your name so I remember you?"

The kid shakes his head as he backs several shuffling paces away from Axle.

"Up yours," he mutters, before he retreats along the street.

Several steps later he turns back to render a middle finger salute. Axle considers that if the box had been smaller, the thief would be in an alley somewhere rejoicing over what he'd stolen. A box of Mom's chicken feed sack dishtowels would surely have disappointed him. Bob appears in the office door at the sound of Axle's elevated voice. He yells after the retreating kid.

"Troy, you little bastard! You stay away from here."

Troy looks back at Bob, his jaw assuming a three-point stance of defiance. There is a fleeting moment before the look passes as though he has suffered a failure of nerve. The kid turns to jog south on the sidewalk.

"Damned little Kraven bastard." Bob mutters. "Them sons-a-bitches ain't nothin' but trouble."

Further along Main Street, Axle notices a police cruiser double-parked with the driver's door open and the gumball light rotating. Shortly, a cop appears from the space between two buildings. He is carrying a black nightstick. He wipes the club with a rag before he climbs into the cruiser. After a slight pause, he closes the door and proceeds along the street toward the filling station. Axle glances again at Troy as he ducks into a storefront more than a block away.

"Probably goin' there to hone his shoplifting skills," Bob murmurs. "Somebody oughta tan his ass and set him right with the world."

"That little sucker tried to steal a box from my trailer," Axle announces.

"Keep your eyes on anybody around here named Kraven," Bob mutters, as he continues to study the street. "Mongo Baron's another one to be leery of. He's the nephew of the sheriff and a meaner bastard never walked than that one."

Bob disappears into the first bay of the garage where he is apparently working on a brake job. The police cruiser pulls onto the station apron where it stops near a far gas pump. The cruiser is painted black and white with a county seal on the door that reads 'Amerada County Sheriff Department'.

A tall, skinny deputy climbs out and dons his smoky bear hat. He slides the nightstick into its socket before he meanders toward the horse trailer with out-of-state license plates. A sail-like nose blooms from the deputy's face. A weak chin adds prominence to his nose. His leather gear creaks under the weight of a gun, handcuffs, nightstick, and spare cartridge pack plus about a pound of keys that hangs from a snap on the left side of his belt. A black leather sap strap dangles from a hip pocket.

A chrome nametag above his left shirt pocket reads C. Kraven. C Kraven wears a tan colored uniform with dark brown pocket flaps and epaulets. A thin dark brown stripe follows his trouser out-seam. The uniform hangs on him like he's lost 20 pounds recently. His feet are shod in brown cowboy boots with glistening silver toe inlays. The peaked hat is tipped forward, which gives him a Marine Corps drill instructor look. All similarity there ends when he opens his mouth. His voice erupts shrilly above the traffic noise. It bears a backcountry hillbilly twang that barely passes for English.

"Is this your trailer?"

Axle shakes his head, as he answers, "No, sir. We borrowed it from a neighbor back home. We're using it to move."

The deputy bumps the side of the trailer with the heel of his hand. The blow makes the metal vibrate. While he scans the trailer he moves to the back entry gate where he peers inside.

"Is this stuff yours?" he asks.

"Yes, sir," Axle responds, as a small ball of anxiety knots in his stomach. C. Kraven zeroes in on a rear taillight lens with a thin crack radiating across the face. With the lens cover clearly in focus, he glares down at the license plate. "Something I can do for you, officer?"

"Oklahoma," the deputy mutters. "Yeah, you can give me your driver's license and registration. I'm gonna write you a ticket for the broke taillight."

"It works," Axle stammers in disbelief, as he steps toward the driver's door. "I'll turn it on so you can see that it works. It's just got a crack in the lens."

"Don't matter," the deputy crows, "we got laws around here about cracked taillights."

That makes about as much sense as a self-inflicted harpoon wound.

"You new hereabouts?" C. Kraven asks, as he opens his ticket book.

"Yes, sir," the boy answers, feeling wounded to the core. "I've been here about 15 minutes."

"Are you gonna live here?" C. Kraven asks.

"Yes, sir."

"Better get new license plates and a new driver's license afore long," the cop says. "People hereabouts don't much like Okie's, includin' me."

Bob materializes from the office doorway. He moves like a target at a shooting gallery.

"I don't want you on my property harassin' my customers and writin' tickets, Clete," Bob offers. "If you're gonna write tickets, do it on the street."

Clete pays very little attention to Bob, as he continues writing.

"I'm gonna forget you sayin' that, Harrison. Do yourself a favor: get back in your office. I'll tend to you later."

A point for Bob, he doesn't give up, instead he shoots right back.

"My property, my business, not yours."

Clete turns his head slowly, as though he can't believe what he's just heard.

"When you're open fer business," he twangs, "this here's public property. Now git."

Bob mutters, "Oh," and retraces his path through the doorway.

He has become as obedient as a plow horse. C. Kraven tears the ticket from his book. He hands the document along with the boy's driver's license and registration back to him. Then, with a grin above his weak chin, he climbs into his cruiser and drives away. There is a self-satisfied smirk on the deputy's face when he departs. Axle wonders aloud as he proceeds to peel the wrapper off another fly specked candy bar.

"I'll probably have to take a vow of poverty to live here."

Bob returns as the deputy drives away.

"God, I wish them people would leave," he mutters. "One Kraven in town is enough, but we must have 15 or 20 hereabouts. Most of 'em work for the sheriff's department. You'll see; they harass the hell out of everybody. Damned Kravens," he mutters again, as he retreats into the service bay.

Axle stares at his first traffic ticket of a lifetime. He speculates that tickets in his new hometown will be as plentiful as sand fleas on a beach. Axle sets the car in motion again. He glances at the ticket lying on the seat, as he turns on Main Street. He realizes that he is white-knuckling the steering wheel.

He's been driving since 3:00 in the morning and feels as though his steel-trap mind has rusted shut. He passes a tattoo parlor on Main Street with an advertisement proclaiming, 'Intimate, discreet tattoo's our specialty'. He decides that he can return for an intimate, discreet tattoo and then when his dad discovers the infraction, he'll end up brightly decorated, but dead. The combination of fatigue, plus the ticket has left him too uninspired to unload the trailer this afternoon. He decides that he will sleep in the car even if he can find the house.

What he wants to do more than anything is to sit at a table in a restaurant and graze on a hamburger with fries for an hour. Eleven hours of staring through a bug streaked windshield, eating hot air and drinking double colas gives credibility to the thought of burger grazing. It is a real charcoal blazer of a day. It is so hot that he has wants to place a fan in his mouth and turn it on.

As he passes the place on Main Street where the deputy had been parked earlier, something catches the corner of his eye. A man sits on the ground in the space between two buildings. He leans against an alley wall as though he is unable to rise. His head is covered with blood. Axle's inclination is to stop and see if he can help the guy, but he reconsiders.

Not stopping goes against everything he has been taught. There is a small element of terror involved, because that's where the deputy had been earlier. He probably did that with his nightstick before he came to the filling station. If he is foolish enough to get involved the deputy might return and do the same to him.

Axle tries to forget the man, while he gamely looks for a place to eat. Karl's Burger Heaven looms ahead on the left side of the road. A new blacktop segment begins just short of Karl's. The asphalt is as black as Texas crude and as smooth as a bowling ball. The town is experiencing a road-servicing outbreak. With guilt prodding him over the man in the alley, he turns left and pulls into Karl's.

Chapter Eight

Sugarloaf Hayes walks through the house where she has lived for the past six months. Before she enters the kitchen, she drops onto her hands and knees so she can see beneath the bed. Atop the bed are two bulging suitcases. The luggage is too heavy for her to carry to the bus terminal.

She uses a small piece of transparent tape to attach a note to the largest bag. The note asks her sister to please send the bags to her by bus and to let her know when to expect them in Springfield, Missouri. Assured that she has packed everything, she rummages through her purse for the essentials of life for a woman. When she is satisfied, she zips the large inner pocket closed before she returns to the kitchen. Her billfold holds a $20 bill along with a bus ticket purchased yesterday.

From a key ring, she removes the house key and places it on the kitchen table. She has one more look around before locking the door behind her. She crosses the footbridge to Birch Street. Her destination is Karl's Burger Heaven. Karl's functions as the local commercial bus stop.

Sugarloaf wears penny loafers. When she has to dump a small pebble from her right shoe, she realizes that she should have worn something more suitable for walking. The lose rim around the top edge of the shoes acts as a funnel for gravel that keeps flipping inside the loafers. Gravel crunches as a rusty old dark-colored pickup approaches her. Mongo Baron hangs his head out an open window.

"Give you a lift somewhere, Sugarloaf?"

She smiles at the very muscular scruffy looking kid as she answers.

"You'd be saving my life if you'd take me to Karl's, so I can catch the bus."

"Hop in, lady. I'm at your command." Mongo smiles through his beard, while he slides the gearshift into low. "Where you goin'?" he asks.

"I'm headed home," Sugarloaf responds.

"What time is your bus?" he mutters.

"I've got an hour," Sugarloaf answers, as she opens the passenger's door.

Mongo waits for her to close the door before he glances in the rearview mirror. With the way clear, he pops the clutch and spins the rear wheels. A shower of oiled gravel cascades into the air behind the truck as the engine roars to life. At the first intersection a block short of Karl's, Mongo makes a sharp left turn. At the highway, he turns left again instead of toward Sugarloaf's destination.

"Hey," Sugarloaf responds, in an anxious voice. "Where you goin'? Karl's is the other way."

"Yeah," Mongo offers, "this'll take just a minute. I need to check the mail before I drop you off. Buy you a cup of coffee when we come back to Karl's."

The truck accelerates to 60 as he heads toward the south bridge and the BARECO refinery.

"You're going to make me miss my bus," Sugarloaf accuses. "I don't have time for a joy ride in the country. Please, let me out. I don't want to go anywhere with you." Mongo accelerates to a higher speed. "Please, stop! I can't do this. Let me out now, damn you."

"This'll just take a minute," Mongo counters. "We're almost there. When I've checked the mail, I'll take you to Karl's."

He slows the truck in order to turn onto the refinery road. For a quarter mile, the road is blacktop before it becomes gravel. At the end of the blacktop, a line of traffic has formed as everybody waits for a train to clear the track that crosses the road. A switch engine is moving a line of tank-cars along the spur where it connects to the refinery rail yard.

Mongo stops at the end of the line. Two vehicles stop behind him. In a burst of hysteria, Sugarloaf opens the door. She leaps from the running board into the bar ditch. She hears the driver's door open behind her. Sugarloaf hits the ground running as she races along the bar ditch as fast as she can. When she has passed the last car in line, she looks back. Mongo is standing on the driver's running board outside the cab staring after her.

In a fit of desperation, she runs to the highway. She flags down an approaching pick up truck. As the driver stops, she leans in the open passenger window.

"I've got someone chasing me. Will you drive me into town?"

"Sure, lady, hop in," the man answers.

There is concern on his face as he stares along the road past the long line of bumper-to-bumper traffic. The line of tanker cars is long with the column moving past the intersection. The road will not open anytime soon.

The driver places his right arm along the back of the seat so he can see the rear window. He then backs at high speed while steering with his left hand. He backs to a culvert turn off bordering a sparsely wooded field. Beyond the fence, a two-wheeled tire track disappears into the trees. He uses the culvert intersection to turn around. When he is moving again, he checks the rearview mirror.

"Nobody's followin' us. Who you runnin' from?"

"Somebody who was taking me where I didn't want to go," Sugarloaf answers, as she glances through the rear window. The man turns left on the highway. Within a couple minutes, they are at Karl's where Sugarloaf gets out. "Thanks a lot mister. Have a nice day. Can I buy you a cup of coffee?"

"Nah," the man offers. "I'll take a rain check. I'm workin' the next shift at the plant, but I was happy to oblige you."

He turns onto the highway and accelerates in the direction of the refinery road. Sugarloaf enters Karl's. The clock above the counter indicates that she has half an hour remaining before the bus arrives. She slides onto a booth in the far corner of the room.

When the waitress arrives, she orders a cup of coffee. Now she can concentrate on making half an hour pass as quickly as possible. A minute later the restaurant door opens to admit a teenage boy. Sugarloaf has never seen the kid before. He is clean-cut, tall and muscular.

He checks the room before he saunters to the only vacant table in the room. The table is adjacent to her booth. The table is round. The arrangement will seat eight people. The kid alights on a chair that faces toward the front of the restaurant. After her initial observation, Sugarloaf ignores the kid. She drinks her coffee in small sips while she concentrates on the front door of the establishment.

Chapter Nine

Axle spends time looking for a parking space at Karl's. Any space he uses must be situated so that he doesn't have to back the trailer. The lot is packed. Karl's is doing some brisk mid-afternoon business for a place situated near the edge of the earth in the boondocks. The fact that the parking lot is full either speaks well of the food, or might indicate that Karl's Burger Heaven employs an exceptional looking, young unmarried waitress. This time of day most people are somewhere with their noses to grindstone earning a day's wage so they can feed the local money machine.

Axle pulls around the building for a second time. The far corner of the lot features a car with a blue-tic hound baying out a side window. Ten feet away, a shorthaired mongrel in a fenced backyard returns the hound's vocal complaints.

The other vehicles are elderly pickup trucks with rust-puckered age spots. There is the occasional Model-A Ford looking black, square and out of place. The vacant vehicles sit scalding in the mid-day sun. Most could function as kilns to bake glaze on ceramic tile. They leak rust granules onto the blacktop beneath them. The parking lot looks like an old junkyard without a new vehicle in sight.

Two late model dump trucks crouch in a row along side the highway in front of Karl's. Signs stenciled on their diver's doors proclaim that they are the property of Barto Excavating. The advertisement features white letters outlined in black on a red background.

As he rounds the building for the third time, a vehicle moves out of its slot near the back of the lot. Axle brings the car and trailer to a halt at the end of an outside row of vehicles. The Pontiac is aimed toward the alley as he kills the engine. The avenue to the alley is unrestricted without a requirement to back the trailer.

During his walk to the front door, he has a look at the building. It's been constructed of concrete blocks that have been painted white and has a shallow peaked roof. Curled paint flakes cover the near wall. The flakes resemble dried garfish scales. Smoke wafts from a ventilator above the kitchen and emits the aroma of fried onions, strong coffee and barbecue.

A mental picture returns of his fantasy hamburger. The image includes a bun toasted open side down on the grill. The top half will be a perfect yellow-brown with caraway seeds on the top. The creation will be warm to the touch with a meat patty that protrudes all the way around the circumference of the bun. The bottom half will be seductively draped with a thin slice of fresh red onion, lettuce, dill pickle slices and tomato. The bun will be slathered with a heavy application of mustard. The remainder of the oversize plate will be devoted to long French fries the color of butter.

Axle faces into a southern breeze as he makes the short trek to an entryway near the corner of the north wall. From a distance, he can hear the faint peal of a large bell. The sound is so faint that if the wind had not been blowing from the south, he would not have heard the sound at all. The bell tone is the same as the one at the small country school he began his education in 11 years ago. He checks his wristwatch. The time is 3:00. What an odd time to be ringing a bell. Perhaps it's a signal for firemen to come save the town, or maybe it's somebody's sick reminder of the fast arriving school year.

The boy passes through the outer glass doors of the eatery into a short entry hall that function as an air lock. He passes through an inner set of gym like double wooden doors, and halts for a moment while he searches for a seat. Across the room, refrigerated air issues from three struggling window units in the South wall. The frigid billowing air provides relief from the stifling heat outside. The drone of southern accents whines softly in the manner of a foreign language. He decides that the crowd at mid-afternoon might be an indication of comfort, rather than the quality of the food available.

There is no spontaneous celebration at his arrival. There is no lull in conversation; everyone drones on. The place sports a genuine ceramic-tile counter top that parallels the east wall where it turns a corner in the direction of the kitchen. The counter continues for four more bar stools before it ends near an entry into the kitchen. The round stool tops feature red imitation leather. They are attached to slim black metal pedestals anchored to the floor.

Menus stand on edge where they are wedged between chrome metal-guards and napkin dispensers on the counter top. Salt and pepper shakers, along with mustard and catsup bottles, are clustered within easy reach. Against the wall behind the counter, two large silver coffee urns gleam in the subdued light.

All counter seats are filled to capacity with pastel guys wearing ball caps, khaki shirts and faded blue overalls. In a far corner, a jukebox plays a country-western tune where someone is dead or dying, left or leaving. None of the crowd seems to be listening.

On the near corner of the counter sits a glass pastry case with three shelves. A hand-lettered sign advertises homemade pies. The bottom shelf contains two-thirds of a coconut cream pie piled high with whipped cream. A large blue bottle fly is wading across the top of the confection. The sight stifles axle's mammoth hunger.

He looks around the room. With the single exception of the fly the remainder of the dining area appears clean. *Maybe the fly is somebody's pet?*

He chooses the only vacant table in the place. His selection is an oversized circular affair with eight chairs grouped around its circumference. The table stands in the southwest corner of the room. Like the others a red-and-white-checkered oilcloth covers it. Silverware lies tightly rolled in a white paper napkin before each chair. He pulls out a chair and sits down facing more or less toward the door.

A harried redhead with a finger-in-the-socket hairdo, a short skirt, and great legs plants a glass of water on the table as she slaps down a menu in a clear plastic cover. She returns to the counter to pour coffee refills before she distributes several orders to individual tables. As far as Axle can tell, she is the only waitress working the place.

Her service will be slow and the tips excessive, because of the way she looks.

Axle opens a four-page menu that features everything but fried chicken lips. While he contemplates, the redhead returns to stand across the table from him with her pencil poised. He settles on a Coke and Karl's Hamburger Deluxe. The second she departs he begins to fret. Will it fulfill his hallucination of the last 100 miles?

The waitress heads for a chest-high window separating the dining area from the kitchen. There she slides the ticket into a round stainless steel ticket holder. A guy dressed in white on the other side of the wall appears to labor over a hot grill. He turns to check the ticket before he turns back to his monumental effort.

Everyone in the joint except the waitress is dressed in some form of faded blue denim. Steel-toed work boots seem the uniform of the day. Counting the waitress, there are three women in the establishment.

At the next table, a 20-something woman of starburst quality nurses a cup of coffee. On a scale of 1 to 10, she is an 18. Somebody's overweight wife sits shoehorned into a booth near a window in the south wall. Presumably, the guy next to her is her husband. She looks like Wallace Berry. He looks like Chester Milquetoast. Everyone else is a southern-fried character study of drawl, grits, and slow mouth movement.

The starburst at the next table passes the first of three physical examinations. She has green eyes, long blond hair in a ponytail and a full blouse. There is a light scattering of freckles across her nose. She wears jeans and a green-checkered top that buttons down the front. Her shoes are brown penny-loafers without socks. A large brown leather purse hangs from her left shoulder. Periodically, male heads turn in her direction for another glorious glimpse of paradise on earth.

She keeps her eyes downcast as she nurses her coffee. Occasionally, she looks at the wall clock behind the counter. Her eyes fall on Axle once. During that fleeting glimpse, they radiate all the warmth of a polar ice cap. Every time someone enters the door, she stares in that direction. She is obviously expecting a heavy date.

Axle's hamburger and fries arrive at about the same time a loud pickup truck with a set of dual glass-pac mufflers idles to a stop outside the building. The driver gooses the engine before he shuts it off. He obviously enjoys the sound of the exhaust system.

The passenger side of the truck is visible through a window. The other half is blocked from view by a portion of the south wall. The crowd has a slight glimpse of the guy getting out of the vehicle, but the drone of conversation slackens. Most sit motionless as they concentrate on the door. The room assumes the humor quotient of an execution witness room.

When it passed a window, the paint job of the truck was composed mostly of spider webs of faded black paint accented by rust scabs. The decomposing color scheme of the corrupted metal appears to have been attacked previously by someone with a bottle opener. The door opens and he enters. He stops inside the entrance where he applies a lighter to a cigarette. Following that, he slides the lighter back into a jacket pocket. He stands with his thumbs hooked in his front jean pockets. Dense long black hair covers his face, head and neck. A few facial features are clustered tightly in a bald spot in the middle of the hairball.

He stands with his feet apart as he studies the room. He appears to be searching for someone. When seen from the back, his head assumes the profile of a hair-covered wart protruding above broad muscular shoulders. The contour of each arm resembles the bowed neck of a Percheron draft horse. Oversized thigh muscles distend and roll with each leg movement. He appears less than 6 feet tall, but there is an aura of brutishness about him that makes him seem larger.

His clothing appears as though he has dressed in the dark from the contents of a rag bin. Jagged holes in his faded jeans at mid-leg frames his kneecaps. The left hip pocket of his pants hangs by a thread. A black shoelace holds his shoulder length hair in a short ponytail. The excess spills down past the collar of his jacket. He wears no shirt. The jacket zipper hangs fully open. There is an abundance of black chest hair that bridges the gap. His appearance is as though someone has screamed, *"Show us hair,"* and he has complied.

Black oiled leather motorcycle boots cover his feet. The boots have run-over heels with small chains that drape across the upper arch of the boot. The chains surround his ankles like spurs. His boot tops vanish beneath grease-dappled pant legs that are without cuffs.

A chain drive wallet bulges from his right hip pocket.

Nobody claps him on the shoulder as a form of greeting. Nobody mutters, *"Glad you could make it."* Instead, all the men achieve a noticeable state of anxiety. All conversation ceases as heads swivel. People recoil as their vision passes over him. The scene is like a room full of trained dogs when their trainer has snapped his fingers. Several people half rise as though a challenge has been issued. Some stand completely upright and head for the door. Some sit back down as in resignation. The room turns from the tortured babble of southern accents to become strangely silent.

Wart Head surveys the crowd like a lion inspecting a zebra herd. Axle stops looking at the stranger, while he disassembles his hamburger. The patty lies as dark and rigid as a hockey puck on the bottom bun. The meat is so over cooked only carbon dating could be used to determine freshness. The onion, lettuce and tomato are fresh, so he shrugs as he squirts mustard on the inside of the top half of the bun. He reassembles everything, while he prays for a flavor that will be better than it looks. The bun is as huge as the patty is small. He unfurls the knife from the napkin roll and cuts the stack in half.

While he hacks his way through his purchase, he observes Wart Head in his quest for recognition. Things aren't getting any better in that direction. Axle fumbles a fry into his mouth. The fries are incredibly greasy. Eating them will rival sucking cooking oil up through a straw.

Axle leans forward to pick up the catsup bottle. He removes the cap as he begins his search for a familiar flavor. He attempts to dislodge some of the ingredients from within the clear glass bottle. First, he shakes the bottle while holding it upside down. None of the contents are forthcoming.

Across the room, Wart Head continues sorting through the crowd as though he is memorizing faces. He moves a step further into the room, which makes several people slide away from their tables. Everybody concentrates on giving him a wide berth. Everyone seems to be inching toward the door. Axle watches the crowd, as he wonders what is happening.

Shake, shake, still no catsup. He tries butting the bottom of the bottle with the heel of his hand. A look inside the neck indicates that the bottle is practically full. Axle takes another glance at Wart Head while he pounds the bottom of the bottle with the heel of his free hand. Wart's gaze finally stops on the quality woman sitting in the booth beyond Axle.

The woman abandons her coffee. She moves out of the booth and backs away from her table. Wart grins at her as he moves in her direction. She looks around as though seeking an ally.

"Mongo, you stay away from me!" she rages.

The only sound in the room is that of Axle ramming the heel of his hand against the catsup bottle and the muted hum of the laboring air conditioners. Nobody is eating anything. It is as though the crowd has contracted an emerging disease. Axle interrupts his battle with the bottle as he ponders the latest turn of events.

Mongo...so that's his name? That's probably short for Mongoose. His beady dark eyes resemble a weasel staring out of a dense thicket. The only hairless things about him are his nose and eye sockets situated beneath a short forehead.

Axle savages the catsup bottle again, while alternating his gaze between the hamburger and Mongo. Buyer's remorse hangs above the table like a giant gnat cloud. He wonders why Mongo's arrival has galvanized the cafe crowd into such total inactivity. A look around the room reveals rapid eye movement between Mongo and the girl. It's as though the crowd is watching a tennis match.

Mongo has settled on green eyes as an object that requires his attention. He moves in a determined saunter between tables. People in his vicinity clear as though someone is carrying a chamber pot.

Axle remains seated, but about 10 nearby customers flee so fast gamblers would have difficulty handicapping the race to the door. To get in the way of the departing would be like wandering into the middle of a buffalo stampede. The room count dwindles by nearly half.

Axle leans back in his chair. The scene reminds him of the time his uncle was teaching him team roping. His horse was untrained, so the uncle suggested somebody saddle up Old Rocket. The crowd around the roping chute cleared in much the same fashion when the horse arrived. Old Rocket had a reputation everybody knew about, and so does Mongo apparently. Axle considers that the owner of Karl's will need a plan for creative money management for the day. Most of the vanishing clientele have disappeared without paying their tab.

Since his arrival, Axle has learned several things. This first day in his new hometown is not about to move anyone to song. Second, the outside air temperature has a chill factor of about 93 degrees in the shade. Third, this is the land where humidity was invented and it feels about a 100 percent out there. Even with these considerations, Mongo stands near the middle of the room dressed in a leather motorcycle jacket. *That better not be the school uniform, 'cause I'm gonna be a reluctant participant to wear leather and grow fungus.* Maybe maintaining an image in this town is harder work than it needs to be.

Mongo squints as the smoke from the cigarette clenched in the corner of his mouth impairs the vision of his left eye. He cocks his head sideways to avoid the smoke curl as he eels his way to green-eyes. He moves in an insolent swagger. Mongo's path is near Axle's table. As Mongo swaggers past, body odor follows him like an aroma-ghost from an old gym-locker. Mongo stands staring across Axle's table at his apparent date for the afternoon. He raises his voice above the rattle of the air conditioners.

"Sugarloaf, get your ass out the door! We're leavin'."

His volume is so excessive he sounds like an escapee from the state home for the loud. As for Axle, the aroma of Mongo up close and personal displaces any further thought of eating. Sugarloaf shakes her head. She backs away from her adversary. She glances frantically around for a place to hide. Her face has the look of a deer caught in the headlights with a complexion as firm and pale as a corpse. Sugarloaf's eyes are twice their normal size and the most brilliant green Axle has ever seen.

Axle resumes his battle with the catsup bottle. He is trying to appear uninterested in the proceedings around him. From outside, there is a deep rumble of motorcycles. Mongo's head swivels to the door as two bikers park their rides. The engine noise subsides.

The front doors open to admit two more horse apples resembling Mongo. It has been some time since Axle has seen that many clothing impaired people in one room.

The appearance of the new arrivals energizes the remaining members of the café crowd into a more compact group near the kitchen end of the counter. Sheep jammed into a three-decker stock trailer would be having more fun. The new arrivals slither across the room to stand near Mongo.

Mongo mutters, "Buddy, take Leon and stand by the door so she doesn't get out."

Buddy has a pair of close-set eyes and facial skin the texture of a well-used cat-litter box. He nods with such force that he resembles Sylvester the cat when he has discovered a mouse the size of a small heifer. Buddy looks in the wrong direction for the door, as though he's forgotten where it is. Once he and Leon relocate the entryway, they collide with each other trying to get there. Someone near the back of the crowd tries to stifle a nervous giggle.

Mongo's clenched fists hang alongside his thighs. There is a pulsing vein standing out on his forehead. The vein is coupled to a facial tic. His eyes are lethal looking. After he glares the crowd into submission, he leans across the table to make a grab for Sugarloaf. She jerks back so that his fingertips only snag the front of her blouse. Two buttons sail through the air to bounce off the tabletop before they rebound to the floor. Sugarloaf's voice climbs several octaves as she shrieks.

"Mongo, you leave me alone!"

Someone in the crowd offers timidly, "Somebody call the cops."

Sugarloaf searches for a safe haven in a recently vacated corner booth covered in imitation leather. The scarlet upholstery is accented by hammered brass round-headed tacks that track in a narrow row up the side and across the top of the seat back. Mongo lunges across her table with an open handed swipe at her head. The blow misses by a fraction of an inch as the table rocks forward with him. The table tips before returning upright.

Axle finds himself flinching for the woman. One of the more adventurous overalls in the corner picks up the wall phone and inserts a coin. Before he can give the operator a number, Buddy takes a step in his direction, grabs the receiver from his hand and jerks it hard enough to sever the metal cord. Buddy throws the apparatus into a far corner and the redheaded waitress faints.

Sugarloaf backs toward the booth. She keeps the table between herself and her tormentor. Mongo slings the table aside. In its flight, it bounces off Axle's table and the resultant movement spills his soft drink.

Mongo kicks two chairs aside. He throws the remaining two more than halfway across the room. The muscular bully has tunnel vision on the woman. Sugarloaf has hit the floor and is worming her way underneath the booth seat with her back against the cinderblock wall.

Axle is enraged. The soft drink was the only palatable thing on the table and it has spilled into his lap. He takes a deep breath as he tries to control his temper. He remembers his father's last words. *Try to remain obscure and whatever you do, stay out of trouble.*

Axle wonders why the day has become such a foray into the art of arriving in a new town. Talk about an arrival not covered by insurance or enduring success. This latest event makes him feel like a sidewalk vendor stuck with a lousy location.

He stands, as he brushes at the front of his jeans with his napkin. Most of his drink soaked in upon contact. He wipes his hands on the napkin while eyeing Mongo's progress with Sugarloaf. He repositions his chair before he sits back down. He takes an absent minded bite of the burger. It tastes like a mustard flavored slab of acoustic ceiling tile. He returns the burger to its plate as he again shakes the catsup bottle. His effort remains unsuccessful.

Sugarloaf is mostly out of sight beneath the booth seat. Her movements are frantic and cat like. She has her back wedged against the cinderblock wall with her neck arched forward. The back of her head rests against the inside of one of the broad legs of the booth seat. Her knees are bent with her feet jammed against the wall. From Axle's prospective all that remains visible of her is an inch of her knees, the toes of her shoes and a fist size glob of blond hair.

Mongo tries lifting the table, but the entire booth system is bolted to the floor. Sugarloaf is making a high-pitched keening noise, as she braces herself. A stray dog would have trouble getting under where she now lies. Axle's temper elevated a couple of degrees when the soft drink fell into his lap, but it wavers every time he looks at the massive, physical presence of the bully. From somewhere far back in his mind, a small voice cautions him.

Keep chewing and don't look up.

Shake the catsup bottle some more, still nothing. In the meantime, Mongo throws another chair in the general direction of the crowd. Axle looks around again. Nobody is doing anything but staring at Mongo who seems violent almost beyond comprehension. More rage seems to consume him with every passing second. Axle has an intense desire to help Sugarloaf, but at 16, he is the youngest person in the room. Being new in town eliminates the impact of home field advantage.

The voice counsels, *what happens if you try to stop this guy, and it turns out she's his wife?* Those kinds of experiences can be meaningful, especially when being wrong probably means spending time in a hospital. He can almost read the headlines: *Dolt steps between man and wife and is beaten to death by the two of them."*

Axle focuses on eating his hamburger just as fast as he can manage. Another bite with two fries, eat faster. He shakes the catsup bottle again, still nothing. Right hand occupied with the bottle, he eats with the left. He wants a swig of his soft drink, but there isn't any.

Mongo kneels on the floor as he tries to pull Sugarloaf from beneath the booth seat by an ankle. He gets one of her shoes. She gives him a big-time attitude adjustment when she kicks him in the face twice with the other foot. He tries again, and she kicks him again. The point of diminishing returns has arrived. For the moment, he is finished prowling beneath the booth.

He stands with a glazed look to his eyes. He still clutches one of her shoes as feels his front teeth, they are all still there. He grabs a handful of napkins from the dispenser on Axle's table and presses them against his face. He gives Axle a sidelong glance, but it doesn't register that Axle is the only one in the restaurant who is gamely trying to eat. Axle reaches the conclusion that Mongo needs a hole in his head, through which daylight and dawning wisdom can enter.

Sugarloaf has become an embarrassment for the bully. His blood pressure appears to climb. From outward appearances, he has come here to retrieve his woman, and she is returning his advances as though they are bad checks. By now he is seeing everything through a red haze. Mongo tries one final time to retrieve the frightened woman from within her hiding place. He bends down to scream at her from near point blank range.

"Come the hell out of there!"

She gives no response and the moment continues to be dismal. A Trailways bus pulls up out front and honks twice, then sits for 60 seconds with the door open before it buttons up and heads back out onto the highway. Axle wants to factor in flagging it down, so he can embark on a week of travel and cultural enrichment. Instead he continues to shake the catsup bottle. The moment drones on like the migration of the seven-year dung frog.

Axle takes another bite of burger combined with two fries. Shake the bottle, still nothing. Mongo's henchmen function like guards at the queen's palace. Buddy seems to be growing more zits by the second. Nobody comes in and nobody goes out. Axle speculates on what will happen when Mongo pulls the woman from beneath the seat. With Mongo's state of rage growing, he will probably be out of control.

Axle attempts to find an ally among the spectators. Nobody will make eye contact with him. All are either watching Mongo or studying the surface texture of the south wall. It becomes painfully obvious that nobody is going to help if he foolishly gets involved. Help? Help, hell, they are all still clustered in the far corner near the counter looking pale and oxygen deficient.

Axle focuses on his hamburger while he weighs all available options. He is embarrassed that he has not attempted to head off what is about to happen. The values of character in thoughts, words, deeds and actions have been taught to him as a matter of every day life. If this were happening in the places where he has grown up, all of the men in attendance would be standing on Mongo's chest while urging him to have better manners. But Axle isn't with his father or the men he grew up around. He is in Amerada in a café with the founding fathers of the local chapter of the Coward's Brotherhood. Most of the active membership is currently engaged in watching Mongo mistreat a woman.

The youngster takes one more look at the men in the room. They resemble denim colored chickens bedecked in bib overalls, various colored shirts and steel toed work boots. At the moment, he'd cheer a knife-welding lunatic as long as the deranged person was on his side. From the deep recesses of Axle's mind, he can hear his father's voice.

You always fight for those who cannot fight for themselves.

With that single thought clear in his mind, his course of action is set. Losing or wimping out will be like hiring a character assassin. From somewhere within his mind, he hears the sound of an uncertain trumpet. Axle clears his throat from his seated position.

"Pardon me."

Mongo doesn't even turn around. Ever fiber of the bully is concentrated on dragging Sugarloaf from beneath the seat even if it involves dismantling the building. Axle's confidence wavers as he studies the muscle structure of the subhuman before him. He twists his upper body around, so that he faces the cluster of men near the counter.

"Anybody else want part of this?" he asks them.

Aside from the intake of air by 20 pairs of lungs, nobody seems to give the idea any consideration. There is instead an underlying current that suggests his request has been met with widespread dissatisfaction. The boy turns back to the action. Those behind him stand poised on their toes ready to flee along the path of least resistance. As a final evaluation, Axle wonders how many of those present can pass through the door at one time without causing a structural defect.

Axle carries a monumental load of self-doubt as he studies the situation for another five seconds. What would his dad would do if he were here? He knows with total certainty what that would be. Mongo would be on his ass in the middle of the room while his dad helped Sugarloaf out from under the booth. Axle's dad is 235 pounds of well-trained muscle with a mean streak. He analyzes his own feelings. The primary feeling is of being scared spitless.

What the hell? If he hits me maybe he'll injure himself.

Mongo grabs the end of the booth table, bunches his shoulders and tears the object from its moorings. Now the entire apparatus dangles from Mongo's hands like a broken barbell. *Impressive,* Axle meditates, as the bully tosses the hunk of tile-covered plywood aside. Sugarloaf's hiding place is vanishing faster than Cinderella's gown at midnight.

"Time to move," Axle mutters, in a low voice. "Excuse me," Axle offers, a little louder.

Anger rends Axle's soul as Mongo kicks the woman's leg. Sugarloaf offers up a yowling noise. She sounds like a wild animal that is about to enter its death throws. She wedges herself tighter between the opposing ends of her refuge.

From somewhere in the crowd, someone mutters, "Oh, shit."

Mongo's concentration on Sugarloaf remains absolute. Axle takes a deep breath as he rises up out of his chair. He grips the edge of his table with both hands before he drives the edge of the table into the back of Mongo's upper thighs. The table pins the bully to the seat back beyond where the original tabletop had been.

As the table strikes its target, the catsup bottle on Axle's table turns sideways and begins its terminal roll to the floor. Axle grabs the bottle in mid flight with his right hand. With all the carnage around him, catching the bottle requires reflex action. He sets the bottle upright on the table surface as he wedges the table edge more firmly against its target. Mongo is pinned face first against the seat back and the wall by the table edge. His obsession with Sugarloaf is finally broken. He manages to rotate so that he can see the fool who has interjected himself into the fray.

Mongo's eyes burn with hatred from within his facial hair bald spot. Axle concludes that he has just lost the element of surprise. The boy's trigger-like mind tells him that Mongo's sense of humor and about 72 points of his IQ have probably been surgically removed through that scar on the left side of his neck. He senses that any criticism must be phrased with great care.

"I don't think she wants to go with you, Ace," Axle growls.

Everyone hears the observation. Another collective intake of air from the crowd is nearly enough to give all those present an ear block. One look into Mongo's eyes reveals that local events are about to get nastier than a comprehensive Albanian history exam.

Mongo makes a growling sound as he exerts firmer pressure against the table. His expulsion of air with the effort reveals halitosis bad enough to wilt a wild garlic plant. The two adversaries strain against the table. The table trembles from the strain of the moment. The shuddering causes the catsup bottle to skitter first one way, and then the other. During the entire event, the bottle remains tenaciously upright near Axle's burger plate.

While the two adversaries oppose each other, Mongo acquires a silly grin. He does not recognize the stranger, but the grin attests to the fact that the newest fish in the pond has just taken the bait. In a matter of three seconds, things have gone from pretty likely, to pretty damned likely, to fairly certain, to all but inevitable. The time to get serious about winning has arrived. Axle can't allow his mind to wander. On the other side of the table, Mongo considers the factors that are now apparent to everyone.

First, Sugarloaf isn't interested in going with him and now everybody knows she isn't. Second, some idiot is complicating things. The third and most immediate proposition is that while the stranger looks young, he stands over 6 feet tall and weighs in the vicinity of 200 pounds. He is not intimidated by the confrontation, nor does he appear to be considering gender alteration.

Mongo clears his throat, as he stops straining against the table. His lack of effort allows the table to wedge him more firmly against the wall. He removes the cigarette from his mouth, as he looks the stranger in the eye. He glances down as he stabs the cigarette butt into the top bun of the partially eaten hamburger. His eyes elevate to his opponent.

"Who the hell are you?"

"Will this be on the mid-term?" Axle asks.

Someone in the cluster of people gives a nervous giggle. Mongo turns his head slightly as he spits on the left booth seat. His eyes narrow into a glazed trance that appears as thin and cold as a sword blade. The moment has more possibilities than a Swiss army knife. After a short pause, Mongo takes a deep breath.

"Before I kick your ass, I want to know your name."

Well, that pretty well sums it up in the old anatomy department.

"Axle Mannheim, from way out yonder," Axle proclaims, as he gives Mongo his 9-millimeter grin.

All room noise has ceased. The air in the eatery is deader than a beached squid.

"You smart son-of-a-bitch!" Mongo screams.

His voice rises as he attempts to move the table. Mongo plants both feet against the bottom edge of the booth seat. With a mighty heave, he pushes his side of the table far enough so that it clears the ends of both booth seats. Mongo places a foot further up onto the seat back as he rotates the table. Axle moves to keep the table firmly between them. They begin a tag contest around the table. Mongo fakes movement one way then goes the other. The entire time he is yelling.

"You're going to have to learn to mind your own business, slick."

"Boy, I'll say," Axle mumbles, as he maneuvers.

"Fuck you," Mongo rages.

The conversation has just entered Boy Scout merit-badge territory, so they both stare at each other for another three seconds as they await the enforcement of speech codes. Axle prays for some bozo to tell them to remain calm. Either that or he is going to need ropes, pitons, crampons and an ice ax to climb out of his current situation.

Axle realizes that any worthwhile transition into his new hometown lies across, through, and over the guy in the leather jacket. This thought is an educational attainment gained from 11 years of fair grades. Every word uttered will be remembered by all of those present.

"Lord, that's deep. I wish I had a lower IQ, so we could talk." Mongo reacts as though he has just been goosed by an electric cattle prod. Axle forms another humiliating suggestion. "Why don't you and the two dog drools by the door leave, and we," nodding at the customers in the corner, "will all count to 20 before anyone moves?"

Mongo shoves the table again. It is now about five feet from the dysfunctional booth. Sugarloaf peeks from around the corner of the bench seat to see who has been dumb enough to get involved. The peek has a look of tempered distrust about it.

Mongo moves to the side, releases the table, raises his arms and shrugs his shoulders. Axle wonders if he is signaling an attack, ordering a pizza or showing despair. Next, he lowers his upper body as he grabs the edge of the table and drives both Axle and the table against the nearest wall. The burger plate and catsup bottle skitter across the tile surface. Axle grabs the bottle once more for no apparent reason. He finds himself pinned while Mongo darts the rest of the way around the barrier.

Axle decides that this latest development is probably an indication that the first trial balloon has floated aloft and been shot down. He needs to get in the first blow. If he doesn't, then he'll be lying on the floor. From that position, he can only hit Wart Head somewhere between the shin and the kneecap. This idea serves about the same function as an appendix. Axle has a fleeting thought of his Dad.

Always take adversity and slap it upside the head.

His dad is the toughest man Axle has ever known. Big Mike is just short of a being a piece of tool-steel with eyes. Axle has lived in adversity for most of his life as the son of a mostly absent military man, while living in various civilian communities. Standing up at the wrong time was necessary, but of questionable merit. When Mongo reaches for him, Axle does the best thing he can think of. His right hand still holds the nearly forgotten catsup bottle that he caught in mid-flight on its way to the floor.

When Mongo decides to dispense with his version of niceties, he makes a sweeping motion as he grabs for the front of Axle's shirt. Mongo is not blessed with raw hand speed. Axle deflects the right-hand lead by elevating his left forearm. He swings as hard as he can with his right hand. The resulting blow makes a brilliant snag with the nearly full, uncapped 14-ounce bottle of catsup. The bottle impacts the left side of Mongo's head above his ear. The explosion blasts catsup onto the ceiling, two walls and a crowd of three inching toward the door. The bottle remains unbroken, but empty. This is a tribute to American manufacturing excellence.

Mongo drops like a stone entering a swimming pool. He makes a half turn to his right staggers backward and attacks the floor in a heap turning over two tables. The act spills everything including the checkered oilcloth coverings onto the floor. When things finally stop falling, the room is deafeningly silent.

Mongo lies in an assortment of food scraps and tableware. Axle turns to face the next menace from the front door. The sound of a sugar shaker rolling across a tabletop before it drops to the floor diverts everyone's attention. Axle figures the remainder of the day can only be described as penal if C. Kraven shows up.

Buddy stands near Leon with his mouth sagging open. While Buddy is distracted with picking his face, a couple more timid souls inch through the door. The stillness of the room is broken by the sound of fast footsteps as Buddy lunges away from the front door. He bolts forward with his right arm cocked to throw a punch. Axle ducks beneath the blow. Axle has reversed his hold on the catsup bottle, so that he is holding it by the neck. As Buddy rushes past, Axle nails him on the back of the head with the nearly empty bottle. The bottle shatters and the jagged edge opens a cut on the back of Buddy's head.

Buddy goes limp in the air as he glances off Axle's left thigh on his way to the floor. He kisses the floor in a slack-bodied face first sprawl before he skids to a stop against Mongo. Leon follows immediately thereafter. He advances as though he is going to make a tackle. Axle drops the broken bottle, grabs Leon by his long hair and left wrist, and runs him head first into the leading edge of a vertical I-beam bracing the roof near the center of the room. On impact, the beam gives a deep metallic hum of vibration as Leon bounces off it on his way to the floor. His normal curiosity of visiting strangers will forever be diminished.

On impulse, Axle grabs his hamburger from its plate. The cigarette butt still protrudes from the top bun. He straddles Mongo's chest, opens the hair-lined mouth with the heel of his hand and jams the burger within. Mongo smells so bad that he has to stifle an impulse to go wash his hands.

Sugarloaf is outside her booth now. She stares open mouthed at the three prostrate leather-bound bullies. Axle stands over Mongo like someone with his shoelaces tied together. Some guy wearing a red baseball cap with a high crown and a long bill grins at Axle from the leading edge of the crowd.

He mutters, "Way to go."

Sugarloaf scurries to Axle. She takes a final look at Mongo.

She says, "The cops will be coming."

She picks up her missing shoe and grabs her purse as she leads Axle toward the front door by his left hand. The remainder of the crowd separates like the parting of the Red Sea. The pair of fugitives burst through the outside doors while Sugarloaf does a couple of one-legged hops as she dons her carried shoe.

She asks, "Who the hell are you?" Axle looks at her with a blank stare. She shakes his shoulder. "Wake up kid, you're in trouble. What are you driving?"

Axle points toward the Pontiac with the stock trailer sagging the rear bumper. Sugarloaf opens the driver's door to slide across the seat. Axle leaps behind the wheel where he jabs the key at the slot in the ignition switch. The key strikes pay dirt on the first try. The rear wheels yelp as the car begins to move.

He has to jam on the brakes to avoid a cop car as it skids to a stop near Karl's front door. Two deputies spill out of the car as they head toward Karl's front door. The crowd boiling from the building nearly tramples them in their haste to depart. The witnesses to the fight of the decade are as resolute as lemmings headed for cliff near the ocean.

Axle and Sugarloaf glance at the front door as they pass. They see Karl meet the cops at the entryway. Karl carries a meat tenderizer mallet in his left fist. He is a medium sized man with dark hair dressed in a cook's uniform. The face below his white cap wears an angry glare. He points into the building with the mallet as he shouts from close range to the first cop through the door. Karl then turns to follow them. He waves Axle away with his free hand.

Axle's car barely clears the cruiser. As he drifts by, he notices that Karl has a tattoo on his right forearm. The illustration spells *Louise* across a heart, encrusted with flowers. Axle speculates on what Karl's wife's name might be and decides probably not Louise.

The boy turns onto the highway in the direction of town. Behind him, loaded dump trucks are grinding out of the parking lot in low gear followed by a herd of pickup trucks. The column resembles a ragged fast moving funeral procession.

Sugarloaf sits with her left arm extended along the top of the driver's seat back so she can peer through the rear window. Axle accelerates along the new blacktop. He passes other vehicles as though he is exempt from all speed laws. Before the first chuckhole arrives, he turns right onto a side street. After several blocks of turn reversals, he draws a comfortable breath.

Sugarloaf asks, "Who the hell did you say you were, again?"

"My name's Axle Mannheim," he answers. "I'm new in town."

She divides her attention between looking at Axle and staring through the back window.

"New," she parrots. "Christ, he can't be more than 16." *He may be young but his arrival was damned spectacular.* "God, you were sensational," she purrs, as she leans across the seat to kiss him lightly on the cheek. "There, take that."

"Pouring catsup on a couple of the local unwashed didn't seem like such a big deal at the time," Axle mumbles.

He grips the steering wheel hard to keep his hands from shaking. *Mr. Black called me the weakest link and I've just demonstrated that. Within 20 minutes of arrival I've fulfilled his prophecy. Jeez. What's Dad going to say? What if they have to abort the mission because of what I've done? The organization will probably fire Dad and he'll install a lightening rod up my backside to give me a purpose in life.* While Axle agonizes over his actions, Sugarloaf startles him back to reality.

"Being new in town, you probably have no idea who that guy was with the long hair and the leather jacket?"

"Some guy with bad manners ridin' in a loud pickup truck?"

Sugarloaf giggles. "That was Mongo Baron. He's the meanest son-of-a-bitch in five counties. You just beat hell out of him and his two buddies with a catsup bottle." She drums the bottom of her fists on the dash. "Yes. Surely, you know that you're in deep do-do."

"How's that?"

Axle rounds another street corner in his drive to the distant tree line of the creek. To his left a house sits elevated on a low-boy trailer. The structure is prepared to be moved.

"Mongo is going to come looking for the guy who made a fool of him in public. He won't stop searchin' until he finds you. And, oh my, yes, something else: his uncle is the sheriff."

Axle stares straight ahead, as he analyzes the significance of her remark. He pulls to the side of the road near a vacant lot and stops. He leans across to fumble through the glove compartment. His hand removes his father's map. While he studies the drawing his mind wanders.

If your name is Kraven in this town, being a cop rivals being president for life. I wonder if they have chain gangs composed of county prisoners in this part of the state. Mop a few floors, then go out and snag brush in the sun for the remainder of the day. I can handle life in the same town with Mongo as long as I keep my back turned away from all windows and doors. I'll need to travel with several large friends. We should always be together and facing in opposite directions. The problem is that I don't have any friends much less big ones. I wonder how endeared the sheriff is to his nephew?

He looks up from the map, while he orients himself. Overhead, a broken cloud layer covers most of the sky. To the west, a disk of sun hangs low on the horizon where it peeks from beneath a cluster of substantial clouds. Sunlight filtering between the clouds gives the houses a subdued bronze cast. Streaks of rain are streaming from the clouds above the town.

Nightfall will arrive early this evening. In a few minutes, darkness and rain will insulate him from the search he knows is coming. He puts the car in gear and turns right onto a street that parallels the creek. His new home should be around the far corner of the next block. A splatter of raindrops obscures the windshield, as he turns on the wipers.

Chapter Ten

Karl shakes the meat mallet at Jeb Kraven.

He yells, "Get that damned Mongo out of my restaurant. The son-of-a-bitch caused a fight and now the place is a wreck."

Jeb looks at Karl. "Ya can tell him yourself, Karl, he'll probably get a charge outta that."

"Not in this lifetime," Karl Mayfair answers, as he heads for the kitchen.

Just inside the kitchen door, Karl's wife sits in a small office in front of a roll top desk. She holds a cold washcloth to her forehead.

"What's going on out there? Has Mongo departed yet?"

"Nope, the cops have arrived, but them three stooges are still lyin' in a heap in the middle of the room," Karl answers, with a smile. He whacks the meat mallet on the butcher-block table in the center of the kitchen. "Man, that kid went through those three like a dose of salt through an eel."

"Yeah, he did," Louise affirms, "but we'll never hear the end of it either. Them Kravens will come in here to bust up the place every chance they get."

"Never thought I'd see Mongo have his clock cleaned by anybody," Karl growls, as he looks at his wife. "You okay, baby?"

"Just a headache. Must have hit my head on the floor when I fainted. I just knew that Mongo was going to beat us all up so he could take that sister of Leah Holmes out of here."

"She left with the kid. I wonder what his name is. Did you ever see him before today?"

"No," Louise says, "and I don't much care if I ever see him again either."

"None of us got the snot beat out of us for a change, and that includes Sugarloaf Hayes."

"From what I hear," Louise comments, as she removes the cloth from her face, "she hasn't been a nun since her divorce. Somebody said she made dirty movies out in California before she came here. I hope she leaves before she gets the idea that she's welcome to stay."

"If that kid comes back," Karl's says, "he's eating free, ya hear?"

"We'll see," Louise says, as she wipes her face with the washcloth. "Anybody started cleaning up yet?"

"Yeah," Karl mumbles. "I sent the dishwasher to hose down the place. I'll have to repair the booth tonight after we close. We got a couple broken chairs to go with the booth. I sure as hell hope that kid comes back sometime. I'd like to shake his hand."

"You better shake your ass," Louise says. "We got to write down who was here and who left without paying. That little fracas cost us a lot of money."

"Yeah," Karl says, "but somehow I feel as though it might have been worth it."

In the dining room, Jeb Kraven leans over Mongo who lies on the floor with a partially eaten hamburger protruding from his mouth. *I know I ain't much, but there lies an absolute cesspool of a human being. Place looks like it's been grazed over by a moving herd of hungry goats. Floor's covered with food scraps and dishes. Buddy and Leon look like a pair of fresh cow pies.* Jeb snares a stainless steel pitcher of ice water from the counter and slops it across Mongo's face. The hairy one rolls his head from side to side as he spits out the soggy hamburger. He feels his head as he groans before he sits up. *The kid's about as coordinated as a wet napkin. Mongo, Buddy and Leon have been cold-cocked by somebody. Who around here is capable of that?*

"If you guys want to sleep, you outta go home," Jeb mutters. His voice drips with sarcasm. "Karl says that you're smellin' up his place. What the hell happened?"

Mongo stands upright. He catches his balance by hanging onto the I-beam roof support in the middle of the room. He looks around for the stranger who punched in, did the work, and punched out. Near the counter, the Mexican dishwasher is shoveling food scraps and broken dishes into a trashcan. Mongo finally looks at Jeb.

"Some tall bastard hit me in the head with a bottle when I wasn't lookin'."

"Who?"

"Hell, I don't know. Somebody I've never seen before."

"He still here?"

"No, I don't see him."

"Better go home and cool off. Karl's mad about his place gettin' busted up."

"Fuck Karl and his place. I want that son-of-a-bitch that hit me," he grumbles, as he heads to the door. He thinks better of sudden movement. He kicks the inert Buddy in the ribs. Buddy moans as he sits up. Mongo looks at the Mexican cleaning the floor. "Hey, Pancho, where'd the woman in the green checkered blouse go?" The man shakes his head. "More than that," Mongo screams, "where did the guy go?"

The dishwasher shrugs as he turns back to his job with the shovel. He wears a thin smile when his head is turned away from Mongo. Buddy looks up from his seat on the floor.

"What happened?"

"We just got our asses handed to us by some fucking kid I've never seen before," Mongo rages. "Get Leon up and go find him for me."

Buddy feels the back of his head. His hand comes away bloody. He stares at the hand for a moment.

"What does he look like, and where do we look?"

"You saw him," Mongo sputters. "You know what he looks like the same as I do. Get your asses outta here and go find him."

"Got any idea what he's drivin'?" Buddy asks, as he realizes that he doesn't want to face the stranger twice in the same day.

Mongo screams, "Hell no! Just go look for a strange car being driven by an unfamiliar guy you ain't seen before. He's gotta be around here someplace."

With his head less than clear, Mongo slams out through the double doors. Buddy and Leon remain on the floor. They feel too rocky to go search for anyone from the seat of a motorcycle. Buddy hears the truck start and spin its tires as it arrows out of the parking lot.

Buddy mutters to Leon, "We better go find that sucker or Mongo'll have our butts instead of his."

Chapter Eleven

Axle stops near the creek while he sits studying the map.

He asks his passenger, "Where do you want to go?"

"I don't have any place to go. My folks live in Missouri and my sister's out of town. Thanks to Mongo, I've missed the bus. There is only one a day, so I'll have to hop another tomorrow."

Axle contemplates her comment. There is a tingle of excitement.

He offers, "You can stay at my place until we can get you on the bus. We've got a house somewhere around here. Most of our furniture is in the horse trailer."

Sugarloaf gets a loopy grin on her face. "Do you mean to tell me that you don't know where you live?"

"I haven't been there yet. Karl's was my first stop."

Sugarloaf glances sideways at him. "Hell of a first stop."

"We can unload and set up some things," Axle advises. "You can spend the night in one of the bedrooms, if you don't mind me being there."

A delicious internal tingle surges through him as he considers the thought of Sugarloaf staying overnight in the same house with him. They will be alone together for a whole night. He probably won't sleep a wink.

Sugarloaf grins. "I'll stay with you if we can find the house."

"Oh, I'll find the house, providing we don't get set upon by some more of your friends."

"Just the two of us there, huh?"

Axle is shy around women. His face turns bright red, but the gathering darkness masks it. He drives for another block before he pulls the car to a stop before a dark house on the far side of a weed choked ditch. He gazes at the structure for an instant.

"If you don't want to do that, there's probably a motel somewhere."

With a mischievous grin, she comments, "I don't have any money, so I need to stay at your place for the night. The bus ticket was the last of the money I had. I also don't have a lot of choices. This car isn't much of a white charger, but you sure as hell will do for a knight in shining armor. I'll have to think of some special way to thank you."

Axle's pulse rate rises as naughty visions race through his mind. The thought of being alone for the night with a grateful woman is almost too much to bear. *Jesus, she's so gorgeous, she is almost instant gratification.* His thoughts soar as they make solid eye contact.

She whimpers in a little girl voice, "Thank you for Karl's."

Is that her special way of saying thanks? His teenage hormones run wild. He envisions other fantasies that have haunted him since about age 10. *Do I dare dream further? Is she suggesting something else by her comment? More than that, how do I find out short of asking her? The suspense is killing me.*

The conversation reminds him of a recurring dream he has. He is participating in the Pamplona Spanish bull run. He starts in the lead and shortly everyone passes him, but the bulls. Then very close behind him he hears the clop of hooves and heavy breathing. He awakens in a cold sweat just before the bull gores him.

Axle snaps out of his reverie as he realizes that his wedding tackle is petrified. He is now the one who is exhibiting heavy breathing. Acutely embarrassed, he glances for a long time at the house out the side window.

This damned woman is dangerous. She's playing with my mind. A person like that should have a handler, maybe even a license.

He looks across the seat in the gathering darkness. Sugarloaf sits smiling as she looks straight ahead through the windshield. She has a naughty flush as she considers what she is about to make happen.

Chapter Twelve

Mongo screeches onto the highway. He races wildly through town, laying rubber on the corners as he honks people out of the way. All the while he wonders what kind of car to look for. The day is giving way to premature twilight as a storm approaches. Screw the car; he'll recognize the idiot stranger when he sees him.

He drives to the pool hall to have a look. No stranger there. He checks a couple of other gathering spots, but both the guy and Sugarloaf seem to have vanished. Finally, he drives north of town where he crosses the bridge. He parallels the railroad tracks on his way into Jose-Heights where most of the Mexicans live.

When he pulls onto Main Street, he slows to a crawl. He observes the sparse crowd as they mill around a park in the center of the small business district. Eventually he finds two young Latino men walking along. He pulls to a stop. With a 16-gauge shotgun shell clutched in each fist, he climbs out of the truck and whips the fool out of both of them at once. The taller one gives him a moderate amount of trouble, but Mongo is too strong for the sorry little bastard.

He leaves the two sprawled on the sidewalk when a small crowd of young women begins to gather. People shout at him in Spanish, while several shake their fists. A pop bottle arcs through the night air to bounce off the truck hood. People spill out of storefronts around the plaza. Mongo sees that the next fight will involve a bunch of adult Latino males who tend to stick together and enjoy using well-honed switchblades.

He climbs into his car and leaves the area. He can see the two guys in the rearview mirror. They are both standing now. They are at the forefront of a mass of people headed in his direction.

As he accelerates away, Mongo brings the index knuckle of his right fist to his mouth where he sucks on a flap of loose skin. Apparently, he caught a tooth with that fist early in the fight. Having blood on his knuckles makes him feel better. He considers rounding the block for a victory lap, but by now there will be a lot of men present with more on the way. Mongo considers the stranger again.

"Maybe not tonight sucker, but there's always tomorrow. Your ass will be mine."

He tromps the gas pedal. Duty calls. Somewhere ahead in the dark river bottom, his uncles are busy with the distillation of moonshine. Moonshine is the main source of income for the Kraven family. Mongo has to deliver a load of hooch up the coast tomorrow night. With that in mind, he makes one more unsuccessful cast through Amerada before heading toward the shack in the river bottom.

"That guy at Karl's sure had fast hands. I didn't even see that bottle coming."

Mongo passes the first of the frequent 'No Trespassing' signs along Marsh Road. Even though the Kravens own no part of the land they live on, they go to great lengths to keep other people away. Andrew Garland, an aged hermit who died alone, had once owned the bottomland. Several of his relatives inherited the property, but they all passed away shortly thereafter. By now the ownership of the land is so lost in title transfers and deceased ownership that a clear title can no longer be established. The only way to obtain clear title would be to purchase the land for back taxes. Since his arrival in town, Harvey Kraven has solved that riddle by paying the annual tax on the land to prevent sale at auction. Nobody since Andrew Garland has bothered to register legal ownership.

Chapter Thirteen

Axle and Sugarloaf sit in the car in front of Axle's new home as the wacky, weird and wild afternoon draws to a close. The house looks like a miniaturized version of a poorly built Victorian mansion. The native sandstone house is a multi-storied steep-gabled affair. It is positively spooky looking. The structure shows evidence of being designed by someone who is not an architect.

The house stands in the middle of a large lot. A massive cottonwood tree towers over the entire backyard. The untrained architect stopped designing the house at roof edge where an eve of less than four inches fights a losing battle as it attempts to keep rain off the sides of the house. The small eve makes the place look like the builder suddenly ran out of wood, money and ideas at about the same time. The vertical stone walls end where the roof begins. Axle cringes at the ridiculous looking place where he has been sentenced to live.

The fugitives pause in the street in front of the place as rain begins to splatter on to the landscape. Sugarloaf removes her arm from the seat back. She resolves to stop toying with the boy's imagination.

"Is this it?" Sugarloaf asks.

"Yeah, home sweet home," Axle mutters, as he opens his door to get out.

Sugarloaf gives a slight gasp. "I'll be damned. You're going to be living right next door to my sister."

They leave the car and sprint through the mini-shower toward the back of the house. The car is parked on the shoulder where it blocks a bridge that spans a significant ditch in front of the place. Axle surveys parking accommodations before crossing the bridge. Backing the horse trailer across a narrow bridge in the gloom of night is something to be reckoned with. Surely, there will be a place to park in back.

They round the south corner of the house to look across the

hedge toward Sugarloaf's sister's house. The structure is a twin to the Mannheim rental. The initial tingle of Sugarloaf's play on words has worn off. Axle is having mixed emotions concerning his invitation for her to spend the night in his parent's house.

"Now you'll have your own place to stay."

"No," she answers, in a meek little girl voice. "I can't do that. They're gone and I left my key on the kitchen table when I headed for the bus."

Axle unlocks the back door, which opens into the kitchen. Beyond the door is a stairway going up. He takes the stairs two at a time to the second floor. At the top he finds a bedroom. Beyond the bedroom is a walled-off attic. His mom had indicated this room would be his. The room is spacious, but so hot from mid-day temperatures that it could be used to bake ceramic glaze on tile.

He returns to the lower level where he makes a hurried pass through the remainder of the house. The lower level contains two bedrooms, a combination dining room living room, a bathroom and the kitchen. Off the kitchen is a small pantry with a narrow passageway leading down into a half basement. He decides to stay downstairs to avoid heat stroke. Sugarloaf follows him everywhere he goes, but upstairs. She comes up to his chin and smells like a flowerbed.

Axle returns to the back door. The creek is a block to the east. As he returns to the car, a large flock of ducks passes overhead. They circle once before they plunge down behind the tree line of the creek. Everything in the neighborhood is going to bed, but him. He still has a trailer full of Mannheim possessions to unload.

Out of curiosity, he walks the distance to the creek with Sugarloaf trailing behind. The rain shower of a few minutes ago has ended. To the west, a thunderstorm rumbles with an occasional flash of lightning. Ahead of them and below the cloud cover, a three quarter moon hangs a scant distance above the treetops.

They walk across the lawn of an empty house. The overgrown yard ends near the top of a slope that lunges down to the creek. Water glistens through a wall of undergrowth at the bottom of the 30-degree incline. Any earth not covered with trees grows nearly impenetrable undergrowth. Across the creek are other trees of unidentified varieties. The tree line stands 100 feet tall. Nature claims everything from the edge of the creek bed slope onward. Somewhere below them, a riffle rustles. The riffle is out of sight, but not out of hearing. The sound increases Axle's acceptance of his new hometown.

Sugarloaf observes, "Beautiful stream, huh? Hardly anyone goes there anymore."

"Why?"

She points south. "Everybody's scared of the Kravens. They live downstream and they don't want anyone on the creek. They shoot at people to keep them off the water."

"Is that so?" Axle offers, in deep contemplation. "They'll have to install naval mines to keep me from fishing there."

Axle moves to the right so he can see the water better. Cypress trees grow at water's edge. Buttonwoods crowd the shallows along the bank. An occasional sycamore stands among legions of immature elms further up the slope. His curiosity satisfied, he returns to the car.

"Will you help me unload, so we can get to bed? I've been driving all day and I'm bushed."

"Certainly, sir," Sugarloaf coos.

Axle backs the trailer along the street before he makes a wide sweeping turn onto the wooden bridge. He gives a giant sigh of relief. Prior to this event he had been terrified of backing the trailer. He parks beneath the giant cottonwood. At the end of the driveway is a one-car garage with a generous tool room on the side.

He wonders how to get his dad to let him park his coupe in the garage and leave the Pontiac outside. His dad will install the Pontiac in the garage and the Ford will be covered with tree sap in short order. Axle preferred to drive his own car here, but his vehicle didn't have a trailer hitch and the Pontiac did. Somewhere during the return trip to Oklahoma, his parents will pass him on the highway driving south in his car while he journeys north for the last load. Their remaining furniture is in an outbuilding on a farm owned by a retired Army colonel, who is now a farmer. The colonel will help Axle load the few remaining possessions before he leaves for the last time. Eventually, someone will have to return the trailer. That *someone* will be Axle.

The boy backs the trailer to the edge of the covered concrete slab that serves as a back porch. After he kills the engine he sits behind the wheel while he considers his unexpected guest who has gone inside to use the bathroom. The invitation for her to stay overnight has become bothersome. Why doesn't she have a friend she can stay with? Nothing is going to happen while she's here. Any thoughts otherwise is purely juvenile fantasy.

His new hometown's main characteristic seems to be a do-nothing blowhard-culture. Why should he expect Sugarloaf to be any different? Sugarloaf returns as Axle steps to the rear of the trailer.

"We better get with it before I develop an allergic reaction from smelling work," Axle mutters.

Sugarloaf giggles. "Are you always this goofy?"

"No, not generally," he says. "Maybe it's the company?"

He drops the ramp on the trailer before the drudgery begins. On his way inside, he flips the light switch near the door with an elbow. Outside, the light of a 60-watt bulb suspended above the back door illuminates their work area.

Two hours of grunt work later they have moved everything into the house including about 100 flying bugs that were attracted by the light. Axle sits on the edge of the porch slab as he reviews the day's accomplishments. His day has consisted of driving nearly 12 hours, fighting three men, and saving both his and this girl's lives. The life saving is probably an exaggeration.

Most of the trailer consists of the larger furniture with uncounted boxes of linens, cooking utensils, miscellaneous crap and clothing. Thank God for small favors: the freezer, the wringer style washing machine, along with numerous boxes of canned goods will be on the last load. His dad can help him unload that stuff. His father is so strong he's like a human forklift.

There is no moving dolly so everything has been unloaded with brute strength. By the time the cook stove and fridge are in place, Axle's energy level is fading. He and Sugarloaf unpack things. They stuff the crumpled newspaper padding back into the boxes. The boxes are then stacked in a corner of the dinning room. Eventually,

Axle finds towels and bed linens. At one point, Sugarloaf disappears into the bathroom. Later, when Axle goes there to drop a box, he finds her bra hanging from the inside doorknob.

While they carry things together that are too heavy or awkward for one person, he is treated to frequent peeks down the front of her blouse, unbuttoned nearly to her waist. The momentary flashes are definitely adding to his fantasy.

The sightings install a lightning rod of purpose on him. Sexual thoughts are something he can't be rid of. Even when the blouse hangs closed, every time he looks at her, all he sees is her nipples outlined against thin cotton material. The fabric pulls and relaxes across each breast every time she moves. The magic moment arrives when they are moving the stove through the kitchen door. She catches him looking, but doesn't bother changing positions.

She smiles. "Were you looking down the front of my blouse?"

He blushes so furiously no answer is necessary. Her bold question nearly causes his tongue to fall from his face.

Following the stove, they move the frame for his parent's double bed into the main bedroom. Axle's set of stacked bunk beds goes into the other bedroom at the front of the house. When they discover his sheets, they take the time to make up the bottom bunk.

They unload the Pontiac trunk. The rear seat has been reserved for clothing. The majority of what is there belongs to his parents. Their things are suspended on hangers from a rod above the seat. He carries in his pitifully small wardrobe and hangs it in his closet. The total sum of the clothing he owns occupies only a third of the closet bar. He spreads the hangers apart so it looks as though there is more than actually exists. Sugarloaf watches him from the doorway.

"You can have my bedroom and I'll stay in my parents room tonight," Axle interjects over his shoulder.

No dummy he, the evening breeze is from the west and will enter through the master bedroom window.

Towels are found in another box. Sugarloaf suggests that he take his shower first. He nods. He is too tired to argue. With the rotation determined, he sets out on his next great adventure of the day. The shower curtain remains in place, a gift from the previous tenant.

While he strips off his clothes, he again notices the bra hanging from the doorknob. The sight causes him to speculate about what it normally covers.

Axle hasn't found his clean underwear yet. Those garments remain somewhere in a box. All the time the water sluices over him, he thinks of Sugarloaf. Once he noticed the bra on the doorknob, she became more noticeably braless with each passing moment. The frequent glimpses of her unrestrained chest through the blouse opening had become an obsession by the time they finished unloading. The thought of what he has seen creates a problem for him. He considers masturbating, but doesn't.

When he finishes his shower, he has to zip his jeans up very carefully. When he is properly trussed inside his pants, he pads barefoot to the back door. He stands with his right shoulder leaning against the door jam while he considers the neighborhood houses.

Sugarloaf settles in the far corner of the kitchen. She leans against a tall stool with a folding step beneath the seat. The stool doubles as a stepladder for his mom. Sugarloaf perches on the edge of the seat with her long legs extended at a slight angle. Her feet are positioned slightly apart.

In addition to the absence of a bra, she is now also shoeless. Her posture pulls her jeans tight across the tops of her thighs. Below her pant legs, two vulnerable looking tanned ankles stare out. One glance and Axle's awareness factor mounts like compound interest. He manages to tear his eyes away from her.

"What's your sister's name?"

He concentrates on staring across the yard at the house. Sugarloaf moves to stand near him. They both peer across the hedge at her sister's dark house. Axle feels the warmth of her cheek on his bare left shoulder. His lust quotient enters overdrive from the sensation.

"Leah."

"She married?" he asks. His voice sounds more strained than before.

"Yeah, to David Holmes. Dave works at the Gold-Line Trailer factory in Shidler." Her voice has a purring quality when she comments, "Dave's hobby is shooting his pistol." She glances up at

Axle's face and smirks. "Leah's a very attractive woman and Dave is a very good pistol shot."

Axle concentrates on the fading scene across the hedge. The lawns of the two houses share communal shade from the giant cottonwood. Toward the back of each lot stands a single car garage. The Mannheim's garage is made of native sandstone, the other of wood. A grape-stake privacy fence marks the far end of the property line. The two houses are separated by 75 feet of mown grass that is divided by a four-foot high privet hedge. Axle has inherited a hedge to trim and a very large yard to mow.

Sugarloaf's cheek radiates heat as though it is a roaring hardwood campfire. He wants to touch her, but is too shy. Axle moves his arm. In the process, he brushes her shoulder as he turns the light off above the door. Her shoulder is as warm as her cheek. His arm recoils as though it is spring driven.

He moves onto the back slab where he peers around the corner of the house. As he wanders, several June bugs crush beneath his bare feet. He resists an urge to rub his arm where she touched him. Even though the light above the door is out, he can still see her standing there with her arms folded beneath her remarkable breasts.

The nearest window on the east wall is covered by a quarter section of unpainted plywood. The wood is bleached silver gray by the combined actions of age and weather. The weeds surrounding the house enjoy fertile soil. Their density reaches nearly to the eves of the old building. Beyond that he can dimly see somebody's tended garden illuminated by a streetlight. There is also a forlorn gray horse in a too small pasture.

From the corner of his right eye, he watches Sugarloaf put both arms above her head and stretch. He shivers as the front of her blouse fills to its maximum capacity. In the far distance, sparse traffic moves across a highway bridge at the edge of night. East of the house lies the sister's house and east of that stands a single row of houses backed up against the creek.

Sugarloaf moves nearer. He tries to think of something else besides the way her blouse is gaping again. Combat squadrons of ducks are elevating and lowering south of town. They maneuver through the sky along with bee-like swarms of shore birds above the marshland. Big Oliver Marsh lies in that direction. He has no idea where the name came from.

He speculates that he can probably get lost in there quicker than the flight of a new cow-pile. With his normal luck, they will eventually rename the place after him following his first opportunity to go exploring. The place thereafter will be known as The Big Mannheim for Axle Reed Mannheim, fool of the century.

Sugarloaf remains near him. Both hands are in her hip pockets. The effect on the blouse is dramatic. He wants to do things he knows would not be allowed, so he moves again. He pads to the car. Behind the driver's seat, an old gray metal cooler sits on the floorboard. He pulls the seat forward to remove the last two double colas from the ice water. The act numbs his hand.

During the return trip to the porch, he picks up a sand spur in his left heel. He hobbles the last few steps on one foot and the toes of the other. He leans against the wall where he dislodges the spur and tosses it back into the yard. He hands Sugarloaf a wet bottle. During the course of transferring the bottle, their hands touch.

She murmurs, "Thanks," in a low throaty whisper.

The sound gives him goose bumps. The boy retreats into the kitchen where he pops the top from his bottle with an opener screwed to the near end of the counter. From there, he surges into the living room to collapse on a reclining chair. Sugarloaf crosses the room to open the front door along with an adjacent window. She sets her soda on the coffee table then plops down on the divan facing him. He watches her by the light from the dim ceiling fixture as she places her naked feet on the edge of the table. Her legs are spread seductively, and her knees frame her face. Her nipples are once again plainly evident in the dim light of the room.

"Well," Axle stammers, in a husky voice. "We've been in a brawl in the neighborhood eatery, narrowly escaped a clubbing by the locals, managed to avoid arrest only by dent of small miracle and I don't even know your real name."

Her green eyes sparkle. "Margo Sugarloaf Hayes, but everybody calls me Sugarloaf."

"Who the hell would name a kid Sugarloaf?"

"You don't talk like a teenager," she moderates. "My mom was a nut. She wanted to name me Winter Wheat, but my dad wouldn't stand for it."

Sugarloaf moves her knees. She spreads them before bringing them back to their original position. Axle glances away as he makes a stab at creating a sentence.

"What have you been doing with Mongo? He seems to know you well enough to think he owns you."

"I was dumb," she answers. "When he offered me a ride to Karl's, I climbed into his truck. When I allowed that much, he decided to claim total ownership."

"Who on God's green earth would want to go for a ride with him, unless you were escorting him on a one way trip to a rendering plant?"

"I was on my way to catch the bus. My penny loafers weren't designed for long distance walking so when Mongo offered me a ride, I took the easy way out."

She moves her bare feet further apart on the edge of the coffee table. She points her toes at him as she allows her legs to loll further apart.

"Didn't your mama tell you not to accept rides from strangers?" Axle mutters. "Mine did."

"Yeah, but it must not have taken 'cause I accepted another ride from you."

They both laugh. Axle takes another pull from his bottle as he thinks about how imported double cola from Oklahoma tastes so much better than the tap water. Her blouse is gaping again. *My God, I can see her left breast including the dark pink area around the nipple.*

"Actually Mongo isn't a stranger," Sugarloaf continues, as she glances down. When she is aware of the view, she studies his face intently. "I've been around him lots of times when I was with Billy Joe, my ex-husband."

"You've been married?" Axle stammers.

"Yeah, for two years. That's something else that didn't take." *Jesus, she's so gorgeous. Why would anyone let her go?* "Anyway, we went to a couple of parties and Mongo was there. I had an initial revulsion of him, but he always seemed to be around so I got used to him. We went to a football game where he scored three touchdowns. I've been around him a lot even when I didn't want to be. You should remember this is the end of summer vacation. He looks grubbier today than usual."

Axle chuckles, as he replies, "Grubbiest hick I ever saw."

Sugarloaf leans forward at the waist to place her bottle on the table. The gaping cloth switches to her right breast before it closes again when she lays back. She places her hands on the couch before she slides further backward on the seat cushion. Another button comes unfastened. The blouse gaps further than before. Now he can see both nipples at once. She moves into a more comfortable position with her hands on her thighs. The blouse closes.

"When I lived at home," she continues, "I was practically under house arrest. My mom is a very strict Catholic. Most of what she said seemed designed to make me afraid of men. When I turned 18, along came Billy Joe Hayes. We married as soon as I graduated. He was 24 and I was 18. We then set about making a complete disaster of our lives." Sugarloaf leans forward to take another sip from her bottle. "The only thing we had in common was mutual lust. We spent a lot of time having sex, which was great, but he couldn't find a job that lasted more than a month. We drifted down here where my sister lives. He found work with a construction company laying blacktop for the county. I got a job at the bank. We had enough money to live on for the first time in our lives." She takes another thoughtful drink. "By then, I knew I didn't want to stay married to him. We never made any plans for the future and we fought all the time. I was afraid I was going to get pregnant. I stayed with Sis and Dave until the divorce was final. Eventually, my presence wore thin at Sissy's. When that happened, I went to California to live with an aunt. The second day there, I discovered the movie industry. Movies and the possibility of stardom provide a trap for dumb young women like me. I ended up living with a second-class grade B movie director who made stag-films. During that year, I wised up a lot. I didn't want to star in porn films for the rest of my life. One night while he was at a promotional, I packed a bag and headed home. I hope nobody back there ever sees any of those films."

She stops talking to stifle a yawn with the back of her hand. The blouse again gaps seductively. She takes another swig.

"I got this far before I ran out of money. I spent some more time working at the bank. While I was here this time, the bank president died. The state auditors discovered that he had embezzled about $200,000 from bank funds. They closed the bank and I ended up living on the dole with Sis again. By then, I had thoroughly worn out my welcome in Amerada. Sis and her husband decided to go away for a week. They want me gone when they get back. They're due back any time."

Sugarloaf moves her knees in another series of spreading motions that turn Axle into an avid observer. Without further coaxing, she takes a breath. Axle looks out the east bedroom window as the lights in the kitchen next door illuminate. By now he doesn't want Sugarloaf to leave, so he fails to say anything. Instead, he concentrates on drinking his double cola.

"Billy Joe was six years older than me. He worked for Barto Construction Company after the divorce. One day, he ran afoul of Mongo. After he healed up sufficiently, he returned to Missouri."

"Mongo have a lot of fights?" Axle asks.

"One a day," she mutters. "Some days more than that. You're going to see a lot of Mongo Baron in the future."

"I suppose, but I'm not going to dwell on that. Why did he jump old Billy Joe?"

"Who knows? Probably over me. B.J. and Mongo spent part of that summer working as flagmen, or whatever they call it. My ex liked to brag about all the women he'd been with; he mentioned me. I guess he blabbed every intimacy we ever shared. When B.J. returned to Missouri, Mongo began to show an intense interest anytime I happened to be in his vicinity."

Axle is more aware than ever of Sugarloaf's blouse manipulations. He decides to move his head to the left for a better view. An end table stands on that side of his chair, but it is out of reach so he stretches in that direction while keeping his eyes on her. He grabs the edge of the table and pulls it toward him.

Jesus Christ an entire breast, nipple and everything.

Axle holds the position momentarily. He glances down to see if his erection is showing. He crosses his legs, but that doesn't work so he drapes one leg over the arm of the chair but that works even less wonderfully. He stands to move to the doorway of the master bedroom. The view of his affliction is even more apparent.

Sugarloaf studies the mouth of her pop bottle from six inches away. Then she brings it to her mouth. She inserts the end about an inch before she pulls it back out to the rim so she can take another swallow.

"When I got in his pickup today, he asked me where I was going. When I said Karl's, he headed in that direction, but he whipped the truck around a corner so that he was headed out the highway. He turned off onto the refinery road. That's when I started getting scared. He kept driving fast with a sort of evil little grin on his face. I imagine he was remembering some of the things B. J. had told him. I knew I had to find a way to get out of the truck. When we came to this railroad siding, a train was blocking the crossing probably three miles from town. I think there is a road on the other side of the track that goes to where he lives in the river bottom." Sugarloaf sits slumped in her seat as she stares at the corner of the coffee table. "When he stopped for the train, I jumped out and ran like the Devil himself was after me. There were three cars stopped behind his truck. The road there is narrow with a deep ditch on both sides. That meant he couldn't back-up or turn around. I ran to the last vehicle in line. It was a guy in a pickup truck wearing overalls and a beard."

"Yeah, that's a pretty standard uniform around here," Axle mutters.

"I begged the guy for a ride back to town. I got out at Karl's and tried to hide in the far corner of the place. I figured Mongo might come there looking for me. You came in, followed shortly by Mongo. While he was trying to get me out of Karl's, I heard the bus arrive and then depart." She pauses for a long time. She takes another hummingbird sip of soda. At this rate, she could probably make a

12-ounce bottle last a week. "My sister says that a lot of young women have disappeared from around here. I knew a couple of them. Old Sheriff Kraven and his boys never developed a clue about any of those missing women."

"The Kraven I met at the filling station seemed barely literate," Axle offers. "Are they all that way?"

"Which one was he?" she asks.

"Bob at the filling station called him Clete," Axle answers. "His name tag said C. Kraven."

"He's one of the smarter ones. Wait until you get a glimpse of the others. They aren't too bright, but they're awfully handy with a fist, a gun, or a nightstick."

Axle sits on the chair again on the pretext of looking at a mar on the tabletop. He gains another glimpse of Sugarloaf's left breast. A one-inch head movement does the trick. He leans a little more to his left where he remains. In the light through the window, her light pink colored nipple is about the size of a dime. Axle's gaze lifts to her face as she begins to talk again.

"When those investigations died of their own accord the families never stopped looking. A brother of one of the missing girls also disappeared. Nobody's heard from either of them since. People say that he went into Oliver Marsh and never came out. After the brother disappeared, everyone seemed willing to accept his sister's runaway theory. I always thought it strange that even after years passed, none of those women bothered to call home or came back for a visit. When Mongo began driving me, all I could think of was that I was about to disappear." She looks around the room as she gives a little shudder. "I'm tired. I want to go to bed."

"Yeah, me too," Axle mutters. "I think I've had enough adventure for one day."

When they both stand, Sugarloaf offers to help him make up his parents' bed. Axle returns to the car where he retrieves two pillows from the back seat. After they have made up the bed, they search for pillowcases by unpacking several of the boxes.

Sugarloaf discovers an oscillating fan in one of the boxes. She insists that he take the fan for his room. When she claims that she's always cold he finally relents. He places the fan atop a chest of drawers in his parents' bedroom. While Sugarloaf shakes down the pillow, she manages to flash both breasts at once. She hands him the pillow.

"Well, I guess that does it. I'm going to go shower if you don't mind."

The thought of her naked in the shower really does it for him. Axle considers peeking through the bathroom keyhole, but chickens out. After she leaves, he closes the door to remain in the bedroom. He strips off his jeans and climbs naked into bed. He covers himself to the waist with the sheet. While he lies in bed he marvels at how good the fan feels.

He tries to take his mind off of what she must look like in the shower. He turns his face to the wall as he stifles an impulse to touch himself. The taste of summer in a strange town enters through the open window. The aroma of honeysuckle, mown grass and the salty tang of the distant marsh drift on the night air. To the west, a thunderstorm pushes a breeze through the open window along with the smell of the oiled dirt road and the horse in his pasture.

Night has arrived. Everything in the middle distance has faded by the time Axle hears Sugarloaf in the shower. His breast-inspired fever is diminished slightly by then. He is finally able to think of other things, but none of them involve sleep.

Somewhere down the block, he hears laughter. He puts on his pants and goes to the front door for a look around. A low-riding, custard-colored three-quarter moon casts a golden glow over the trees at the creek. The town lies bathed in suffused moonlight.

Sugarloaf continues her shower. Axle is suddenly hungry. He is as wide-awake as he has ever been. Instead of eating at Karl's cafe, he had joined in the disruptive flow of events there. He pads back to bed where he strips off his pants and lies down. He is abnormally restless.

The cooler in the car contains a slab of hard salami with a wedge of longhorn cheese. There is half a loaf of bread in the back seat. He imagines that he can hear the sound of peanut butter hitting a cracker. His hearing seems nearly as acute as the family pet. The dog can hear a refrigerator door open from two blocks away.

He considers striking out barefoot through the sand spurs again to retrieve an evening meal. While he savors the thought of cold hard salami on fresh bread, the door opens to admit Sugarloaf. She wears one of his T-shirts. The thin covering is just long enough to hang at mid-thigh on her. It is the sexiest thing he has ever seen.

She turns her back toward him as she softly closes the door. The moon-glow highlights her breasts from where the too large shirt drapes the material away from her stomach. She makes an exaggerated movement as she pulls the shirt off over her head.

The accompanying adrenaline surge he experiences gives his heart a jumpstart. His manhood assumes the rigidity of a railroad spike. She stands before him arched spectacularly in the moon-glow as she stands holding the shirt. The sight creates an image that would add authenticity to anybody's photo album.

She drops the T-shirt on the floor and shakes her hair in place. She touches her tresses to feel where they are. They are down past the nipple line in front and undoubtedly bellow her shoulder blades in back.

She murmurs, "Are you awake?"

"Incredibly," he answers, in a hoarse response. His throat feels as though it has been packed with gravel. She places one luxurious knee on the edge of his mattress. Her appearance has sculptured an erection on him that feels the size of Florida. "Maybe we should have supper or something."

"Or something," she repeats. "I have not properly thanked you for what you did in Karl's today. What you did took a great deal of courage."

She leans over him. The kiss she gives him is open mouthed and searing. His night becomes more glandular than at any other time in his life. She comes up for air.

He offers, "Thank you. That should do it." When he tries to get out of bed, she places a hand on his shoulder to restrain him. "I'll get the food from the car. You can go with me," he offers in his gravely voice, as he attempts to rise.

"Later," she murmurs.

Her hand dips beneath the sheet. She fondles him the way a monk handles prayer beads. Her lips move from his mouth downward.

They trace a burning trail over his chest where she hovers while she investigates each nipple with a tongue as frantic as a bee ravaging a blossom. Her exploration encompasses everything in its path as it traces a resolute path that terminates below his beltline.

In the flash of an eye, she has turned him delirious with need. Her gorgeous mouth terminates in an exploration that he has only imagined in dreams. Her slippery wet pursuit ends in the detection of everything essential to a lover's reward. Before he can enjoy the fruits of her discovery, it is too late. There is no turning back. The alarming sense of urgency that consumes him is frightening in its intensity. The velocity of his cum-shot is volatile, but she does not shrink from his termination.

She plows a flaming path up along his body in reverse order until she has returned to where she started. She stands to hover astride his hips. Their eyes lock as she lowers herself on to his immensely inflamed digit. In an instant, they are firmly and deeply coupled. The night sizzles and throbs around them as linear thought becomes impossible.

The next morning, Axle comes awake following a hard night's rest. He feels the need to hold an icepack to his wounded body part. Just to prove that life isn't going to get any easier, Sugarloaf parades through the house, drop-dead gorgeous in her birthday suit. Her movements are those of a wild creature in heat. By 10:00 AM, they have christened nearly every horizontal surface in the house.

When she has finished going down on him for the third time, she says, "The bus comes at noon and I need to be on it."

Following a final blazing moment of orgasmic agony, they climb into their clothing. Sugarloaf wears what she wore the day before with undies hand washed in the bathroom sink. The sight of her panties hanging over the shower curtain rod is the most erotic thing that Axle has ever seen.

At 10:30, he unhooks the trailer. They drive to the truck stop in Shidler that functions as a bus terminal. Their route of travel avoids Karl's. They are oblivious to everyone in the truck stop while they hover over breakfast.

As they eat, they remember the continual paroxysm of pleasures that had exceeded the powers of both their imaginations. While every trucker in attendance admires Sugarloaf from afar, Axle remembers the coral pink naked woman flesh that had inspired every heated motion. He maintains a manic ardor for the beautiful sex panther who seduced him. There was the shattering intensity of first time sex for him. The look of her sends molten flashes of need racing through him even in this public place.

What an experience the night had been for her. Both cock and tongue had wounded her the first hour in his bed. She had intended to offer a single reward to him for saving her from an uncertain fate with Mongo. What a joke that thought had been. The first stuttering movements of his tongue on her nipples changed all that. Her reward had been to quickly give him oral. He had then responded in kind. She had guided his inexperienced tongue to her clit. The liquor of her cunt's passion along with her screams of pleasure had inspired him like no other man she had ever been with. He had taken to cunnilingus the way a frog takes to water.

The thought of rewarding him for saving her from Mongo vanished when his tongue discovered her clit. She was the one being rewarded when her release was suddenly upon her. He required little guidance after he discovered the reward of listening to the vocal pleasures offered up by a mature woman when he stroked the needy jewel between the luscious lips of her cunt. His inexperienced efforts had given her responses that she had never known before. His youthful vigor inspired her to spread her legs wide when he slid his mammoth cock into her.

Afterward, she realized that she had granted a man total access to her for the first time. She had held back nothing. Granting total access was not a normal feature of her physical makeup. The feeling of such fevered arousal was something new to her. Before, it had been a matter of making a living and nothing more.

The magic of his inexperience had even caused her to orgasm during foreplay. That was also a first for her. Sugarloaf did not seek out men for sexual pleasure. When she wanted pleasure, she had merely engaged in prolonged bouts of masturbation. The actions of the men she had been with seemed to be merely a need for stimulation that was not her own. Until she engaged this marvel of a young man in the acts of cunnilingus and coitus, she had been the best lover she had ever known.

He had become so aroused by her vocal eruptions that he had placed his immense cock and thrust into her. She had received the rigid offering with a pleading voice that cried out for mercy, but none was forthcoming. Her body turned rigid when he entered her, because the penetration had occurred as her raptures peaked. She had screamed a fluttering groan of satisfaction when he slid all the way into her. The sounds of her pleasure inspired him further.

He was in her for scant seconds before her body reacted to the glow of the pubic blow when he bottomed in her. She had clawed his back then as she gripped him with her vaginal muscles. During the violent penetrations, she had shot off again.

While she was in the midst of explosive coital pleasure, she realized that she had never truly orgasmed before. His ministrations had been wondrous. She couldn't get enough. This inexperienced kid had seduced her in the manner that she had wanted to be fucked for her entire life. She had given him the knowledge of her clitoris and he had taken the ball and ran with it. She had always faked orgasms for the camera, but not this time.

There was no faking allowed when this bed devil had his way with her. This man of the universe had made her russet nipples project with agate-like hardness. She had lost count of the number of times he had sent her tumbling over the edge into the abyss of a death-like orgasmic paralysis. There are no words to describe the ecstasy she found with him. His young cock seemed too big for her, but in the end he had been the perfect size for her hungry cleft.

His cock had fit so snuggly into her that it stretched the muscles of her vagina. The feeling had been frightening at first. Her face became flushed from suffering the numerous passions of pleasure. She taught him to pinch her nipples firmly during intercourse and then harder as her orgasm neared. Everything he did resulted in the final gasp of a singing pleasure that curled her toes and caused her to cry out with every stroke he gave her.

While they attempted to eat, they both remembered every agony of last night's many orgasmic moments. At 11:30, depression set in when the loudspeaker announced the departure of her bus. They walk hand in hand to the boarding area where Axle kisses a woman in public for the first time.

"Why don't you stay for another day or two?" he questions.

All the while he has a lump in his throat the approximate size of Cuba. Sensing his problem, she moves firmly against him.

"Don't get all wet eyed on me. The first time is special for everyone. We'll see each other again. I'll be back in a little while."

She kisses him on the cheek, as he puts his arms around her. She presses her face against his chest as he hugs her. Hugging her is his way of keeping her for a while longer. He feels her warm breath against the hollow of his neck. The bus driver stands by the door impatiently. Finally, he clears his throat.

"We have to get going, miss."

"Yeah, I know," she whimpers. She gives him another kiss on the mouth featuring a lot of tongue. She boards, as the last passenger of a nearly full bus. From an open rear window, she calls to him as the bus backs up. "Watch out for Mongo," she cautions, in an elevated voice. The bus stops, shifts gears and then pulls away. She yells at him, "I'll write you a letter!"

He waves at her, as he says, "I love you."

She blows him a kiss. The bus turns onto the street to disappear half a block later when it moves up a slight grade onto the highway in route to Houston. Across the street from the parking apron near an abandoned service station, a dark pickup truck pulls onto the highway to follow the bus. Axle walks to the parking lot where he climbs into the family Pontiac. He wipes wet eyes with a handkerchief. *What a memory. I hope she returns real soon. I already miss her.* Their night together had passed faster than a speeding bullet.

At home, he takes a quick look around before he locks up. When he is certain there is nobody near the house he removes the telegraph key and earphones from the door-facing. He sits up the Hallicrafters radio. When it is good and dark and the set is fully warmed up he tunes to a prearranged frequency. He transmits his first message without encryption:

NIGHT OWL, NIGHT OWL, RIPTIDE X
NIGHT OWL COPY X
RIPTIDE GO X
CONFIRM NAME OF FORTUNE TELLER X
MADAM GLUBA X
RIPTIDE MSG FOLLOWS X RIPTIDE IN PLACE X OTHERS
FOLLOW X WILL BE OFF STATION UNTIL ARRIVE X TRIP
UNEVENTFUL X NOTHING TO REPORT BUT COMO LINK
X SINGER SAYS HELLO X
NIGHT OWL COPY X
RIPTIDE CLEAR.

Axle returns the equipment to the door-facing. He secures the house and proceeds to couple the trailer to the car. As he kneels to fasten the safety chains and couple the tail light circuit to the car he hears footsteps. He turns to find a pretty woman standing close behind him. She appears to be a slightly older, nearly twin version of Sugarloaf, but with light brown hair.

Green eyes apparently run in the family. She wears short shorts, a halter top, cork soled medium heeled sandals, a smile and a waist length ponytail. She owns the same type of incredible legs Sugarloaf wears. Her long naked legs seem to go all the way to her ear lobes.

"I'm your next door neighbor, Leah Holmes," she offers, as she holds out her hand.

Axle accepts her hand with its long fingers and manicured nails. "Axle Mannheim, ma'am."

After an extended period of silence he realizes that he still holds her hand. He drops the digits as though they have become a venomous snake. Her smile turns even more dazzling when she detects his discomfort.

"I've come to offer you the use of my lawnmower, if you need one," she murmurs. "The last family moved away. They didn't mow the grass before they left."

The boy inspects the grass following a deep shuddering breath.

"Thanks for the offer. I have to retrieve the last load of our furniture. I'll be gone for a couple days, but Mom and Dad should be along later this evening or tomorrow."

He avoids any mention of Sugarloaf. He senses that it would not seem right if she knew that her sister had spent the night with him. She would assume what had happened and the thought would probably annoy her. Sugarloaf had made the earth move on its axis last night.

Leah offers, "Welcome to Amerada. If you need anything, just holler."

A naughty thought crosses his mind. "Thank you. I'll see you in a day or two."

Axle pulls the car onto the driveway in preparation to back the trailer across the bridge. The event concludes without a hitch. Leah follows his progress along the driveway. She watches him with her left arm flexed behind her slender back, and with that hand gripping her right elbow. The pose tests the material of her halter top. The image prosecutes a naughty notion of mouths joined with hands busy.

Axle waves through an open window as he begins a final drive to Oklahoma. He receives a farewell wave. There is another brisk mid-day business is in progress when he passes Karl's. He wonders when Mongo will arrive to liven up the diners evening.

He spends a portion of the next four hours remembering Sugarloaf, as he listens to the hypnotic effect of tires striking the seams in the roadway. About 1:00, he stops at a roadside rest area where he stretches out on the front seat and sleeps for a while. He awakens with the distinct feeling that the occupants of the Overholt Turkey Farm have paraded across his tongue.

Midnight finds him back at the farm where he sleeps in the car as he awaits daylight. He awakens to the crow of a rooster. He wonders where Sugarloaf is and when she will return to him. Mom and Dad are somewhere on the road to Amerada, or maybe they're already there. He hopes that they didn't stop at Karl's for a meal before going to the house.

Chapter Fourteen

The bus discharges its passengers in the parking area of the Houston bus terminal. Sugarloaf consults the agent at the ticket counter where she determines that there is a three-hour layover before departure to Little Rock. The depot restaurant is being remodeled so she walks a half block to the recommended eatery. The place is an old railroad dining car sitting on a concrete foundation. To the west, the sun begins to vanish behind tall clouds. Overhead, a modest cloud cover suggests rain in the near future.

When she is seated at a table in a low backed booth, she orders a grilled cheese sandwich and a cup of coffee. A sign on the wall near the cash register proclaims free coffee refills. During her meal, the bus station intercom announces that her bus departure will be delayed yet another hour for mechanical repairs.

She idly sips coffee while considering last night's adventure with Axle. A shiver of delight passes through her as she remembers some of the more exquisite details. For an instant, she wishes she had remained another day in Amerada, so he could further scratch the itch within her that never seems satisfied. While her mind races, darkness settles over the town.

She becomes aware of a bearded man in the booth across the isle from her. The man seems vaguely familiar. While she considers him, he abruptly vacates his booth. He leaves behind a newspaper spread out on the table. He pays the cashier before he leaves. Only then does she take the paper into her own booth.

She kills time reading the paper. Three cups of coffee later she has read the entire edition twice to include the want ads. In something just short of an eternity, the loud speaker on the corner of the bus terminal announces her bus's departure. She goes to the restroom before she ventures through the front door on her way to the depot.

The entrance to the bus station is less than half a block away. An alley separates the eatery and the corner of the bus terminal.

The entry to the alley is a black cavity without any form of light. She glances up at the corner of the building where a green porcelain covered light fixture dangles from an arched metal mounting. The socket contains the remnants of a broken light bulb. She could have sworn there had been a light burning in the fixture when she passed by on her way to the diner. She only noticed the light because it was burning during daylight hours. Now that night has fallen, the insubstantial light fixture is no longer working. The absence of any form of light makes the alley appear more menacing than normal.

She has feared dark places since she was a little girl. Her mother would leave the bedroom door ajar at night so she could see the faint glow of the hall nightlight. She quickens her pace as she nears the void between the buildings. She is almost beyond the opening when two large shadows dart out.

One shadow places an arm around her neck with a hand across her mouth. She struggles as she screams into the large calloused paw. The other silhouette secures her legs in a vice-like grip. Her captors were visible to her only for the wisp of a second, but during that time she identifies the man who sat across from her in the diner.

She struggles against the powerful arms that hold her. As they near a vehicle, something strikes her head. There is a bright flash of heavenly bodies as she falls away into another dark nothingness.

A long time later, Sugarloaf awakens. She can feel the vibrations of movement and the smell of hot oil. She turns her head to discover a man's booted foot depressing the foot-feed. A deep throbbing headache coupled with dizziness makes her want to throw up. There is an instant of consuming terror when she discovers that there is a restriction around her neck and a gag in her mouth. The gag tastes like an oily rag.

When her senses fully return, she identifies her place of confinement. She is on the floor of a vehicle traveling at high speed. Her face rests on the transmission case. Her body is wedged face down against a rubber floor mat. She can feel the vibration of tires on a highway. When she tries to move, she discovers that her hands are tied behind her back. She finds that her legs are bent with her ankles restrained. The rope from her ankles is tied to her neck. She is consumed by an overpowering fear as she bucks against her bindings. Any movement to unbend her legs tightens the rope around her neck, choking her. A foot finds the middle of her back to press her against the floor. Eventually, a hand pulls her face away from the floor mat using her hair as a handle.

"Hold still, girlie," a shrill voice mutters. "It'll be better in a little while."

Her face thuds back against the floor bruising her cheek. Sugarloaf Hayes screams into the gag as she realizes that she is about to disappear. While the truck rolls along, she fights the ropes while she cries hysterically.

A long time later, there is a passage of lights outside. The vehicle jounces along for a long time before it stops in the darkness beneath trees. Insects keen outside in the black night. There is the smell of water and the rustle of tree leaves in a slight breeze. In the distance, a night bird cries.

The man on the rider's side opens his door. The dome light does not illuminate. The rope between her ankles and neck is cut before powerful hands pull her out through the open door. When she is outside, the man stands her upright so that she leans against the side of the truck bed. Her legs are numb from confinement. They tingle as the circulation returns.

The other man remains in the truck with the lights on and the engine running. The man holding her upright is tall. She stands only as tall as his chest. She strains to scream against the gag. He rips the tape from her mouth and then removes the rag from her mouth. He cuts the restraints from her arms. Her mouth is dry. She is so frightened that she can't scream now that her mouth is free.

The other man opens his door before he turns off the engine. His door closes with a soft click as he strides around the front of the truck. As her eyes adjust to the darkness, she realizes that both men are bearded. They smell of old sweat. With the headlights off, their features remain invisible in the darkness.

The moon comes from behind a cloud. A splash of moonlight reveals the bearded face of the man from the booth seat in the restaurant, the one who left the newspaper. His partner wears a floppy brimmed black hat with a tall round crown as though it is homemade. His face remains in constant shadow. The hatted stranger grabs the front of her blouse and rips it open. Buttons fly in every direction. He turns her around so he can rip the remaining portions of the blouse from her body.

With the blouse gone, he slides a knife beneath her bra strap and gives a gentle tug. The keen blade slices the elastic with little effort. The cups of the bra sag forward freeing her breasts. She feels the cold metal of the blade as he cuts through her brassiere shoulder straps. The man in front fondles her breasts after her best lacy bra falls away.

When he is finished with her breasts, he leans down to cut the tape above her knees followed by the wrap at her ankles. He slits her jeans up the front of each leg. When they are hanging free he cuts the waistband in two places. The denim lands in a puddle near her feet.

She stands before them bathed in moonlight wearing only white lace bikini panties. She had marveled only that morning as she stared at herself in Axle's full-length mirror, how well her sun-kissed body looked in white panties. He cuts through both sides of the waistband of her panties. The scraps of clothing are retrieved from the ground to be tossed into the truck bed.

A flash of moonlight reveals her naked pubis as she leans against the pickup bed with her legs slightly spread. The tall man cups her pubis in the palm of his hand. Even though she is scared spitless, the touch of his palm against her protruding clit sends a shiver of lust racing through her body. This night of horror is turning into a scene from one of her movies. She is about to be raped and her body imagines how good it is going to feel.

She rasps, "I'll do anything you want, just don't hurt me."

The last part of the comment ends in a thin whimper of panic.

"You bet you will, girlie," the man offers, as he slaps her full across the face.

Her head quickly rebounds to center as she glares at him. Sugarloaf's only thought is to stay alive; nothing else matters. There is nothing they can do to her that someone has not already done countless times before, except kill her. The tall man probes her woman's wound with a thick finger.

"Her cunt's already wet and as bare as a baby's bottom. You're gonna enjoy what I've got for you, honey bunch. It's gonna stretch that tight little pussy of yours. Poor little pussy," he laments, as he unfastens the top fasteners of his bib overalls.

The garment falls to puddle around his ankles before he steps out of it. He stands before her in brogans without underwire. His hard cock is long, thick and slightly arched with a gross looking large flared head. Sugarloaf gives a whimper as she stares at his offering. His balls hang pendulous in their sack. The monster cock protrudes from a fluff of dark black hair. The dramatic presentation is much like a redwood tree protruding above a lodge pole pine forest.

The tall man grips her by the back of the neck as he propels her away from the truck. She staggers and nearly falls. When they are in the bar ditch, he forces her to her knees in the soft sand below the edge of the unmaintained roadbed.

"We saw your movie, honey; now you're gonna tend Oscar the way you did for them other guys. Later, we'll get around to them other things, but now I want your mouth around it."

The hatted man has also dropped his overalls and exposed himself. He is as well hung as his partner. Both men are equipped to dispense punishment to any woman. Both are uncircumcised. When she is face to face with her project, he strokes himself several times in a well-practiced manner before he presents himself for service.

Her face is still aflame from the open handed slap, so she does not hesitate. She slicks the foreskin back with a firm grip around the base of his well-starched cock. She cradles his balls in her left hand while she strokes the shaft several times in a jacking motion. She licks her lips. In return, he begins to fuck her hand. She guides him so that each fore stroke ends only when it bruises her lips. With each bruise, her lips part a little further. She is blessed with a generous mouth. At long last she grants him entry into the Valhalla he seeks. As she moves him, she scrubs the underside of his cock head with her she-devil-tongue.

She feels him tremble. Sugarloaf deep throats him all the way to the root of his cock base before she withdraws him. She is more stuffed full of cock than the stud stars in those movies. She aims his unscrupulous inflexible dick so that she can apply the favored strokes designed to bring him off. As she prepares for the ejaculatory spasm, his apocalyptic whimper announces the arrival of the event. The production is accompanied by a mighty thrust followed by a recoil that splatters into her with the velocity of a large caliber rifle round.

She continues to gently stroke him beyond the pleasurable agony of ejaculation. Eventually, his pleasure turns to the suffering of sensitivity. Only then does he begin to fight the pleasure of her mouth. No matter how many times she performs a blow job, the final event continues to remain startling.

She deep throats his member one final time. In the end, her excessive sized captor has been reduced to a brogan shod naked adolescent. Sugarloaf has been in full charge of her captor during the entire event. Her talent as an experienced fellatrix will keep her alive. She had put everything she knew into his blow job and he had been mesmerized by the event. He would want the delicious favor every time he saw her pretty mouth that had so indulged him.

From the corner of her eye, Sugarloaf watched his co-conspirator standing with his overalls around his ankles. While he watched her perform, he stroked himself. Both men are fully engaged in their own form of sexual gratification.

Sugarloaf's first seducers cum-shot had been accompanied by a loud gasp of pleasure. He had gripped her head and gave a mighty final thrust at ejaculation that forces his swelling armature all the way into her throat with a single stroke. She was barely able to accept the violation without injury. The flared head of his dick had filled her throat. She could not breathe when he was fully inserted into her throat. She had pulled back before she began to bob her head in the short terminal strokes that men favor during the production of their final crisis.

A short time later, he had fully expended himself. She provided him with the final effort of her first oral commitment as a sex slave. She must remain slightly sadistic, but cooperative. Men want to dominate during sex, but only Axle had been able to accomplish the feat. She is perplexed by what has happened during the past 24 hours. She has gone from being saved to becoming a sex slave. She is gripped by an icy fear that accompanies her situation.

This is no worse than being the sex machine at a private holiday celebration where she might do 20 cocks before she is finished for the evening. She knows that there will be other acts to follow this one, but fellatio will occupy most of the action for these two. They are addicted to fellatio the same way they are addicted to breathing.

Her second prospect offers her a can of cold beer from a cooler in the truck bed. She rinses her mouth and spits before she takes a couple swallows. The beer tastes terrific. Before she can finish, the man leads her to the soft sand where she again assumes the position of sexual servitude. Sugarloaf has been kneeling in front of men since she was a teenager. She had been taught the act by her first sex partner who was 10 years her senior. She had learned her trade well enough to star in countless lurid movies. The films sold even before they could be produced. The only difference between then and now is that she will not take home an ample paycheck. If she is lucky, she will be allowed to remain alive.

Sugarloaf rests with her buttocks on her heels as she settles into the stance she has occupied countless times before. Because she has a large, lurid looking mouth with perfect lips, her movies featured close-ups of her engaged in the act of fellatio. She keeps her pubis waxed so that her protruding clit is on permanent display. The simple motions of walking caused the pressure of her panties to grant her an orgasm several times a day. She has been a slave to her clit since discovery at age eight. The persistent contact of clit on cloth has kept her in a near constant state of orgasmic excitement for most of her life.

The hatted man instructs her to go slow so that he does not completely lose control. If she properly pleasures the second man, who has shown her pity, he will keep her alive for his personal pleasure. Sugarloaf is a fellatio artesian who understands exactly what men want. This one will never want a quickie. Under normal circumstances, he would want to be tied spread-eagle on a bed and be sensually tortured to ejaculation. She would talk to him about what she was going to do. She would bring him to the brink of ejaculation and sit watching his cock pulse while he begged for fulfillment. His pleasure would consist of multiple starts and stops. Unfortunately, as things are now, he will merely fuck her face to conclusion.

Sugarloaf Hayes does what is demanded of her, because the better she services her captors, the greater chance she has of staying alive so she can eventually escape. When the second man has met his gobbling, screaming conclusion, he lifts her upright. She uses the still cool beer and the back of her hand to clean up with.

Before they return her to the truck, her arms are again bound behind her back. Mosquitoes are bothering her nakedness. The taller man gets behind the wheel. When they begin to move, the one with the hat puts a thin white cotton sack over her head. The shock of having her head covered causes her to gasp. The effort pulls the sack flat across her open mouth.

She is seated between them. The passenger's hands are never idle. He is constantly feeling her up the way a teenage date would act. The position of her bound arms forces her forward onto the edge of the seat where she begins to cry softly. Eventually, she must lean forward to rest her forehead on the dashboard. Apparently they are not afraid of being seen, otherwise she would be back on the floor.

Before her head was covered, the moonlight allowed her to see the area around her. They were on a little used trail with grass growing between the wheel tracks. The land was densely wooded with a lot of insects and night noises. Birds made night calls, while bullfrogs drummed in the background. The frogs indicate the nearness of water? There are other creature sounds, things she cannot identify.

She hated the smell of her captors and what they made her do. The motions of movement finally stop again and both men get out. She can hear them talking in low voices as they urinate in the darkness.

When they are finished, the engine starts and the rocking motions continue. She leans back in the seat. After several miles, the vehicle stops. She can hear the faint sounds of waves lapping a shore. There is the smell of brackish water. They move her to the tailgate of the truck bed for more sexual favors before resuming their journey.

This time they fuck her girl-goody instead of her mouth. *Thank God for the IUD I had installed two months ago.* The thickness of their endowments made her orgasm a sure thing. She screams in rapture for them four times before they are finished with her. She is not slapped again. They enjoy her the way they have probably not enjoyed a woman before. She feels fear mingled with being entirely sexually satisfied.

Chapter Fifteen

Axle's second arrival in town with the last load of furniture carefully avoids Karl's Burger Heaven. He parks the Pontiac in the backyard before he leaps from the car and runs through a rain shower into the kitchen. Wet cardboard boxes litter the lawn beneath the tree where they have been discarded during the unpacking process.

He is greeted by the smell of fresh baked bread. On the stove, the family Dutch oven sits half full of black-eyed peas soaking in water. The sourdough crock, covered by a white dishtowel, stands on a counter top beneath a row of cupboards. The family never seems to have enough money for store-bought bread, so his mother bakes twice a week. The loaves are almost always sourdough with an occasional twist of dill bread thrown in. Breakfast commonly features sourdough biscuits, fresh butter, gravy and homemade wild berry jelly. Home seems re-established as the familiar smells blend around the boy. There is the soothing sound of a waltz on the radio.

In Wyoming, they'd had their own Guernsey cow named Bessie. Fresh butter was churned twice a week and they had sold fresh milk and butter to friends. Axle hopes that they never own another cow. The fresh butter and milk were great, but he hated hoeing out the stall. Moving manure in a wheelbarrow and loading bailed hay into the barn loft were two of his least favorite chores.

His mom is nowhere in sight, so Axle goes to the fridge for something to eat. The appliance yields part of a two-day-old meatloaf. The remnants of the last meal eaten in Oklahoma have been imported across the border into Texas. He uses a serrated knife to cut two slabs of gold encrusted bread from a loaf on the cooling rack. The first slice is the heel. He eats that out of hand with a lot of butter. The slices remain warm from the oven. He puts the next slice on a plate with a companion. These receive a generous amount of sandwich spread from a half empty jar. He piles on a thick slab of meatloaf and a large leaf of iceberg lettuce from a new head in the crisper. Next comes two overlapping slices of beefsteak tomato from a roadside stand. The tomato slices are nearly as large in diameter as the lid of a coffee can.

He returns the perishables to the refrigerator before he pours a glass of Kool-Aid from a green cut glass pitcher. A shelf near the bottom of the ancient Cold Spot refrigerator yields a jar of homemade bread and butter pickles. He takes six spears, so he won't have to return for seconds. He flops down at the kitchen table where he begins to munch.

He hears his mom shuffling things in the other end of the house. She's probably working in a bedroom. He tunes the kitchen radio to a station carrying the St. Louis Cardinals baseball club who are playing an afternoon game.

He has remained mindful of their assigned mission, but every day he finds himself wondering where the danger lies. Periodically, the slide of agent Pine's dead face flashes across his mind. Regardless, the Grouer All-Wave Radio, the sandwich and the smells of home make everything seem as though there is nothing to be feared in the entire universe.

Maggie is a real class act. She is disappointed that Axle does not share her enthusiasm for manual labor. They always have a huge garden so she cans massive amounts of vegetables. Axle can imagine hoeing down the weed patch next door so his mom can have a garden the size of a small truck farm. Canning was the ticket to surviving the Great Depression, even though his dad was never without a fulltime job. Maggie returns to the kitchen carrying an armload of dishtowels.

"Oh, good," she offers, "you're home."

She stuffs the towels into a deep cabinet drawer before giving him a peck on the cheek. She squats in front of a floor level cabinet door near the stove. Once in position, she begins to transfer pots and pans from the counter top to the cabinet shelves. Axle glances at the counter top where he vividly recalls Sugarloaf's bottom gracing that particular surface.

"How'd the trip go?" his mother asks.

"Great," Axle mumbles, around a mouth full of sandwich. "No

problems. I made it back in 11 and a-half hours this time. The trailer had a flat before I left Oklahoma, but Noey Hastings helped me fix the puncture."

"Did it ruin the tire?"

"Nope, just a small nail," he answers. "We patched the tube and put it back together like the pros we are."

"Your dad's really going to be glad you're home. We both worried about you driving all that distance by yourself," she says, as she slams another stack of pans into place. "I've got some important news for you. We're going to have a visitor for a while. He'll stay in your room with you until his parents arrive. I don't really know when that will be, but it shouldn't be long."

Axle poses three questions. "Why does he have to stay in my room? Why can't he stay upstairs? Who is this?"

"We don't have any furniture for the upstairs bedroom," she answers, as she reaches for a column of stacked bread pans. "His family is being sent here by the organization. The boy's name is Toby. He's supposed to be your second cousin from Louisiana, your father's half-sister's son. The organization decided that we would probably need backup before the operation is finished, so another family is moving in to live around the corner from us."

"What does Dad think about all this? They said they weren't going to send any other operatives."

"At first he was outraged. But then last night he decided it would be comforting to have someone around in case we need help. He knows the man from the war; they trained together."

"What's the boy like?"

"I've never met him," his mom continues, as she moves a stack of cast iron skillets to the front of a shelf. "Mr. Black says he's a really nice, intelligent boy. He plays football, wrestles and boxes. Mr. Black says you'll like him."

"Did he order me to like him?" Axle asks, as he puts his half-eaten sandwich back on the plate, "or was that merely an observation?"

"More on the order of an observation. How can you not like someone you've never met?"

"I just know this is going to be an idiot I'll hate on sight," Axel mutters. "He'll be about as much fun as a course in creative tooth decay."

"He's supposed to be on the 3:00 bus. I'm glad you got home when you did, 'cause your dad's working and I didn't have any way to go get him."

"How am I supposed to recognize this creature?"

"He's 6 foot 5, weighs 235 pounds, has dark hair and looks like a professional wrestler. Just look for someone who's young and the approximate size of your father. Mr. Black says he will be wearing something with the word *Louisiana* inscribed on it." She stands upright to snag her purse off a counter top. She produces a $5 bill from her billfold. "Here, you can stop at that little restaurant on the highway and buy yourselves something to eat."

Axle slips the bill into a front jean pocket. He remains thoroughly numb to the idea of living with a stranger.

"This is turning into a quasi-religious experience. I'm supposed to accept some stranger living in my room. Before I can get over the shock of that, I'm expected to feed the newcomer who is the approximate size of a Brontosaurus, and I'm supposed to suppress his mammoth appetite with only five bucks."

His mother smiles and gives him a peck on the cheek. Axle consults his wristwatch. The dial shows 2:45. It's time to get up and stride briskly into the future.

"Are you all right with this?"

"Yeah, sure. What if this guy turns out to be some speckled dweeb, what do I do then?"

"He won't," she assures him. "I trust Mr. Black's judgment."

"You've got more faith than a revival crowd," Axle mutters. "I sure hope you're right, so I don't have to bury him in the woods somewhere." Maggie glares at her son. "I'll bring him back alive if he's on the bus." Axle heads out the door. "See you in about an hour." The screen door slaps its door jam and he is gone. "Hot damn. First, identify the new arrival, and then lunch at the local tiger's den."

The last time they took somebody aboard, it had been his father's mother. She had died two years ago. It had cost the family several thousand dollars to bury her. That had been money they didn't have.

The rest of her family was composed of cousins who lived out of state. None of them were interested in body disposal. Axle had loved his grandmother dearly, but after that, he couldn't help wondering about every other enterprise that washed up on the family shore.

Axle finishes the rest of the sandwich on his way to the car. His '36 Ford is parked beside the Pontiac in the driveway. Before he can move his car, he has to back the trailer into an unloading position near the back porch. Backing the trailer is much easier this time. Maybe he's finally getting the hang of backing. With the trailer in place, he unhooks and cranks up the trailer tongue before he pulls the car forward to clear the driveway.

Across the hedge, a load of Leah's washing hangs from a clothesline. Her panties flap there in a gentle breeze. Axle jumps into his car and heads for Karl's. The new Smitty dual-exhaust system he had installed in Gillette generates a pleasant echo within the cab.

Memories flourish like buzzards on a sheep carcass as he drives to Karl's. He drives sedately, so as not to attract another ticket. The only slot available is at the edge of the lot to the rear. The alley files between rows of residential buildings that resemble decaying teeth. Sheets of unpainted plywood cover most of the windows. The wood has turned gray from constant weather exposure. The cops are probably involved in a shift change otherwise they would have flagged him down by now. He maneuvers through the parking lot a second time before accepting the parking slot near the alley.

As he climbs out of the car, a bus arrives out front. He leaves the car unlocked as he lopes to the front of the building. As he trots toward the bus, he glances back at his car. The newly painted coupe looks resplendent where it peeks out from between an assemblage of local rust buckets. Axle stands near Karl's front door until he is certain the last person has de-bussed. Apparently this is a planned stop. The passengers assemble inside where they prepare to eat.

When Axle is about to turn away, a guy who has to turn sideways to make it through the door steps down. Nobody else matches his mother's description the way he does. The dude resembles a toad scanning for flies as he studies the entrance to Karl's. Finally satisfied, he yawns and stretches. The guy is rumpled looking as though he's been asleep since he boarded the bus in Cajun country. His nose is slightly warped. There are patches of mild scar tissue around his eyes. Obviously, he has encountered fists in the past. This one is definitely not a choirboy. Axle takes a step forward.

"Are you Toby?" The question is preceded by a half hope that he isn't.

"Yo," he booms. His drawl nearly stretches the word into two syllables.

Toby resembles a Walt Disney impression of a lumberjack. He is all of the promised 235. At least a 150 of those pounds are devoted to shoulders, pecs, biceps and arms. His black hair is cut flat on top with a duck's tail finish in back. His eyes are dark brown, almost black. His massive arms protrude from a ragged, sleeveless, faded gold-colored T-shirt that looks more like a tissue thin upper body stocking than a shirt.

Across the front in blue letters are two lines with the words, *Staff, Louisiana State University*. The shirt strains in a thin web across his incredible chest. Below the shirt his jeans are faded nearly white with dark blue patches on both knees. The belt loops hang empty. His sneakers are so thoroughly worn out that they consist mostly of a dense collection of strings held together by a white rubber sole.

Axle looks at him as he tries to think of something clever to say without entering into a period of dumbness. The Cajun glances at him while he peers around the parking lot. His presence seems to block out the sun. He's large enough to create his own weather pattern.

"How does it feel," Axle asks, "to be passing through life without a neck?"

"You outta know," Toby retorts, as his attention returns. "You got the same problem."

"Welcome to a small town famous for intrigue and law enforcement," Axle offers, as he extends his hand. "It took me all of 10 minutes to get my first ticket." They shake hands. Toby's paw feels like five skin covered railroad spikes. Axle takes his hand back as he stifles an urge to flex his fingers. "I've got some good news and some bad news for you. What you want first?"

"Give me the bad news," Toby says, as he studies Axle's face.

"The kids in the high school are so tough they have their own cemetery," Axle mutters.

"That sounds about like where I came from. My last school boasted that 90% of its graduates eventually made parole. What's the good news?"

"We've got a complement of local hillbilly-bullies to occupy our time, along with a police force who hates anybody from anywhere that ain't named Kraven. There's more: football practice starts tomorrow and we can hit people without being arrested."

"My kind of place." Toby grins full out. "Are there any girls?"

"Yeah, I guess so," Axle mutters. "Apparently some of them keep disappearing and nobody knows where they've gone, at least nobody we know of anyway." Axle pauses. "Are you hungry?"

"Absolutely," Toby answers. "I'm always hungry."

Axle winces, while he considers that this sucker will walk into Karl's and order the entire left side of the menu while considering that it's only the first course. Axle decides that he knows what is coming. He regrets that he has only $5 for such a memorable event.

"You got any bags?"

Toby nods. "Yeah," he says, as he makes a snapping sound the middle finger and thumb of his right hand. "I'm glad you reminded me."

He turns back to the bus. By now the driver is kneeling on one knee as he pries luggage from the belly of the beast. He produces five containers. The first four are cardboard boxes held closed by silver duct tape. Toby takes up the four boxes, two beneath each arm. He then gestures to a cheap tin suitcase. A piece of cotton rope reinforces the latch mechanism and hinges of the item.

"That's mine, too." Axle retrieves the suitcase by its handle as they launch themselves toward Axle's car. Toby lumbers along carrying his boxes as though they are four brown paper lunch bags. "I understand that we are supposed to be related in some manner."

"Yeah," Axle answers. "Cousins or something like that, distant at any rate. It's gonna be a tough sell though, seeing as how I'm so much better lookin' than you are."

Toby gives an incidental snort. "Where we headed?"

"I thought we'd go to the local tattoo parlor and have our ears pierced so we'll whistle in a high wind."

Toby stares at him until Axle chuckles. "You're jivin' me again. You must be some sort of a wise-ass?"

"I've been called that and worse," Axle acknowledges.

There is a thought process developing for Axle. He has been in town for a combined total of three and a half days without a friend in sight. After an initial hesitation, Axle decides that he wants to be related to Toby. If at some point in the future, the organization sends him bear hunting with a switch or enters him in a knife fighting contest, he wants this human muscle machine on his side. Mongo still lurks somewhere in the background and Axle figures he can certainly count on meeting him again.

"I like a little smart-ass in a guy," Toby murmurs. "I see you're into weight liftin'?" he booms, as they arrive at the place where the car is supposed to be.

"Yeah, sure, six days a week," Axle answers.

"I thought so," Toby growls.

"Every morning I run two miles. Six days a week I lift," Axle offers, as he stares at the hole in the row of trucks where his car is supposed to be.

Toby responds, "We can work out together. I'm into power lifting. I want to be in the Olympics."

"No wonder you look like a five ton truck-jack. It's okay by me, but I have a hard time running with anybody. I doubt that I've got enough weight plates for you."

"Anything will do 'til my stuff gets here." Toby glances at the abandoned buildings. "Is this place dyin', or what?"

"It looks a little under populated," Axle answers, "but they've still got an oil field and a refinery hereabouts. It's just not a boom-town anymore."

"The way downtown looked along Main Street, the school will probably be a tent."

"I haven't been to the school yet," Axle offers, as he arrives at a decision. "We might as well stop by school and register. Football practice starts tomorrow and we need to sign up today."

"Okay by me."

This guy can probably press my entire weight set with me sitting on the bench. Maybe he can lie under the car and I'll run back and forth over him to toughen him up till his weight set gets here? Axle looks at Toby.

"What size jacket do you wear?"

"Triple-X large, long," Toby responds. "I have a terrible time with shoulder pads. I always end up wearing the ones they give interior linesmen." Axle nods in fascination as he wonders what has happened to his car that was parked here. "Last month my grandma died, and Mom tried to buy me a suit to wear to the funeral. A 52-long suit coat fit just fine, but the pants had a 46-inch waist and I need a 32." Axle stares at Toby in disbelief. "The salesman claimed that if he took the waist up that much, the hip pockets would be touching. It was sort of embarrassing."

"So what did you do?"

"I went to the funeral in a gray sweat suit with a draw string tied in front. I don't think anybody even noticed."

"What a glorious, moving moment that must have been," Axle observes.

"Yeah, I don't think my aunt will ever forgive me." Toby looks sideways at Axle. "You got any idea why I am favoring you with my presence before my parents get here?"

Axle shakes his head. "Nope, I only know that it wasn't my idea."

Toby gazes into the distance. "I got in trouble back home, so Dad sent me here ahead of time while he waits for a transfer to the oil field to come through. The delay will make our move seem more believable."

"Sounds reasonable," Axle agrees.

"Besides," Toby continues, "I gotta play football, so I can get a scholarship. That's the only way I'll ever be make it to college."

"I hope I get to go to college."

"Dad figures it'll take about a month before they can make the move," Toby continues. "Dad claims trouble follows me like a bad dream. I can't seem to shake trouble or bad luck." While he talks, he continues to stare into the distance as though he is lost in contemplation.

"I'm really glad you came along when you did," Axle offers. "You'll need to stick to me like white on rice 'cause I got a bully chasing my ass. He just hasn't caught me yet."

"Welcome to Bullyville," Toby mutters under his breath as he gives a broad grin.

"I figured I'd need a Ph.D. in adolescent, child psychology to handle you when Mom told me you were coming," Axle allows, "but now that you're here I have another idea."

"Involving the bully, right?" Toby asks.

Axle grins.

"Okay, what does the guy look like?"

"He's muscular, not as tall as either of us. He has a bad case of face and head hair. His nose looks about like yours. If he has a neck, I didn't see it. He is the local ego king. He probably has to have a fight every day to maintain his reputation."

"Oh, one of those," Toby says. "How old, approximately?"

"I don't know, older than me and I'm 16," Axle answers, "how about you?"

"Sixteen, starting my last year of high school," Toby answers, "I'll be 17 next month."

"You skip a year of school the same as I did?" Axle asks.

"Yep," Toby offers, "I skipped the sixth grade."

They are now standing in the gap where he had parked the coupe.

"What the hell? My car's gone!" Axle says in a loud voice as the tin suitcase hits the gravel.

Toby says, "Yo," again as his contribution to the discovery.

The cavity in the line of cars looks like a gap in somebody's front teeth. The boys stand where the coupe had been, while Axle entertains a brain lock. He can't imagine why his car isn't there.

Axle's dances in a small circle as he tries to dispose of the thought that he's just encountered another of life's snags. The only difference this time is that for once he's not alone. He moves further into the alley that runs north and south. To his right he sees the rear bumper of his car disappearing around a distant corner. A kid is propelling the vehicle by sitting on the rear bumper as he pushes with his legs. Axle emits a growl of discovery as he heads along the alley in overdrive with Toby in hot pursuit. They round the corner of the far building to find the car at rest in the middle of the east bound lane of Elm Street. Four adolescents are busy trying to hot wire the ignition. Their problem is that none of them seem to know the exact procedure.

Two kids are in the car. Another boy lurks outside near the driver's window. The outsider leans in through an open window as he offers advice. The kid sitting on the rear bumper sees Axle first. He simply leaps up and races off down the street without telling anyone. The others remain oblivious to Axle's arrival. Getting caught by the owner of a recently stolen car causes a condition some might describe as "Severe adversity."

The window looker's back is to Axle while he issues instructions to the kid in the driver's seat. Axle advances quickly to the guy leaning in through the driver's side window. In perfect stride, he kicks the thief between the legs from behind. The kid grabs his crotch as he drops to the street. From there he rolls onto his left side with his knees drawn up near his chin. With the apparent supervisor immobile, Axle turns his attention to the driver. The driver is concentrating on the ignition switch, which is near the steering wheel on the dash. The arrival of the owner comes as an immense shock when the thief finds himself in the clutches of a pair of powerful hands.

Axle grabs the kid by the hair with one hand while his other fist assumes a vise-like grip on the kid's upper left arm. He then proceeds to hoist him out through the open window.

Axle gets a look at the kid's face as he extrudes him through the opening. The face is familiar. It is Troy Kraven of earlier attempted theft fame.

As Axle threads Troy out over the window sill, he mutters, "Howdy Troy, longtime no see. It looks as though you've climb another rung up the ladder of criminal success."

Troy is caught red handed with a semi-stolen car in his possession. No need for an improvised story this time. Talking to Troy is like talking to a wildcat. The young thief is a scratcher and a howler.

Troy comes through the window with Axle's hide under the nails of his free right hand. While he claws, he makes sounds that suggest a squirrel fight in progress somewhere in a river bottom.

While Axle handles the near side crooks, Toby rounds the far corner of the vehicle where he catches another kid coming through the passenger door. Toby grabs him by the nape of the neck and slams his head four times face first against the edge of the door jam. Toby's arm pistons as though he is casually sawing a board in half. When he turns the thief lose the kid drops to his knees on the street where he kneels while holding his head.

The thief on the bumper who saw Axle first, is high-tailing it along the street with enough head start to make chasing a losing proposition.

Toby looks after him as he asks, "You want me to run down the other one?"

"No, three's enough for a lesson learned," Axle mumbles as he looks into Troy's face from close range.

Axle has Troy by the throat with one hand while he hangs onto an arm with the other. While he talks with Toby, he slams the back of Troy's head twice against the car. The thief's head rebounds off the edge of the roof. The act leaves Troy limp. The kid's feet dangle about an inch above street level. As a final gesture, Axle double-punts him at the belt line with a right knee. Troy has stopped scratching and screaming by now. With the application of the knee, he folds over smoothly to grab himself while he experiences the need for someone to pump air into him. Axle releases the kid's throat whereupon he slowly puddles onto the street. Breathing is no longer an easy process for him. Axle knows the feeling.

The first offender still resides on the street about five feet away. The kid is making mewing sounds while attempting to knee walk out of range. For his effort, Axle kicks him on the side of the head. The kid straightens out as limp as a rag before he embraces the asphalt road bed face first. Axle hopes that he acquires second degree burns from the sun scorched black-top.

Axle turns back to grab Troy by the hair again. He lifts him upright against the side of the car. From that position, he forehands and backhands the kid's face with an open palm. The act feels so good he does it again. He then begins to wonder how much pressure it would take to tear out a clump of hair.

Three people of a four person car theft ring are now residing on the street near the car. Toby looks at Axle as he nods toward the rear of the vehicle. They both turn to watch as a Sheriff's cruiser pulls to a stop behind the Ford. The deputy turns on the roof light. A tall skinny cop who looks like a bad erector set selection opens the door and climbs out. His name tag reads J. Kraven. As the deputy passes the rear bumper of Axle's car, he says, "Stop what you're doin' and grab some paint."

Toby looks at Axle. His eyes are bright with mirth as he mutters, "Why go eat when we can have a meeting?"

Axle grins. The cop continues, "Turn the kid loose and put your hands on the car roof, step back and spread your legs." When nobody moves, he says, "I ain't gonna tell you again."

Axle releases Troy. Instead of doing what he is told, he decides to talk which at 16 is his favorite pastime. Axle has a teenage condition his father describes as *inoperable stubbornness.*

For speech therapy, he gets a whack across his left collar bone from the deputy's night stick. Further argument is resolved when he realizes that unlike his parents, the cop expects the total obedience of a feudal Lord.

Axle and Toby assume the recommended position with their hands along the edge of the roofline. From that position, they watch the individual members of the auto theft ring recover sufficiently to stand upright.

Axle mutters in a low voice to his new friend, "This is like playing third fiddle in a bad band."

Toby tries unsuccessfully to stifle a giggle. The deputy whacks him across the back of a thigh with the night-stick. Toby gives a yelp of appreciation.

Axle favors his left shoulder as he leans against the car. He holds his left arm tight against his chest. He wants a sling for the arm more than just about anything. No sling arrives. Instead, he receives additional creative policemanship.

"Troy," the deputy says, "what in hell are you doin' here?"

"He stole my car," Axle offers in a loud voice, "that's why we're all standin' out here in the sun."

The deputy says, "Shut up."

Axle answers, "Yes, sir." Additionally he shifts to place his forehead against the edge of the roof gutter. From that position, he rubs his collar bone with his other hand.

Troy takes a deep breath before he whines, "Uncle Jeb, we was just funnin' this dude when he started wailin' on us."

Troy's voice sounds like a motor bearing about to fail. The kid maintains his small high pitched voice throughout the conversation. He responds as though he's had a lot of practice pleading for sympathy.

Jesus Christ, another Kraven with a badge. It's like we've all died and gone to a funny farm.

Uncle Jeb is cut from the same cloth as Clete. He is tall and skinny with a pinched faced. He remembers Clete while looking at Jeb. The observation results in an enlightening experience. Put the three of them together and it would be like staring into a rodent cage. They all resemble weasels. Uncle Jeb has something else going for him though. He has enough facial wrinkles to win any prune look-alike contest.

In addition to the comical uniform, J. Kraven wears a Sam-Brown belt and holster set. The array was probably stolen in the distant past from a deposed Peruvian General. His feet are shod in dark brown cowboy boots that sport silver toe inlays. The entire uniform resembles something an insane person would wear to a food fight.

While Jeb speaks to Troy, he regards Axle and Toby as though he is looking at fresh cow chips on the street. Uncle Jeb grips and re-grips his night stick with both hands as though he would enjoy using it again. Meanwhile, Axle is forming a cramp in his neck from leaning awkwardly against his car.

Jeb growls at his nephew, "Troy, you get your ass home. I'm gonna talk to your Dad this afternoon and I want you there. Do you understand me?"

Troy scuffs a toe on the ground while he shrugs his shoulders and sticks his hands in his front jean pockets. Eye contact is not Troy's long suit. Instead of eye contact he stares at the pavement. Uncle Jeb speaks again a little louder when he asks, "Do you understand me, boy?"

"Yeah, Uncle Jeb."

"Then git, I'll talk to you later."

Troy walks unsteadily away, accompanied by his two running mates. All three are marked by combat. They limp as they walk which is a new feature acquired from their latest journey into thievery. One has a mass enlarging near his right temple. He walks as though he is straddling a short fence line. Another has forehead lump the size of half a cantaloupe from enduring Toby's continual ramming effort against the door frame. Both his tongue and nose are bleeding.

The back of Troy Kraven's head is forming a very large welt. Both cheeks are scarlet from being slapped. He walks in the stooped manner of a very old person.

The balance of payment for Axle is that he has a bruised collar bone and is missing several inches of hide from the outside of his left forearm. The arm appears as though he has been in a cat fight and the cat won. Toby remains large and unmarked.

"Hey," Axle says from his angled position, "wait a minute, those kids stole my car from the parking lot at Karl's. Aren't you going to do anything?"

The would-be thieves carry their latest learning curve across the street where they stand in the shade of a green awning in front of Wilson's Drug Store. From there, they watch their adversaries being harassed by Troy's pet deputy. The kid who fled first joins them. They all seem about 14 years old.

Uncle Jeb looks up and down the street before he says, "Yes I am."

"You mean this car?" he says as he raps the left rear fender with his night stick. The blow leaves a small dent.

"Yes, sir," Axle answers.

"This car appears to be illegally parked," the deputy observes.

"But they stole my car from Karl's parking lot," Axle stammers again in disbelief.

"What you think we are around here?" Jeb asks. "Stupid?"

The words cowardly, sneaky and unacceptable come to mind.

With his observation fresh in his mind, Jeb returns to the squad car where he retrieves a leather-bound booklet. He proceeds to write Axle a ticket for illegal parking.

Axle and Toby turn, so as to lean their backsides against the side of the Ford. The best part of getting the ticket is that the deputy has to lower his face to write. The act of writing allows the two law enforcement casualties a temporary relief from staring at his features.

Later, with the second ticket lying on the seat between them, Axle fires up the car and returns to Karl's where they retrieve Toby's belongings. *Anymore tickets, and I'll have to begin a career as a professional pedestrian.*

Chapter Sixteen

The tin suitcase lies flattened in the parking lot near the edge of the alley. It now resembles a thick silver pancake encircled by a loose cotton rope. The boxes remain in their original condition only because they were out of the line of traffic. The boys load everything into the rumble seat of the Ford before moving to a new parking spot near the front door of Karl's.

Toby's arrival seems a lot like a carbon copy of Axle's last trip to the establishment. There is an aroma of destiny about the place. Last time it had been trouble with Mongo. This time it's trouble with teenagers followed by a deputy. The day now includes another driving infraction. It seems that eating at Karl's is always going to be a hazardous undertaking. The next stanza will probably be as predictable as a Swiss watch. Mongo will show up to continue the grand arrival adventure.

The peeling paint on the side of the place hasn't healed itself. There seems to be about as many vehicles in the parking lot as before. As the boys pass through the inner door into the dining area, about 30 heads swivel in their direction. Axle notices that nobody jumped up to flee the way they did when Mongo arrived.

Axle elects to sit at his former table in the far corner facing the door. The same waitress delivers water and menus.

"I read somewhere that Wild Bill Hickok got shot from behind," Axle mutters. "So I've decided to die facing the door."

They take a few minute to survey the culinary delights awaiting them in the kitchen. While Axle studies the menu he glances at the next table where a guy is eating something that resembles a small animal road kill.

Probably better to eat what's delivered than to go into the kitchen and be threatened with a cheese grater.

Axle mutters, "Don't try the water, get a Coke, the stuff tastes like swamp scum."

Toby tries it anyway. Only the naive are caught by surprise. He screws up his face as he mutters, "Man, that's bad with a capital-B."

The waitress arrives. Axle knows better than to order the hamburger so he asks for an open faced, hot beef sandwich. He has decided that it will be hard to screw up something that's covered with gravy. They both order soft drinks.

Axel doesn't mention his previous ordeal eating here. Without warning, Toby orders a hamburger. Axle plays with his silverware while he glances around the room. Nobody makes eye contact, but nearly half those present cast oblique glances in their direction. As before, only two women are in attendance. The local teenage girls remain strangely absent. Axle is beginning to feel like a Hun on a village pillaging mission. Since his arrival, the parents of the hamlet seem to be hiding their daughters.

"I sure hope I don't get another teacher that matches the one at the last school," Toby comments. "I had one in Louisiana that was as mean as a snake. She had a hair-do modeled after an ancient Teutonic helmet and the temperament of a cornered wolverine."

Axle keeps an eye on the front door while he listens with only one ear.

"Her name was Joyce Barnwart," Toby continues. "She looked about the way her name sounds. She came complete with a face that would stop an 8-day clock. She had all the curves of a third grade school girl."

Axle gives a little chuckle as he glances away from the door.

"Old Joyce enjoyed calling on me to answer questions in class, and of course I'd screw it up every time. She'd then hold me up for ridicule. I got a ration of that every day. Before long, I began to hope that she'd go outside and catch herself a few moths for lunch."

Axle stifles a giggle. The mirth is interrupted by the arrival of their meal. Toby's hamburger looks like something from the cover of a food magazine. Axle's hot beef sandwich looks as though it has been spawned by the same place the water came from.

The cook is watching them through the kitchen order window. The accompanying mashed potatoes are suffering vegetable defamation. Axle figures that he can probably choke down meal down providing Mongo doesn't show up to ask for another dance.

They eat in silence. Toby's hamburger is magnificent while Axle's dead cow sandwich turns out to be not as bad as it looks. As they finish eating, two pieces of pumpkin pie overflowing with whipped cream materialize, unordered.

Axle motions the waitress to the table as he points at the pie. "That's not ours," he announces in a low voice.

"It's on the house," the red head answers as she turns to leave.

In the space of a five second conversation, Toby has initiated a flurry of fork manipulations that allow him to inhaled his pie before Axle can even get his fork into position.

Toby offers, "Pie's great. What's the free food thing about? You got a secret admirer?"

"I've been here before," Axle answers, "I guess they remember me."

"They remember the way you handle a knife and fork, or what?" Toby mumbles.

"Something like that," Axle mutters around a fork full of pie. "Maybe I'm an art surgeon with eating utensils."

"Okay," Toby says as he drops his fork on the empty plate, "out with it. I always like to know what I'm up against."

"Probably just a coincidence," Axle answers as he stares straight ahead while talking.

There is a long pregnant pause before Toby comments, "I'm still waiting and I've got all afternoon."

Axle pauses between bites. He looks down at his plate as he wishes more was there. Finally, he begins reluctantly to recite his last ordeal when he was here. When he finishes, Toby grins knowingly before asking, "Wow, what happened then?"

"I went home," Axle offers. "We spent the night and I went back to Oklahoma the next day for the last load of furniture."

"No, not that," Toby growls, "I mean what happened to the woman you left with?"

"Oh, her," Axle says. "She spent the night at our house. I put her on a bus the next morning at the Shidler truck stop."

"That's it?" Toby mutters, in a sarcastic tone. "Aren't you leaving something out?"

"No," Axle answers. "Even if I were, you're too young to understand." Following the last comment, Axle gives a low test chuckle before adding, "Nothing really happened but a hard night's sleep."

Toby tries to keep a straight face when he mutters, "I take it that mummy and daddy weren't home when she visited?"

"Nope."

"Can you be a little more specific about your nighttime adventure," Toby questions. "What about the hours between dusk and daylight?"

"No comment," Axel responds.

"Why do I suspect you aren't telling me the entire story?" Toby accuses as he leans back in his chair to display a look of complete disappointment.

"Oh, well, forget that for an instant," Toby offers. "What did she look like?"

"She was nothing more than the usual run-of-the-mill-blond with green eyes and all the other optional equipment."

Toby continues to grin as he compresses the last few crumbs of pie crust onto the bottom of his fork before eating them.

They each finish off a Coke refill apiece. Axle stands to drift over near the cash register. He glances back at the table where Toby glares at the plate where the pie had been. Left alone in a restaurant with an unlimited bankroll, he'd probably injure himself eating. The redheaded waitress with the big hair stands behind the register. Her hair-do today appears to have been assembled by the use of an explosive charge.

Axle says, "I don't have a ticket, what do we owe?"

A dimple appears in each cheek. "No charge," she murmurs, "welcome to Amerada."

"Are you sure?" Axle stammers. She nods while still dimpling. Her teeth are very white and even. "Did we win a contest or somethin'? What'd we do to rate free food?"

"My name's Louise. I'm Karl's wife."

She offers her hand across the counter. Axle grips it. He releases her hand as she restores her dimples. Toby ambles up in time to hear the last of the conversation. Axle glances at the long serving counter where 10 guys sit grinning as they monitor his obvious discomfort.

He turns away from them and leans across the counter.

"I'd really rather not does this. Just give me a ticket so we can pay and be on our way?"

Louise replies, "I'm serious, there's no charge. After you left the other day, some of the customers took up a collection and gave it to Karl. Then Karl and I put some more with that. We made a little ledger for the cash register. It's sort of like a bank account. Any time you come in here, you're eating free. If they hadn't taken up the collection you'd still be eating free. That's our way of saying thank you for yesterday." Louise draws a small breath. "Food's cheap. What you did was not."

Axle's face burns a brilliant crimson. He is embarrassed beyond description. He glances along the counter where every cornea in the place is turned in his direction.

He stammers, "My appreciation to you and Karl and everybody else. Thanks a lot."

He suddenly has a burst of the 'timids'. He bolts for the door with Toby trailing behind. As Axle passes through the first set of doors, somebody in the background begins to applaud. Others join in. As the outer doors close, Axle jets for the car. Toby follows at a walk with his left hand in his front pocket and his right guiding a toothpick in his mouth. Axle slides into the car starts it and puts it in gear. When Toby enters the other door, Axle pops the clutch and they are under way.

"Boy, that was impressive," Toby growls. "It's really great to be traveling with a local celebrity."

Axle glances at the paint flakes on the side of the building as he heads toward the highway.

"They made more of what happened than it was worth."

"Yeah, sure. Trust me. I'm not smart enough to teach quantum physics at Podunkville-U, but I'm smart enough to know that people dressed in work clothes don't make more of anything than it's worth."

Axle changes the subject. "Might as well go sign up for football. You do play football when your not making stupid comments, don't you?"

"Absolutely," Toby says, "and quite well, I might add."

Chapter Seventeen

Sugarloaf is forced to walk naked and barefoot for a distance. She still wears the hood with her hands tied behind her back. A door creaks open, then closes behind her. There is the snap of a match against a fingernail as a flare of flame precedes the hiss of a gas lantern. She feels the chill of metal against her left ankle followed by the snick of a padlock closing. An unaccustomed weight drapes against the top of her left foot followed by the rattle of a chain as she moves her leg. The cloth bag is pulled from her head.

She is alone with the bearded man in an odd looking room. She finds that she is chained by the ankle to a bracket in the wall. The restraint is a long length of what appears to be dog chain. The chain is fastened to a bracket in the wall by a bright-metal nut and bolt. The other end is secured to her ankle by a small padlock. To her right, a nearly waist high spring mattress set rests atop an elevated, wooden platform. The springs are elderly. The blue and white ticked material of the mattress is stained. The crumpled white sheet is badly in need of washing.

Near the center of the room is a gray metal office chair with padded arms. The chair is bolted to the floor. The chair legs are pierced by new nuts and bolts that also pass through brackets protruding from the concrete floor. The brackets twinkle in the flickering lamplight.

The bearded man prods Sugarloaf to the chair where he bends her over the backrest facing forward. Her ankles are loosely tied to the rear legs of the chair above the metal rungs. A knife is used to cut the ropes that bind her arms. The man holds her by the nape of the neck. She bends forward from the waist across the back of the chair. She grips the armrests to remove the strain from her lower back. He handcuffs each of her wrists to a chair arm. The man ties a black cloth, across her eyes.

For the brief moments when she can see, she notes that the inside of the structure resembles a storm cellar. There is a dome shaped concrete roof with shelves along both walls. The shelves are lined with canned goods. The floor, ceiling and walls are concrete. There is the smell of earth in the room.

Behind her, she hears shuffling footsteps and the sound of a door closing. There is the sound of a zipper with another shuffle of feet. A man enters her from behind. Sugarloaf drops her head as she begins to sob. In her mind, she vows to survive.

Chapter Eighteen

Mongo pulls into the parking lot between the field house and the side door of the high school. A pipe and cable barrier arrangement surrounds the schoolyard. Four motorcycles sit with their rear wheels against the curbstones. The remainder of the parking lot at the field house is filled with cars. The motorcycles indicate that part of his crew is present and drawing equipment.

His people are the best of the football team. They wait until the last day to register. Mongo sits in the truck for a while as he feels the knot above his ear. He memorizes the other cars in the parking lot. No strange vehicles are present. He knows who owns them all.

He watches Sarah Woodling float along the sidewalk toward the field house door. Mongo watches her until her backside disappears through the swinging doors. For a brief instant, he considers why he's never been able to get to first base with her. First base, hell, he hasn't even found the road to the ballpark.

"Wonder why she's hangin' out at the gym?" he asks. "She's probably looking for some jock to torment the hell out of for the remainder of the year."

Mongo climbs out of the truck and struts toward the door. He grins. He is the local football stud who excels in running over people on the football field. This is his time of year. How fun to hit the bigger guys and make them cry. Last year, he'd scored touchdowns at will, but a sprained ankle caused him to miss the final game. Without him, the team lost the conference championship by two touchdowns during the one game he couldn't play.

"Have to do some drivin' around after while," he mumbles, "in case the new kid doesn't play football."

He thinks some more about yesterday. The guy was big enough. Surely, he'll show. Mongo enters the gym where he meanders to the counter separating the equipment room from the locker room. He stands on the scales while an assistant records his weight and height next to his name at the bottom of the list on a clipboard.

Sarah Woodling stands 10 feet away talking to Coach Palmer about the girl's basketball team. Mongo glances at her. The look of her causes a familiar inner tremor to course through his body. Too bad she's such a stuck-up bitch. When she turns, she gives him a 100-watt smile.

"Hi Mongo, you ready for your last football season?"

"Sure am, gorgeous. We're gonna win the conference this year. You gonna be homecoming queen again?"

"Not me. Once was enough. I've got to watch my grades so I can go to college."

"I ain't watchin' grades. I'm gonna become independently wealthy."

Mongo drifts into the equipment room where he draws his equipment. He puts his gear in a locker with his name stenciled on the front. Then he walks to the front door. Sarah is directly behind him.

"Hey, Sarah, want to go for a ride out to my place and back?"

About that time something strikes him from behind and everything goes black.

Chapter Nineteen

Axle drives north on Birch Street. All he knows is that the high school resides on the northwest corner of town. Ahead, a flagpole with the stars and stripes waving in a gentle breeze stands before a large single-story, blond brick building. The field house sets apart from the school with the lights of the football field plainly evident close behind the building. There is a parking lot between the two buildings.

Four motorcycles squat in a regimented row near the front door of the field house. The bikes are aimed outward as they await their owners. He wonders if they are the same people he met at Karl's. Two are Harleys, and the others are Indians. All are painted black.

Toby mumbles, "Looks as though the local motorcycle gang is having a meeting. I'll bet that they're all scruffy lookin'."

As the new arrivals fast walk toward the door, Toby says, "Race you." They both sprint for the door.

The building has double-spring hinged, swinging doors. There is an outer pair, and then behind them a twin inner pair. The manner of construction acts as an air lock to prevent drafts from entering the building. The doors are substantial looking, well made with a large, bright, metal kick-plate at the bottom.

Axle still carries a load of adrenaline from his second traffic ticket. That causes him to enter through the doors with more velocity than necessary. Toby trails by half a step when the doors swing inward.

There is a momentary resistance on Axle's door at mid-swing. Thereafter, the inner door fully opens. Beyond the door, some husky dude does an imitation of a dying swan onto the floor where he kisses varnish before sliding nearly a yard.

The guy lies absolutely still, face down. When he doesn't move, Axle wonders if he's killed somebody. When he realizes what has happened, he expects a deputy to emerge from the equipment room to issue another ticket for assault with a door. The guy on the floor shakes his head as he tries to rise. The victim turns onto his left side as Axle bends down to help him up.

"Jesus, I'm sorry," Axle stammers. "I didn't realize anyone was standing on the other side of the door."

The guy on the floor wears a maroon and gray high school letter jacket above faded jeans. He rolls to a sitting position with his eyes glassy. The name on the left breast of the jacket reads Montgomery. The other side of the jacket bears a big, red, chenille 'A' with a bunch of stripes, metal emblems and devices.

Axle grasps Montgomery's upper left arm as he tries to help him up. The guy shakes off the hand. Axle again bends down in an attempt to help lift the guy to his feet.

While Axle adjusts his grip for better leverage, he notices a scar on the left side of the guy's neck. He stares again at the face before him. Suddenly, he realizes that it's Mongo from Karl's, with a bath, no beard and a haircut.

Axle releases the arm before he recoils upright. Axle would not be surprised to learn that everyone in the room is named Kraven. People are surging in their direction from around the end of an equipment counter. One is obviously the coach. The others resemble younger assistants. Beyond them, ten other people stand grouped in a corner. A stupendous looking blond earth-nymph stands clutching books to her chest about five feet to Axle's right.

Axle makes a final desperate attempt at damage control by offering his hand to help Mongo to a standing position. Mongo no longer wants help. Instead, he issues a low growling sound that hints of recognition. A look of rage rifles across Mongo's face. Nobody can mark the exact instant when Mongo decided that he wants to be standing over Axle's rapidly cooling dead body.

While Mongo attempts to stand, he becomes increasingly loud. A rumbling-sound issues from his throat that resembles a diesel engine running in somebody's basement. Axle takes two baby steps backward so that he is temporarily out of range. This will be their second encounter. For some reason, every time they meet, Mongo gets hit in the head with something.

Once again, they have reached a momentary flash point. Axle

decides that he doesn't want any footprints across his chest so he moves further away to avoid the rush that he knows is coming.

In the background, people continue to close in on their position. If Axle bends over backward any farther with an apology, he will need medical help to return to vertical. For an instant, he gives consideration to returning briskly through the double doors on the way home.

Axle takes his eyes off Mongo only for a second as he searches again for the incredible looking blond girl. Where the hell is she? Oh, she's leaning on the equipment engaged in an uncontrollable laughing fit.

My ass is a sieve.

Mongo is upright now with a second lump forming on the back of his head. This one is the approximate size of half a new turnip. It has surpassed the one above his left ear by nearly half an inch. Axle needs no further education to realize that Mongo is insanely angry.

Mongo stops feeling the back of his head for just an instant, then takes a step forward. A devilish look of pleasure forms on his face. He has at last found the idiot stranger from Karl's. Finding him is like an answer to a prayer.

Mongo surges forward with an agility that would put a silverback ape to shame. He grabs Axle's shirt front with both hands. Axle lunges backward, and the front of his favorite T-shirt fails at both shoulder seams. The cloth comes away in one solid piece that leaves Axle's chest bare. With his plan of attack as yet unsatisfied, Mongo drops the cloth and gropes for Axle's nearest arm with his left hand. The hand offers a grip strong enough to make an oyster wince.

While Mongo hangs on with his left hand, his right arm is drawn back as though to throw a punch. Axle prepares to deflect the blow with his left forearm as he circles counter-clockwise.

The coach and four other people arrived at about the same time that Mongo shredded the shirt. A big kid nearly the size of a Hereford steer with a hormone imbalance grabs Mongo's right arm while the coach hangs onto his left. Both are screaming, *"Mongo"* at the top of their lungs. The coach wears a white ball cap with the name Palmer stenciled below the word 'Coach'.

The confrontation quickly reaches a centrifugal absurdity. Four people stand welded together in a tight formation as they fast-dance in a circle. At the center of the orbit is Mongo who still grasps Axle's arm while trying to free his own right fist. The coach and the Hereford dangle from him at an obtuse angle while being slung to the outside of the orbit. By now, Toby is also hanging onto Mongo's right arm along with the steer like kid. The scene continues to grow like fungus on a tree stump.

Ten seconds ago, Toby and Axle came lumbering through the door wondering what football season would be like in their new hometown. Now, they are both worried about what Axle's facial configuration will be later in the day.

Other bystanders close in. Five more kids latch on to Mongo. The mass continues to dozy-doe in a circle with nobody calling the square.

For the time being, everybody is safe, but that is like having faith in the safety and security of the Titanic. Nobody feels as though Mongo is going to continue through life with people chinning themselves on his right arm and with the coach surgically attached to his left shoulder.

Most background noise ceased when Mongo struck the floor. The single exception continues to be the hysterical giggling blond and the snare drum of Axle's accelerated heartbeat.

The remaining people in the room stand around like patrons watching a rodeo bull riding event. More reinforcements leap into the pile. Six of the locals manage to tear Mongo away from his only known advisory. Everybody is so excited they couldn't have scored a four on an intelligence test.

The anger in the room reduces to a low rumble as everyone begins breathing again. The event is similar to Axle's initial arrival at Karl's. Axle decides that he doesn't want to hang around for desert.

The coach finally detaches himself from Mongo. He then turns his attention to the two new arrivals.

"Follow me," he says, as he leads them behind the equipment counter. While they move beyond the substantial barrier, coach makes a mental appraisal of the two latest arrivals. The big one looks like a middle linebacker, the other one maybe a line backer, running back or end.

Coach Palmer maintains an eye on Mongo while he helps the new kids with their equipment draw. All the football gear is laid out on long cafeteria style tables. Most is used, very little is new. The shoes are new and in boxes. All are low quarter, a departure from Wyoming where everyone wore high tops.

Bubba and several of Mongo's friends corral him in a far corner while they attempt to extinguish part of the burning bridge that opening the gym door created. Toby follows Axle like the horse trailer he was dragging earlier in the day. Together, they sort through gear as they search for what they need.

During the melee, Toby has maintained a contented little grin on his face as though savoring the arrival of another meal. While they move between tables, Toby offers a personal observation, "That must be one of the guys from the other day?" he mutters. "Or can we expect more?"

"Yeah, Mongo's the primary bully in town," Axle answers while glancing over his shoulder. The other two are here some place. I saw their faces slide past while we were hugging each other."

"Boy, when you pick an enemy, you don't mess around." Toby offers. "Couldn't you have picked someone a little less sizable?"

"His choice, not mine," Axle mutters. "I was defending the woman of my dreams when he took acceptation to my presence."

In the background, on the far side of the room, Mongo continues to generate growling sounds. The sounds are sandwiched between expletives. Axle finds it difficult to walk and select things while looking over his shoulder. Together, they sign for their gear. Axle sees the name immediately above his on the hand-printed equipment list. The name is Montgomery Elwood Baron. There are three Kravens listed as well, probably hear no evil, see no evil and speak no evil. Further up the list are four kids named Forest.

Seeing Mongo's full name, Axle forms his own personal title of endearment. He decides that he will call his new enemy "Elwood."

That's probably a name he hates. Axle knows that he would hate that name if it was his. The guy obviously detests breathing the same air that Axle breathes and the feeling is mutual. Axle considers the fact that he's been in town only a little over three days and already he has a major hate relationship going based on intense loathing. He has placed himself in the spotlight that Dad and Mr. Black had mentioned. The low profile they suggested had vanished the instant he entered Karl's Burger Heaven.

While Toby talks with the coach, Axle watches the beautiful girl as her hair catches the diamond glint off a sunbeams from an upper window. The golden glow becomes a search light of interest for him. He lowers his vision and almost instantly locks eyes with Mongo's giggling female friend. She is stunningly beautiful in a cotton dress that features a red plaid pattern with a white lace yolk and collar that encircles her slender neck. Their eyes remain locked.

Brown eyes, dark and deep.

Something in his soul gives a little click as though a door latch has just dropped into place. The moment becomes strangely exquisite as following the instant she hit Axle with a smile so radiant he'd have impaled himself on a sword for another one. A feeling that he never wants to be out of her sight engulfs him. From the moment when he first he saw her, he knew that he wanted to look at her for the rest of his life.

Axle tears himself away from the bewitching vision of the earth goddess as he stows his gear in a locker. Toby hands him a grease pencil. He writes his name on surgical tape attached near the top of the door. Toby takes the locker to his immediate left. They snap on the combination-locks provided and head for the car. As they depart, the coach is nose to nose with Mongo. They are engrossed in a heated discussion. Coach keeps turning Mongo around as he talks to him, but Mongo seems only interested in one final look at his latest mortal adversary.

Axle waves at him as he yells, "Hey, Elwood, don't be a stranger."

Mongo screams, "You son-of-a-bitch! I'll take care of you tomorrow!"

"There'll always be a tomorrow for us, dummy," Axle advises in a raised voice.

"Maybe not for you!" Mongo screams with his face contorted

into a grimace of pure hatred.

Following his last comment, Mongo lunges against the restraining arms of coach, the young Hereford and three other people who are again hanging onto him for dear life. The entire pile tumbles to the floor in a heap as Toby grips Axle's arm to propel him through the swinging doors.

Mongo is yelling at the top of his lungs from behind the closed doors, "Tomorrow, you're mine!" he rages.

By now, Mongo is nearly overpowering five people who are valiantly attempting to control him. The departure from the gym seems a few points shy of a swell send off.

Mongo is furious because he can't shake free of the gym rats and the new guy is getting away again. That fact enrages him further, to the point that he kicks a couple shins and even jabs Bubba in the eye with an elbow. They all hang on until Coach Palmer is certain the new kids are gone. At that point, they all turn lose and jump back. Mongo charges through the doors into the parking lot.

The new guys are nowhere in sight and that stupid Woodling bitch is probably still laughing at him.

Mongo can barely hear the coach yelling at him from inside the building, "You either knock it off Mongo, or I'll suspend you before practice even starts."

Mongo couldn't have cared less about school, but he doesn't want to miss any part of the football season. He suspects that coach ain't about to suspend his star running back who is the best player in the history of the school. However, Mongo resolves that he won't miss a game this year because of anything he does to the new kid.

Mongo stands with clenched fists as he considers that he has been decked twice in two days, once with a bottle and now with a fucking door. He decides that he'll nail the new kid's ass tomorrow on the football field. *No bottles or doors out there, just him and me. Tomorrow, we'll decide who's the local stud.*

Mongo pounds his fists on the front of both thighs in frustration. He then runs back through the double doors where he goes straight to the coach's clipboard. He flips through the list until he locates the last two entries. The lines read Axle Reed Mannheim and Toby

Graham Fitzpatrick.

"Axle?" he mutters. "What a stupid name."

I'll make him squeal like he needs grease. I wonder what position that big bastard plays that's with him? Probably muscle-bound and can't run. Watch your ass tomorrow, Mannheim, just you and me, baby. Elwood! That asshole is going to regret calling me that name. Nobody calls me Elwood, ever. I hate the name. My mother gave me that stupid middle name, because it had been her father's name. Grandfather Woodrow 'Woody' Elwood Hayes died of alcohol poisoning at age 43. He was the victim of a bad batch of his own moonshine.

Mongo drives home where he parks the car in the shade of a big gum tree near the riverside boat dock. He undresses and swims upstream for 40 yards before he returns to hold onto a big rock below the home riffle. He lets his body stream with the current. He loves the feeling of cool water swirling over his body. Later, he moves along the under cut west clay bank where he checks for resting catfish beneath the over-hang. He finds three before he is finished. The two biggest ones surge away at his touch. The smaller one weighs about 10 pounds. The big cat allows itself to be noodled and taken home for supper.

Luther taught the boy to noodle catfish when he was barely big enough to swim. Noodling had very nearly cost him his life when he slipped his arm through the oversized gill cover of a 30-pound flathead. The fish was nearly as large as the boy. If Luther hadn't been there to pull both him and the fish out onto a gravel bar, the creature would have drowned him for certain. It clamped its jaws around his arm hard enough to leave a scar, and then it swam to the bottom of a deep hole. The skin on Mongo's arm still bears the indelible marks of the big cat's teeth. The beige hide of the bite differs in texture from the rest of his arm.

He swims back to the floating wharf one-handed as he tows the still active catfish. He places the cat in a live-box attached to the dock. He rockets out of the water to sit on the damp wood of the dock with his feet trailing in the current. He mulls the thought of how to find Axle, the fool.

At sundown, he drives into town where he hangs out at the pool hall for several hours. About 7:30, he drives the streets. About 8:00, he comes upon a young bicycle rider doing circles beneath a streetlight on the south side of town. Mongo doesn't recognize the kid. He pulls to a halt beside the youngster who stops at the edge of the road beneath the streetlight.

"Hey kid," Mongo growls. "Do you know of a new family moved into town somewhere around here?"

The kid answers, "Yeah, somebody named Mannheim moved into the old Adams place."

"Thanks," Mongo says, as he slams the truck into gear and moves out.

The tires squeak on warm asphalt as he heads for the Adams place. The house is two blocks further along the street. A block from the house, he slows the truck as he turns off the headlights. The truck drops off the asphalt surface onto oiled gravel near the entry to the Adams driveway. He stops short of the bridge. From there, he surveys the front of the place.

While he watches, he slips the truck into gear. He allows it to idle forward until he can see through a break in the hedge above a wrought iron gate. The house is fully lit with only the window shears drawn. He feels behind the seat where he pulls his .22 cal. squirrel rifle from the window rack. He points it out the window before he jacks a round into the chamber.

"Here's to you Mannheim," he mutters, and squeezes off a shot.

Chapter Twenty

Axle drives home at a leisurely pace. He constantly searches the rear view mirror to see if anyone is following him. The family's new home now functions as a siege zone. It seems that every departure or return may involve a dash for survival.

Axle crosses the bridge before he remembers the trailer, which remains in the backyard where it awaits unloading. The thought brings the thinnest of smiles to his face. Now he has someone to help him with the grunt work. That thought alone is heady stuff. Since his departure earlier in the day, he has gained something amounting to an instant brother. Maybe his luck is changing.

He parks the coupe and sits looking at the trailer. Axle breaks the silence. "I just returned from Oklahoma this afternoon," he mutters as he gestures toward the trailer. "Hope you're not too exhausted from watching me dodge Mongo. We've got a trailer to unload. Everything has to go inside the house, be unpacked and put away. It looks as though you've arrived at just the right time."

Toby stares at the four horse trailer piled high with boxes. He pauses so long Axle wonders if he'll have to give him a wake up call. Finally Toby mutters, "I'll help and we can get through it in a hurry."

"Come meet Mom before we get to it," Axle offers. "I'm hitting the sack early 'cause practice starts at 6:00. We need to be there by 5:30."

The two boys enter the kitchen carrying Toby's imitation luggage. Maggie Mannheim stands near the stove stirring seasoning into her large cast-iron Dutch oven that sits on a front burner. The aroma of ham, black-eyed peas and Cajun spices fills the house. The aroma stimulates two young appetites. Maggie turns without missing a revolution as she says, "Hello Toby." She gives him a hug with one arm before she slaps Axle's hand as he reaches for the tasting spoon on a trivet near the burner.

"My, you're a big one," she observes. "Hope I've fixed enough supper for us."

An elevated wire cooling rack on the far corner of the counter top holds two bread pans covered with white dish towels. Axle flips the nearest towel aside to find yellow corn bread with a golden crust staring back at him.

Maggie says, "Get out of there, your father will be along shortly and we'll eat." Axle reluctantly spreads the towel back in place as he thinks to himself, *Zowie, black-eyed peas with ham and corn bread for supper.*

Toby watches Axle's every move the way a bird watches a tree snake. One of Toby's several failings is that anytime someone mentions food he suffers instant hunger.

Axle jerks his head toward the front of the house, "I guess we're not wanted here, let's go have a look at my room."

The boys leave Axle's harried mother to her cooking as they move to the front bedroom where Toby unpacks his stuff. Axle sits on the bottom bunk as Toby takes things from the travel boxes on the floor and out of the tin pancake. One of the boxes contains a bunch of wire coat hangers atop the clothing. Toby shakes wrinkles out of things before he puts them on hangers. He then installs them on the closet cross-bar to the left of Toby's few meager possessions.

Toby's clothes are about like Axle's. There isn't much without a hole or a patch somewhere. The closet measures a little over a yard wide and consists of a door, an upper shelf and a hanger bar. When Toby finishes unfolding and hanging, they both survey the end result. Together, their combined clothing doesn't fill the cross bar. The title of, *'Poor White Trash,'* crosses both their minds. Their families appear to be about one rung above barely endurable poverty.

Axle gives Toby the lower two drawers of his dresser.

Toby dumps his socks, shorts and other folded items in the assigned space. They finish the clothing inventory before they file back through the kitchen to the trailer. There, they begin their pre-supper exercise program.

First on the order of unloading comes Axle's weight lifting set. That goes into the garage to be set up in the tool room. The garage will hold about a car and a half with a tool room on the side. The tool room contains a work bench and his father's mammoth red stacked tool boxes.

Together, the boys get the weight-set and bench in place in the assigned space of the tool room. They decide to use the main garage for their work out so they put the bench against a wall in the corner. The weight plates and bar go on the floor to be stacked neatly in the same corner.

The car will fit in the garage with room to spare. When they work out, the car will need to be outside. In those instances, the vehicle will sacrifice its paint job to the elements.

Moving the weight set is a work-out all by itself. The bench is made of two-by-twelves held together with round-headed carriage bolts. The original weight set has been joined by various other add on plates and miscellaneous items found at second hand stores. Axle can make up a bar bell that weighs 320 pounds by putting everything on at once. He can bench press that weight four times, providing he has an attendant to be sure the lift doesn't collapse on him. He almost never has an attendant so he rarely lifts that amount of weight. Once, when he tried a fifth repetition, he couldn't get the bar back up onto the support. The bar had slowly collapsed onto his chest. He managed to tip the bar sideways. One end fell to the floor but he had to wiggle out from under the other end. The blunder very nearly injured him, but it cured any future desire he might have to work beyond his capacity.

Unpacking household items takes the better part of two hours with both of them working like pack mules. An afternoon rain shower sends the humidity to the top of the scale. Even when they are inside, sweat condenses as though they've been working in a rain forest.

Michael Mannheim arrives home from his new job as the last box enters through the back door.

"Great timing, Dad," Axle jokes, "I figure you were sitting down the block waiting for us to finish before you drove across the bridge."

His dad laughs as he puts his left arm around his son's shoulder in a gruff hug. "Sorry I missed the fun," Big Mike offers, "but I'll make up for it tomorrow. I'll be working overtime for a while. The company has six engines down and nobody but me to fix them."

While they stand in the living room near the last box, Big Mike shakes Toby's hand with his massive paw. "Did he help or did he Tom Sawyer you into doing most of the work? You've gotta watch this guy, he'll work you if he can."

Toby nods sagely, as he responds. "I discovered that right away, Mr. Mannheim."

Axle whacks him on the shoulder with a fist following the good natured lie.

Everybody washes up and sits down to supper. The Mannheim's dining room furniture came from Germany when Mike's grandparents emigrated. The table is round, and the top sets on a massive center pedestal with five claw foot legs radiating outward. Eight matching chairs fulfill the arrangement. Everything is solid oak with a dark finish. There is a matching China cabinet in the corner with curved glass in all the openings. There is also a buffet against a second wall.

The elderly cast-iron Dutch oven contains the main course. It consists of ham chunks in black-eyed peas. The iron pot rests on a lazy Susan near the center of the table. Michael Mannheim stands as he ladles food on to plates as they are passed to him. On either side of the lazy Susan, corn bread is stacked high on two platters. The bread is cut in four inch squares with the plates covered by tea-towels.

There is also a brick-shaped block of soft room temperature butter. A green cut glass pitcher of milk completes the setting. Over the years, the Mannheim family has had sufficient food, however, there were occasionally hard times during the war. Axle can remember his mother making meals that consisted of slices of home made white bread covered with milk and sprinkled with sugar. Times are better now than they were then, but Axle will always remember the milk, bread and sugar meals.

With an extra mouth to feed, an awesome quantity of food disappears. The cast iron kettle is empty by the time the meal is finished. Outside, the overcast sky turns a dull slate-gray with distant thunder.

Maggie clears the table. Axle and Toby both jump up to help her. Axle's dad slides his chair back from the table as he fires up a cigarette. He looks over his shoulder.

"Have you been to Karl's Burger Heaven since you've been in town?"

"Yes, sir," he answers. "I stopped there when I arrived with the first load, and again today."

"Hear anything worthwhile?" his father asks, with a sly look on his face.

"Nothing concerning what we came here to discover. Why?"

"Oh, just wondering. Perhaps you should be less reckless with your allotted time on earth."

Oh, boy, here it comes, death by lecture.

Axle knows better than to pursue the conversation, because his dad doesn't think much of fighting although he had his share of personal combat when he was younger. Michael Mannheim instilled certain values in his son. One of those values concerned fighting. His philosophy was that you walk away from a fight unless you're cornered. When that happens, you give the assailant more than he bargained for.

His 'what would Dad say?' guideline had defused a number of predicaments. It kept him out of a lot of trouble. His father will have more to say about Karl's later, but not in the presence of their new houseguest. With the dishes out of the way, the family sits around the table where they discuss everything but Karl's.

Finally, his dad says, "See you in the morning. I have to get up early."

With that he stands, walks around the table, and exits toward the bedroom.

Chapter Twenty-One

The first drops of rain are falling as Mongo aims the rifle toward the front window of the house across the ditch. He squeezes the trigger. At the report, the window sheers-buck as the bullet passes through. The bullet enters higher than he intended. He drops the rifle on the seat as the front door of the houses bursts open. A large body comes hurtling through. Mongo slams the truck into gear as he moves slowly away with the lights off. The figure crosses the foot bridge and closes the distance between them at an alarming pace. Mongo is not prepared for the speed of the stranger so he tromps the foot feed. The rear wheels spin, the truck fishtails as the glass-pac's bellow. The tires throw oiled gravel toward the runner.

"That'll show em," Mongo mutters.

The bullet had struck the wall inside the dining room, directly behind and above Michael Mannheim's chair. The slug made a slight knock sound like a single knuckle rap on a table top. The bullet path is slightly right of Axle's head. Tiny glass fragments sprinkle the floor at the base of the sheers. The sand like particles glint in the light for the short time the room remains illuminated.

The bullet missed Mike by a foot and Axle by less than that. Had the shot occurred ten seconds sooner it would have taken Mike in the center of his forehead. At the unmistakable whap of the passing round, Mike charges the front door. He is out the door before anyone else can react. Axle follows his father. Toby slaps the light switch as he sails through the front door.

Maggie Mannheim moves to stand behind the door jam of the kitchen door where she remains motionless. When there are no more shots, she hugs the wall as she inches into the living room. When she is in position, she pulls the drapes across the wide front window.

The window is composed of an interconnecting series of diamond shaped clear glass panels in a continuous series of locking lead frames. The window is constructed in the manner of a stained glass window. The beam of a flashlight reveals one damaged pane near the center of the panel. The glass contains a web of tiny cracks radiating away from a small diameter hole.

Outside, Big Mike has stopped chasing the pick up and returned across the foot bridge. The light from a corner streetlight had revealed a nondescript older, blacked-out pickup moving slowly away to the east. Mike had raced after the vehicle. Initially, he was able to close but as he neared the tailgate the driver accelerated away.

The bright backdrop of a nearby streetlight shows only the outline of one head on the driver's side. The sound of the trucks engine had revealed the presence of a three-quarter race cam. That means that the vehicle is powered by an abnormally powerful, probably race tuned engine. The roar of the engine sounds like a dragster under load.

When gravel pelts Mike in the face, he turns aside to abandon the chase. The truck pulls away to disappear around a far corner. Everybody returns to the house.

Axle stands in the middle of the road where he had watched his father chase the truck. He cannot remember ever seeing his father run before. He is impressed with the way his dad covered a short distance. The truck had the distinctive sound of a custom exhaust system. The sound was familiar.

With the shears in place, nothing can be seen but the bright vagueness of a lighted window. The table is not visible nor is anything else distinct through the brightly illuminated sheers.

"They apparently weren't shooting at us," Axle mutters. "They were shooting at the house. There's no way that anybody could see a target through those window sheers."

"Jesus Christ, what's happening?" Mike mutters to his son, as he turns to face him. "We've been in town less than a week and already somebody's shooting at us. It's almost as though they knew we were coming."

While he speaks, he gazes at his son. "Is there's a message here somewhere?"

"Maybe someone besides me doesn't like the looks of this house," Axle mumbles solemnly.

When they return inside, Axle considers what to tell his parents. When the family is gathered in the living-room, Axle drops onto the arm of the couch. His father regards his son intently as Axle volunteers the story of his arrival in Amerada. When he is finished, his mom looks scared. His dad nods only once as though in resignation.

"Could be the guy from the cafe, or we might be compromised. Watch out for yourselves," Mike mutters as though thinking out loud. "Somebody has just registered displeasure for whatever reason. From outside, they couldn't see anything to shoot at, just a lighted window. I guess maybe we should call the cops and report the event."

"The cops are all Mongo's relatives, "Axle mutters. "It won't do any good to call them. If it was Mongo, nothing will happen. We'll just look like a bunch of goobers from Oklahoma and they'll all laugh at us. This thing will work itself out if it's Mongo. He has high hopes of revenge at the first opportunity."

"Yeah, maybe," his dad says. "I'm mad right now. If it happens again, we will have to do something about it. I don't especially like the thought of eating our meals from a reclined position on the floor."

Toby gives a short tentative giggle.

They all move to the table to sit for a while. Periodically, someone casts a furtive glance toward the front window. Maggie Mannheim finally speaks, "After tonight, I'll always view that window with suspicion."

Axle takes a roll of silver tape from a kitchen drawer and places an almost square strip across the bullet hole from the inside. The tape will hold the remaining glass in place.

"This new tape sure is slick," Axle says, to his dad. "Where'd you get it?"

"Got a case of the stuff while we were in Gillette," Mike answers. "It's called Duck Tape, something they developed during the war to seal ammunition boxes for shipment. The stuff is supposed to be waterproof."

After a while, the family retreats to their respective bedrooms. Half an hour later, Mike comes to his son's bedroom door where he comments, "We should notify Night Owl of our problem so that they remain informed. It's part of the intelligence gathering process."

Axle springs out of bed to retrieve the sending-key and ear phones with Toby watching. He sets up the radio before he encrypts a message. Following encryption, he establishes a link with Night Owl. He then relays the following message:

RIPTIDE REPORTS A SHOT FIRED INTO OUR DWELLING X SHOOTER DRIVES DARK PICKUP TRUCK WITH LOUD EXHAUST SYSTEM X BELIEVED TO BE MONTGOMERY ELWOOD BARON X AGE NINETEEN NEPHEW OF SHERIFF KRAVEN X NO INJURY X SUBJECTS WARY OF BEING COMPROMISED X RIPTIDE OUT.

NIGHT OWL COPY X WILL RELAY X OUT.

With the radio equipment again secure in the door jam, Axle lies staring at the chain link pattern of the metal web beneath the upper mattress. He grapples with the sheet as he tries to cover his feet where they protrude beyond the end of the bed. The pair of stacked GI bunk beds is something less than a blessing. The problem is that they are too short for a pair of over six foot tall boys.

Toby leans over the edge of the top bunk, and asks, "You awake?"

"Yeah, can't sleep."

"Worried about tomorrow?"

"You bet, tonight, tomorrow and the rest of the time we're here," Axle mumbles in the dark, "I've never been shot at before."

"Don't worry about the shot," Toby answers in a loud whisper. "I think we both know who that was. The problem is that he now knows where we live."

The "we" word Toby offered sounds really good to Axle's ears.

"Tomorrow's going to be a continuation of today," Toby speculates. "We can count on Mongo trying to intimidate you at practice. He'll probably jump your ass when it's over. I think you already know the drill. It'll be at his convenience, 'cause he won't want anybody like the coach breaking up the proceedings before he's finished."

There's a long pause while they both consider the reality of the situation they will be faced with. Eventually Toby mutters, "I love football almost as much as I like breathin'."

"Can you play any sort of musical instrument?" Toby questions as he leans over the edge of the bunk again. The radiance from the streetlight out front streams in through the open window where it illuminates Toby's face that is bright with pleasure.

Axle squints up at him before he eventually says, "No, why?"

"I was thinking maybe you should go out for the band instead of football?" Toby suggests before he giggles silently in the dark.

"Band?" Axle mutters, "I can't even play a Kazoo, much less a real instrument. I'm stricken with athletic ability, not musical talent."

"They'd teach you," Toby continues, as his voice breaks again. "You can learn to play something small like maybe a flute or a piccolo, that way when Mongo shoves it up your ass, you'll still be able to walk." Toby rolls onto his side, pulls his knees up against his chest and collapses into an uncontrollable laughing fit.

Axle envisions himself marching along with a gold plated band instrument protruding from his posterior while braving hard stares from the game day crowd. At first he giggles before the giggle turns into full blown laughter. A couple minutes later, Axle's dad is at the bedroom door.

"All right you two, go to sleep or go sleep in the car so you can laugh all night and not bother anybody."

Both boys answer, "Yes, sir."

In the dark, Axle whispers to Toby, "Get off the damned band instruments thing, I can't stand anymore." With that comment he turns and buries his face in the pillow, so his dad can't hear him laughing.

"You play offensive or defensive...flute?" Toby asks, several seconds later. Once more, the stifled giggles turn into laughter muffled by a pillow.

"I go both ways," Axle offers "End on offense, linebacker on defense, how about you?"

"Don't pick a tuba," Toby concludes, as he covers his face again. The bunks shake as they laugh in tandem. "End on offense and linebacker on defense," Toby wails in mirth, his voice is high and flute-like in the dark.

Axle says, "Are we going to be rivals, or what?"

"Not if I can help it," Toby whispers toward the ceiling. "What side of the line you want?"

"Left end and left linebacker," Axle mumbles.

Toby looks over the edge of the bed as he whispers, "I'll take middle backer and right end. Coach needs nine more players and we've got ourselves a team."

Axle stares at the top of the window in the dark stillness as he considers tomorrow. Outside, the rain has stopped. There is the sound of insects bouncing against the window screen before they hover to bounce once again. Toby comments, "While we were stowing our gear, I talked to that big kid that helped coach break up your second introduction to Mongo."

"Which one," Axle asks.

"The one who plays center and looks like a 300 pound Fig Newton," Toby mutters. "His name is Bubba Bentley. He seems to think your ass is grass tomorrow."

"Him and probably every other kid in town," Axle observes.

"Bubba claims that Mongo had a fight last week behind Karl's," Toby continues. "A brick layer from Dallas thought Mongo said, 'stand up' when he had in fact said 'shut up.' By the time the guy realized he'd made a mistake, Mongo had him horizontal in the air. A short flight later, he struck the ground neck first."

"Sounds about right," Axle offers, "The guys got arms like oak tree limbs."

"You can worry about his arms if you want," Toby says, "But I'd spend some time dwelling on his legs. After the brick layer was down, Mongo went nuts. He spent some time kicking him while he was down. I guess he punted him around most of the parking lot before Buddy and some other guy's got Mongo under control. The victim looked like regurgitated dog food by the time Mongo was finished with him."

"Hmm," Axle murmurs.

"The guy's friends took him to the Shidler hospital," Toby offers. "I guess he's screwed up pretty bad. He won't be laying bricks for a while. He earned a broken jaw, nose, ribs and other assorted injuries."

"I'm not a brick layer," Axle whispers from below.

"Yeah," Toby says, "You're an entertainer. You are perhaps the Bob Hope of Amerada. Ever since you arrived in town, you've provided local entertainment. You're destined to be the bride at every wedding or the corpse at every funeral. Tomorrow ain't gonna get any better."

"I'll figure out a way to handle Mongo," Axle mutters.

"Maybe you can show up at football practice wearing catchers gear and carrying a baseball bat," Toby offers after which he starts giggling again. "You can claim you got your sports mixed up and refuse to change." Giggles muffled by pillows again fill the room.

In a little while, Toby continues, "Bubba's sure Mongo will start a fight sometime tomorrow. Old Mongo's 19. He's more 'n two years older than you and he has more experience. According to Bentley, he's whipped just about every guy in town who'd fight him, including an impressive number of grown men."

"I ain't everybody," Axle responds.

"Yeah, well this guy is somebody," Toby continues. "The school district held him back for two years in grade school so his mental process could catch up but it apparently never did. The teachers keep him eligible to play sports. If they didn't, then they'd be on somebody's hit list because the local athletic program wouldn't amount to much."

Toby pauses before he adds, "Bentley claims Mongo started fighting about the third grade and has fought nearly every day since. He never loses. He's slowly worked his way through most of the male population is three Counties."

Toby leans over the side again as he mutters, "Bentley says when him and the swamp Kravens come to town for supplies, survival becomes the major sporting event of the month. The whole town is scared to death of the entire family, which includes everybody but the Forest boys. I guess the Forests live somewhere in the middle of Big Oliver Marsh. Mongo and the marsh Kravens live on this side of the marsh where the creek enters.

"Bentley says that everybody remains out of sight when any of the river dwelling Kravens come to town. I guess there's a couple of really mean people in that clan. One is named Luke and another is Luther. Apparently, the town folks don't want to attract their attention. Even with that effort, one of them is always able to find some poor wretch to pound hell out of. Mongo generally supervises. Mongo's going to be in town tomorrow. I hope you've got enough sense to be scared of him?"

"Maybe I ought to stay home?" Axle offers in mock fright.

Toby looks down at him before he says, "You're jivin' me, right?"

"Yeah, but he's built like a tank," Axle observes. "I've never fought anyone that looks the way he does."

"Don't worry about how he looks," Toby says, "He'll have some weakness you can exploit. Maybe he's slow or somethin'. I figure it's only a matter of time until he gets around to me. I look impressive enough that most people leave me alone."

Then Toby offers a minor chuckle before he says, "I'm sort of one-dimensional. I've spent the last couple years fighting Golden Gloves in New Orleans. Last year, I lost a decision in the semi-finals to the guy who won the state title in the heavy weight division. He head butted me. That opened a gash in my right eyebrow. The ref stopped the fight. I kept gettin' in trouble back home. I either had to come here or join the Marines. I don't dare get in trouble here or they'll have my ass."

Toby is silent for a while before he continues, "If you want me to take care of Mongo tomorrow, give me the word and I'll flatten him."

"Are you tryin' to horn in on my fight?" Axle mutters. "This is going to be the biggest brawl in local history without the words World War as part of its title."

"Oh, that's okay, I'll wait," Toby answers. "I wouldn't want to detract from your moment in the sun," he whispers.

"How about you," Toby asks, "have you fought much?"

"I haven't had to fight very often," he answers. "I generally have two fights at every new place we've lived. The local toughs try me once to see if I'll fight and then again to see if I was lucky the first time. After that everybody leaves me alone."

Toby looks down over the edge of the bunk at him as he says, "I've got some gloves in the closet, want to get up and put 'em on for some pointers?"

"Nah," Axle says, "I'll be all right."

Axle closes his eyes. His mind skips back in time to when he was ten years old. That was the day he got his clock cleaned by another kid who was 12. His father helped his mother repair the damages following the fight. His injuries consisted of a bloody nose and a black eye.

Following the repairs, OSS officer Major Michael Marston began to instruct his son in close combat training. His dad taught him weight-lifting and several forms of the martial arts. He also gave him an insight into the ways of the world. His idea of the world pretty much revolved around survival of the fittest. Among other things, his Dad was a philosopher. Because of today's activities, his third postulate of existence seemed to apply: *Live as an anvil, be patient and strike like a hammer.*

During the war, Michael Marston's world consisted of learning to survive in foreign lands. His body carries several scars attesting to just how hard an education survival had been. During his travels, he developed other axioms to live by. He claimed that most of them were based on ancient Chinese philosophy:

"Good fortune favors the strong."

"Better an enemy overestimates your stupidity than your intelligence."

"All victories and all defeats are temporary."

"Speed never has a bad day."

"Silence makes no mistakes."

For the first six months, Axle had worked on weight training and every day his father introduced him to some new kick, throw, or manner of delivering a blow. Everything progressed at a fast pace until his father departed to do battle in some distant land. Axle lifted weights five days a week the way he'd been taught. He then rested two days. He progressed rapidly in strength and ability. When his dad returned from wherever he'd been, they reviewed everything Axle had been taught. When abilities were up to Big Mikes satisfaction, Axle was left to his own devices. When his father was around, Axle's days began early with Tai Chi. Evenings after school were devoted to full contact sparing. The time spent with his dad was always serious stuff. There were no tournaments, no colored belts, just learning and practicing what he'd been taught. By age 12, Axle's world consisted of doing knuckle push-ups in his sleep. He learned rapidly as he gained confidence. Then came the day when his mom sent him to the store for a bag of flour.

At the time, they lived outside a small town in California. Some kid from the edge of town decided to show off for his sister and her girlfriend. About the time the idea of showing off developed, Axle came ambling by on his way to the store. The kid was four inches taller than Axle and a year older. He held Axle by his shirt front while he described to his audience what he was about to do to the stranger. While he was busy talking, Axle hit him a straight punch to the solar plexus followed by two kicks to the head. The kid went down and stayed down. Axle stood poised in his fighting stance as he waited for the bully to get up. When he didn't immediately recover, the girls helped him up. They then guided him across the street to his home. The next day, the bully's older brother knocked on the Marston's back door and asked to see Axle outside. The older brother was two years older than Axle and a lot bigger. When the brother wouldn't take no for an answer, Axle stepped through the door. He headed for an open space behind the garage. Once there, Axle proceeded to kick the kid in the crotch before kneeing him in the face. While he was trying to get up, Axle nailed him on the side of the head with a round-house kick.

When the boy showed up asking for Axle, Maggie sensed a problem. She prodded her husband awake from a nap then suggested he go and find out what was happening behind the garage. Michael made it through the back door in time to pick the big kid up and help him into the family car. He then drove him home. Those two episodes had ended any further thoughts of revenge by the local talent.

Axle works out every day. He does Tai Chi and karate forms before he practices a variety of kicks on a heavy bag. His exercise program had been interrupted by the move. The Ironstone hand-to-hand combat instructors tested Axle's ability as the family prepared for their assignment in Amerada. Axle had proven to be more than a match for the instructors. As he lies in the dark, Axle remembers another of his dad's favorite sayings.

"Any enemy who wants to hang himself can easily be led to the noose."

Axle speaks aloud in the dark.

"I will be pure in motive and direct in action."

The response from the top bunk is a soft purring snore. Axle lifts his leg until his foot is against the chain link bottom web of the top bunk. He pushes sharply upward. Toby shoots into the air about a foot before he returns to the mattress.

"Now is not the time for you to go to sleep on me," Axle counsels.

Toby mumbles, "Sorry, I drifted off."

"I wanted to put your mind at rest before we go to sleep, or are you interested at all?"

"Yeah, sure."

"I promise I will win if anything happens."

From the back of Axle's mind he remembers another of his father's quotations. *"A promise weighs less than nothing."*

Chapter Twenty-Two

Following the shooting, Mongo watches the rearview mirror. Half a block behind him, he sees a big dude in the road beneath a streetlight. He wonders who the guy is. He presses the accelerator hard as he listens to the glass-pac's bellow. After he turns a second corner, he flips on the headlights and heads for the highway.

"Your ass is mine, Mannheim!" he shouts, as he hammers the steering wheel with the heels of both his hands. "Now I know where you live, dude."

Finding Axle has made Mongo's entire day. Wet, drooping limbs whip the sides of the truck as he nears the shack. Green leaves stick to the edges of the windshield where they are untouched by the wipers. He parks near the front door of the shack before he runs through the rain to the front door. Luther sits at the slab-wood table eating deer-meat stew and tortillas. He also has a bottle of warm beer on the table before him. Luther belches loudly.

He mutters, "You better get over to the still. Luke's already come across once. He wants you to relieve him."

Mongo helps himself to a bowl of stew along with several tortillas before he drops onto the table seat to eat.

Between bites, he says, "Luke ought to pay closer attention to the still instead of worryin' about bein' relieved. I bet the lazy son-of-a-bitch hasn't purged the cooker. He probably wants me to relieve him, so I'll have to do that."

Luther agrees, "Yeah, probably."

Luther knows from experience that it's never a good idea to disagree with Mongo.

Mongo mutters, "I got to drive all tomorrow night deliverin' hooch, so I need to get my sleep. You go help Luke purge the cooker. I expect the cooker to be washed in the creek before you start the next batch. The two of you can handle the still until Clyde returns from Arkansas. That'll probably be tomorrow. He'll relieve you then."

Luther starts to say something before Mongo cuts him off. "Do as I tell you before you make me mad. You remember how it goes when I get mad?"

Luther nods, as he gives a low, "Um," of acknowledgement.

He then turns up the bowl to drink the last of his stew.

"Go on now, get," Mongo growls.

Luther stands to pump water from the hand pump at the sink into his dish. He walks through the door into the rain without further comment. Luther is 6 feet 7, and weighs 300 pounds. Luke is 6 feet 3 inches tall, and weighs 240 pounds. In spite of the fact that they both tower over Mongo, they are both scared spitless of their nephew.

Several months earlier, Luke and Luther had decided that they weren't going to work the still anymore until they received their monthly pay. Payday was a week overdue. This particular month, Clyde Kraven had not collected from his dealers in time for that to happen.

While Clyde was away tending to business, Mongo came home to find the fire extinguished at the still. Both of Clyde's brother's were lying in the shack drinking beer. The resulting conversation angered Mongo. He grabbed a pick-ax handle standing in a corner near the back door. He had beat hell out of both men. Once the dust settled, Luke and Luther limped back to the still. Two days later, Clyde returned from his trip with the money. Over the years, Luke and Luther had been reminded on more than one occasion that their nephew turned practically insane when he fought and he had a really short fuse.

When Mongo finishes his stew, he makes a trip to the privy before he hits the sack. Across the creek, Luke and Luther grumble about their lot in life while they purge the cooker. They wash the vessel in the creek, install a new load of mash and get everything operating again.

Mongo lies in bed while he considers with some degree of satisfaction that Luke and Luther will tend the still as instructed until Clyde returns. Clyde will bring with him another relative to help for a week or so. That will allow the brothers to take a break from the family business. Mongo wonders if he hit anyone with the rifle shot through the window at the Mannheim home.

He falls into a restless slumber. While he sleeps, he dreams of what he will do to the two new arrivals during tomorrow's football practice. Subconsciously, he considers the fact that the kid at Karl's had really fast hands. Mongo hasn't had a fight in two days. The process of waiting until tomorrow does not allow him restful sleep.

Chapter Twenty-Three

Axle sleeps badly. By the time the day dawns, he has run out of things to be fearful of. The morning features a bright sunrise with clear skies. When Toby climbs out of bed, he finds the bottom bunk already empty. He quickly dresses and sets about mentally preparing himself for the first day of football practice at a new school.

In the kitchen, Maggie Mannheim is busy at the stove. A glance out a kitchen window reveals Axle involved in Tai Chi exercises on the back porch deck. Toby lumbers through the door as Axle finishes his last series of moves.

When his new friend is finished, Toby asks, "You through dancin' yet?"

When his remark produces no results, he asks, "What you got planned for today at school, slugger?"

"Survival," Axle answers.

"What's for breakfast?" Toby growls in response.

"Probably oatmeal," Axle answers as he bends at the waist to clasp his ankles. He stands with his upper body pressed against his legs for nearly a minute.

"Oatmeal is for patching holes in plaster," Toby offers, with a slight smile.

The kitchen timer rings as they enter the house. Several minutes later, they sit down at the table before large bowls of hot oatmeal. Maggie Mannheim drinks her coffee while she watches the boys attack their breakfast. They sprinkle cinnamon and honey over their oatmeal before adding milk. Sourdough bread helps fill the void in two cavernous stomachs. The meal is eaten in silence. Near the end, Axle says, "Let's leave the car home and jog to school."

Toby nods in agreement as he offers, "Sure enough, honey pie." While he talks, he wipes the inside of his bowl clean with a piece of bread before he pops it into his mouth.

"You two have a good day at school," Maggie murmurs as she

rises from her chair to move toward the bedroom, "I'm going back to bed."

Axle gives his mom a peck on the cheek as he heads for the door and his first day introduction to a new school. The direct path to school would be through a green cotton patch along the west side of town, but doing that would probably irritate the farmer. With that in mind, they jog along streets and sidewalks. Cross country, the school is about a half mile distant. By their manner of travel, it is perhaps a quarter-mile further. The boys move along the sidewalks as they pass other kids headed in the same direction. Heads swivel as they pass at a respectable lope.

The faces of the town kids display both apprehension and curiosity as a common mask. The only youngsters abroad at this hour are prospective football players. As the new arrivals advance along their route to school, other kids begin to jog. They fall in behind the newest arrivals in town. The other youngsters remain well back so as not to be considered friendly with the strangers.

The teenage grapevine has spread the news of the previous day's events. The news of Mongo's latest hostility has traveled faster than mercury droplets racing across a linoleum floor. Everybody knows of the confrontations at school and at Karl's. In their minds, the newcomers are about to be handily caught and maimed by the local bully.

As Axle and Toby approach the school parking lot, the area contains only four vehicles. None of them are motorcycles or the Kravenmobile.

The joggers arrive outside the gym where they spend a short time walking in circles, cooling down. Near the entrance through the perimeter fence, three big boys sit in a door-less flat-bed truck. They watch Axle and Toby with particular interest. The truck bed has the words, *"Forest Seafood,"* painted around the circumference of the edge.

When Axle and Toby are ready to enter the field house, everybody's problem collides head on with a solution. Mongo turns a far street corner in his pickup. The truck contains four of his band.

Four motorcycles trail the vehicle closely. The rusty truck

is obviously the one from Karl's. The mufflers also sound like the vehicle that figured prominently in the nighttime rifle shot.

The field house becomes the latest place of choice to experience fear, claustrophobia and a rapid heartbeat.

The Kraven truck is spectacular in its elaborately dilapidated appearance. The body consists of spider webs of rusted metal amazingly held together by faded black paint and expanding rust granules. The vehicle approaches the school parking lot slowly with the engine idling raggedly. The rough idle most likely indicates the increased power of a dirt track racer. The rattle of the three-quarter race cam makes the modification plainly evident. The glass-pac mufflers are just as loud today as they were last night.

The Mongoids ride two in front and three in the truck bed. The three in back sit well forward where they lean against the cab so they are out of the direct wind blast. The riders continually survey the sidewalks as though they are conducting a witch hunt. Every eye is thoroughly involved in a search for someone to burn at the stake. Their greetings are loud as they connect with other members of their local fiefdom.

Axle and Toby enter the gym about the time they are noticed by the people in the slow moving caravan. Each motorcycle has two pack-lets astride them. Once assembled, the hoodlum pack consists of 14 members. Their trademark manner of dress is black leather motorcycle jackets with chair drive wallets and oiled leather motorcycle boots. They represent a formidable force.

One kid in the truck bed jabs his buddy in the ribs with an elbow as he aims an index finger in a shooting gesture toward Amerada's latest teenage addition. The parade of vehicles enters into a massive parking effort in the lot near the field house. The engines are shut off in unison followed by everyone dismounting as though they are part of a mounted cavalry exercise.

Axle and Toby filter through the building to the locker room with no visible display of terror. The Forest kids follow close behind them. There is an extended space that separates everyone from the leather bound Kraven militia.

Toby and Axle drop onto a pair of long well anchored benches that run the length of the locker room. A view of the room reveals about two dozen other kids who are obviously not joiners. They are hurriedly changing into football gear.

The two latest additions to the Amerada athletic program receive no evident form of greeting. Their arrival is apparently to the utter disbelief of most.

The Forest boys drift along the bench to their own lockers. The eldest member is last year's quarterback. He nods as he lifts a fist in a pumping action as he mutters, *"Woo-Woo,"* as though he is a train whistle. With the sound, he launches a grin at Toby. Toby smiles back before he growls, "Same here, Slick."

Moments later Mongo barges through the door. His arrival has all the presence of a German Tiger-Tank crushing through a French hedge row. He assumes a position before his locker. Several other nearly-dressed members of his clique ease into place so as to be nearer to him in a show of solidarity. Within moments, everyone has shifted into the accepted social pecking order. There are now about 20 in Mongo's group of devotees.

The entire pack seems to be headed for self destruction over a cliff somewhere at or near the football field.

When the Forest boys are nearly dressed, they walk over and sit on the bench near Axle and Toby. Todd Forest, the eldest of the three mutters in a low voice, "Welcome to Amerada High, I hope you're as durable as you look."

Man-mountain Bubba Bentley shifts from his locker to a place on the bench near the Forest contingent. A couple other non-Mongoids move to stand in his shadow. Lines in the local litter box have been drawn and loyalties selected before anyone has drawn a straw or flipped a coin.

While Mongo dons his gear, he inspects the group with the interest of a dog looking for a place to bite. He does everything but point and laugh. His intentions are so clearly evident that conversation is deemed unnecessary. His eyes steam with obvious venom.

With the single exception of Mongo, none of the Mongoids are physically imposing. Mongo is clearly the most muscular member of his clan.

Buddy appears to be second in command. He is about six one with a face so ravaged by early acne that his entire head appears to be a pimple. If anyone hits him in the face, they'll need to immediately disinfect their hand or cut it off before it ferments. In his current state, he would be better off if someone took him to a clinic and had him put to sleep.

Third in line of ascension is Leon. He was the third figure at Karl's who helped guard the door. Leon's upper forehead sports a pair of twin scabs. They are the apparent points of the I-beam impact. His flaming red face with no facial hair is perched atop a long neck. After only one look, Axle associates him with a sign he saw in Denver one time when the family was traveling to California. The sign was a giraffe with an extended neck. Neon tubes outlined the entire structure. Leon immediately becomes, *Leon the Neon Giraffe.* No other nickname fits the way that one does.

Another Mongo devotee is referred to as "Brisket." He wears a fat face with buck teeth atop a fat body. These physical characteristics combine to make him resemble a fat gopher.

The rest of Mongo's crowd falls under the heading of "Other." A general comparison would be to a colony of army ants adrift in a forest. They would probably swarm should any of them feel threatened.

A contingent of Mexican kids keeps to themselves at the far end of the locker room. They apparently have the inside track on the great wisdom of the universe. They aren't buying into anything the gringos are selling. They are small, lean and muscular. Their muscle structure has been acquired by performing stoop labor for most of their lives. They speak Spanish to each other in soft differential tones.

Mongo glanced at them as he growls, "I told you last year, either speak English or shut up."

They stare back as they fall silent.

Mongo follows his last comment with, "What are you lookin' at?"

Following that question, the Latino's devote major time to adjusting equipment. A tall slender kid named Jose Flores fails to cower the way the rest of them did. Jose carries a gravity knife with a well honed six inch blade. He favors the instrument over fists.

Axle and Toby remain on the bench. The Latino kids move to stand near Bubba Bentley and four other nondescript players of medium build. The Forest kids are middle sized individuals that appear as tough as alligator hide. They keep their eyes open and their mouths shut. Mostly, they watch Mongo and his crew with great suspicion. They do not appear to fear Mongo or his pack, but are leery of them.

Might as well start, Axle decides.

Axle looks at the nearest Mexican kid as he utters the only Spanish words he knows, "Buenos Dias." The greeting is loud enough for everyone to hear. The kid grins back and nods before answering, "Si."

At the greeting, Mongo's head snaps around to glare across the room in an attempt to identify the conversationalist. Axle glares back as he loudly proclaims, "International diplomacy."

Toby chuckles as do about half the Latinos. The Forest kids launch wide needling grins as they peer across the room at their common adversary.

Bentley concentrates on putting on his cleats without looking up. Muffled snickers emerge around the room. The sounds of merriment are similar to the low volume bleating of instruments being tuned before a scheduled band practice.

The other players in the room accelerate their dressing process when Mongo begins to eye the line of prospective players. With the exception of the Forest faction, Bentley and the other four defectors, everyone else in the room acts as though they want to be somewhere else. If they dress any faster, they'll probably forget something, like perhaps a shoe.

Toby dons several items of special equipment he has brought with him. Before he climbs into his shoulder pads, he dons a quilted well-padded vest-like garment that covers his shoulders and hangs to mid-rib length. Instead of a jock he wears something that looks alarmingly like a panty girdle. It comes to mid-thigh and becomes an undergarment in place of hip pads. Nobody laughs or makes comment concerning his apparent corset. He dresses entirely unmolested by criticism from anyone.

Black elastic pads cover his elbows. He wears padded gloves with half-fingers on his hands. Knee pads cover his knees in addition to the knee pads sewn into his pants. He paints *No-Stick* on his feet and ankles with a dauber. When his feet are dry he leans forward on the toes of first one foot and then the other while he wraps both ankles with a double layers of tape. Two pairs of athletic socks go on each foot. His shoes are a size larger than his normal foot gear. He carries his jersey to the equipment counter where he cuts the lower half off, about six inches above the belt-line. Everybody watches his dressing process, if not directly, then indirectly from the corners of their eyes. By the time he finishes slipping into, taping on and wrapping up, he is probably wearing nearly as much body armor as a medieval knight. Before he closes his wall-locker, he takes a boxers mouth piece from a small paper bag. The mouth piece goes into the top of his left glove. There is no doubt in anyone's mind; Toby Fitzpatrick is a sports bomb with an apparent interest in hitting someone. While he dons his equipment, his attention span is absolute. His concentration is as though his mind has entered a new dimension where nobody exists but him.

When he is nearly finished, he drops onto the bench near Axle. From there, he surveys the opposition.

To their left, the Mongoids have assumed what appears to be a protective formation. While Axle finishes lacing a shoe, Toby says, "We can expect a modest amount of discomfort on the practice field. I haven't been watching them closely, but I imagine that it probably takes about five of them to lace and tie one shoe."

Axle giggles.

While Toby pulls on his jersey, he glances again at the Mongoids as though they represent the entire rodent population of the town dump.

"If you are any good at this," he continues, "we are probably the toughest duo in the state and those fools don't even suspect. Do you want any of his friends or can I have them all?"

"Bite off as much as you can chew," Axle mumbles.

Toby stands and turns his back to Axle. When he is ready, he growls, "Do me."

Axle pulls Toby's jersey down over the neck roll and the rest of his gear. Toby is more noticeable in size than anybody with the single exception of Bubba. The shoulder pad roll behind his neck gives him the appearance of a bull rhino with an ingrown horn. Everything about him is round. He wears round shoulders, round thighs, thick round wrists, and a round butt. The overall effect is of raw, round power. As previously advertised, the only shoulder pads he could find that fit were a set of linesmen pads complete with rib protectors.

The cut off jersey shows six inches of belly. The modification is an effort to help combat heat. The trimmed jersey looks like a good idea, so Axle elects to do the same with his. A pair of scissors from the trainer's table does the job. Now the two boys are pretty much a matched set.

The Forest kids follow suit. Next in line at the table is the Mexican contingent. Nobody in Mongo's crew moves to comply.

Toby leans close to Axle's ear as he mutters, "I feel like a bastard at a family reunion. Practice will be like fighting a war armed only with tire chains."

Axle puts his arms through his short jersey sleeves before he turns so Toby can pull the jersey down over his pads in back.

"Suits the hell out of me," Axle mutters.

Toby puts on his helmet. He then leans at an angle before he violently rams the side of an empty end locker with his right shoulder pad. The collision approximates the sound of a car crash. Upon contact, he screams at the top of his lungs, "Kill!" The utterance is not unlike the roar of an enraged beast. Next, he turns to glare across the room at the Kraven contingent before he does it again.

While Axle stands bent over as he reties a cleat, Leon of the long neck shuffles across to stand over him. When Axle turns his head Leon growls, "Hey Okie, we're gonna bust your ass today."

Toby turns from ramming the locker. There is a quick burst of motion as he hits Leon just below his chest protector with a fist. The blow is a left jab that flips Leon backward over the nearest bench seat. His velocity propels him across about four feet of locker room floor on his back. Leon ends up lying in a fetal position as he gasps for breath. He projects his usual minimal personality from that position.

Toby grins a mischievous little smile as he loudly mutters, "Hey piss-ant, if you want to try for seconds get up and come back over here."

Leon struggles to a kneeling position but wisely remains on the far side of the bench. He is quickly surrounded by Mongoids. Thus ends his dream of intimidation.

Toby looks at his running mate, as he mutters, "No lifeguard on duty in that gene pool."

From across the room, somebody offers a low test, "Wow."

At the far end of the locker room, people in various stages of undress begin to shuffle toward the door. One guy wears one shoe and carries the other as he limps through a side door.

Mongo had looked up when Leon sailed across the bench to assume his final destination. He now stands facing Toby but does nothing, which is probably an insightful thing.

Toby has just entered the equation as an unknown hole card. The Forest kids and the Latinos shift restlessly as they await a reaction from Mongo.

After a short pause, Axle and Toby leave by the nearest of three doors. The path to the football field leads around the perimeter of the basketball court on a walkway covered by a carpet runner so cleats won't mar the varnished surface. Halfway to the outer door, in a small alcove hangs a little used speed bag. The pear shaped item is complete with swivel and a wooden overhead suspension board. Toby stops at the device where he makes the bag dance in response to very little fist movement. His hands barely move, but the bag becomes a maroon blur. He stops after about a ten second demonstration. He grins at Axle as they depart the gym. Behind them the bag continues to swing.

"Impressive," Axle observes, "hold that thought, you may need it later. We can now go spend quality time attached to Mongo's sternum."

"The speed bag is mostly for show," Toby mutters. "The heavy bag is where the work is done. I wanted to feel something with my fists. I love hittin' a speed bag."

Outside, those who fled the locker room earlier stand in a group at the near end of the football field. Axle and Toby begin trotting toward them. When the two newest kids in town reach the border of the cinder track that outlines the playing field, they both turn and head along the track at a fast jog. Half a dozen of the more energetic among the spectators decide to follow.

The boys do two laps before the coach arrives with a pair of assistants. They are followed shortly thereafter by Mongo and his contingent. The team's practice gear is left over game uniforms from past seasons with a scattering of new white practice jerseys above wheat-colored pants. Mongo wears a several year old game uniform in the traditional school colors. Fully dressed and padded, he resembles a maroon and silver, rail-splitting wedge.

Toby comments in a loud voice, "That jersey looks like a particularly ugly Christmas shirt I once received and immediately burned so I wouldn't have to wear it."

Before Mongo can form a response, coach blows his whistle. Everyone clusters around him and the assistants near mid-field. On command, everyone divides into offensive and defensive units according to the positions they played last season. The Forest boys all play backfield on both offense and defense. Axle and Toby stand in place until coach asks them, "What position do you guys play?"

He seems to be mostly looking at Toby when he forms the question.

Toby answers, "Middle linebacker on defense and end on offense."

Then he switches his gaze to Axle, Axle responds, "Linebacker and end."

"You guys look like a couple of book ends," the coach offers, with a wide grin on his face.

Lacking anything better to do, he sticks them both on defense.

Everybody in attendance has played several years together except for Toby and Axle. As new arrivals, they represent a pair of unknown variables. All the players but the Forest boys and Bubba remain a safe distance from Mongo. Everyone makes an obvious effort to avoid talking to either of the new guys. The two main characters in today's drama have become an instant social liability.

Tackling practice follows warm up, first on a dummy and then one-on-one with a running back carrying the ball. Axle waits his turn in the tackling line until Mongo emerges as the ball carrier. When Mongo is first in line, Axle steps in front of the two kids ahead of him to face his acknowledged advisory. No firestorm of protest erupts. Everybody remains in position, watching.

Mongo has just been bayed.

A light bulb of discovery illuminates when the two adversaries line up head to head for the first time.

The coach starts the back and tackler approximately ten yards apart. Blocking dummies and the remainder of the team define the boundaries of the impact zone. The outline around the battlefield has finally been drawn.

Coach slaps the ball into Mongo's middle and the fun begins. As a ball carrier, Mongo doesn't try to dance or stutter-step; he just lowers his head and comes like a runaway locomotive. His obvious intent is to go over the tackler as opposed to going around. Axle moves two steps forward, where he leans low as he concentrates on Mongo's belt buckle.

As the moment of impact nears, Axle lowers his upper torso so that he is below the battering ram that consists of Mongo's helmet and shoulder pads. Axle impacts Mongo on his thigh pads well above his knees. The solid sound of pad impact ends with Mongo horizontal in the air above the tackler's left shoulder. Axle wraps his arms around the ball carrier's legs as he propels him backward onto the ground. Axle has a momentary flash of dim moonlets orbiting the radiant sphere of earth before getting up and making his way to the end of the tackler's line.

Following contact, there is a round of scattered applause from the rear of the crowd. Mongo stands and whirls to see who the culprits are. Toby, the Forest kids and Bubba Bentley are in plain view clapping vigorously. Bubba is the approximate size of the Gadsden Purchase with weight no longer recorded in pounds but by displacement. Somebody has stenciled the words *"wide load"* across the butt of his uniform in white lettering.

Bubba comes from a farm family near the outer boundary of the school district. He's spent most of his life on the end of tools with handles on them. When he isn't doing that, he is shot-putting bales of hay onto a wagon. He resembles one of those multi-tired compression vehicles construction companies use to compact road-base before they apply asphalt.

Mongo Baron glances at Bentley and the Forest kids before he whirls to the coach, where he yells, "He can't do that again!"

Coach nods, and says, "We'll see." He motions for Axle to return to the head of the line. Axle assumes a three point stance. From that position he growls, "How's it goin' Elwood?"

Mongo's face turns purple.

Coach slaps the ball into Mongo's belly whereupon Axle cuts him off again just above the knees. This time, Axle receives a knee to the helmet. This time, he sees Jupiter, Mars and the outer rings of Saturn before he returns upright.

Mongo slams the ball on the ground where it rockets into the air as though launched by a cannon. One of the waiting players tosses it back to coach.

The local bully from the Kraven Republic of Amerada has registered displeasure with a solid left knee. Mongo limps slightly as both players stagger to the rear of their respective lines.

Axle's head is spinning. While he waits for his head to clear, he wonders nonchalantly if he could locate the men's room with a flashlight, a compass and a seeing-eye dog.

The lines advance again. When another Mongo/Axle confrontation looms, Toby taps Axle on the shoulder as he mutters, "My turn. Why should you have all the fun?"

Coach hands Mongo the ball once more and he charges his opponent. Toby stands his ground and at the last second, puts a hammer lock around Mongo's head, turns sideways and levers him in an arc that ends in a body slam with Mongo flat on his back. Toby follows through by dropping hip first onto his chest. Toby stands and jogs to the back of the line. Mongo lies inert as he waits for someone to pump air into him. He has been leveled for a third time in much the same fashion as a dozer flattening a large tree. Mongo and his challengers spend the rest of tackling practice with Axle calling him Elwood and Mongo giving Axle the word. The word is always an expletive.

Toby, Bubba and several other robust linesmen nowhere near the size of Bentley join-in as they conduct cheer-leading rehearsals without short skirts or pompoms. Every time Mongo comes to the head of the line, either Axle or Toby switches places with someone so they can hit him. Axle lives for the time when Mongo can't get up, but he always does. The practice field adversaries seem condemned to each other's company.

After ten Mongo/Mannheim/Fitzpatrick replications, coach and everyone else has had about as much of tackling practice as they can stand. Coach divides the players into offensive and defensive units. He places Toby at middle linebacker with Axle at left outside linebacker. They play a four, three, four defense. Mongo remains undisputed at the fullback position on offense. The placement of anyone else on the playing field is of little consequence.

The three arch-enemies form a tripod of animosity spanning both the offensive and defensive formations. After years of being Mongo's only adversary, the Forest boys are practically incontinent with delight.

The offensive team walks through a play three times to pickup blocking assignments before they run it full speed. Practice continues with the offense learning plays and the defense trying to disrupt them. At one point, Axle gets a shoulder pad on the ball and Mongo fumbles. Toby rakes it in with one enlarged paw and runs through the offensive team like a buffalo plowing through a fence. When he finally steps into the end zone, the offensive side of the line looks as though a grenade has exploded in their midst.

Football plays at Axle's and Toby's former schools always involved some form of finesse. In Amerada, the plays generally involve, Mongo left, Mongo right or Mongo up the middle. There are only three basic blocking schemes for the offensive line. When those are established, then Mongo does the rest.

After the third play, Toby growls to Axle, "Perhaps the star is a little too stupid to understand and remember play diagrams?"

Several minor scuffles evolve following contact late in practice. Coach, his assistant and the uninvolved linesmen quickly extinguish these. By the mid-point of practice, no shots have been fired but it quickly becomes apparent that something further will happen before day's end.

Thus far, Mongo has run the football 18 times and has accounted for minus three yards with a fumble. Axle and Toby have anchored the defensive team like an anvil and a hammer.

When the active part of practice ends, the team engages in conditioning. They do wind sprints and laps before jogging back to the gym. Axle and Toby both peel out of the return to the gym to run up and down the aisles in the spectator stand on the home side of the field. The home stands are made of concrete and brick. The visitor stands are pipe with wood seats. The boys run up the first vertical aisle on the home side of the field, across the top row, down the second isle, across the bottom row and then up the next isle. The entire section contains eight isles in all. The steps are 20 steps up, 10 seats wide and 20 steps down. Nobody else attempts the drill although the Forest boys observe from the north end zone. Coach stands outside the gym door and watches.

After practice, Mongo doesn't waste any time confronting his primary antagonist. He stands in the locker room with his pads off but he is still in his pants and socks when he braces Axle in front of his locker. All he says is, "I'll see you outside."

Mongo strips and jams his legs into his jeans.

Toby looks at Axle as he mutters, "Did that sound like a threat to you? It did to me."

"Practice probably scrambled his brain," Axle observes as he strips away his own uniform.

One of the assistant coaches lounges near the far end of the dressing room. Following the confrontation, the assistant slips along a wall and then out a door. The movement goes unnoticed by practically everyone but Axle. Axle decides that coach will be notified and will stay around to break things up.

Whew, good thing. Now I probably won't have to fight.

The assumption is that he is safe from the local bully for the time being. That thought makes Axle even cockier than normal. That is to say that he becomes practically insufferable in his comments concerning Mongo.

Axle grins at Mongo as he states flat out, "Elwood, you're mildew. If you can't hit any harder with your fist than you do when you carry the ball, then you're in trouble. Would ya care to debate the merits of this latest decision? It will be to your benefit to withdraw the invitation."

Mongo screams so loud that beads of spit fly from his mouth, "Get your ass out to the parkin' lot, idiot! Coach ain't gonna be out there to keep me off you. You're in this one all by yourself."

Toby comments with a big mitt-eating grin, "Maybe not, but I'll be there."

Everyone but Bentley and the Forest's flee the presence of the two about to be combatants. People leave with all the concentrated drive of a buffalo stampede.

His dad's logic comes zooming from somewhere way back in his mind: *When you don't show fear it makes the enemy uncertain of your ability.* Axle knows his dad is right, but inside he is sacred nearly spitless. The trick will be not to show fear. Mongo is shorter in stature than Axle, but in build and muscle structure he doesn't even appear mortal. Axle's last remark caused most of his ball practice shenanigans to achieve fruition.

With his last comment, Mongo's rage enters over-drive. He tears off the remainder of his gear and dresses without a shower. What is apparent is a mental development arrested in mid-stride by an all-consuming hatred. His eyes leave Axle only while he ties his sneaker shoelaces. The difference between Mongo and sanity is the difference between day and night, or about 8,000 miles.

With his sneakers finally tied, Mongo leaps up and heads for the door. He is carrying his shirt. Axle hollers after him.

"Hey, Elwood, don't leave before I get out there! I always hate it when my date stands me up."

Mongo nearly tears the doors off their hinges as he lunges through them. Most of the team follows as fast as they can manage. People disdain personal hygiene to facilitate a more favorable spectator vantage point.

After Mongo's departure, Axle gives a violent inhalation. The motion is his first obvious attempt at breathing in the past three minutes. All he can hope for now is that Mongo has a short attention span and forgets who he's waiting for by the time Axle and Toby are dressed, or that coach will be waiting outside to break things up.

"I wish I was home at the kitchen table attempting to establish a new nacho record," Axle mutters, to his new running mate.

While he talks, Axle secretly prays for an instant Cholera epidemic that will place Mongo in the hospital and perhaps thin the crowd a bit.

"Didn't take him long, did it?" Toby observes, as he strips off the last of his gear. "I believe that we have inherited a really dedicated enemy."

"Yep," Axle says. "If you think we've spoiled his day so far, wait until he tries me on outside."

"Don't screw him up too bad," Toby offers. "He's the only back we've got that can move the ball. All the others just go through the motions."

"Maybe you should try talking him out of his attempt to try and kill me. That should be a snap for a silver-tongued devil like you."

Toby considers the comment for a second before he shakes his head.

"No. Go ahead and screw 'im up; he's got to learn some time. It might as well be you instead of me, 'cause I'd kill him."

Axle asks, "What was your problem in Louisiana?"

Toby grins, and answers, "Fightin'. I can ruin smiles faster than tooth decay."

Axle looks at Mongo's number-two man, who still remains on a bench across the room. He is obviously acting as a rear guard.

Axle asks him, "How about you, Buddy? Why don't you go try to talk him out of getting his ass whipped?"

Buddy gulps air as he shakes his head at being addressed directly. He finishes tying his shoes before he moves to stand near the main exit door.

What is going to happen when I go outside? What if I'm unable to subdue him and end up on the losing end of an actively bad fight? Not much else to do, but go face the music. Following a win, I intend to short circuit Mongo's love life with that neat looking little blond. Following a defeat, I can join a passing Gypsy caravan.

The two latest additions to the Amerada athletic program take their time showering and getting dressed. Axle wants to be sure coach is in position to deflect the fight before it starts. Everybody but Buddy has dressed and departed before the two latest social outcasts are ready for their lesson in Kraven diplomacy.

Toby observes, "This is like fighting a Golden Glove event. By now, the crowd will have sung, danced and trifled itself into chaos and slavery. All you have to do now is win." Toby looks across the room at Buddy. "How about you and I fight a prelim before my friend does the main event?"

Buddy swallows hard at the prospect. He's had enough close contact with the two social outcasts. He quickly passes outside. Once Buddy has disappeared, Toby goes to one of the locker room windows facing the parking lot. The walls of the room are painted white, including the windows. That is probably an effort to discourage people from looking in through clear glass. Toby takes a knife from his pocket and then hangs by one hand from the windowsill. He scrapes away a small portion of the paint. He makes a minor adjustment in peephole size before he chins himself again on the window ledge. A majority of the parking lot is visible through the hole.

"Boy, would you look at that?" he offers. "There's full force excitement in effect out there beneath a searing summer sun. People are flocking into the parking lot like seagulls to a chum line. Most of the student body must be standing in the parking area. And there's not a cop, coach, or teacher in sight."

Axle hangs on the ledge himself. "Looks about like that New York street they photographed for Movie Tone news on VJ day."

Toby glances at the front doorway where Leon is visible.

"Mongo says for you to get your ass out of here so he don't have to come get you."

His message delivered, Leon retreats. His departure leaves a door swinging on its hinges.

When the door stops moving, Toby mutters, "Take your time getting out there, the more we wait the more antagonized he'll be.

The madder he is, the more likely he is to make a mistake. Anger works against you in a fight; it makes you careless."

Axle sits down on a locker room bench where he adjusts a shoelace. He leans forward with his elbows on his knees as he stares into space. Toby leans against the wall with his arms folded. Outside he can hear a loud hum of voices.

Four or five minutes pass, before Toby says, "Time to boogie."

When he speaks, Axle nearly jumps out of his skin.

Chapter Twenty-Four

Outside, Mongo paces in the parking lot like a caged animal as he watches the Field House entrance. Leon, along with the rest of the mice, stands nearly motionless in the background. Mongo tosses his shirt through an open window of his truck before he begins shadow boxing. Everybody has by now cleared the locker room except for Mongo's two latest projects.

Leon holds up his hands while Mongo practices hitting them. Mongo still has a light sheen of sweat from football practice. He makes a couple more lunges at Leon's open palms before he walks toward the center of the half-circle fighting ring created by the spectators.

All those present stand butt outward in a crescent formation like a herd of musk ox. The forward part of the group has their horns facing the gym door.

Mongo looks toward the building as Buddy comes scurrying out. Buddy walks across the parking lot to where Mongo stands waiting.

"Where the hell is he?" Mongo asks. "Am I going to have to go in and drag him out?"

Buddy swaggers to his leader where he announces, "The guy is really stupid. He asked me if I wanted to try and talk you out of gettin' your ass whipped."

"Say what?" Mongo screams.

"He seems to think he can whip you." Buddy follows his comment with an uncertain little chuckle as though the thought is so completely ridiculous it doesn't even merit consideration.

"When I've finished with him," Mongo responds, "I think I'll attend to the big one. The two of 'em outta be about right for an afternoon work out."

Mongo turns to Leon as he growls, "Go tell him to get his ass out here. I've got other things to do."

Leon passes through the outer doors. Almost immediately, he

bursts back out as though in flight.

"I told you to go get him," Mongo rages.

"They're on their way," Leon offers in a firm voice as he considers Toby's offer to throw him through the door.

Everybody continues to stand around, watching and waiting while tension mounts. Mongo is becoming more visibly angered by the second.

Inside the building, the two victims take turns hanging from a window ledge while they study the proceedings outside.

Toby drops to the floor for the last time before he asks, "Ready to go kick some butt?"

"Ready as I'll ever be."

Axle takes one final glance through the peep hole. Mongo is standing in the center of a half-arc of people, staring at the gym door.

As they pass through the inner doors Toby says, "We have now arrived at the apologizing, groveling portion of the day. You can beg him not to kill you, or you can just act loose as though we are on our way to a picnic."

This is one of the long narrow loops of time Dad always refers to. The ones he claims will hang in the mind like a vapor, many years later.

The two friends open the outer doors as they pass through line abreast. They are gabbing and grinning as though they've just won the Irish Sweepstakes. Once outside, they stop to look at what awaits them.

Toby mutters in a low voice without turning his head, "Last year's history teacher told us the Ottoman Empire added refinement to military exploits by executing Generals who lost battles. I don't want to have to attend no funeral, General."

Axle glances at him before he grins.

Across the circle Mongo leans slightly forward as though restraining himself.

Within Axle, a small inward hum of uncertainty revolves like a bench grinder wheel running at low speed. His face is completely passive although a slight grin comes and goes as though he is considering some gleeful internal joke. The facial expression is no mean feat since what he actually feels is abject terror.

He watches Mongo's face as they move along the short sidewalk that approaches the edge of the parking lot. For the first time all day, he sees a flicker in Mongo's eyes that indicates a small element of doubt. Whatever the look is, it has stuck its head out, had a quick look around and then disappeared.

Axle's mind races in a circle. He so immersed in the idea of survival that he can barely think. Above the crowd, the spotlight of a six-trillion candle power Texas sun burns down on most of the teenage hair-dos in town. It appears that the entire student body has misread the schedule and is assembled in the parking lot. The moment fairly bristles with anticipated disruption. The major-mess-watchers have not been caught off guard. One forward observer utters the nervous comment of, "There he is."

Everybody else is nearly wetting their pants in gleeful anticipation. The anticipation of Mongo and the newcomer duking it out is the local event of the year, or maybe even the decade. All of the football team, the hopefuls, the passers-by, and the bulk of the student body are either in or near the parking lot with the expectation that accompanies the usual thrashing of a newcomer.

Most of the people in town, along with the bulk of western civilization, probably agree on what is about to happen. The general thoughts running through the crowd contains words like ambulance, splints, glucose and blacktop burns.

As the scheduled victims pass from the concrete sidewalk onto blacktop, Axle looks at Toby as he mutters, "Time to consider possible escape maneuvers. We can try sailing right on through the parking area and out the other side."

Toby chuckles as he shakes his head, "Nope, too late. The far observers are standing with their arms locked."

Then he offers, "We can locate a bear proof dumpster, get inside and close the lid. Barring that, we can always thumb our noses and run." They both laugh.

Toby's presence doesn't seem to count for much because he is thought to be sport for another time. Both boys' realize that they are squarely in the midst of subjective victim selection. The Mongo-Ass-

Kicking-Derby is about to begin and Axle is the hands down first selection.

"I've never had a chance to fail on such a grand scale before," Axle mutters.

"If he proves to be too much for you," Toby comments in a low voice, "I'll step in. The local news on this one is not going to read, *Arrived late, gave ground, no factor.*"

Axle surveys the crowd again; neither the coach nor either assistant are anywhere in sight. That observation is chilling. He decides that they are probably all in the same vehicle headed for the Gulf for some late summer fishing. The cocoon of comfort he so recently rationalized for himself about the coach being here to intercede suddenly evaporates. As the aura disappears, he finds himself in a sort of a ready-fire-aim situation.

While he visualizes the prospects ahead, Axle's mind races with things his father has taught him. He settles on several of the finer points of mind control. Near the edge of the parking lot, he comes to attention with his feet together. He bows his head and places his palms together in a praying motion in front of his face. He does a Tai Chi move that ends with his elbows outward like the wings of a bird. From this position, he readies himself. His eyes are open but display only whites as he gazes upward to the center of his forehead. As though from a third eye, he observes Mongo across the circle. His thoughts focus: *Find your center. Find your energy. Clear your mind. Find pure motivation. Make your mind as calm as a moonlit pool surrounded by darkness. Find the true reflection of this moment. Here on the battlefield, there will be no enemies or opponents, only those who are one with you, as you become a celestial warrior. Look deep into your inner self as you contemplate this person who boasts of mayhem and personal injury. Walk the bridge alone along the path of ultimate destination.*

The posture and thought process require only seconds before he comes out of his apparent momentary trance. Finally, he speaks to Toby, "How about you keep the rest of them off my back?" Axle mutters over his left shoulder.

"Uh huh, my pleasure," Toby offers as he stops near the edge of on lookers. His eyes never leave the Mongoids.

Everybody roasts in the midday sun, but no one seems to mind. The members of the football team form the front row of spectators. Beyond them, other people perch on the tops of cars. Some stand balanced on the short pipe fence posts that ring the parking lot. There are people poised atop every vantage point. The anticipation involved is electric. The crowd emits a dull humming sound like a far away diesel engine driving an air compressor.

To one side, a group of high school girls act as though they are enrolled in a shrieking, fainting and pants-wetting contest.

In his mind, Mongo has formulated a plan to pummel and kick Axle's ass around the circumference of the parking lot. The new kid is to make no input into this venture except to serve as an earth leveling device.

The sky is sharp with detail. The heavens promise sunburn to those without a top covering. To the west, a meadow lark launches its flute-like call from atop a fence post. A hundred yards further, a large black turkey buzzard plops down onto the cross-arm of a tall utility pole. Axle imagines the laws of unintended consequences at work. Perhaps the buzzard has been sent as a prophecy of things to come.

Mongo struts before the crowd. His muscle structure covers him like a cobble stone street. He turns to face Axle, and then moves toward him. The exhilaration of the moment gooses everybody's breath rate.

Axle's mind is completely clear. The terror has vanished. He recedes into himself to search his mind for his father's teachings.

All we need now to create folklore is a throbbing song and an intricate dance. A year from now, only a meager number of the onlookers will recall what they were doing on the first Monday afternoon of the school year. Few will chose to remember that they were jumping up and down and screaming in the high school parking lot.

At the center of the circle, Mongo wipes his forehead with his right hand, flexes his shoulders and does a few jabs in the air. He is showing off for the crowd. By his actions, he does everything but sell peanuts and event programs.

He looks at the newcomer as though he is destined for the same outcome as an arena bull in Juarez. Mongo is about to claim both ears and the tail in the first round.

Mongo reiterates in a loud voice, "You've been a pain in the ass since ya been here Mannheim, now it's my turn."

"You sure you want to go through with this, Ace?" Axle offers with a note of resignation in his voice.

Mongo says, "Fuck you," thereby issuing a strategic vision impact statement as he moves toward his opponent the way he has done 1,000 times before.

"Okay, zoo breath, your move," Axle answers as he stands lightly balanced with his left arm up parallel to the ground, his left foot slightly forward and with his right foot significantly back.

Improvise, improvise, improvise something.

Suddenly, Axle snaps up an arm that points south as he comments in a loud voice, "There's trouble."

All heads in the crowd turn in that direction including Mongo, who partially turns. While the crowd looks at nothing, Axle aims his left heel at the target and in a flowing swirl of motion delivers a round house kick with his right foot to the point of Mongo's chin.

Mongo has only a glimpse of blurred motion from the corner of his right eye before the overwhelming force collides with his chin. His world turns black as the blow fells him like a cow in a slaughter house kill-shoot. As he drifts into darkness, Axle strikes his head twice more with the same foot before he can reach the ground. Only three blows are delivered. All involve the front side of Mongo's face. By the time the crowd looks south, comprehends, and then back again, the fight is over. A renewed view of the contestants reveals Axle standing over Mongo's inert form while looking in the direction he originally pointed.

Across the circle, Toby chimes, "Bing-bong, total elapsed time about three seconds."

Axle stands lightly balanced, sucking air and waiting for one or more of Mongo's followers to enter the contest.

People wear furrowed brows as they look at each other. Eventually someone mutters, "What the hell happened?"

Toby bounces on the balls of his feet in front of Mongo's followers who are now uttering, "son-of-a-bitch" repeatedly. They sound like a phonograph needle hung up in a groove.

"End of fight, game, set and match," Toby storms in an elevated voice.

Axle glances down at Mongo, who is face up but inert.

"Maybe now that he's down," Toby mutters, "we should tether him to the bumper of a car with a long rope and do once around the block in celebration."

Axle glances along the arc of the event circle in time to see Toby slap Buddy full force with an open hand. The blow makes a meaty sound like a melon hitting the ground. There is another report as he back-hands Buddy's face back to center. The Cajun's hand speed is nearly as fast as the snap of a finger.

The front row of people utters an, *"Oh,"* as they shrink backward.

Toby looks left, then right as he growls, "Anybody else want to go a few rounds?"

Toby looks as hard as a steel projectile while he faces down Mongo's crowd of people. He stands with his fists balled and his arms half raised. He is obviously ready to give someone a reverse face lift.

There are no takers. Instead, everyone seems to have a prior engagement elsewhere. With the single exception of Buddy, they all shrink from the challenge.

In the background, the audience is so apparently bored with the after fight sequence that a couple of boys pummel each other on the shoulder to keep themselves amused.

People begin moving. Some hop across the cable between pipes as they move off school property. After a few steps, most turn back to see what will happen next. Buddy stands riveted in place while he touches his flaming cheek to shake the cobwebs from his head.

Toby offers a second challenge, but apparently nobody wants anymore unknown quantities for the day. Mongo's friends swagger out of range with their thumbs hooked in their front jean pockets. All apparently wish that they had not attended this exhibition. The two newcomers who were invited to an after practice celebration have turned into the guests from hell.

Axle finds no pleasure in fighting. He always finds the aftermath disturbing.

The gorgeous blond from the gym remains with what was the front row of spectators. Her tousled, blond hair is casually stunning above eyes that radiate an unspoken promise.

Axle decides that the young woman was probably sinfully beautiful the instant she was born. She gives him a smile. In that shallow instant, a small charge flows through him that resembles live current.

Bubba "Fig Newton" Bentley, the wide-bodied linesman steps away from the crowd to hold up Axle's right hand as he announces, "You've won. Now we can all go home."

With that comment, Bentley steps over Mongo on the way to his Model-A. He glances back only once as he chugs out of the parking lot.

Axle tears his eyes away from the blond girl. "Let's get the hell out of here before the cops arrive."

He begins to jog home. Toby calls after him.

"Wait a sec!"

Axle turns around. Toby walks to Mongo's truck. He reaches inside where he pulls the squirrel rifle from its rack in the rear window. He smells the barrel.

"Recently fired," he announces.

Toby steps to the nearest open-top pipe supporting the suspended cable that outlines the perimeter of the parking lot. He thrusts the rifle barrel into the pipe to mid-length, leans back and bends the barrel to a 90 degree angle. In that configuration, the rifle will be good for shooting around corners, but the sight picture will be significantly distorted. Toby tosses the gun back through the truck window where it bounces off the seat on its way to the floor.

"I'm probably the only one here who saw the entire fight," Toby offers, as they jog home. "Even with my excellent attention span, I got bored when the blow-score reached three to nothing. I gotta admit, my concentration lapsed and then I started looking for a stretcher."

Chapter Twenty-Five

Mongo feels someone shaking him. He opens his eyes to find Buddy bending over him. Mongo's entire head throbs, his mouth most of all. He sits up and looks around.

What happened? Hey, there's a lot of somebody's blood on the front of my shirt. Wait, where's everybody goin'?

He feels his mouth. His hand comes away bloody. That's when he realizes that the blood on his chest is his. How can this be? He's never lost a fight before. His head throbs. The earth revolves as he tries to stand. His mouth and upper lip are numb, but starting to hurt. A tentative feel finds a wide gap above his front teeth, where his lip has separated.

The son-of-a-bitch didn't fight fair, he sucker punched me.

Mongo stops moving as he feels his front teeth. One of them seems to be missing. Two others move loosely when he touches them. His lower jaw has a strange electric tingle to it when it moves.

"Somebody's needs to look at that lip," Buddy says. "It's gonna need stitches. He knocked out one of your teeth, come on, I'll drive."

Mongo looks around the school ground unsteadily. He sees a mass of kids walking away, probably going home. Only a few remain and those won't meet his gaze.

Coach Palmer appears out of the peripheral crowd to ask, "What's going on here?"

Coach bends down to inspect the damage. "Well, it's finally happened hasn't it?" he announces, "I always figured if you kept lookin' you'd eventually find someone you couldn't whip."

"Huh," Mongo mumbles, still dazed and senseless.

"You better leave that new kid alone," the coach offers. "He's different. You keep foolin' with him and he'll cripple you." Mongo nods. The movement hurts his head. Coach remarks further, "No more black top drills in the parking lot, okay?" Coach grips Mongo's chin and moves it from side to side. There is a grating sound along with an agonizing electric shock of pain. "Come on," the coach mutters, as he looks at the muscular kid with the body of a man. "We'll go to the Shidler hospital. I'll tell them it's a football injury and our athletic insurance will cover it."

"Okay," Buddy mumbles, "whatever you say."

Buddy helps Mongo up.

"You're going to be on the side lines for a while with that jaw," Coach Palmer says, "but it can't be helped. While I'm thinking about it and you're receptive, don't fool around with his buddy either. Those two are more than any of us realize. Stick to playin' ball and stop fightin' altogether."

Coach takes Mongo's left arm while Buddy holds his right. Together, they propel him toward the coach's car. The trip to the car requires a dedicated effort by both of them to hold Mongo upright.

Buddy follows the coach in Mongo's pickup as they drive to the hospital. Mongo's nose and jaw are both broken. Both eyes are starting to blacken. His entire face is a disaster area. During the time he is under anesthetic, they wire his jaw, and pack his nose. It takes 23 stitches to close his upper lip.

Hours later in Mongo's hospital room, Doctor Woodrow informs him, "Those teeth will probably firm up in a week. If they begin to swell or hurt more than now, come back. No way to tell about nerve damage for a while. If the nerve is injured, they'll have to be extracted. What happened?" the doctor asks.

"He got hit in the face by a helmet," the coach says. "First day of practice and my star running back is injured. How long do you think he'll be out with that jaw?"

"Without complications? Broken jaws generally take about eight weeks. Looks like he got hit more than once," Doc Woodrow observes. "He'll have to stay here a couple days anyway. Before he can go home, he needs to learn how to feed himself. He can't chew, of course, so food has to be reduced to a liquid. He'll be eating through a straw until he gets unwired." The doctor completes the process of bandaging the upper lip. "That's a bad place for an injury. Infection in that area can be fatal. It needs to be disinfected daily and kept surgically clean." The doctor examines both of Mongo's eyes. "I'll need to see you every day so I can keep an eye on that lip. Come to my office every morning. Do you understand me?"

Mongo starts to nod then thinks better of the motion.

"Sure, doc."

Mongo feels the back of his neck as the orderly wheels him out of the recovery room toward a bed in another part of the hospital. His neck is stiff from practice and from being struck repeatedly by the new kid. He feels like throwing up from the lingering scent of ether. His face feels like someone worked him over with a hammer.

This ain't over yet, he thinks. *I'll get even. Nobody's gonna do this to me and get away with it.*

Chapter Twenty-Six

"We got to find work so we can earn some money," Toby offers as the boys drive in Axle's car along Main Street. "Got any ideas?"

"How about yard work?" Axle offers. "There seems to be a lot of yards that need mowing in town."

"To do that we need to find a pickup I can afford," Toby offers. "I've got some money from flying pipeline surveys for my dad."

"What's flying surveys?" Axle asks.

"Dad's got an airplane in Louisiana," Toby answers. "It's a PA-18, Super Cub. We contract with oil companies to fly along their pipeline right of way to search for leaks."

"You fly with your dad, right?" Axle confirms.

"No. I fly alone," Toby replies. "That's how I made the money."

"Don't you have to have a license or something to fly an airplane," Axle wonders aloud.

"Yep, I got that when I turned 16," Toby answers. "I've got just over 2,000 hours. I also have an instrument rating."

"Wow," Axle murmurs. He is impressed almost beyond description.

"Flyin's easy," Toby says. "Dad says I got a natural aptitude. I'd like to fly in the military later after high school, the same way he did."

"Think your dad could teach me?" Axle asks.

"Sure," Toby answers, "unless of course, you've got two left feet or somethin'."

Toby bangs him on the shoulder with a closed fist that results in them both have a short laugh. Axle turns into Harrison's filling station. When the attendant arrives, Axle forks over three dollars for gas. As he pays the attendant, he notices a flyer thumb tacked to a small bulletin board near the door. The flyer reads, "Exceptional, Model-A pickup for sale, $400." Toby records the phone number on a piece of scrap paper from a nearby wastebasket.

When they arrive back home, Toby calls the number. Several

rings later a young male voice answers, "Hello."

"I'm calling about the pickup for sale," Toby says. "You still got it?"

"Yeah, but you need to speak with my dad," the voice mumbles. "Hold on a minute."

In a little while a man answers, "Are you callin' about the truck?"

"Yes, sir," Toby answers.

"I got one more than I need," the man growls. "You want to come have a look at it?"

"Yes, sir, where are you located."

"We're 16 miles west of Shidler on Ventura Road. Look for a farm house on the north side of the road with a mailbox mounted to the grip of an old plow. The name's Mayhew on the box," the man offers.

"Be there within an hour," Toby mutters, "please hold it for me."

"I don't expect anybody else," the man answers. "You're the only one that's called."

Toby hangs up as he mutters, "Mayhew? Ain't that the name of one of the missing girls?"

He stares across the room before answering, "One was named Charlotte Mayhew. They could be the same family or maybe a relative."

Axle thinks for another instant before commenting, "She had a brother named Mark who's missing as well. If that's the same family, then we need to turn this trip into a fact finding mission without arousing suspicion."

"We'll think of something," Toby muses as they head out the door.

Axle stops for a second before he returns to the front of the house to tell his mother where they're going.

Forty minutes later, they turn down a country lane lined by huge Cedar trees. A white farm house sets at the end of the lane. Ahead, numerous out buildings radiate away from a large red barn. Mules graze in a pasture on the right. Further in the distance, a man rides a mule drawn cutter-bar, mowing hay. As they turn onto the lane, guinea hens began calling from the crown of the barn. The guineas make a cackling racket as they alert anyone within hearing distance of the arrival of strangers.

They come to a stop, and a huge Rottweiler scampers around the end of the house before he charges the car. The dog stands nearly as tall as the windowsill as he confronts the driver. The dog appears to contemplate eating the occupants of the vehicle as soon as it stops moving. Near the corner of the house, a smaller version of the same breed watches from a distance. He delivers a continuous growling sound deep in his chest. The back door of the house opens as a teenage boy exits.

"You the guy that called about the truck?" he asks, as he approaches the car.

"Yeah," Axle answers. "That's an impressive animal you've got there."

The teenager hooks a finger around the chain link choke collar encircling the animal's neck. He holds him less secure than Axle would have liked. The canine never takes his eyes off the new arrivals. The other dog remains at a distance, where it watches suspiciously.

"This is Buster," the boy says, as he pulls on the chain collar. "He don't much like strangers since my brother and sister disappeared."

"When was that?" Toby asks, faking ignorance.

"End of last year. I thought everybody in three counties knew about what happened."

"Just moved to town a month ago," Axle offers. The kid looks about 16.

"I don't remember seeing you at school," Toby comments. "What grade you in?"

"I'm a junior at Shidler high school. You probably go to Amerada, 'cause you got here awfully fast."

"Right on," Toby answers.

"Name's Wagner," the boy says. "Come on in the house while I get the key. The truck's out back in a shed."

The boy does not offer to shake hands, but he does invite them into the house. They enter through the back door. Buster accompanies them to lie alertly on an oval hooked throw rug. The dog is forever aware of their presence.

"My brother just relieved me in the hay field, so I'm kind of dry," Wagner says. "How'd you like some lemonade?"

"Love it," Axle answers.

The boy produces four glasses from the kitchen along with a sweating clear glass pitcher of lemonade. The pitcher has ice cubes and lemon slices floating in the mix. Axle wonders where the fourth person is, when Wagner sets four glasses on the table. There is a creak of floorboards and an older man passes through the hanging beaded screen of a nearby door. He carries a pump shotgun at port arms. The man glances at the new arrivals before he places the weapon on a pair of pegs above the doorway. He extends his hand by way of introduction.

"I'm Mark Mayhew," he volunteers. "I talked to one of you on the phone."

"Yes, sir, that was me," Toby volunteers, as they shake hands.

Wagner pours the lemonade.

"I heard you say you're new around here," the elder Mayhew comments. "We got a little shaky after my son and daughter disappeared. Before that, we didn't have the guinea hens or the Rottweilers. Now we got both."

"The dogs are really impressive the way they greeted our arrival," Toby offers.

"Wished I'd gotten 'em years ago," the elder Mayhew says. "Those damned guineas near drove me crazy the first week we had 'em. We got use to 'em in a hurry, though, and now they're the best sentinels anyone could want. Anything moves outside, they raise hell and we all go have a look."

"Them dogs sure got my attention," Toby mutters. "The big one must weigh near a 150 pounds?"

"You didn't miss that far," Mayhew says " He's 165. You got a dog?"

"Got a black and tan coon hound back in Louisiana, where I came from," Toby answers. "He'll arrive when my mom and dad get here in a little while."

"Don't see many coons around here anymore," Wagner says thoughtfully. "Probably too many coyotes. One thing we got though is quail. Lots of those runty little bobwhites, but mostly what we got is scaled quail. Those are the big ones with the little white topknots."

"Huntin' coon at night wouldn't be much fun around here," Mark says. "Too many rattlers, and the weather barely gets cold enough most years to make 'em hibernate. Finish your drink and we'll go take a look at the truck."

Ten minutes later, they adjourn to a shed behind the barn where a metallic-blue, Model-A pickup stands awaiting a new owner. Wagner starts the engine and pulls it out into the sunlight. The truck is flawlessly finished, with a paint job that matches its pale blue, tuck and roll interior.

"Truck belonged to my son that disappeared," Mark, Sr. offers. "The wife wants me to sell it 'cause it reminds us all of Junior. Part of the healing process I guess."

"I hope you don't mind me asking," Axle offers, "but how'd you lose your son and daughter?"

Mark studies the boys before he answers, "I guess you don't know, do you? Somebody kidnapped my girl and then Mark, Jr. disappeared while he was looking for her. Both of them vanished without a trace. The sheriff tried to tell us that they ran away to find a better life somewhere else. He theorized that they were probably tired of farmin'."

"Where'd your daughter disappear from?" Axle asks.

"Right here," Wagner answers.

"I think Junior must have discovered something important, that's why he disappeared," the elder Mayhew offers, as his voice clots with emotion. "The kid was fond of huntin'. He was a good tracker. He made a cast of some tire prints he found beyond the home hill where they took Charlotte when they captured her. Junior didn't trust the sheriff and his crew so he didn't show the casts to them when they came here nosin' around. We was all pretty much afraid of the deputies. They acted like we'd done something with our own daughter that we was ashamed of."

"Dumbest bunch of people I ever saw," Wagner chimes in. "They didn't have a clue when they got here, nor when they left. They didn't seem to know what to look for or where to begin."

"Of course by then," the father observes, "Mark had figured out what he thought had happened. We used to sit around the supper table while he told us what he'd discovered that day and where."

While his dad talks, Wagner enters the truck shed. In a few moments, he returns with a pair of long plaster casts of tire treads. He places them on the truck tailgate. When the casts come out, Mark, Sr. heads for the house.

Over his shoulder, he says, "You want the truck, let me know and I'll get the paperwork ready."

The boys watch Wagner's father disappear before turning their attention to the casts. One cast is unremarkable. The other has a small cavity in a valley in the tread. The form has been circled by a faint pencil mark.

Wagner points to the mold, as he says, "Mark claimed that this tire print is from a Lee tire and the small crater he circled is a tire plug used to repair a puncture. Before he disappeared he did a lot of looking at truck tires on vehicles around Shidler and Amerada without finding anything that caught his attention."

"That would be quite an undertaking," Toby offers, "especially in a country where most everybody drives a pickup truck."

"My brother spent every available minute searching for a match," Wagner mutters. "One day when we'd finished hayin', he said he was going into Amerada to look some more. That was the day when I changed the water pump, so this truck was down while I worked on it. Because of that, he drove Dad's Desoto sedan. We never saw him again. The car turned up in Bailey about a week later."

"How long ago did he make these casts?" Axle asks as he runs a hand over the tread on the mold.

"Last November," Wagner says. "I can't believe it's been damned near a year."

"You sure he said he was going to Amerada?" Toby asks, "or did he just say he was going to look around?"

"He said he was going to Amerada," Wagner answers. "He spent a lot of time in parking lots around truck stops and anywhere else where vehicles tend to congregate."

"How'd you like to have to check every pickup in the county lookin' for a tread match?" Toby ponders as he glances at Axle.

"You'd end up checkin' a lot of 'em more than once," Axle speculates.

"Mark had a notebook where he wrote the license plate numbers in and the descriptions of trucks he'd checked," Wagner offers. "I doubt he checked many trucks more than once."

"Woowee," Toby says in an appreciative voice, as he makes a sound like a hog call.

"Mark said these tire prints came from a half ton pickup, and the tires were practically brand new," Wagner offers. "He also said two men carried her away and that a third man was at the truck waiting for them. They all wore size 12 work boots except for one. That man wore tennis shoes, the kind with those round sucker holes on the sole that athletes use on a basketball court."

"The problem with that clue is that every third kid around here has a pair just like 'em," Axle mumbles absently.

"Yeah, but these was different," Wagner says. "One of the shoes had a crack across the ball of the foot, as though the sole had split most of the way across."

Wagner is obviously very proud of his brother's investigative ability. The longer he talks the more enthusiastic he becomes. The longer he talks, the more things he brings out of the shed. The next item produced is three sets of foot print castings. The tennis shoe imprint shows a crack running across the sole at the flex point beneath the ball of the foot.

Wagner puts another set of castings on the tailgate of the truck as he says, "The other two men wore boots with Cats Paw soles and heels. Mark claimed they had been half-soled 'cause shoes only have Cats Paw soles after they've been resoled. He also said that one of the men walked like a duck with his toes pointed outward."

Wagner looks at his audience as he says with a note of pride, "My brother was better at investigatin' than the sheriff ever thought about bein'."

"Did he have anything else to go on, that you know of?" Axle asks.

Wagner thinks for a moment, and says, "He said all the men smoked a lot and that they smoked roll-your-own cigarettes. They used wooden matches to light-up with. He had a burned Half-and-Half tobacco tin he found where they squatted around a small fire pit near the truck. The paint on the tin was mostly burned away, but you could tell what brand it was. That don't help much either," Wagner continues, "Lots of people around here roll their own cigarettes with Half and Half. Probably a hold over from the war when they couldn't get anything but the makin's."

"Man, he really got into this sort of thing, didn't he?" Toby says with awe in his voice, "I wish I could have met him. Did you ever go looking for truck tires after your brother disappeared?"

"I looked at a number of trucks before Dad made me stop," Wagner continues. "He made me stop because he said that he didn't want to lose me too."

There is a moment of silence before he continues.

"I used his notebook to eliminate vehicles in Amerada. His notebook indicated that he'd looked at about 200 by the last entry."

"You still have his notebook?" Axle asks in disbelief. "Why wouldn't he have that with him when he disappeared?"

"Forgot it, I guess," Wagner answers. "Or maybe he started a new one for some reason."

"Boy, I'd like to see that," Axle mutters. "I'd like to do some looking for that tire plug myself."

Wagner reaches behind a cabinet in the shed and produces a small spiral ring notebook, the kind that fits into a shirt pocket. The cover is red and severely worn. Inside are about 200 licenses plate numbers with an "X" recorded in the right hand margin. The booklet is divided into two segments, one begins on the last page and is entitled Shidler. The others are registered from the front. The front of the notebook lists Amerada trucks. Axle takes the booklet from Wagner and seems to idly glance through it as he slowly turns the pages. The index finger of his right hand follows each line. He studies every inscription as he moves slowly through the book. Axle turns the booklet around and then studies the other entries from the back of the book. When he is finished, he hands the notebook back to Wagner who also glances at his brother's notes.

"Junior was obsessed with finding the people that took Charlotte," Wagner growls. Then he says in a lower voice, "and I think he probably found what he was looking for."

Wagner shivers slightly. Then all at once, he seems to realize that he has told more to complete strangers than perhaps he should have. His mouth clamps shut as he withdraws from the conversation.

"You guys want to drive the truck?" he asks.

"Yeah, you want to go with me?" Toby asks brightly as he slides behind the wheel. Wagner moves the plaster casts to a work bench in the shed before he climbs onto the passenger seat. Toby fires up the truck, and together they head along the tree-lined lane toward the main road where they turn left and accelerate away. The engine has a full-throated solid sound as though it has recently been overhauled.

After they are gone, Axle studies each plaster cast individually. He holds each mold in the sunlight so he can see even the slightest detail. The tennis shoe with the cracked sole also has a narrow triangular shaped segment missing from the rear edge of the heel print. Only careful study of the cast reveals the small shallow detail. There is a faint pencil line trace around the defect on the mold. Obviously, someone noticed the tiny gash and outlined it.

In a few minutes, the boys return with the truck. Toby announces, "I'll take it." Following the statement, he sets behind the wheel where his hands fondle the custom made polished wood steering wheel. The truck is in perfect working order.

Everybody adjourns to the house where the elder Mayhew sits at the kitchen table sipping an amber colored liquid from a clear squat glass. The giant Rottweiler sits by his side. Mark, Sr. looks up through blood shot eyes as the boys enter.

"Toby wants the truck, Dad," Wagner announces softly with an obvious note of regret.

The old man nods before he goes into a back room. In a short while, he returns with the title to the truck. "Truck's a little over-priced," Mark, Sr. says. "I guess I was hoping nobody'd buy it."

Toby announces, "It's worth every penny."

Following the comment, he produces four 100 dollar bills and Mark signs and dates the document on the back, to transfer title. They shake hands before the three boys return to the shed where the truck stands gleaming in the sunlight.

"I'm going to miss this baby," Wagner mutters as he runs a

callused hand over a fender.

"Me and Mark did a lot of sanding, leadin'-in and stuff before we painted her. Mark really loved this beauty. It belonged to our grandfather."

"She's a real nice truck," Toby observes. "I'll take good care of her. Considering the circumstances, I figure I'm lucky to be gettin' her."

"We'll have a look at a bunch of tires," Axle offers. "Somebody might as well keep lookin', who knows what might turn up."

"Take the notebook and the molds with you," Wagner volunteers. "They're just more memories we might as well be shed of."

Toby picks up the booklet and tucks it into his shirt pocket. The boys load the molds into Axle's rumble seat. They all shake hands before the two Amerada kids head home. Wagner waves good-bye from the front of the shed as he slowly closes the doors.

Chapter Twenty-Seven

That night after supper, with the dishes cleared away and the drapes pulled, the family clusters around the dining room table. Mike turns serious when he announces, "Okay, it's time to get organized so that we're doing what we came here to do. We need to itemize all the information we have before we transmit the substance of what we know to the Ironstones.

"Since the Kravens appear high on the list of possible perpetrators, we need to investigate every deputy to see if we can establish a link to one of the missing women. We'll do the deputies in town first, then we'll check on the others living around the county."

"What do you mean check on?" Toby asks.

"We need to establish their routine so we know more about them. It wouldn't surprise me to find one of the missing women living in a basement of one of their houses. Nobody's searched there, I'll bet.

"We want to know where they live and what they do when they're off duty," Mike answers. "We'll establish a living pattern for each individual before we file the information with the organization. Maybe something useful will turn up. Temporary notes will be kept in the door jam with the transmitter key. We'll transmit information every 24 hours providing we have anything to report."

"Man that's going to be a lot of leg work," Axle observes as he speculates on what he'll be doing with his nights in the future. He had hoped to spend most of those with Sarah Woodling.

"Yes it will," Mike answers, "and that's where you boys come in. Kids your age are expected to be out nights doing things like playing pool at the pool hall, dating girls and milling around town. I've arranged for a couple of bicycles you can bum around on."

"Bicycles?" Axle says in astonishment. "We're a little old for bicycles, Dad."

"You can't use your car," Mike admonishes. "You're going to become window peepers which is considered to be a crime in most localities. Parking the car somewhere and then setting out on foot won't work. You can hide a bicycle by just laying it down behind a bush or in a ditch. You can either ride a bike or go on foot, but no car. Got it?"

"Yes, sir."

"Okay," Mike continues, "let's start our list of the people we need to check on."

"We may be looking for someone who's not known to us," Toby observes.

"Never mind that," Mike mutters, "we have to start somewhere."

"The Group is already suspicious of law enforcement people in this area so that seems to be a good place to start," Axle comments.

Mike takes a sheet of paper from a Big Chief writing tablet and writes down the name of Harvey Kraven along with every member of the Amerada sheriff's department known to the family. Any known address goes opposite the name.

"We'll keep a roster of suspects as they become known to us, but the Kravens will head the list," Mike details. "They'll be scattered all over the community. We won't know some of them so we'll need to write down license plates of the people who work at police headquarters. The Group can then identify the owners for us. Tonight we'll start with all people named Kraven listed in the local phone book."

Maggie asks, "Are there others besides the deputies that the Group is suspicious of?"

"Perhaps," Mike answers, "They haven't told us yet. We'll need to query Night Owl on that one. As I remember, there are several relatives in other segments of the local government that were persons of interest but I don't remember their names," Mike responds. "Discovering who they are shouldn't be difficult for a couple kids in a small town."

"While we're skulking in the bushes," Axle mutters, "what are you gonna be doin'?"

"Initially, I'll help you gather nighttime information when I can," Mike answers, "but mostly I'll be covering the places where Agent Pine hung out. He discovered something there that got him killed, so I'll give pool, beer and dominoes a shot."

"Lucky you," Maggie chirps brightly.

"Honey," Mike says, "you're specialty will be circulating in the community where women gather and listening to gossip. Sometimes gossip is more revealing than anything."

Maggie nods. "Several women have invited me to quilting sessions."

"There's a Methodist church on the north side of town," Mike announces. "This Sunday the three of us will begin attending there. Toby, you give the Baptists a try. They'll have social functions we can attend that may prove productive."

"Whoopee," Toby says. "Just don't make me attend any Holy Roller revivals."

Mike consults the local telephone directory, which is only about ten pages thick. He records several addresses for various Kravens who are not associated with the police force.

"I'll take the two of you out tonight and show you how to watch without getting caught," Mike says. "We'll start after it's good and dark."

Mike looks at the boys before he says, "If we get separated, we'll meet back here at the house at a designated time."

The boys look at each other and grin.

"When you go to an address," Mike says, "make a note of anyplace that has a dog. Dogs present special problems, they make us watch from long range."

"What we gonna prove with this," Toby asks.

"We won't know until we give it a try," Big Mike answers. "Being covert requires that we know our enemy above all else. From here on, we need to be extremely careful. If you think you need further inclination to be cautious, you can recall what Agent Pine looked like when they fished him out of the irrigation canal. Out there somewhere is a person we've been paid to find. Nighttime surveillance might identify him for us, or it might turn into an exercise in futility. We won't know until we try. It's a starting point that we must explore. If anyone has a better idea, I'm willing to listen."

Everyone shakes their heads, and so a search pattern is

established. At 9:00, Toby, Mike and Axle strike out on a casual stroll around town. They move randomly through the night to eventually end their walk near Jeb Kraven's house. The house is a small wood frame dwelling painted white. The place is dark with no sounds from within. Jeb's pickup is gone and the place is locked tight.

The three window peepers move to Clete Kraven's house. His place is also wood frame but painted gray with white trim. There are untrimmed bridal veil bushes along the east side of the structure, which screen all the windows. The only lighted window is in the kitchen. The room presents a study in organized chaos. Dirty dishes form an immense pile in the sink, and the kitchen table is a mound of litter.

Deputy Clete is barefoot and in his underwear at the kitchen table nursing a quart bottle of beer. Two empties are on the table along side his revolver. One bottle later, he remains in the same position where he stares blankly at the wall in the general vicinity of the refrigerator. After another hour of waiting for paint to begin pealing from the wall, the three peepers prepare to leave. At that precise moment, Officer Clete strips off his underwear and begins masturbating. As he begins his project, a soft feminine voice from the next room, says, "Why don't you bring that in here and let me take care of it for you?"

Officer Clete rises out of his chair to stagger through the doorway. She leads him to a distant bedroom that is illuminated by a dimly burning kerosene lamp. The peepers move to a bedroom window where they watch the Widow Hampton prepare Clete for his adventure. She loosely chains his arms spread wide to the legs of the bed frame. She then lifts his rather large scrotum as she brings his legs together. She wraps a military type belt around his legs just above his knees. She wraps a chain around his ankles. The chain is loosely fastened to the footboard of the double bed. While she works at securing him, she reiterates what she intends to do to him when he is in position. The woman uses every dirty word the boys know to enliven her description.

When her subject is secured, she stands astride his raging hard-on and slowly lowers herself down onto the thick spike as she assumes a cowgirl position that faces him. She must slowly work her way down onto his immense erection. When she has accepted all of it, she sits perfectly still with her head handing in submission. Her long dark hair hangs down onto his chest.

Her hands are on the bed as though she is about to begin doing a series of push ups. Suddenly, she engages in a prolonged wailing shuddering fit that announces the arrival of her orgasmic event. She shudders while she curses him for making her do this to herself. The deputy makes no sound. His only revelation is to remain intent as he provides her with every element she needs to abuse herself.

When her orgasmic impulses have ended, she begins to work him off. Not long after her first circular motions, Clete begins to suck air as he strains against the chains that bind him. When he screams, "Oh God," for the first time, she stops all movement. He lies whimpering for several seconds before she again applies a circular hip movement. With her second effort, he grabs a pair of bars in the headboard before he offers up his next loud response. Again she stops all movement. She begins to counsel him in a sexy low voice that has its effect on the young men outside the window.

Several minutes pass before she again offers up additional hip rotations. Each time she moves, less movement is required to attain more of the same results. Finally he begins to beg for release. She gives him a low throaty chuckle of recognition as she suggests possible courses of action for him to take. When he is babbling incoherently, she begins the slow hip rotation that quickly brings him to the brink of near insanity. His orgasmic screams fills the night as he bucks up into her.

"Go to the sheriff's house and see what's goin' on there," Mike advises in a husky whisper. "I'll watch here until something else happens or they go to sleep."

Axle mutters a near silent, "Okay," as the two boys scuttle away in the dark. It is difficult for them to walk in their advanced sexual condition.

They are careful to walk on the sidewalk and avoid dew laden grass that might leave a trail. Two blocks later, they are at the sheriff's house, where they filter behind a row of oleander bushes that surround the dwelling. The house is blacked-out except for a dim light issuing from the eastern window furthest from the street. The illuminated room has two windows. One is on the east wall and the other is around the corner on the north wall. Both are screen covered with windows and shades fully raised. There is an occasional rustling noise as a gentle breeze rattles the wooden pull bar of the roll-up window shade against the window facing. A gap below the shade offers a wide viewing slit above the sill.

The boys take a quick glance through the window furthest from the street. The dim inner light reveals a large floor fan oscillating in a far corner. The fan shuffles warm air back and forth as it scans the room. The air movement causes the window shade to chatter against the frame.

Five feet from the window, Harvey Kraven lies naked on his back in the center of a bed. A slender and equally naked woman kneels between his outstretched legs. The woman is providing an oral sexual favor still banned in most states. The two subjects are so thoroughly engrossed in her performance that the onlookers could have paraded the Texas A&M marching band past the window without being noticed.

The woman suddenly rises up to lower herself onto the sheriff's cock. When she is totally impaled, she begins to work herself off. Her pleasure arrives after a short burst of movement. When she has concluded her pleasurable suffering, she rises up to withdraw him from between her narrow hips. She then moves to again kneel at the altar of her partner's sexual fulfillment.

She takes him into her mouth and begins a slow deliberate act that causes the sheriff to babble incoherently for a considerable time. She stops when he nears conclusion and starts again when he has regained control of his emotions. She tortures him in this manner for nearly 15 minutes before she grants him total fulfillment from his condition. His ejaculation rocks her head back but she does not relinquish her oral grip on him. Her movements continue at the same pace as though nothing has happened. Shortly after, the sheriff begins to scream for her to stop, she grants him his wish.

When she is finished with her performance she parades naked

to the bathroom. The Widow Barlow is magnificently proportioned with long legs, narrow hips and small firm breasts that point magically upward. Later, she draws on a bathrobe for the walk to her house next door.

When the sheriff regains mobility, he turns off the light and shortly thereafter begins to snore. Later investigation reveals that the woman is Sheriff Kraven's office manager, Marge Barlow. The boys listen to the sheriff snore for less than an hour before they leave. During that time, they witness the lights extinguish in the Barlow household. With the residents of both houses now engaged in sleep, the boys head for home. They are jogging in tandem down the middle of the street when Toby breaks the silence.

"Clete and the sheriff both have themselves a woman, so they probably wouldn't need to kidnap other women for their pleasure."

"Yeah, seems like both of them were about pleasured out when we left them," Axle observes. "Talk about convenience. How about having someone that eager livin' right next door?"

Toby muses, "I wouldn't get any cumulative ideas about engaging in the same activity with your comely next door neighbor."

There's a chuckle, and Axle replies in the dark, "I remember what her sister told me about her husband. I've always admired anyone who is an excellent pistol shot."

"Uh huh," Toby responds in the dark.

"Besides, the thought never occurred to me," Axle murmurs.

"The hell it didn't," Toby responds as they round the final corner near home. "It occurred to me the first time I saw her in those shorts so I know it occurred to you. First liar ain't gotta chance."

They both giggle as they cross the bridge.

At home, they sit in the dark until Mike returns. Following his arrival, they pull the living room drapes before they surround the kitchen table. For the next 15 minutes, they consolidate their meager information.

Mike mutters, "I've got nothing to report. Clete leads the dullest of lives. The only near lethal act he performed was to kill four quart bottles of beer, and then go to bed. If he's a predator, I'll eat your socks. If I drank that much beer, you could iron clothes on me. I'd sure hate to have his hangover in the morning. After he went to bed, I didn't think there'd be any further activity so I came home. He doesn't live with anyone and he appears to be a beer alcoholic. What went on at the sheriff's house?"

Both boys look at each other while they wonder why no mention was made of the sexual activity Clete was subjected to. Eventually they both draw the same conclusion. Mike had not mentioned the sexual presentation because his wife was present.

After Maggie stifles a yawn before announcing that she is going to bed, the gloves come off and all is revealed. Shortly thereafter, Mike goes to bed.

While they remain at the table, Toby immediately imagines the fate of Axle's mother later tonight before he considers what he is going to do for himself later.

Later in the night, the activity in the master bedroom is long and slow. While Axle sleeps, Toby listens to the faint sounds of married sex in another room.

He imagines Maggie being brought to release with cunnilingus before she responds in kind with fellatio administered in a slow, loving manner. While he thinks of them, he masturbates furiously into one of his socks that is destined for the clothes hamper in the morning. His release is powerful, with his release muffled by a pillow so as not to awaken his bunk mate.

Their earlier conversations in the dinning room had concluded that, "Sheriff Harvey certainly had a spiritual awakening with the woman from next door before they went their separate ways."

Big Mike had concluded that they would see a lot of sex both regular and irregular while watching through windows at night. "There's not a lot of other things to do for entertainment around here, so sex will probably be the largest entertainment package available. Present company excluded."

Axle had nodded sagely as he wishes he could engage in some of that same local entertainment himself. He wishes that he could enjoy Sugarloaf Hayes at least twice night for the rest of his life.

"I suppose that we'll hit a couple more addresses every night until we've checked them all," Toby mutters. "If by then we haven't discovered anything worthwhile, we'll start over again or maybe we'll find some other avenue to explore."

The boys mutually wonder how much more of what they witnessed tonight they can endure before they both need to find action of their own. Axle was barely able to walk when they departed Clete's bedroom window.

"Hopefully, before we are either bored or hornied to death," Toby relates to his audience, "something new will develop."

"Something damn well developed while we were witnessing Barlow in her chosen profession," Axle mutters.

"Yes, it did," Toby replies. "Have you ever had a woman do that for you?"

"Only on one occasion," Axle replies.

"Was that following your initial experience at Karl's." Toby asks.

Axle responds, "Mongo was entirely responsible for any education I might have experienced since I've been in town."

Shortly after that comment, Axle wanders to the bathroom where he jacks off into a basin of warm soapy water in the hand bowl. Now fully released from his individual predicaments, he climbs into his bunk to rapidly discover sleep.

They explore various dwellings every night for a month. During that time, they discover that a lot of erotic activity happens in the village after the lights go out. Aside from that, they discover nothing of investigative interest.

Maggie joins a women's league that bowls once a week at the Shidler Bowlerama. The women travel together in cars, generally four to a vehicle. The only thing Maggie learns is that Mongo Baron has tagged several of the housewives she bowls with. Those events happened after he had physically assaulted their husbands. None of the women relating the information were on the receiving end, but the women in the car were all properly horrified. All the comments seem reliable.

Mike spends a lot of time in various beer joints in both Amerada and Shidler. He frequents every pool hall/domino parlor in both towns. A general dislike of the Kravens is evident. One night over a snooker game, he meets a missing girl's father. The man is Morton

Cane. After the last ball enters a pocket, the two men adjourn to a local tavern. Over several beers, Morton describes his daughter's disappearance.

Morton and his remaining family members live about five miles out of town on a dirt road. His daughter had taken the family car to a slumber party in town on a Friday night, but never arrived there. The car was later discovered in the Shidler Truck Stop parking lot. The keys were in the ignition. The windows were left rolled down, with the doors unlocked. The sheriff's department never developed a clue. Sheriff Kraven claimed that the girl had left town on a bus. That was his explanation for why the car was found where it was.

Morton is one of the most negative and depressed people Mike has ever met. He is highly suspicious of the competence of the sheriff's department. He also does not believe his one and only daughter ran away from home. After nearly an hour of conversation, Mike goes home.

The Ironstone Group investigation lumbers along without discovering anything worthwhile. In the process, weeks turn into months. The boys continue to search tires on trucks in various parking lots without success. Everyone is discouraged by the continuing lack of evidence.

Chapter Twenty-Eight

Monday November 14th arrives with a prior commitment. All the boys in the senior class are invited to attend a Rotary Club meeting in the basement of the Methodist Church. Most of the pillars of the community are present. There are several guest speakers in attendance. All give a sales pitch for their particular area of civic responsibility.

The third and last speaker is at the podium when people begin yawning and nodding out. Half an hour later, he still drones on in a style that couldn't motivate fish to remain in water. Axle is barely conscious when he decides he'd like to amputate the speaker's lips. The speaker is Sheriff Harvey Kraven. Sheriff Kraven has all the tact and desirability of a persistent ear infection. His county vehicle bears a license plate holder featuring the emblem of treason: the stars and bars of the confederacy. He is even less lovable on this occasion than any other day Axle can remember.

The senior male students are being integrated into the adult side of the community even though they are only teenagers.

Axle glances along the row of folding chairs where he notices Mongo eyeing him as though something is hanging out of Axle's nose. He is probably fantasizing some form of revenge, but Axle anticipates that it will not be a direct confrontation. Perhaps another shot through a window after he has his rifle barrel straightened.

That afternoon at school, Toby is voted captain of the football team. Melissa St. Claire is the homecoming queen. Homecoming occurs the following Friday night. The queen is crowned before the game, but in Axle's estimation, Sarah Woodling will be the most beautiful girl present.

Friday night arrives and Melissa is radiant in her crown and gown. Melissa stands five foot three, weighs 100 pounds and is the star of the local gymnastic club. Amerada high is too small and rural for a gymnastics program, but a club composed mostly of European immigrants from Scandinavian countries keeps the sport alive and flourishing in the area. The members live mostly on farms around the county. One farmer maintains a small gymnasium in an out building on his property where the club practices.

Time flies and Amerada High wins all their football games for the season. Since Amerada beats everybody on their schedule, they become the undisputed conference champions. Mongo misses the first six games, but when he returns, he is just as good as a running back as Sugarloaf had indicated. He also plays the position of third linebacker on defense. Mongo plays along side Axle and Toby with only mild annoyance. In general, he remains as cordial as a cobra at a mongoose convention. The good news is that combined, the three are probably the best small school line-backing corps in the state. Amerada high is too small to receive prominent attention so no major scholarships are harvested.

Mongo, Bubba and Toby each receive a scholarship from a small college with a compass point in its name. Bubba decides to attend but Toby can't because he is on assignment with the Group.

Mongo eventually declines because he simply isn't interested in either school or moving out of the area. The rest of the football team concentrates on getting through the remainder of the school year.

Football season departs with its short-lasting flush of victory. Next comes the sport Axle despises most of all: basketball. The only thing he likes about basketball is the fact that the school has both boy's and girl's basketball teams. Both teams ride the same bus to out of town games. Both Sarah and Melissa play girl's basketball. The night time trips on a school bus with Sarah snuggled close aboard and the lights out are special. Axle's heart soars like a homesick angel. He is in love for the first time in his life. With the lights out, Axle remains in an advance state of tumescence while Sarah plays the part of a blond temptress.

Toby teams up with Melissa and they become a foursome everywhere.

Mongo plays all the sports and remains a mystery to everyone. He is a loaner who never acquires a permanent girl friend. Axle and Toby think that is strange because at their age, girls are nearly all they think about. Everyone else in school is paired off in a somewhat normal fashion. It is as though they have enrolled in a year long petting contest. Everyone but Mongo participates. He remains aloof and girl less, without apparent interest. It isn't that women aren't interested in him, quite the opposite is true. The local sports hero is a unique marriage of both muscle and speed, but he dwells beyond the fringe of polite society.

After home ball games, Karl's turns into teenage-central. Everyone goes there for shakes and burgers. Everyone but Mongo... he goes home.

The boys and the Mannheim family keep their eyes and ears open but there remains no indication that anything concerning the vanished women is happening anywhere within Amerada.

There are two things that are noteworthy. There is the continuous aggravation caused by the cops and the sale of moonshine by the Kravens. Together, the boys check a lot of tires on pickup trucks without finding a plug in the correct position.

On November 25, 1949, Toby checks a spare tire mounted in a truck bed. The tire carcass bears a plug in exactly the desired location. Mongo Baron drives the truck. When Axle checks the tire, he spies a small, dirty scrap of white cloth peeking from beneath the edge of the tire. The shard is fairly new looking and rectangular in shape. The narrow end is raw as though it has been cut by something sharp. Three sides are hemmed. There are three small eyelet's attached to the uncut end. The fabric is glossy, elastic and looks familiar. Axle is drawn to the object so he stuffs it in his shirt pocket. Later that night at the supper table, he brings out the scrap for examination.

"Anybody got any idea what this is?" Axle asks as he drops the scrap on the table top.

Maggie takes one glance before she says, "That's part of a bra strap. Where'd you get it?"

"From Mongo's truck bed," Axle answers, "right next to an incriminating spare tire with a fiber plug in a tread valley."

Big Mike picks up the scrap and studies it. "It's been cut by a blade of some sort," he observes. "Whatever cut it was so sharp that the material is hardly frayed. Wonder why Mongo would be carrying around part of a bra strap?"

"Since we've been here," Toby elaborates, "Mongo hasn't had a girlfriend. Could it belong to his mother or a sister we don't know about?"

"Mongo don't have a sister or a mother, at least in this town," Big Mike answers. "I've already checked his family background. Except for the time when he was recuperating from his fractured jaw, he's lived with his uncles in the creek bottom near Big Oliver Marsh."

"Who'd he live with when he was injured?" Maggie asks.

"He lived with Clete in town so he could use a food blender to feed himself," Mike answers.

"Clete's not married either," Toby offers. "We've checked out all the deputies by personal observation. There's no woman involved with any of them that we know about. Near as we can tell, they only work, drink and sleep. That seems a pretty dull existence for a bunch of swamp rats."

"Maybe we need to have a close up look at where Mongo lives," Axle muses.

"You guys stay away from there," Mike growls. "I'll do any lookin' out there that needs doin'. I'm trained for that function and you're not."

That night, an encrypted message is sent by short wave:

NIGHT OWL, NIGHT OWL, NIGHT OWL, RIPTIDE.
Several identifiers later:
NIGHT OWL COPY X GO RIPTIDE X RIPTIDE ASKS NAME OF BOSS X
BLACK IS BOSS X
AFFIRMATIVE NIGHT OWL X RIPTIDE MESSAGE FOLLOWS X POSSIBLE LINK BETWEEN ABDUCTIONS AND KRAVEN-BARON FAMILYS THEORIZED X WRITTEN EXPLANATION FOLLOWS X WILL REPORT ADDL INFO AS AVAIL X RIPTIDE CLEAR.
NIGHT OWL COPY X WILL RELAY X NIGHT OWL CLEAR.

Prior to finding the fiber plug and bra strap, nothing has seemed out of line but the cops and the moonshine operation. They rule the local populous like an arm of the Waffen SS during WWII.

Another strange thing happens during the second week of the current month. Leah Holmes comes calling. She arrives at the garage where Axle and Toby are lifting weights on a Saturday morning. As usual, she wears short-shorts that reveal the total length of her incredibly long legs.

We've seen you with less than you've got on right now Mrs. Holmes, the boys think. *We've watched you make love to your husband. The fact is that you didn't just have sex, you put on a clinic.*

"I understand you escorted my sister out of Karl's the day she was supposed to leave for Missouri," Leah accuses as she leans on the garage door jam. While she speaks, her arms are crossed beneath her monumental breasts. She speaks directly to Axle as though Toby isn't even there.

"Yes, ma'am, I did."

"Did you also give her a ride back there the next day so she could catch the bus?" Leah asks as she studies his face.

"No, ma'am," Axle answers as he stares her in the eye. "I drove her to Shidler. She caught the noon bus for Springfield, Missouri from a truck stop on the east side of town. I put her on the bus and then watched the bus depart for Houston."

"That was the day after Mongo made a fool of himself at Karl's?" Leah speculates thoughtfully.

"Yeah," Axle answers as he sits up on the weight lifting bench to dry himself with a ragged white towel.

"She never made it," Leah offers. "She is missing and nobody knows where she went."

"I saw her ticket," Axle says. "It was for Springfield. It was an express bus. The first stop was to be Houston and then Springfield."

Leah continues to lean on the door jam as she studies Axle's face.

"Maybe after she got to Houston, she decided to go back to California," Axle offers.

"If she did, none of her friends out there know about it," Leah responds. "I don't think she'd go there again. California was a bad experience for her."

"That was some time ago," Axle notes, "how come you're asking me now?"

"My mom filed a missing persons report. The state police came to see me as part of their investigation," Leah continues. "They said she was seen at a restaurant near the bus stop in Houston, but never left on the bus to Springfield."

"How'd you know I took her to the bus stop," Axle asks.

"Word gets around in a small town," Leah offers. "If the state cops call me again I'll tell them you were the last person to see her in Amerada. They'll probably want to talk to you."

"Okay with me," Axle mutters, helpfully. "If you've got a number, I'll give them a call."

Leah produces a business card from a blouse pocket. The card has a number with the name of a Sgt. Monroe in Houston printed on one side. Axle places the card on the end of the tool room work bench. In the background, Toby busies himself amassing more weight plates on the bar as he readies himself to begin his bench presses.

Axle turns back to Leah, "I'll call him as soon as I'm finished here," Axle's says as he positions himself to tend the lift for Toby.

Toby lies on the bench, checks his grip and rapidly does six presses before slowly straining a seventh. He mounts the bar back atop its rest before he sits up. As he wipes down with a towel, Leah locks eyes with him.

"How many pounds are on that thing?" she asks. Her face is slightly flushed as she traces her lip line with the tip of her tongue.

Toby wipes down as he smiles at her. "About 380," he acknowledges.

"My God," she says. "You just lifted more than twice what I weigh."

Toby smiles, and tries to act modest. She turns away and walks toward the backyard gap in the hedge. Her hips move in a saucy cadence. At the short, wrought iron gate in the hedge, she turns facing the garage to fasten the latch. Both boys are watching her retreat.

Leah's respiration increases as she enters the house. She pauses to lean her back against the nearest wall inside the kitchen. *Damn him, why'd he have to do that while I was watching.* She enters the bathroom, where she strips and masturbates while taking a hot shower.

Chapter Twenty-Nine

Five months have passed and spring is in full bloom when Toby's parents announce their long anticipated move to Amerada. The boys are now 17, approaching graduation and the end of high school. Adulthood looms on the horizon with an urgent requirement to work for a living. The boys have no prospects for employment and no idea where to look. There are no goals to be attained, because they have no ambition in mind. They have no philosophy of life, unless eating, drinking and voiding can be considered a philosophy. Every morning, they climb out of bed to find that they can barely contain their bewilderment as life races past them.

On January 6, 1950, Toby's mother calls Maggie Mannheim with the news that they will begin moving on the weekend. She asks for the boys to come and help. Toby's father arrives that same day. He rents a house a half block from the Mannheim residence. The Fitzpatrick backyard abuts the creek.

The investigation to this point is stalled in the middle of nowhere. Axle's greatest and most recent find consists of a paper cut he received while thumbing through a book in study hall during a staring session with Sarah Woodling.

The Ironstone families will live half a block apart. Axle and Sarah have been going steady the better part of the school year. In late December, Sarah's father is very nearly transferred out of state. The fact that she didn't leave represents a prayer influenced by impatient grace. Axle has lain awake nights praying that Sarah wouldn't be forced to live in some far distant place. It would not have seemed right to knock on God's door with a prayer and have him not answer. Within a week, her father receives a promotion and remains in town.

Chapter Thirty

Toby's dad is Cecil Beckwith, but their Ironstone family name has been changed to Fitzpatrick. Cecil works for the same oil company as Michael Mannheim. The transfer has been easily managed because the Group has a retired OSS agent who is employed in a high position within the company. During World War II, Cecil flew British Spitfires and P-51 Mustangs in Europe. He first flew for the Canadian Air Force, and then later the British Royal Air Force. When the U.S. Army Air Corps arrived, he was transferred to fly with his own nation.

Cecil was inducted into the OSS at the midpoint of the Battle of Briton. While he was recovering from a lower back injury, the OSS came calling. It had not taken long for his knowledge of the German language to gain the attention of this covert organization. He also possessed a unique knowledge of explosives from civilian employment in mining operations. The OSS taught him infiltration. Cecil's career crossed paths with Mike Marston in France, where they conspired to drop several bridge spans simultaneous with D-Day.

When Cecil was released from active duty, he was recruited to join the Ironstone Group. His knowledge of mechanics plus his love of flying presented the rarest of opportunities for them. He was able to obtain an Aircraft and Engine mechanics certification using his GI-Bill. Following his licensing in that capacity, he began to work on private aircrafts.

His certification to work on aircrafts created a unique position for him within the Ironstone Organization. While he worked as a field mechanic for an oil company, he also worked on airplanes at local airports. In addition, he also flew pipeline right-of-way inspections for several oil companies on weekends.

To this end, he had purchased a Piper Cub airplane. The aircraft was purchased at a government surplus auction. The machine was one of many declared surplus to military needs.

The end of the war had found the Army Air Corps involved in a gigantic pilot training program. Training pilots became an occupation that was no longer needed when the war ended. So the training program was dismantled and the aircraft disposed of at auction. The Army Air Corps became the newly formed United States Air Force and a reduction in force occurred. Cecil bought the Cub at auction in Barksdale, Louisiana at a price that came dramatically close to stealing.

He installed a larger than normal engine in the J-3 Piper Cub. The aircraft was then registered as a PA-18 Super Cub. Other than the engine mounts being reinforced, very little else was changed. The larger engine meant that the craft had more power than before. It could now more easily perform simple aerobatic maneuvers like loops, stalls and spins. The wing was not stressed for negative G-forces so rolls were not performed. The plane could do lazy-8 maneuvers, chandelles and a sloppy, positive-G, barrel roll but nothing more. It spun beautifully and had to be flown out of the spin.

Considering the hours it had flown, the Cub was an elderly air ship by any standard. Cecil had stripped the airframe to bare metal. With the frame laid bare, he then dust-blasted the airframe so he could repair any structural defects. Several cracks were found and welded, and the area strengthened with gussets before reinstalling new fabric.

His A&E certificate allowed him to perform the work himself. During the course of a year, he completely reconditioned the machine from the trailing edge of the rudder to the prop nut. By the time he was finished, he owned an elderly Cub in mint condition. The craft remained traditional Cub yellow with a graduated black stripe along both sides of the fuselage.

When Toby's dad arrived by car to rent the house on the creek, the boys returned with him to Louisiana. The Cub had to be flown to Amerada from a sod strip north of New Orleans. The person who would fly the aircraft to Texas has yet to be decided.

Cecil and the boys arrive in Louisiana at mid-afternoon, Thursday, January 12, 1950. To a man, they were grainy eyed and weary. Because of the energy of youth, the boys were able to help the movers pack the last of the family possessions into a moving van. By the time of the evening meal, everybody involved was in a state of physical exhaustion. Supper consisted of steaks so large they very nearly cut off the oxygen supply to the charcoal in a borrowed barbecue grill. Following the meal, Cecil speculates, "Somebody needs to fly the Cub to Amerada."

Of course Toby can do the flying, but more probably it will be his father. About the time Axle was praying for a Genie to show up and grant him a wish, Cecil offered, "I guess you guys better take the plane so I can drive Rebecca in the car. I wouldn't want her to be at the mercy of a couple of teenage racing enthusiasts."

The moment was rarer than Steak Tartar. Only seconds before the announcement, the boys were exhausted. Now they are both wide eyed as they construct the flight in their minds. The decision that the boys will fly the bird to Texas nearly surpassed Axle's concept of human tolerance. That night they sleep in a neighbor's home where sleep arrives with about the same frequency as a solar eclipse.

Axle has never flown in an airplane before. The closest he'd come had been when he was securely bared to a seat mounted on the outer circumference of a circus Ferris wheel. He was skeptical of Toby's flying abilities to the point that he feared a crash somewhere along their route home. While they lay in bed that night on folding camp cots, Axle asks suspiciously, "Do you really know how to fly one of those things?"

"You bet, nothing to it," Toby answers. "I've been flying since I was ten. I used to sit on Dad's lap and fly the thing before I was tall enough to reach the rudder pedals."

"How long will it take us to get there?" Toby asks.

"I don't know, we'll do a flight plan tomorrow and then we'll know right down to the minute," Toby answers. "Dad's a stickler for knowing how much fuel the bird will have when it lands."

Axle lies awake far into the night until sleep finally overwhelms him.

Before Cecil and Rebecca depart for Amerada, Cecil maps a proposed flight route on navigational charts. Toby calculates time and distance, plus fuel endurance by using a circular slide rule.

Cecil checks every entry on the navigation card before he gives final approval. His attention to detail is inspiring.

The range of the Cub is not very far, so frequent refueling stops are plotted on the map. The trip is about 470 aerial miles. The route is mostly along the Gulf coast.

The following day with Toby at the helm and with Axle in the back seat, the Cub lifts off headed for Amerada. Their departure features an azure blue sky with the sun a golden wafer behind them. Ahead the heavens are cloudless. The Cub rides the thermals as light as a kite.

Toby has limited cross country fight experience, but he has more than 1,000 hours of flight time that has mostly been accumulated while flying pipeline surveys. He is able to navigate by time and distance while using a map. He flies with the same attention to detail of his flight instructor father.

Five minutes into the flight, Toby yells at Axle above the engine noise, "Take the controls for a while."

Axle takes the stick in his hand with rudderless ambition. His inexperience causes him to roam all over the sky. Toby whoops and hollers so much he nearly makes himself sick with laughter at Axle's attempts to steer the Cub in a straight and level flight.

The substitute for satisfaction is patience. After nearly 15 minutes of frantic gyrations, Axle becomes confident enough to steer the feather-light Cub reasonably well. Near the first stop of their journey, Toby demonstrates several stalls, followed by five spins and their recovery. Next, he talks Axle through six more of each maneuver before they enter the landing pattern. Finally, Toby shoots a touch-and-go landing with Axle following him on the controls. Following that, Axle does six more landings before they land and taxi to a gas pump for fuel.

Over the next two refueling stops, Axle makes a total of 12 landings without Toby on the controls.

There is a spreading sense of doom following the third refueling stop when Toby says, "Get in the front seat for the next engine start, takeoff and landing."

Axle immediately decides that prayer vigils should commence

in earnest. He's been watching everything Toby's does in the front seat. He is certain that he can start and taxi the beast, but he lacks confidence. At first Axle is hesitant to do anything lest he make a mistake. He is trance-like as he considers what to do next. When he hesitates during engine start Toby mutters, "Either do something or whine all summer."

When Axle hesitates further, Toby says, "Come on, pard, we've made 28 landings, done a total of ten spins along with 14 power-on and power-off, stalls. I'll be in the back seat. I'll follow everything you do on the controls. There's nothing to worry about.

In reality, flying seems about as natural to Axle as walking. The maneuvers performed were over for him quicker than he would have liked. Everything involved has been an elaborate thrill. The problem with flying is that when something goes wrong, you can't just get out and walk to your destination.

Axle hesitates momentarily before he climbs through the door into the front cockpit. He straps himself into the front seat so tightly that he nearly loses circulation in his lower extremities. After the initial dramatics are finished, the rest is like learning to add and subtract all over again, but without flash cards. Starting the engine is easy. Taxiing while using the brakes, rudder and throttle prove to be simple. The takeoff is an adventure in combating torque with the rudder pedals. Once airborne, they proceed to the next landing site.

They enter the next landing pattern where Axle is required to make four touch-and-go landings. The wind is calm and the landings flawless. After the final touch-down and roll-out, Toby instructs, "Taxi to that gas pump over there near the edge of the apron."

The ground attendant motions them into a parking spot opposite the fuel pump followed by a cut-engine signal.

Toby says, "Leave her runnin'."

Toby then gets out of the back seat. While he leans in to fasten the lap belt so it doesn't interfere with the stick, he says, "Take her once around the pattern, land and taxi back to the pump."

Axle stares at him in a terror stricken daze. Eventually he responds with a sound that resembles, "Duh."

"Just keep your head out of your ass and look around," Toby

mutters. "You can fly this thing nearly as well as I can."

Crunch time has arrived.

Axle mutters, "What if I hurt your dad's airplane? I've never done this before."

"The hell you haven't," Toby says. "We've done 31 landings and you did most of them. You need to get with it so we can get home before dark."

With that final comment, Toby closes and latches the door. He then walks away from the aircraft to stand with the attendant near the gas pump.

Axle stares dumb-struck at the instrument panel for a few seconds before giving the engine a touch of throttle. The bird begins to roll and he is on his way.

He taxies to the active runway where he gets a green light from the biscuit gun in the tower. He then lines up on the centerline, checks the mags and takes off. Initially he feels like a giraffe in a high wind. As the wheels clear the ground, he suddenly remembers that Orville Wright's first flight was 120 feet long and occurred on December 17, 1903. Axle's flight is longer, but probably just as thrilling. Axle flies crosswind, downwind, base leg and lands like he's been doing it all his life. After landing, he taxies to the fuel pump, kills the engine and gets out.

"Man what a boost!" he shouts at his buddy.

Toby hands him a cold Delaware Punch soda to christen his maiden solo flight. They have a swig apiece before Toby claps him on the shoulder, before he says, "I originally bought some marshmallows for the bonfire I believed would ignite off the end of the runway at takeoff. When that didn't happen, I traded the bag for these two bottles."

The boys have a chuckle at an old pilot's solo joke while they watch the fuel attendant service the bird. When the aircraft is topped-off and the fuel paid for, Axle returns again to the front seat for the last leg of the journey. During the flight, Axle makes a mental note. Some day he is going to qualify for a pilot's license.

There is a lighted sod airstrip six miles north of Amerada where the bird will be hangared. Cecil and Toby will fly out of there. By the end of the trip, Axle is in love for the second time in his life. This time the object of his affection wears yellow-and-black, doped fabric and never changes clothes. The Cub makes him yearn for a multi-zeroed salary so he can own one of his own.

They arrive over Amerada late in the afternoon.

They decide to tour the local area before landing for the last time. By air, the Gulf coast is amazingly close to where they live. After seeing everything from above, they vow to make a trip to Matagorda Island sometime in the near future. They fly the deserted Gulf-side beach line along Matagorda Island for several miles before they turn northward to tour Discovery Bay.

Eventually, their lazy orbits bring them over Oliver Marsh. Beneath them lies a treasure trove of potholes, waterways and tall saw-grass flats that tweak their imagination. Fishing there would be wonderful beyond imagination. They spot The Hundred-and-Forty-Foot-Hill towering above the north side of the marsh. West Clear Creek enters the marsh at its northeast corner. The main channel is easily traced until it disperses into a maze of slender channels near the center. The marsh is huge. There is only one road to the marsh, and that terminates at a small open bay about a mile from where the creek enters. A truck is parked beneath the trees where the road ends.

From the small bay, several channels wind their way into the heart of the marsh. Near its center a clump of houses stand elevated on stilts above the water. A small fleet of boats sits clustered near and beneath the houses. One boat is noticeably larger than the others.

The marsh lies several miles from town. There is a silver colored pipeline hanging in suspension across West Clear Creek near where the creek enters the marsh. The pipe elevates above ground to span the creek before it disappears once more beneath the earth. On the south side of the creek, near the emergence of the pipeline is a small, dark-colored building with a green roof. They can see a smoky haze above the trees on the north side of the creek directly abeam of the house. They descend through 80-degree air to an altitude of less than a foot above the tree canopy. The haze smells of wood smoke. Axle stands the bird on a wing tip above the house as he marvels at how well they can see everything. Unknowingly, they have just violated the air space above Amerada's most feared family.

While they watch in fascination a destructive panorama unfolds below them. Someone emerges from the sack to stand in the clearing holding something in the air above his head. Whatever that something is, it flashes in a sequence. Suddenly, a hole appears in the left wing of the Cub. That's when they both realize that they are being shot at. The hole is about three feet outboard of the fuselage. Toby is slightly quicker on the uptake than Axle. When Toby sees the hole appear in the wing, he grabs the controls, rolls wings level, applies full throttle and dives away from the shack heading east. He makes a large clearing turn around the shooter before he heads for the sod landing strip north of town.

A post-flight inspection reveals three bullet holes in the aircraft. Obviously, mundane flying above the house on the creek is not in the best interest of a fliers' health. Why would anyone shoot at a low flying airplane anywhere in the United States? The shooting adds to a growing list of things yet to be determined.

Cecil is going to find fault with whoever shot his precious Cub, no news flash there. Both have a sudden chill as they realize that a bullet hole in doped fabric is probably about the same size as a bullet hole in living flesh. They now jointly want to know more about the people who live on the creek near the marsh.

Chapter Thirty-One

It becomes increasingly apparent that eventually somebody is going to have to make a trip down the river to see what is happening at the Kraven compound. Big Mike and one other person will make that voyage. With this thought in mind, a request is placed with the Ironstones for a canoe. The request is approved. The canoe will provide a means of fishing the creek when it is not involved in reconnoitering the activities of the Kravens.

Two weeks later, the canoe arrives. It is 17 feet long, has a square stern for an outboard motor and an aluminum keel that keeps it from being tippy. It is made of olive-drab-colored Fiberglass, with aluminum gunnels and seats. The canoe also comes with two paddles and a pair of seat cushion-style life preservers.

The dainty craft arrives on a Bee-Line motor freight truck at 2:00 on a Thursday afternoon. By 2:30, the boys are on West Clear Creek. By 2:45, they have boated their first bass. The two-pound largemouth succumbed to a Guinea feathered Shannon spinner with a red tail. Toby buzzed the bait along the surface, beneath a cypress tree skirt while using a long cane pole with two feet of line. The fish charged from underneath the tree overhang and nailed the bait. Toby has doodled their first fish from the new craft and they aren't even wet yet. The odds are that a lot more fish will follow.

The canoe floats like a gull on the water. The boys are smitten by the way it glides with just one paddle stroke. Without question, it is the greatest thing to happen to them since they discovered fishing.

Late that afternoon, when they return home, they clean fish for half an hour. When they are in the freezer, they string a drop light behind Toby's house where they construct a storage shed to house their latest toy. They attach the structure at waist level to the rear wall of the Fitzpatrick back porch.

When the enclosure is finished they install a pair of carpeted bunks for the canoe to rest upon in an upside down manner. They then affix a pair of hasps and padlocks to the door and paint the structure white to match the house. The canoe is home, properly christened and housed. They are set for life.

Chapter Thirty-Two

Sugarloaf's days and nights in the root cellar become a blur of debauchery. She loses track of the number of days of her imprisonment. At least five men a day visit her crib. She is rarely out of bed. With the exception of Mongo, her captors are brutal. She recedes within herself as she concentrates on surviving. She dreams of an opportunity to escape.

On a shelf in the depths of the cellar, she finds a wooden bowl containing a hand full of nuts, and a hinge-handled, metal nutcracker. The nuts are small, native pecans. Among them is also a nutmeat pick. She eats the nuts, and while cracking the third one, realizes that the nutcracker has a use beyond its intended designed. Perhaps she can use it to remove the nut from the bolt securing her chain to the wall ring. She puts the bowl back on the shelf before she applies the hinged handles to the castellated nut. Before she can finish working on the wall bolt, the door lock of her crib rattles in its hasp. She tosses the nutcracker beneath the mattress before dropping onto the edge of the bed. The visitor is Clete Kraven for his usual, once a day favor.

When Clete departs and locks the door, Sugarloaf rinses her mouth and uses the chamber pot before retrieving the nutcracker. She is able to remove the nut from the bolt. She stares at the nut, unable to believe her good fortune.

The nut is returned to the bolt, but installed only finger tight. Nobody will notice unless they check the chain at the wall bracket. Anytime they remove her from the cellar, they unlock the padlock at her ankle. The chain remains attached to the wall.

She returns the nutcracker to the bowl and for the first time begins to plot an escape. The first problem will be to pass beyond the locked door. The second problem will be getting back to town before her captors realizes that she has escaped. While she considers the problem, the lock on the door rattles again as Mongo pays her a visit. Mongo always stays longer than any of the others. He has the sexual stamina of youth.

The other men smell of old sweat and rarely bathe. Mongo and the deputies are the exception. Mongo seems to care about her, where as the others don't. Everyday he brings her food and water in a water crock. He dutifully empties the chamber pot and sometimes takes her to the creek to bathe.

The second day following her arrival, he even brought her a toothbrush, some tooth paste and a bar of soap. Mongo enjoys watching her while she scrubs herself before returning her to the cellar. Following the bath, he always requires additional sexual service when they arrive back at the cellar.

The root cellar remains relatively cool at midday because it is below ground level. The earth atop the roof insulates the cavity from the sun. The cellar is near the bottom of a hill about 50 yards into the brush, behind the shack. Long ago, she decided that she is better off in the cellar than she would be in the shack or at the still. She had been stationed at both those places early in her captivity. Both places were hot during the day and the shack was bug infested. While there are bugs in the cellar, they are mostly roly-poly's and earwigs. Neither are especially annoying, unlike the mosquitoes and roaches at the shack.

Two days after loosening the nut on her chain, Mongo arrives with a screen door. A heavy gauge, steel, security panel has overlaid the fine screen mesh in the door. Mongo installs the new door with spring hinges that return it to the closed position when released. There is even a little rubber ball mounted on a dangling wire so the door won't make a loud slapping noise when it strikes the jam.

When Mongo leaves, Sugarloaf inspects the door. The heavy screen overlays the inner frame. It is secured with round headed bolts drilled through the wooden frame, with the heads on the outside. The bolts have a square shoulder beneath the round head. This feature keeps them from turning in the wood when the nut is tightened. Inside, the bolts pass through an open segment of the heavy screen, then through a large, flat metal washer topped by a lock washer. An ordinary nut caps the installation. The door has a hasp and uses the same padlock as before

Sugarloaf's heart gives a little flutter when she realizes that she can remove the heavy gauge screen and escape the cellar. All that remains now is to plan her departure and develop enough courage to follow through. The only clothing she is allowed is the top sheet from the bed. Her kidnapers aren't interested in clothing. They want her naked when they visit.

The next day while at the creek with Mongo, she looks more closely at her surroundings. She can smell the refinery and is certain Amerada lies upstream somewhere. Traveling cross country, barefoot will be nearly impossible. She notices a pair of boats tied to the dock. When Luke drops into one of them he carries a dead coon he found somewhere. She watches him start the engine and notes everything he does to get it running. He squeezed a little round ball on the black hose running into the engine then flipped a lever on the side of the cowling. Next, he pulled out a knob on the front of the engine cover. Finally, he pulls forcefully on a black T-handle near the top of the engine. The handle is attached to a rope that comes out nearly three feet when he pulls. She decides the lever on the side is a gearshift and the knob in front must be a choke.

When the engine starts, it doesn't make very much noise, until he gives it the gas and roars away toward the marsh. She begins to understand how she can travel without shoes. All she has to do is steal a boat.

That night in the wee hours of the morning, after Luther has visited her and gone, she loosens all the nuts on the door using the nutcracker. When she is ready, she removes her chain from the wall. She then unscrews the nuts from the screen door and slithers between the wooden segments of the door frame.

Outside the cellar, she gathers up her ankle chain and carries it with her left hand. The night is not given to moonlight, so she occasionally strays off the smooth surface of the path leading to the clearing. When she encounters grass, sand spurs hobble her. She passes the shack quietly and then creeps down the river bank to the dock. Both boats remain tied to the wharf as before. She drops into the nearest one, unties the rope to the dock and pushes free. The slow current of the water moves her downstream. She feels for and finds the black ball on the fuel hose and squeezes the bulb several times. It hardens in her hand. She feels for and finds the lever on the left side of the engine cowling that she supposes is a gearshift. The lever has three positions. She places it in the middle position.

Her hands move over the engine until she locates the little round knob she figures is probably a choke. She pulls that out. The boat bobs in the current, as it turns gently sideways toward the bank. She pulls the starter rope twice before the engine coughs to life. It makes a lot of noise before it dies. She pulls the rope frantically several more times. The odor of gas tells her she has flooded it. She pushes the little knob in as she tries again.

After three kicks the engine fires and catches. She rotates the throttle on the tiller and the engine revs, but does not move. Then she remembers the gearshift lever and puts it in reverse. The gears clash as the engine comes down from high RPM, but remains running. The boat backs further away from the dock.

Atop the bank, a dark form hurries down hill to the dock. At the center of the stream, she shifts the lever into forward, gives the motor more throttle, and turns the tiller all the way to the left. The boat shoots forward headed upstream.

The dark form on the dock drops into the other boat. She wishes she had thought to disable the second boat before starting this one. In the dark tunnel of the night, bugs smack her in the face. The night is unusually black and she strives desperately to see ahead.

The boat careens off something, probably a log, then rights itself. She can tell where the bank is only because the trees are darker than the water. She aims between the twin rows of darkness. The boat makes good time for a long while before the bow rises high above the water and the boat strands itself on something. She is hurled forward across two seats.

The engine dies. She picks herself off the floor, and feels over the side with an arm. Her hand finds the roughness of a log. She hears the other boat in pursuit. It is not far away. She feels the log again and decides there are two of them tied together. There is a large cable running between them. She scoops up her chain and climbs onto the logs.

She drops to her hands and knees, then inches toward the nearest band of darkness. Balancing is difficult, because the logs are slippery with moss. She clutches the leg chain to her chest with her left hand as she struggles along. The sound of the pursuing boat is much closer. She moves along the logs toward the bank as quickly as she can. The end of the logs arrives. She clings to the bare cable for support. She thrusts one leg toward the bank, but finds only water.

The boat charges up onto the logs near mid-channel. The motion of the logs knocks her off balance. She falls into the water and sinks beneath the surface. In panic, she releases the chain and struggles to swim toward shore. The chain catches on something beneath the water and holds her fast below the surface. Sugarloaf fights against the chain until the air in her lungs gives out and blessed darkness rolls over her.

Chapter Thirty-Three

The Amerada school year ends a month early on May 6, 1950 when the high school partially burns. The volunteer fire department responds, as do firefighters from Shidler. By the time the inferno is under control, it has destroyed half the auditorium and most of the classrooms in the main building. The field house is a total loss. The blaze is well established when discovered by deputy Jeb Kraven who is performing a routine nighttime patrol.

The boys receive their diplomas the following Friday at noon on the front lawn of what remains of the high school. Their graduation from public education occurs during a light spring shower with gusty surface winds. For graduation they receive identical gold, Elgin wrist watches with ornamental gold bands. Each watch has their name engraved on the back of the case.

Toby and Axle make the startling discovery that they are out of high school, unemployed and under educated. They both recognize a trouble zone when they see one. That very week, the boys reach income immobility when they discover nobody wants their lawn mowed, trimmed or otherwise touched. That is also the day when they begin looking for jobs in the classified section of the newspaper. The paper contains nothing they are qualified to do.

During the early spring of 1950, Amerada remains almost totally without work opportunities for young people. There is of course the oil refinery staffed by middle-aged men and a rather large, declining oil field. All the new oil fields are in the Midland area. The coolies in the oil patch tend to remain in place until they die. Much is lacking in the boys employment future.

Axle's father tells him he need not find employment right away, but he also reminds him that when he turns 18 he has to register for the draft. Axle doesn't mind registering for the draft, but he still wants a job so at some point in the future, he won't have to live under the south abutment of a highway bridge. The boys feel that were it not for the fact that they are still involved in seeking information for the Ironstones, they would be pushed out of the nest and neither feels ready for that event.

The mystery of the missing women remains unsolved and they seem no closer to a solution than when they arrived. Mr. Black is becoming impatient and threatens to send other agents into the area.

Chapter Thirty-Four

One morning, Toby mutters, "We need to get the Condor finished and in the air so we can see if it flies.

Axle nods, as he offers, "Yeah, I knew that was coming."

They postpone further thoughts of fishing and journey into Toby's basement where they have a very large model-glider under construction on a Ping-Pong table. The thing has an eight foot wingspan and is supposed to be a non-powered, soaring glider. The plans call for it to be hand launched from some place with a height advantage like a water tower. An alternate means of launched flight is to be pulled by a tow line attached to a car bumper. The model needs to be towed at a speed that will cause it to climb steeply. When the glider reaches a certain angle above the tow vehicle, the tow line will automatically disengage from a hook beneath the nose.

The boys finish the original model and try the suggested tow rope launch procedure. The half-baked idea doesn't work. They have to reconstruct a portion of the left wing following the crash that occurs about 40 feet from the launch point.

They decide to alter the design after the tow rope incident. They rightly suspect that the sheriff's deputies aren't about to allow them to launch from the town's water tower. Their next version of "hand launching" will involve throwing the model into the wind with an unintended engine and folding propeller installed in the nose.

They go back to the drawing board. Toby has a well-seasoned Olsen & Rice 23, model aircraft engine. They buy a folding propeller through an advertisement in a model airplane magazine. The prop is designed for a powered glider. The concept being that when the engine quits, the prop will fold and streamline along side the nose.

They mount the engine vertically with a slight downward cant. They make a small gas tank from a portion of an eight-ounce tomato juice can. They continue to modify and reduce the size of the tank until the engine runs for only 20 seconds. They figure the model will climb better with the engine angled downward. The downward cant will create more lift by pulling against the cord of the wing. When the engine stops running after 20 seconds of powered flight, the Condor will begin to soar on its own. They correct the weight and balance of the craft after adding the engine by gluing split-shot fishing sinkers inside the fuselage near the tail.

The model is covered with flesh-colored silk-span, and lightly coated with clear, hot-fuel-proof dope. The large wing generates lift from the slightest breath of air. They boys have high hopes for a successful mission on the next launch. They do a test run on the engine and the airframe seems eager to become airborne. The engine is designed for a less massive model, so the Condor should climb slowly.

They finish the model the following morning and pile the thing into Cecil's Chevy, with the end of the wing hanging out a rear door window. They drive to an area north of town, near the airport. The terrain out there is more to their liking than anything near town. The model is assembled a mile north of Amerada at the edge of a Mesquite orchard. They use rubber bands to strap the wings atop the fuselage before they fire up the engine. Toby holds the bird in a launch position over his right shoulder while Axle primes the tank with one last surge of fuel. Toby runs forward and throws the monster into a barely noticeable breeze. The launch looks like someone hurling a cumbersome winged javelin into the air.

The model staggers momentarily before it rights itself and climbs straight ahead. It immediately strikes an air thermal and rises alarmingly until it is a mere dot in the clear blue sky. The engine quits and the Condor begins to soar. The upper air currents are prevailing south.

The model does a chandelle that points it toward town. The boys give chase in the car. The model passes town a half mile to the west, headed in the general direction of Oliver Marsh. The boys charge along back roads at break neck speed trying to keep the thing in sight. Money and several weeks' work have been put into the contraption and they don't want to lose it. Axle especially doesn't want to lose the engine.

They stop periodically to lean out open doors, stand on running boards and watch the thing through a pair of old Japanese binoculars. The field glasses were a present from Axle's adopted Uncle following the war in the Pacific. One lens is slightly out of focus. The Condor leads the boys down roads they never knew existed. They struggle to maintain sight. Finally, the craft runs out of favorable lift and begins a terminal glide near the west edge of the marsh.

The boys run out of road and ideas about a half-mile from the obvious landing zone. The model is about 100 yards above the earth when they abandon the car and head cross country on foot. After leaving the car, they perform high speed running and wading through briars and cactus plants. They ford one small, pearling creek they didn't know existed. There is a final significant run across a short grass, cactus strewn prairie, before the bird disappears behind the trees near the edge of the marsh. The boys traverse a game trail through the trees. They soon find themselves standing on a slight rise above water's edge. Although they have seen the marsh a number of times from the Cub, this is their first time to see it from land.

The marsh is massive in size, startlingly green, lush and beautiful. The same thought strikes them both. The slack water below the mound has to be densely populated by largemouth bass. They both envision slow fishing augmented with spurts of fish feeding frenzy in the greatest fishing spot in the known world.

They see the model about 50 yards away where it hangs cradled in the top of a saw grass clump. The bird dangles above water about ten feet from shore. To their immediate left, an old bronze bell hangs bolted to a large water oak tree. The fulcrum arm of the bell has a short brass chain attached. The bell is about ten feet above the ground.

The boys look at this out-of-place ornament located miles from civilization. They wonder what purpose it serves. On an impulse, Axle pulls the chain and the bell gives a loud clang. The sound peals across the marsh where it disrupts the contentment of a mass of waterfowl. Every water bird within 200 yards thunder into the air to mill around in a whirlwind like swarm.

The mound beneath the bell is about 12 feet above the water

line and directly in front of an open, muddy, pool. The pool edge is outlined by Lily and Dollar pads. The grass and cattails on the opposite side of the pool slowly part. An incredibly large alligator emerges. The creature swims smoothly toward the base of the bank. The gator has an enormous girth and length.

"Jesus Christ," Toby mutters, "look at the size of that critter. That son-of-a-bitch is worth a fortune."

The boys stand with their mouths hanging open as they watch the thing eel through the water. They are both ready to throw in the towel and migrate out of there, when the gator stops at the foot of the bank. From there, it lies peering up at them. They involuntarily back up a couple of steps as they stare into large reptilian eyes. The eyes are flat yellow, dead looking, and without expression. The gator looks at them as though they are being surveyed as a prospective meal.

While they watch, a clear protective covering rises up to cover an eye before the film slides back into its protective receptacle. The gator has winked at them as though to share some dark hidden secret of the marsh.

The beast places its front feet on the edge of the incline and chatters its jaws like castanets in a cabaret. Then it pulls a third of its considerable bulk upward at an angle onto the bank. The gator seems to be evaluating how well the boys would fill a void in its diet. The reptile lies there sunning itself without fear as it expectantly watches the two of them.

"I believe I've heard that bell before," Axle offers with a shudder, "at the occasional odd moment."

Toby just stands looking downward with his mouth half open in stunned surprise.

"I thought that gators are supposed to be shy and evasive. I thought they only fed at night. I'm thinking that someone occasionally comes here, rings the bell and feeds the gator," Axle mutters. "What would one feed a hungry beast of that size...obviously something very large and often."

Toby says, "Better yet, why would anyone want to feed it anything. Let's get the glider and get the hell out of here before that thing decides to have one of us for lunch."

With that thought foremost in their minds, they charge along the top edge of the mound at a canter. Toby sprints into water to mid-calf and snatches the glider from atop the grass. He cradles it lovingly as he wades back to shore. The boys hastily inspect the craft for damage, while watching the water for any sign of motion.

To one side, the bank shows signs of where a boat has been beached. Grooves from aluminum bottom stiffeners are plainly evident on a firm, gently sloped, clay bank. A couple minutes pass before the boys remove the glider's wings. With the glider disassembled for travel, they move back along the trail to the top of the incline. Axle edges to the lip of the bank where he looks down. The gator has disappeared. That discovery gives both of them the willies. They want to know where it is but not enough to conduct a search.

Toby leads them back along the game trail as he studies the hard packed surface ahead. The trail has claw marks both old and new along its entire length. Following this revelation, they come to an abrupt halt. Could the gator have the knowledge and ability to perform an ambush somewhere ahead?

"I hear them things can move really fast out of water," Toby says. "They're fast enough to catch an unwary cow or horse in a short dash on shore."

While the boys ponder their next move, they receive an immediate answer to their question. From somewhere ahead on the trail comes the sound of a struggle, followed by a shallow bleat. Three, small, white tail deer nearly run the boys down as they hurdle along the trail, their eyes are wide with terror. Behind the deer the bleating and thrashing continues, gaining in momentum before ceasing altogether. The boys creep forward until they can see around a bend in the trail.

The gator lies across the trail, where it has just captured lunch in the form of a yearling deer. The gator is busily shaking his head and torso, as it attempts to tear off the animal's head. The deer is dead by now but the gator continues shaking the carcass. Finally it settles into chewing on its prey.

The boys leave the trail. They make a wide detour around the ambush site with the vision of the dead deer clearly etched in their minds.

"This is not a place I would care to come unarmed or unwary," Axle mumbles.

"Roger that," Toby agrees.

Once they're out of the tall bottom growth trees, they break into the shuffling trot perfected during high school athletics. Axle glances to their right, where The-Hundred and Forty-Foot-Hill stands about a quarter mile distant. The side of the hill bordering the marsh is very steep.

The car comes into view in about 20 minutes. They huff up to it and stow the Condor in the back seat with the wing tip again protruding through the open rear door windows.

"Don't bother asking me to swim out into the marsh to retrieve this thing again," Axle mutters.

"Took the words right out of my mouth," Toby answers. "My God, did you see the size of that critter? He could kill and eat a horse."

"Or a person, or a cow, or even maybe half a cape buffalo at one sitting," Axle offers.

"The son-of-a-bitch could probably consume a gray whale, given enough time and opportunity," Toby comments as he grins at his own wit.

"He could also capsize a boat and eat the occupants or come into town and lay waste to Main Street," Axle continues, and then chuckles. "What a monster, I never knew anything like that existed anywhere around here."

"I saw gators like that in Louisiana," Toby comments. "That's just an old one that's lived a long time unmolested by people."

"Knowing something like that lives in the marsh gives bass fishing here an entirely new prospective."

"One gator's not logical," Toby says. "There has to be others just as big or bigger."

Chapter Thirty-Five

They return from fishing the creek one day to discover that Melissa St. Clair is missing. Anxiety in the area comes boiling to the surface. Prodded by this latest development, the boys set about placing their most recent investigative idea in motion.

As a starting point, they will look for the still. They know very little about where to look, but figure somewhere along the creek should be a prime area. Entry into Kraven country by car is from an extension of the refinery road south of town. Going anywhere near the shack by road would be like entering a minefield. They begin by traveling a little used road that runs near the back of The-Hundred-And-Forty-Foot-Hill. They have decided to create observation point somewhere on the slope that faces the creek.

The headlights of the car reveal numerous 'No Trespassing' signs nailed to fence posts. As the sun peeks over the eastern horizon, the boys exit the road to park in a grove of tall live oak brush about a quarter mile from their proposed observation point. They are as close to Kraven country by auto as they are ever likely to get without being noticed.

"This ain't Barney Pepper Cress or Welsh's Milkweed we're wading through," Toby whispers. "This stuff's got thorns."

"We'll need a transfusion if we do this very often," Axle agrees, as he plucks part of a blackberry cane from his left thigh.

A lot of trudging brings them to the summit of the hill. The first thing they see below them is a blue heron flapping across the fire of the sun. To the east, the waving grass of the marsh gives up its chlorophyll tint as it undertakes the gold of dawn. They bear witness to the crushing silence that fills woodland at the first shallow instant of sunrise. Below them at the edge of the marsh stands the slight rise where the school bell is fastened to a tree. A clump of gum trees marks the place where the giant reptile rules that part of the marsh.

The side of the hill nearest the creek is steep and covered with dense shrubs, blackberry briers and a poison oak thicket. Everything is dramatically clear from the crest of their observation hill. They can see a lot of the marsh, a fair section of the creek and a weathered tarpaper shack on the far side of the streambed.

South of the shack in the water near a gravel bar, another heron stands hunched over a riffle like Dracula lost in a time warp. The bird fishes successfully for several minutes before it lifts off in a great struggling flap of wings to glide deeper into the marsh.

Their attention returns to the shack. They discover that their daunting opposition lives in a hovel resembling a cluster of abandoned packing crates. Toby takes one look at the shack through binoculars.

He whispers, "If I ever need a supply of rat pelts, I know where to set the traps."

Down slope from the crest of The-Hundred-And-Forty-Foot-Hill, the boys find a large tree stump in a dense thicket overlooking their area of interest. The stump is four feet across, irregularly shaped, very old and in an advanced stage of decay. A dense layer of limbs and leaves screens the stump from prying eyes that might search the hillside from below. The boys are plainly visible from above, but figure that won't matter since the Kravens are not likely to be airborne.

The boys check each other for anything that might reflect sunlight. Finding nothing, they use their pocketknives to trim away small limbs. The act creates a narrow field of vision downward from the stump. From a sitting position on the old tree bole they can see part of the creek, the front of the shack, a garden and all of the clearing around both productions. They can also see a dense barrier of brush at the bottom of the hill. There are tall trees on both sides of the creek. Their observation post is unfortunately above the upper canopy of the taller trees along the creek bank.

The boys rub damp earth on the freshly cut limb stubs so they are less noticeable. They will carry the fresh cut limbs with them when they return to the car at dusk. Somewhere along the way, they will thrust them into the earth butt first. This act will hide the limbs by making them appear as dying brush.

With the field of view finally prepared, they begin their

observation from beneath an unrelenting sun. Within minutes, they begin to feel like ants under a magnifying glass. The area looks inviting for what they need, but it takes only a few minutes for them to discover why they haven't done this more often. The stump and the surrounding area prove to be home to at least 1,000 nickel-back wood ticks plus a multitude of large black ants.

While on the stump, they quickly become a component part of the tick and ant colony. In addition to that discovery, the area around the stump is densely screened from all sides by heavy brush. The foliage will vector any breeze above them. As time passes, the sun scorches down so hot that sprinkler water wouldn't have been able to reach the ground.

Aside from the insects, the first day constitutes a fascinating new pastime that passes slowly. On this first day, they have infrequent sightings of people moving around near the shack. Clyde and Luther take turns weeding the garden. All three of the current residents work individual shifts at the still.

The garden is an interesting plot. It contains stepping-stones between the rows that allow the men to weed and harvest even when the earth is wet. The Kravens bring water from the creek to the plants by means of a carry-yolk with a bucket dangling from each end. They pour the water into individual underground containers buried at the base of each major plant. The boys speculate that the containers are large tin cans with holes punched in the bottom. Nearly everything grows upward as the plants climb aloft on columns of concrete reinforcing wire. The cylinders are about two feet in diameter and about five feet tall. The columns are kept upright by being wired together in clusters of three. In that fashion they form a triangle that supports the aggregate columns. Tomatoes, pole beans, squash, cantaloupe and cucumbers grow up the columns. The things not grown on cylinders are okra, carrots and potatoes. Pole beans out number the other plants in quantity by more than two to one. Whatever else the Kravens are doing, they are eating well from the fruits of their own labors.

Observing work at the garden, while interesting, produces no worthwhile information. By day's end, they vow to prepare themselves better for their next observation session.

The Kravens move back and forth across the creek by means of a footbridge built atop a large pipeline spanning the stream. The top of the pipe has been modified with cables and wood to create a suspension footbridge.

The following morning, they hose down the area near the stump with an aerosol can of DDT. In less than an hour, the odor dissipates along with the insects. Their kit now includes a boat cushion apiece to sit upon. They also bring two olive drab military style ponchos for when it rains. They also bring two large glass Clorox bottles filled with water.

Day two finds them hunkered down on their stump of choice just before daybreak. Several hours into the interminable watch they are both filled with an almost debilitating depression. For yet a second day, nothing is happening below them. The scene turns into hell with a river view.

The boys call it quits at dusk and return home. The first two days of spying by the young global talent pool on the hill has been something less than disappointing.

They are able to return to the stump for the third day only because the earth remains too wet for them to work at blasting a stake line. By mid-morning, the sun has appeared behind clouds, but it continues to radiate more than 100 degrees of heat. No breeze circulates through the brush at the stump level, so by 10:00, they are thoroughly uncomfortable. The brush-enclosed area of the stump is as stifling as though they are waist deep in a stagnant pool. The observers watch in slack-jawed silence as they sweat in earnest.

By the time the sun reaches its zenith, they are ready to be turned and basted. Babies are undoubtedly born and weaned while they stare at the area of the creek, the shack and the pipeline bridge. At dusk, they gladly trudge to the car. They are both painfully aware that they are again leaving their observation site without any useful information.

Daybreak Thursday finds them back on the stump. Memories of the preceding days have become emotionally persuasive. Axle wears a dark green colored extra-long billed cap, of a type favored by saltwater anglers. Toby brings along a discarded elderly black fedora that originally belonging to his grandfather.

One look at the black hat causes Axle to remark in a low voice, "That thing on your head will become a fully functioning inverted barbecue pit by 10:00."

Toby makes no comment. He merely sits and sweats. By mid-morning, the black hat occupies a position on the limb of a bush behind the stump. By noon, the temperature has cooled to a modest 93 degrees of wet heat. Humidity reigns. All the observers have accomplished so far is that they are another two and a half days older and Toby has sun burned the top of his head.

Axle mumbles in resignation, "If this is the leading edge of a rescue mission, I wonder what the main body will feel like?"

Aggravation multiplies by the square of the day's discomfort.

While the boys bathe in sweat and humidity, the theme song from Gone with the Wind begins to play in Axle's head. Songs of the mind are something that happens to him frequently. Sometimes he hums the tune for days on end.

While the tune runs its internal gamut, he remembers a comment by an old banjo guru from Wyoming. Axle had asked him one time why he learned to play the banjo. The old man pondered the question before answering, "My dad had a banjo. If he'd had a guitar I would probably have played that. I imagine a tune and it comes out through my fingers but don't expect me to tell you why. It's like there's something in my soul that music touches. I listen to a song and it transports me somewhere else, even perhaps back in time. If you took away my banjo it would be like cutting off my hands."

Axle speaks to Toby in a low voice, "Can you play a musical instrument?"

"Naw," Toby says, "I got probably less musical skill than your average bullfrog."

"I can't either," Axle mutters before he begins to chuckle at the comparison, "but I always wanted to be able to play something so I could write a song. Somethin' classical like what we heard in that movie the other night, *"Tiara,"* I think it was called. Anyway, that song is hung up in my mind. I can't make myself stop wantin' to hum it."

Toby looks at his buddy for a while before he says, "Well, don't start now. If you do then one of the Kravens will doubtless climb up here and shoot us."

Axle smiles as he stifles a giggle. In less than a minute, he is busy trying to suppress another giggle. Suddenly they are both engaged in trying to stifle laughter. Not laughing requires a mighty effort before their giggle reflexes finally subside. Nearly ten minutes pass before they are finally over the idiotic burst of humor. Shortly Axle hums a couple of muted bars of the song, and then for the next few minutes they writhe in an agony of unexpended mirth.

"If we had paper," Toby says, "we could practice origami." Immediately, they have returned to the violent mirth mode.

While they fend off laughter, they never lose sight of the fact that they don't know what they are doing. Given time, they will probably come up with a suitable solution to their problem but chances are it will violate the cruel and unusual punishment provisions of the constitution.

Time drones on. The view below them is only slightly more interesting then the biography of a necktie. Hours pass at a terminally dull plod with frequent glances at Toby's wristwatch.

"After thought orphan that I am," Toby growls in a muted voice, "I can imagine the Kravens finding us up here whereupon they will use us as though we are a roll of toilet paper. Nobody's gonna come lookin' for us here when we turn up missing. If we're caught, nobody will know where to look."

"When we decided to come here," Axle mutters, "I wouldn't have given you a set of poorly done retread tires for our chances of finding anything useful. After this many days of wasted energy, you can forget the tires, I wouldn't give a fig for the idea of coming here."

"Your dad's knowledge of how to research these people would be useful," Toby whispers. "Anything else is less so."

"Maybe," Axle agrees, "but he ain't here, and we are. Now we're gonna have to make the best of it."

"Have you come up with any other ideas about what we should do?" Toby asks as he peers through the lop-sided set of Japanese binoculars.

"Only this," Axle says, as he slaps a bug climbing upward inside his pant leg. "We're probably going to have to start doing this solo until the weekend arrives. In another day, the ground's gonna be dry enough to work."

"We'll have to go to work on Monday for sure," Axle speculates, "unless it rains this weekend."

Friday arrives and it rains all day. The boys sit in the rain for several hours as they achieve a new degree of misery. That is when they decide to crawl down the hill to see if the still is where they think it is, beneath the tall trees. Wood smoke and the odor of sour mash have tweaked their imagination long enough.

Thirty feet from the stump they have to ditch their ponchos. The rubberized cloth keeps snagging beneath their knees. Additionally the fabric makes a distinctive sound every time it touches foliage.

When they are free of the ponchos, Axle authors a round-about route to the grove beneath the hill. Crawling is slow going. The blackberry briars are unrelentingly torturous. In about an hour, they find themselves within 20 yards of their objective. At that point, an impenetrable wall of brambles stops them. The only thing the extended crawl has accomplished for them is that they have accumulated about a half-pound of chiggers apiece and a handful of wood ticks. The parasites are their only reward for time spent beneath the brush trying to approach the still.

In the end, the boys crouch about 20 yards from the moonshine cooker while they view the clearing around the apparatus. What they can see is the top of the contrivance. The device is screened from three sides by brush and stacked wood. There is a tin roof of corrugated metal near where a long copper coil snakes along an eave. The coil disappears from view below the roof.

They decide that the still is about eight miles from town by road. By creek, it's about two miles, maybe more. Moonshine is being manufactured 100 yards from the Kraven shack, but on the west side of the creek. The still is hidden beneath 100-foot tall trees and surrounded by undergrowth taller than a man's head.

The only thing they have determined thus far is that the Kravens live in an unpainted, severely weathered wooden structure at the base of a short hill, about 50 feet from the creek. Green mineral coated tar paper covers the entire structure. The original shack has additions scabbed onto it in random fashion. The total effect is of dynamic competition as to what part will collapse first.

Drinking water appears to come from a well near the center of the clearing. A privy is situated about 30 yards downstream from the house at the edge of the creek bank.

About 50 feet from the shack, a 12-inch pipeline painted-silver surfaces from the earth at a shallow angle. The pipe spans the creek supported by a suspension system composed of steel cable slings and pipe trusses. The pipeline has been turned into a suspension bridge by the use of wooden planks and additional cable. The total length of the bridge appears to be more than 20 yards.

One of the three men is always in attendance at the still except for one rare occasion. On Friday, the rain hampered the still's operation so Mongo went there for only an hour. When he crossed the bridge, he carried a large green-colored dinner pail.

"Road kills are living better than the Kravens," Toby mutters, as he peers through the binoculars.

The binoculars have a lens out of focus. During a time when nothing is moving below, Toby takes the optical device apart to see if he can fix the defect. He can't see anything to repair. The hour-long episode nearly turns both of them into thumb suckers when he drops a small screw into the humus near the stump. For the rest of the afternoon, one of them is always on their knees searching for the screw.

"You've got the mechanical aptitude of a cow," Axle whines in disbelief as he combs the ground around the stump with his fingers for the hundredth time. An hour later, Axle puts the heel of his hand on the screw. He feels the object before he sees it.

"Don't tell me you found the damned thing?" Toby mutters in exasperation.

"Hell, yes," Axle responds, "now don't drop it again."

They both giggle. Axle produces the screw. Toby has a hell of a time putting the thing back together but he eventually succeeds.

After all that effort, the eyepiece remains out of focus. The boys continue to stare through the good lens with one eye closed.

The single eyepiece allows the observers their first close looks at Luther, Clyde, and Luke while they are in their own element. Since the fight with Mongo, the boys have avoided the Kravens like the heartbreak of psoriasis. Now they study them in close detail while they are on daily parade.

While Toby studies Luke through the binoculars, he observes aloud, "These people are so tough they probably all use the same toothbrush."

The boys decide that Luke looks like a throwback to the Neanderthal period. He stands about six foot seven and weighs an estimated 300 pounds. Part of that is devoted to a hard looking oversized belly. Neither of the boys are fooled by his appearance though, he is also strong. The part of his face not covered by hair is pocked with the ravages of early acne. All visible skin appears to have the surface texture of a concrete aggregate wall. Dramatic craggy eyebrows protrude from a shelf above each eye. They resemble giant forehead-dwelling dark caterpillars. His beard is a curly tempest of black and silver hair that begins just below his deep-set eyes. He has about a 16-inch forehead. The boys judge him to be in his late thirties or early forties. His only clothing appears to be a pair of unpatched faded blue overalls.

Luke rolls his own cigarettes. He has a powerful muscle structure with arms that appear to long for his body. His normal facial expression is a deranged glassy-eyed stare. He incessantly breathes through his mouth. A fact worth remembering is that he dwarfs Mongo. All future caution will be fueled by their memory of him through the binoculars.

There is another person at the still periodically. His name is Luther. Luther is very reclusive. He rarely ventures outside the shack. Luther is a scaled down slightly less impressive version of Luke. The boys learn his name when Mongo yells at him one day from across the creek.

Clyde Kraven is seldom in residence. The boys speculate that he's probably on the road somewhere expanding the bootleg business.

Clyde is more normal looking than the others but with the same profusion of dark hair as Mongo. He has no unusual physical characteristics. Physically he is about as imposing as an accountant.

There does not appear to be any women in residence, which is a small wonder considering the primitive conditions and the nature of the people living there. Any woman willing to stay at the shack would need to possess the mentality of a mushroom. Even then, a chain and collar might be required as a diversion against a momentary burst of sanity.

All the Kravens' waking hours are devoted to supporting the fire at the still, which they tend 24 hours a day. To this end, they cut vast quantities of firewood, but none is apparently harvested near the still. They truck wood to the shack with the pickup. They employ a wheelbarrow to transport the wood across the bridge to the still. The boys figure they use either wood or kerosene for cooking at the shack because no power line or propane tank is evident.

Wheelbarrow labor is performed with little apparent effort. Cords of stacked wood cover the area around the shack like the walls of a medieval fortress. The men carry .22 Cal. semi-automatic rifles everywhere they go. The boys can anticipate taking more bullets then Bonnie and Clyde if they screw this up within range of any of the Kravens.

Moonshine is dispensed to the public in fruit jars with zinc lids. There are a lot of jars stored in their original cardboard containers beneath the porch overhang at the shack. The boxes are transported back and forth to the still by means of a two wheeled furniture dolly with oversized tires. The finished product is taken to the house to await distribution. The wheelbarrow explains Mongo's overly developed neck and shoulders. The boys speculate about how many wheelbarrow trips it would take to produce that sort of muscle structure, probably a gazillion.

The Kravens have a trotline spanning the creek near the shack. Somebody runs it twice a day. Every three days, a pair of them seines a shallow slew at the edge of the marsh. The bait from the seining expedition is dumped into a hardware cloth live-box attached to the shack-side boat dock. What they seine from the slew appears to be crawdads, small fish and minnows.

The catfish, drum, buffalo and carp taken from the trotline go into a larger live-box at the dock. The live-box eliminates the need for a refrigerator. For water travel, the Kravens employ two 16-foot aluminum John-boats powered by fairly new, 20 horsepower outboard motors.

The only thing that points toward a woman being in the area is the trip across the bridge by Mongo when he appears to carry food in a lunch pail. Food is taken across the footbridge every day about noon.

The distribution area for the rot-gut booze is apparently somewhere far removed from Amerada. Mongo makes deliveries in the truck twice a week. The route of distribution is unknown but it takes him about ten hours to make delivery and return. The truck leaves at dusk and is back by daylight.

Neither Axle nor Toby have seen any moonshine at the various local parties they've attended. Mongo never flashes it around the school kids or carries any in his truck at school. The boys have surveyed the vehicle at every opportunity. Since the fight, the boys are operating under clouds of discontent wherever the Kravens are concerned. Unfortunately, they run the risk of discovery every time they approach the vehicle.

The boys will continue to watch from their stump until further observations are considered unnecessary. Time spent at the stump has been nearly as boring as watching paint dry or cement crack.

The boys return to the stump before daylight that day. They return to stump watching only because they don't really have anything else to do. By 9:00, a blue bird day has blossomed with sunshine of sufficient velocity to start Kingfishers chattering in the trees along the creek bank. That's when good old Sheriff Harvey makes an appearance at the shack in his official county vehicle. Mongo and Clyde meet him near the front door. Harvey talks with Clyde who continually jabs Harvey in the chest with a forefinger as he speaks. Heated words are exchanged. When the conversation ends, Mongo goes into the shack and returns with a cardboard box that he loads into trunk of the sheriff's car. Following the exchange, Harvey walks across the pipeline bridge. He remains at the still for nearly an hour. After visiting the still, he returns across the bridge and immediately departs.

"What's he doing at the still?" Axle wonders aloud.

"He's obviously not splitting fire wood, I'll wager," Toby offers. "Maybe he's performing some sort of sacred male, bonding ritual."

By the time he departs, the boys have established a professional conflict of interest that was previously only assumed. In their minds, they hear the sound of an assumption shattering. Clyde, not Harvey, is the apparent brains of the operation.

The next day at various intervals, police cruisers visit the shack. There are always two occupants and they both cross the pipeline bridge to the still. They return one at a time at about half-hour intervals. The boys wonder what the attraction is at the still. If they wanted moonshine, all anyone could ever drink is stacked just inside the front door of the shack.

Is it possible there is a woman at the still?

An hour after the cops have departed, an unidentified vehicle with out-of-state license plates visits the compound. The two occupants go to the still for a visit. Late in the day, the mayor of Amerada pays a visit. He also goes to the still. He is a cousin of the Kravens'. His name is Ralph Corbin.

We need to have a look at the still.

Stump sitting has extended to 14 days. The information gathered extends only to tick, chigger and mosquito bites. The weather has been cooperative, with six days and nights of rain during the 14 days. The rain has kept the ground too wet for them to work.

A liquid, golden-orange sunset puts Tuesday, August 15, 1950 to bed, as the boys jog back to the car by following a deer trail that intercepts the road. They have planned a canoe trip for Thursday night, two nights hence. A beautiful sunset concludes another Wednesday too wet to work, but just right for stump sitting. This will be their last day before the canoe trip.

"We've spent damned near two weeks modeling in-active wear for the insects in the brush on the slope of the hill," Toby growls, as he hurdles a blackberry clump. "Our trips out here have raised more questions than answers."

"Yeah. Blackberry brambles is an ordeal that makes me wonder why I'm doin' this."

"We've just spent another day locked in a green hell," Toby mutters. "I'm gonna sleep like a baby tonight."

"We've still got tomorrow to look forward to," Axle offers. "Maybe things will get better."

"They can't get much worse, that's for certain," Toby sympathizes. "Unless the Kravens take exception to our being up there and decide to have a look around."

"You ever think about what we should do if Mongo comes up top on a scouting mission?" Axle asks. "Do we stand and fight or run?"

"We do whatever the occasion seems to warrant," Toby answers.

Chapter Thirty-Six

They leave Toby's truck in his parent's driveway while they eat supper. They return to Axle's home after the meal. As they enter the house through the back door, the phone rings. Axle answers. It's Pearl Woodling.

"Is Sarah with you?" she asks, with apprehension flooding her voice.

"No, ma am," Axle answers. "I haven't seen her for a couple days."

"She went to the store over an hour ago," Pearl wails. "Her father went looking for her and found the car in the store parking lot with the driver's door open. The keys were in the ignition, but Sarah was nowhere around."

"Maybe she went somewhere with a friend," Axle answers, as a knot of anxiety forms in his stomach. "I'll be right there Mrs. Woodling." Axle hangs up and turns to Toby. "Sarah is missing. Let's go."

This can't be happening, not to Sarah.

Axle and Toby go to the Woodling house. Afterward, they scour the town with their emotions hovering near the surface. For the next three hours, they nearly drive the tires off the truck as they search for her.

Everybody who lost someone did this very same thing, and found nothing.

Axle feels as though he is about to have a nervous breakdown. All he has remaining are the scathing bittersweet memories of a love lost. He recalls the things first time lovers remember: first touch of hands, first moment alone, first kiss, first promise, and first joyous heart. What remains of her in his mind are the memories to be cherished for as long as he breathes. The next eight hours feature aimless driving.

Axle says, "Remember that quotation from English class? Miss Biggs said it was by Edmund Burke an 18th century British statesman:

the only thing necessary for the triumph of evil is for good men to do nothing."

"Yeah," Toby answers. "As I recall it was one of your favorites the first time you heard it."

"Well, what we've got here is good men doing nothing. It has to be the Kravens. We've got to go there in the canoe."

"Yep," Toby agrees, "we've got no other choice."

"Tonight, about midnight seems right," Axle mumbles, as he turns toward home.

"Okay," Toby growls, "done deal. We won't tell anyone; we'll just go."

"Let's have one last look from the stump," Axle comments. "If they've got her out there, maybe we'll get lucky and see her."

Chapter Thirty-Seven

Dawn Thursday morning finds the boys back among the bugs on their stump. The day dawns with low hanging clouds. The threat of rain is in the air as they watch the hovel across the creek. The good lens of the binocular still shows the same old scene. <u>While they are busy grappling with the definition of lawlessness as it applies to the Kravens, the gasp inducer happens.</u> Luke emerges from the shack prodding Sarah ahead of him.

She wears an unbuttoned men's blue work shirt but is otherwise naked. She is without shoes, socks or pants. Her hands are bound behind her back as he propels her toward the creek bank. Axle is looking through the binoculars when the procession emerges from the shack. He does a double take before he jabs Toby with an elbow almost screaming, "Sarah."

Toby comes up off the stump in a half crouch while he stares hard at the clearing. A light mist rises from the ground as rain begins to fall. Luke and Sarah continue their walk across the hard packed earth to eventually disappear below the creek bank.

Suddenly, the boys know everything they need to know. The Kravens are the ones who make women disappear. This latest knowledge brings a cold chill of reality that settles over them like morning fog on a marsh. What must happen next is terrifying for them. They must devise a plan to make the Kravens disappear.

Luke and Sarah have been out of sight for perhaps two minutes when the stillness below them is broken by a sharp skirling scream that ends too abruptly. Shortly thereafter, there is the unmistakable sound of an outboard motor starting. Within seconds, a boat appears headed downstream into the marsh. Luke is at the tiller. Sarah sits on the middle seat in front of him. She is staring straight ahead.

Axle turns toward Toby with gigantic eyes as he utters just three words, "The gator hole."

They both rise as a single simultaneous thought rifles through their minds. They now understand the purpose of the bell. They both believe that Sarah is about to die. They leap from the stump as they begin to race uphill through brush.

Years of running two miles almost every day with an occasional ten miler thrown in now means the difference between life and death for Sarah.

The boys have always carried at least one gun with them when they visit the stump. Today, Toby is carrying Axle's scope sighted, Mossberg, M-151, semi-automatic .22 Cal. rifle. The gun had been his birthday present at age ten.

Toby has the rifle and a slight lead as they emerge from the tall brush at the top of the hill. Ahead, a terrace of laced vines drips downward across their line of flight. The vines make running difficult. Axle stumbles repeatedly as Toby's lead increases. They pass the edge of the vine orchard to jet into an open space filled with Pin Cushion Cactus plants.

The boys plan to intercept the game trail they both remember from when they retrieved the condor from the marsh. Their path lies through rough terrain that fords at least one creek. There will be an abundance of brush, weeds and trees packed into the creek bottom. While they run, reality comes flooding back from wherever it had taken a hike to earlier.

Toby carries the rifle at port arms, as they run. For perhaps the first time in their lives, they push themselves beyond their physical limits. They are suddenly engaged in the race of their lives. They move easily, with their breath surging through open mouths and flared nostrils. From their left comes the faint sound of the outboard rising and falling as Luke maneuvers along the maze of channels in the marsh. Even though they are running flat-out, Axle feels like they are moving with all the speed of Skippy the Wonder Sloth.

Axle remembers something his dad told him as an inspirational thought for high school sports. "There are two kinds of heart, one lives in your chest and pumps blood. The other lives in your soul and pumps courage." Axle's soul heart is pumping overtime.

They plunge through brush before they cross the creek. They plow through unfamiliar terrain near the stream bed at a dead run.

Finally, the entrance to the game trail comes into view. As they turn onto it, they hear the school bell toll. It rings three times before it falls silent. Above them, the sun gleams like a freshly minted gold piece as it peeks through a break in the clouds.

The boys pound along the trail as they attempt to run quietly. They both feel as though they sound like a stampeding buffalo herd. Toby slows as they round the last bend before the lip of the incline. Thirty feet ahead, beyond a brush screen, lay the top of the clay bank. From the undergrowth ahead, they can hear the sound of Luke talking. They are perhaps 15 feet from the school bell when Sarah screams. Luke's joyful cackle splits the morning stillness.

"Ya see 'im, girly?" he growls. "Ya do what yer told or I'll feed ya to 'im."

The boys hesitate for only a second as they peer through a gap in the veil of greenery. Sarah screams again, "Oh, God, oh God." Her voice condenses before it trails off into nothing.

Through the mint-colored leafy scrum of brush they can see Sarah kneeling at the top of the bank. Luke stands behind her holding her in place against his thighs.

Toby surges through the last wisp of undergrowth with the rifle held high. As he emerges, Luke turns toward him. As Luke turns, Toby gives him a horizontal butt stroke with the rifle stock that strikes the giant near his left temple. The blow sounds like someone hitting a side of beef with an ax.

Luke is propelled sideways from the force of the blow. The butt stroke produces immediate unconsciousness. Luke's body turns limp as it topples in a slow somersault that passes over Sarah. His passage bends her forward. Everything seems to move in slow motion as Luke turns in the air to impact the bank halfway to the waterline. His body is slack at impact where it rolls once, before it slides to the edge of the water. Luke lies as limp as a down-filled pillow.

The yellow unblinking eyes of the gator stare at what he has received. With a dramatic lunge, Luke's head disappears between opposing rows of teeth. The gator and his prey vanish beneath the surface of the pool.

Riled mud and disturbed water plants boil to the surface for a long minute before the struggle ceases. The rolling water awards the occasional flash of gator and various man parts. As suddenly as it began, the frenzied motion ends. The surface of the pool swirls as it bubbles sluggishly before it calms once more. To one side of the pool near the crown of the fallen tree, a streak of blood emerges.

As Toby administers the butt stroke, Axle grabs Sarah by her long hair in the same motion. Luke's body drags her forward, causing her to slide over the edge of the embankment. Axle's grip on her prevents her plunge into the reptile's lair. At the conclusion of the butt stroke, Toby grabs her upper arm. Together, the boys hoist her to the top of the incline. While Toby concentrates on the gator hole, Axle produces a pocket knife. He cuts the rope from around Sarah's wrists, arms and neck. At first, Sarah stands facing away from her rescuers as she stares downward toward the gator hole. She stands transfixed by the still barely rolling water. Everyone is mesmerized by what has happened.

Suddenly Sarah begins to back away from the bank. Her movements are made powerful by a fear driven need to flee. With her bonds removed she quickly turns to run. Her eyes are wide with terror.

She slams into Axle's wide open arms with a hint of recognition. The tears come then. While terror engulfs her, she clings to him trembling as she cries with great racking sobs. Toby alternates his attention between the two of them and the gator hole. He stoops to pick up the mass of rope where it lies knotted in a pile. He flings the white clot into the muddy water. The cotton rope floats half submerged for half a minute before it slowly sinks.

He growls, "Let's get the hell out of here before that thing decides to come back for dessert."

The three of them proceed along the trail toward the distant car. Sarah still wears the man's shirt, but she has no shoes. The boys alternate carrying her piggyback. While they travel, Sarah has moments of silence followed by sobs of hysteria.

"Who brought you to the shack?" Axle asks, her during a period of silence.

"Mongo and Luke kidnapped me in the parking lot of the store. I was struck from behind with something. When I awoke we were on the road to the shack in their truck."

"How many people know you're here?" Axle asks.

"For sure all the Kravens at the shack and probably all the ones on the police force," she says. "Clete came out last night. He took his turn raping me. Others were invited for today. They planned to welcome me into my crib."

"Holy Christ," Toby mutters.

With that comment, he turns to run backwards so he can watch their back trail.

"I wasn't very cooperative," Sarah sobs, "so Luke brought me to the gator hole for an object lesson. The trip was successful. I would have done anything to prevent a return visit to that place."

"We saw you leave in the boat," Axle pants. "We ran all the way from The-Hundred-And-Forty-Foot-Hill."

Against all apparent odds, we have solved a more than 10-year-old mystery.

They stop so Toby can take over the carry. Sarah clings to him in a kind of stunned silence. Her facial expression is as though the predatory animals living at the edge of the swamp have stolen her soul.

She wails, "Last night was my worst nightmare. I'll never get over what happened."

"Were there any other women out there?" Axle asks, as he turns to look behind them.

"I didn't see anyone. While Clete took his turn, I heard the others talking about someone else. There may be another woman over there, I don't know. Oh God," she wails, as she begins to sob anew. When she is able to talk again, she whimpers, "Last night, I dreamed everyone in town got up and closed their windows so they couldn't hear me screaming."

Her voice makes a slight hiccupping sound before she returns to sobbing. Axle puts his hand on her shoulder. She turns her head to press his hand hard against her face. Her body continues to shudder as she rides Toby's back. In a while, they swap the carry again. Axle lasts another 150 yards before stopping. One more swap and Toby carries her the rest of the way. The one not carrying always carries the rifle as he watches the back trail for any sign that they are being followed.

"Wonder how long we've got before they miss Luke?" Toby mutters. "Any ideas what they'll think happened to him and Sarah?"

"If we're lucky," Axle answers, "maybe they'll think the gator got 'em both. The problem is that gators don't generally eat large prey immediately. The gator will stash Luke at the bottom of his hole underneath that water-logged tree. Several days from now when he's properly aged, the feast will begin. If we're lucky, they won't look for him. They'll figure the gator got them both, so they won't do anything."

"There's one thing for sure," Toby growls. "Ain't nobody gonna go into that muddy pool looking for a body. Our problem is that we can't count on them not lookin'. Whatever we do, we can't take Sarah home. We have to stash her someplace where she won't be found if they decide to search for her."

"They might figure she got away," Axle considers. "It's not rational for them to think that the gator got them both."

"What we gonna do with Sarah?" Toby asks. "Can't take her home, that's the first place they'll look."

"I want to go home," Sarah sobs.

"Can't do that, honey," Axle mutters with grim determination. "If they decide to look for you, the first place they'll look is at your parents' house. We have to stash you in a place where they'd never think to look."

"We've got her back", Axle considers aloud. "The cops are in on this thing all the way to their eyebrows. We have to hope that they don't believe she's a living witness. We'll hide her in the abandoned house in the weed patch next door to our place. They'd never look there."

It's midday when the fugitives arrive at the car. They decide that Sarah must not be seen during the ride home. There is but one place with that much security. She has to ride in the rumble seat with the lid closed.

She reluctantly agrees to be locked in the rumble seat before they begin their trip home. At first, she is a bit claustrophobic, but she eventually settles down for the short ride to the Mannheim residence.

Near the edge of town, a patrol car begins to trail them. It follows their vehicle most of the way home. Half a block from their destination, the cop turns on his gumball light. Axle pulls onto the ditch bridge before he stops.

Jeb Kraven climbs out of the cruiser. As he approaches Axle he twangs, "Goin' a little fast there, weren't you sonny?"

"I was doin' 20," Axle replies, as he leans against the body of his car adjacent to the rumble seat.

"Your speedometer must be wrong," Jeb offers as he proceeds to write a ticket.

Before he makes the first entry on the form, Jeb's radio summons him to his squad car. He climbs in and listens intently before he responds into the mike. He then digs out on the gravel street at high speed. He rounds the first corner to be rapidly lost from view. Both boys give a sigh of relief.

Axle pulls forward to the garage. A full-bloom sunstroke sort of mid-afternoon is now in progress. Puffy gray clouds to the south show thin shards of rain stringing down from them. Overhead, the sky is nearly clear. Sarah has to be removed from the car without anyone seeing her.

"You suppose that sucker will come back when he's finished with the call?" Toby speculates.

"Probably," Axle growls with a note of resignation. "Open the garage. No need to tempt fate anymore than necessary."

Axle puts his face close to the rumble seat before he says, "Can you hear me Sarah?"

From inside the trunk, Sarah answers, "Just barely."

"Don't make a sound," Axle offers. "We just had a close call with Jeb Kraven. He's gone now but he might come back. I'm gonna put the car in the garage and close the doors."

Sarah gives a muffled, "Okay," then retreats into silence.

After the car is parked deck first inside the garage, the boys climb out and then race into the house. When they're safe inside, Axle makes three ham sandwiches and takes a bottle of Delaware Punch from the fridge. After he pops the top with the counter mounted bottle opener, he returns to the garage. Sarah is claustrophobic again and wants out. Axle has to crack the rumble seat lid so he can hand her the sandwich and pop bottle.

Before he closes and locks the rumble seat, Axle places a hand through the opening onto her arm.

"I can't let you out, sugar; all our lives are at stake. That fact overrides any other emotion any of us might have. You've got to stay in there until it's dark or until it begins to rain. That's when we'll be able to move you."

Sarah answers, "Okay, I'll make it. Just get me out of here as soon as you can."

"Don't answer if anyone talks to you. If it's us, we'll open the lid before we say anything. Kraven could return. If he does, he may try to inspect the rumble seat. We'll deal with that if it happens."

Sarah gives a diminutive, "Okay," from inside the car.

She is now more afraid of being found than of confinement in the locked compartment. The boys sit on the rear deck of the house until a steady downpour begins. When that happens, they sneak into the backyard of the weed-choked lot next door.

They make a roundabout entry through the weed patch that originates along the back fence. At the back door, they find a very old hasp screwed into the door jamb. A thoroughly aged padlock secures the hasp. Axle returns to the garage where he retrieves his lock picks. The lock snicks opens in just a few seconds. They enter into the darkness of a long abandoned building.

The house is quite old, but remains fully furnished with aged furniture. A layer of dust covers everything. There are clothes in the closets with an oilcloth cover on the small, square, dining room table. The table is set for two with place mats and miscellaneous silverware still in place. It looks as though someone went somewhere for food and never returned.

There are three Aladdin kerosene lamps in every room. There is a bathroom with an old claw-foot bathtub. A toothbrush lies on the washbasin near a flattened tube of toothpaste. Axle tries the tap. The water has been turned off. That fact will necessitate carrying water for the commode to flush and for drinking.

The rain continues in sheets. The boys release Sarah from her confinement and sprint her into the house. Toby, in a fit of ingenuity, finds the main water valve in a cast iron receptacle in the ground near the front door. Axle picks the lock securing the gate valve. They use a monkey wrench to turn on the tap. Now they have water for their fugitive.

One corner of the living room contains a large table with books between bookends on the top. Between the legs of the table is a partially filled five-gallon can of kerosene. The kerosene will provide fuel for the lamps. The stove is also a kerosene-fired model, but it can't be used. Smoke or condensation coming from the vent pipe would give away the hiding place. They will need to carry food from next door. With that arrangement, Sarah can hide there almost indefinitely. The old house provides a temporary hiding place.

"Where do we go from here?" Toby mutters.

Chapter Thirty-Eight

Luther awakens from sleep at the still around mid-afternoon. He sits up on the cot where he stretches before he looks around. He pulls his pocket watch from a bib pocket. It's past time for the shift change. *Where the hell is Luke*, he mutters to himself.

He's probably pestering the new girl at the shack. Luther brings the boiler fire back to life with several slivers of wood. When the fire is to his liking, he peers across the creek. Not much is visible through the undergrowth, so he crosses the bridge to the shack.

Mongo lies stretched out on a cot in his underwear. Luther shakes him awake. "Luke's gone and I got no relief," he mutters.

Mongo rubs his eyes with the back of both fists as he growls, "He took Miss Sarah to have a look at Lucifer so she'll be more cooperative. He's probably enjoyin' himself so much he's forgot to come back."

"Yeah, I know, but I been over thar fer nine hours an' I want some grub."

Mongo says, "Ya'll could stand to miss a few meals, Uncle. We'll let him be. Go back to work, I'll be along directly."

Luther leaves by the front door. When he's gone, Mongo goes outside in his skivvies to relieve himself at the edge of the clearing. When he returns to the shack, he grabs his rifle. He walks to the creek bank where he checks the boats. One boat remains missing. He moves to the center of the bridge. There he leans on a cable hanger while he studies the marsh. There is nothing unusual out there, just the usual tall marsh grass waving beneath low flying birds.

He scratches himself as he considers what his Uncle is up to. He's probably teaching Miss Sarah to play the skin flute. That most preferred act has been something Miss Sarah has been reluctant to perform. His cock springs to life as he considers what it will be like when she fully submits to their most favored form of sexual servitude. Next will come anal intercourse, another favored perversion. The problem with normal intercourse is that she will eventually become pregnant and need to be disposed of in the usual manner. Sex slaves are becoming harder and harder to come by.

Melissa, on the other hand, has proven more acceptable to instructions. Shortly, he will determine how well she has adapted to her newest occupation. His man-meat stiffens at the prospect of watching her service his cock.

When he tires of the view of the marsh, he returns to the house where he serves himself a bowl of deer meat stew from a black-iron kettle on the stove. When he's finished, he drinks water from the dipper in the water crock. Finally, he concedes to the thought that he must go work the still. He pulls his overalls on over a white T-shirt. There is the slight tickle of an uneasy feeling as he crosses the bridge to relieve Luther.

When Luther has departed, he prods Melissa awake. She addresses his need from a kneeling position while he lies back on the cot. His head is constantly elevated so he can watch her perform. Watching the rise and fall of her head gives him a sense of sexual power that he has rarely known. She has learned her new trade well. He now allows her to perform without holding her head the way he normally does.

When Luke still has not returned after three more hours, Mongo crosses the creek to the shack. Luther is on his cot asleep. Mongo nudges him with his foot before he mutters, "I'm gonna go have a look for Luke. Maybe he had motor trouble. I'll be back shortly."

Luther grunts before he returns to sleep.

Mongo drops into the remaining boat. He starts the outboard and then heads along the creek channel into the marsh. Mongo rarely goes to the gator hole. It has been some time since his last trip. Consequently, he makes a wrong turn and he has to backtrack to find the right boat-road.

He finds Luke's boat nosed onto the shore in the usual place. The motor is tilted up out of the water. Mongo beaches his boat alongside Luke's before he treads the path to the top of the clay bank.

The water hole below is muddy but the Alligator is nowhere in sight. Neither is Luke or Sarah. He studies the pool in a search for an answer. He notices a hank of white cotton rope snarled among the water weeds on the far side of the pool. Mongo's heart skips a beat when he concludes that Luke has fed Miss Sarah to the gator. Lucifer has obviously eaten everything but the rope. He didn't want that to be the case because he enjoyed having Miss Sarah around. Her presence has kept him in a constant state of arousal.

Miss Sarah is the prettiest woman they have ever captured. There hadn't been the usual family discussion to decide what they will do to her first. They always enjoy the look of pure terror on a woman's face when they openly discuss what they are about to do to her. They had eventually stripped her naked before they tied her face first over the back of the lap dance chair. They had made a three way girl out of her before they cut her loose. She had revealed that she was entirely virginal during their use of her. They were surprised to learn that her boyfriend had not yet used her before they captured her. They had allowed her to rest for three days before she assumed sex slave duties in the root cellar. After that, she was introduced to every member of the clan within four days. Teaching to administer oral sex had been a pleasurable experience for her tormentors. Mongo had especially enjoyed Miss Sarah's attention. He had gone to see her three times a day for the first week she was in the cellar. Every time had been an adventure.

Mongo glances around the edge of the gator hole but finds nothing else worthy of his attention. He yells loudly several times but there is no response. Finally, he drifts back to his boat. On an impulse, he stands in the boat and shouts again for Luke as loud as he can manage. There is no reply. The only sounds are the wing beats of several hundred ducks and a couple acres of herring gulls disturbed by the sound of his voice.

He decides that Luke's absence is an unusually strange occurrence. He develops a cold, crawly, sensation along the nape of his neck as he considers other possibilities. What has happened to Luke? Maybe Luke didn't feed the newest woman to the gator after all...maybe he's back in the woods using her and doesn't want to be disturbed. That's probably it.

Mongo decides to take Luke's boat and leave his for him to use. He wants to know for certain that the motor runs the way it should.

He transfers to the other boat. He pushes away from the shore with an oar. When water depth permits, he drops the lower unit of the tilted motor into the water. The gas tank is about half full. When it quits dragging on the bottom he gives a couple pulls on the starter rope and the engine roars to life. He shifts into gear and heads back along the boat-road toward the shack. Mongo decides that Luke will most certainly be along in a while. When he reappears, Mongo'll make him work a double shift.

Mongo ties the boat to a cleat on the still-side boat dock. He walks up the bank to the boiler. Only Melissa is there. She watches him as he purges the spent mash from the cooker before he starts a new batch simmering. When everything is working, he lowers his jeans to his ankles before he sits down on the cot in the screen-covered room. Miss Melissa proves to be most accommodating.

After a short nap, he arises to stoke the fire again. He spends the rest of the afternoon working the still himself. While he tends the still, he works himself into a silent rage. All the while, he considers what he will do to Luke when he returns.

At dusk, he builds up the fire before he finds sleep. About 9:00, he comes awake to feed more wood to the coals. He has one more look around before he returns to the shack. Luther is snoring loudly, but Luke is still missing. Mongo returns to the dock. The other boat is obviously still at the gator hole.

Something has indeed gone dramatically wrong. Miss Sarah has become a great cock tender, but Luke would never stay in the marsh this late, not even for the best pussy on earth. Mongo crosses the bridge to the shack. There he finds Luther sitting at the table eating stew.

Mongo mutters, "Luke's still missin'. Somethin's bad wrong. I'm goin' to town fer some help."

Luther growls, "What ya want me ta do?"

"Go mind the still 'til I get back. I changed the mash. Harvey and his cops can go look for Luke in the marsh. Maybe playin' with the gators out there will scare some lard off Old Harv."

Mongo drives to Harvey's house on the north side of town. He enters through the back door without knocking. Amerada's finest lies sprawled naked on the living room couch. His mid-section is partially covered by a white cotton sheet.

The Widow Barlow is fully invested in a cup of coffee at the kitchen table. She wears a thin cotton smock open down the front. When Mongo enters she holds the garment close around her. The cloth is thin so the smock conceals very little. Mongo wonders why such a fine looking woman would shack up with a slob like Harvey Kraven. He very quickly answers his own question. She puts out for job security and to keep her son out of jail.

Mongo stares at the widow. There is a dramatic challenge in the fixed stare she gives him. The widow appears to be driven by an insatiable measure of lust.

Mongo considers the situation, before he mutters, "Go home and send Buddy over."

Marge pulls the smock front together before she leaves by the back door. Mongo returns to the living room where he kicks Harvey on the sole of a bare foot. Harvey utters a sound of protest before abruptly sitting up.

"Hidy, uncle," Mongo blares. "You better get yourself dressed; we got us a problem."

"What now?" Harvey mutters. Mongo is one of his least favorite people.

"Luke's missin," Mongo declares, as he takes a pull from a warm nearly full bottle of beer sitting on the coffee table. "His boat is at the gator hole but no Miss Sarah or Luke anywhere around. I think the gator got both of 'em. You guys need to go have a look."

"At night, in the marsh," Harvey challenges in disbelief. "You gotta be kiddin'?"

"Who better then your guys, Harvey," Mongo offers with a grin.

Harvey mulls a reply before he concludes, "If the gator got 'em, goin' at night ain't gonna bring 'em back. When its daylight, then we'll have us a look see."

Mongo growls, "Suits me. See ya'll then."

Buddy comes through the door, as Mongo is about to leave. He takes Buddy with him to the shack where he will become a full time replacement for Luke. While he drives, Mongo considers the situation. Buddy has been his running mate since grade school. He has worked the still before. Mongo knows that Buddy is so afraid of both himself and Harvey Kraven that he would never divulge anything concerning what happens at the riverside compound. Buddy fully understands the consequences of breaking the code of silence that surrounds the Kraven family's activities.

Mongo relieves Luther. He then spends half an hour showing Buddy what he needs to do. When he is satisfied that Buddy understands what is expected, he rewards him with full access to Miss Melissa before he leaves.

With his duties fulfilled, Mongo heads for town and the Widow Barlow's house. He intends to respond to the challenging look she gave him earlier. During the drive, he again considers the problem of Luke and Sarah. He has an uneasy feeling about their disappearance. There aren't enough explanations apparent for what has happened at the gator hole.

Harvey will be the one to untangle the mystery of the missing people. Mongo parks his truck behind the grade school building. He walks the two blocks through the alley to the widow's house. The back door is unlatched. He latches the screen behind him after he enters. Inside, he turns on a small lamp in the living room so he can find his way into the bedroom. A short thick vanilla scented candle burns fitfully on a night-stand near her bed. The flame bathes the room in a dim erratic light.

"That you, honey?" comes a sleepy voice from the bed.

"It's only me." Mongo unbuckles his jeans. "I'm about to take the sass out of you for that look you gave me earlier. Uncle Harv isn't giving you what you need, so I've come to take care of what ails you. You shouldn't look at men that way unless you are prepared to accept the consequences."

Marge gives a startled gasp at the sound of an unfamiliar voice. The cotton sheet falls away from her magnificently proportioned upper torso as she sits up in bed. The sheer sexiness of the woman has the anticipated effect on him. Her nipples are startlingly erect. She gave him that yearning stare of challenge earlier.

The sight of her naked body turned him rock hard in an instant.

He has been living in the sustenance void of the Bambi-like creatures of high school age at the shack. He has yet to discover the quality of a mature woman who knows her way around a bedroom. But then this one has no idea what her challenge has brought into her bedroom.

"Uncle Harvey's an old man," Mongo mutters.

"I've wanted you since the first time I saw you," Marge whimpers, "but Harvey better never find out about this or we are both toast. Harvey will make us disappear."

"No, he won't," Mongo challenges, as he steps out of his pants. "He won't even know it happened unless you scream too loud."

Mongo strips off his T-shirt before he turns to her. A surge of lust overwhelms her as she stares at the biggest cock she has ever seen. The man before her is young, excessively muscled and magnificently endowed. He is carrying what appears to be 10 inches of the thickest cock she has ever seen. Her body gives a shudder when she realizes that she is about to be boned beyond her comfort zone. This is the creature of her erotic dreams, the one she has masturbated to countless times since puberty. Her cunt floods at the thought of what he is about to place between her legs. All she has to do is be able to cover what he has to offer. For the first time ever, her astonishment at seeing a naked man is genuine.

She throws aside the sheet as she reaches for the main course of her preferred man-diet. There is a fishbowl moment when she grips his swollen member with both hands. She strokes the thick offering as animal passions surge through her. She trembles as she prepares for the total invasion she has always wanted. Several of her lovers had been long, but none have been this thick before. The feeling of it as it stretches her will be divine.

She moans as she considers the torment involved when he makes her cover it. The challenge causes her to lose every inhibition. The end of the chase nears when he positions her in a sitting position against her headboard. He moves her with such little effort. His body seems to simmer with erotic energy as he straddles her perfect thighs to stand tall on his knees before her. He grips the back of her head with one hand as he offers his immense cock to her mouth. She holds the fully fleshed-out muscle with both hands as she prepares to indulge him. She utters language that indicates she is eager for what is about to happen.

"You expect me to suck your cock, do you? You need to remember that I want that in me before you expend yourself and become limp."

"I don't become limp, sex machine," he growls. "I intend to fuck the ass off of you before morning."

She has reacted exactly the way he wants his women to react. She had been properly astonished by the size of his equipment. There had been no terror or protestations, no fake denials about not doing *that*. His new fuck-buddy is entirely compliant. His first thrust knocks her head back.

He slides his stiff dripping dick into her mouth. Her tongue titillates him before he buries himself with lustful fury all the way to the hilt. She gives a gagging cough when he enters her throat, but she does not dodge the thrust or withdraw. The act he had intended as punishment reverses itself. He feels her weigh his scrotum in the palm of a hand. The long graceful fingers of her other hand grip the base of his cock with a firm fist.

Her pussy floods as she surrenders to the passion. The grossly flared head requires a generous mouth like hers. This virile stud of a man is the person she has always wanted. She trembles as she suckles him. All the while, her mind envisions the orgy that will occur when he uses her vaginally.

She elevates her eyes. His face is a mask of pure pleasure. He grips the headboard as he begins to fuck her face. She must ration her hunger or she will bring him off too quickly. If that happens, she will have cheated herself out of what the future holds. Dirty words flow from his mouth as he indulges himself in his favorite form of sexual fulfillment.

This is nothing like doing Harvey, Marge thinks. If he will allow it, she resolves to torture him before she allows him to cum. She expels him from her mouth.

"Why don't you allow me to be in charge? I can do it better if you let me be on top."

He withdraws and drops on the bed beside her. She moves off the mattress to stand looking down at him. She instructs him to move to the center of the king size mattress where she has him lie with his arms outstretched. She fastens thick well oiled leather straps around his wrists. The straps are attached to metal chains fastened to the adjacent legs of the bed frame. She leaves his legs unbound for the moment. She moves to a nightstand where she removes a bottle of baby oil. His eyes follow her every move. His erection seems to grow in size with every passing second.

When his arms are secure, she knee walks onto the bed to kneel between his muscular thighs. She places a hand around his majestic cock just below the corona. She dribbles a generous amount of oil from a flip top bottle onto the head. She slathers the oil so that it totally covers his cock and scrotum. He is nearly insane with lust. He writhes on the bed like some large muscular snake.

"Do you like?" she inquires. He quavers. "Poor baby."

His hips move, so that he is fucking her hands while she applies the oil. She grasps his manhood in a double-handed grip. She performs a wallowing motion that encompasses just the corona. His eyes close as he whimpers in time to her movements.

"That's it, lover, enjoy what your slave is doing for you."

After a few strokes, she lowers her mouth to envelop the massive head. Her tongue presses firmly against the roof of her mouth while she works him with her oral cavity. The cock-head presses against the underside of her tongue providing the illusion that she has taken him all the way to the back of her throat. His eyes remain closed as he fucks her face with powerful short strokes.

She imagines his thick pork spreading the lips of her cunt at entry. She is near orgasm the entire time. She will be fully packed with cock for the first time in her life. The thought has kindled a flame in her that had been missing for a very long time. Pre-ejaculate and saliva cover her chin as she prepares him for his desired happy ending. She massages his balls as she orally strokes him. All the while she studies the way he reacts. He obviously enjoys having his dick covered by a warm, wet mouth.

When he begins to tremble, she expels him again. She decides to try his cock on for size. She desperately wants to feel his thickness inside her. She suckles him some more, but relents when his body forms an elevated arc above the bed. His reaction is beyond dramatic.

Five glorious strokes later, she slides him all the way into her throat. Sheriff Harvey had insisted that she learn to deep-throat. She had swallowed a great many peeled cucumber before she was able to perform the feat to his satisfaction.

She has to remove this very thick offering from her throat, so she can breathe. Her tongue cushions his fermium with firm short strokes. She feels him tremble again. His urgency is apparent. She removes all physical contact. His hips continue to move even after he is denied her manner of entertainment. When he is again under control he tests the chains with his powerful arms.

He sobs, "Why did you stop? I was about to go off."

"Of course you were, lover. I intend for you to suffer a lot of delicious agony before I allow you to cum."

Between panting breaths, she gives his fermium a long delectable licking. He gasps at the deliberate enticement.

"Do it, you wonderful little cock-sucking bitch," he wails. "I need to cum."

"Not yet you don't, you incredible stud," she pants. "I intend to torment you for a very long time before you will be allowed the release you crave."

"Oh, fuck," he mutters. "I don't think I can stop. Here it comes." She grips the base of his shaft with an intensity that causes him to wilt, but his incredible lust causes him to quickly recover. His cock weeps a single clear tear of pre-ejaculate. "What a surly bitch you are. I'm going to fuck the ass off of you when you let me up."

"Promise? I've been looking for a big dick like yours my whole life long. Your uncle only uses me for blowjobs. I've had to supply my own gratification since the day he hired me."

Mongo watches her as she lowers her mouth back onto him. Her eyes are locked with his. This is the greatest X-rated production he has ever witnessed. The view of her mouth around him is as hot as anything he has ever been a part of. Even the teenage slaves are not this enjoyable, not even the first time. She lunges onto his cock, so that she takes it deep. She gags slightly as he passes into her throat.

He loves the sound of his dominance over women. He loves

to listen to them beg for mercy, but none is ever forthcoming. The housewives he has taken after beating their husbands nearly to death have merely begged for mercy, even as they held him in position to enter them. He found that act quite stimulating. One had even begged him to fuck her the instant he dropped his jeans. Everyone had wanted to be fucked, but they acted as though they didn't. It was a rare thing when he found a woman capable of deep-throating him. He especially enjoyed the young ones who had rotated through the cribs at the shack. He loved the look of total horror on their faces when they met his cock for the first time.

Marge makes him feel as though every inch of him is being treasured by the most perfect muscular orifice in the entire universe. This one is more than an amateur. Perhaps that is what has been missing before. The sex slaves were there to be used by their captors, but Marge wants to be used, because she loves it. She is performing graciously where the others were performing an unwilling task.

Mongo has never been dominated by a woman before. This one is different. She is driving his urges. She is torturing him where the others merely wanted to be finished with the chore. For once in his life, he is being made to feel submissive. The widow's behavior drives his lust factor off the chart.

Mongo is suddenly jealous of his uncle. When this assignation is concluded, he will tell his uncle that Marge is no longer his exclusive property. He will tell him to keep his hands off of her. In the future, she is to perform only as his secretary, nothing more. And he'd better not hassle her about her change of status. There is something to be said for having a woman who dominates him. He imagines coming to her house every day for this same event. The instant he sees the chains he will become submissive to her demands. She can use him as she pleases.

His prime pleasure begins to claw for its final elevation. When he whimpers, she expels him from her gorgeous mouth. She again applies a grip to the base of his cock with such force that he loses his erection for a fraction of a second. He quickly regains the cast iron rigidity she was tending before. Minutes later his torment begins anew.

"I thought you were about to cum, lover, what happened?"

"You made it stop, you gorgeous slut. I don't want you to do Harvey anymore, you hear. I want you to be mine exclusively. I'll have a talk with him."

"But I'll lose my job. I can't afford that."

"No, you won't. He's more afraid of me than of anything else on earth. He knows I'll kill him if he does anything but what I tell him to do.

"How's this for you?"

"Oh, fuck, that's good. Don't stop, don't stop, don't stop."

Five times she brings him to the brink of ejaculation, but every time she denies him release. He is barely able to move inside her before he feels doomed to completion. Finally, on the sixth elevation, she grants him the final tribute to her efforts.

His orgasm is a loud scream in the quiet shadows of her bedroom. She accepts his final thrust and the massive discharge without flinching. She grips his buttocks as she milks the last of his pulsing dick. When he is too sensitive to allow further manipulation, she holds him steady as she concludes the scarlet act with faint swallowing motions. She reluctantly allows him to escape. She loves the final torment she inflicts on her victim. She loves the violent gyrations they go through when they try to extract themselves from nirvana.

She wipes her mouth with a small hand towel from beneath a stack of pillows. Incredibly, she enjoyed every aspect of blowing him. He remains trussed on her bed. She strokes his rigid length.

She utters, "There, there, poor baby. What would you enjoy now? If you tell me what you want, then maybe I can give it to you.

"Turn me loose," he whimpers.

She continues to stroke his perfect peter until he squirms.

"You have not yet experienced a ruined ejaculation," she accuses. "You must endure that before you will be allowed to fuck me."

"Aaaah, aaah, oh God," he whimpers, beneath her touch.

"That bad, huh? You seem incapable of speech. Why don't we just do it again?"

She lowers her mouth onto him to administer slow fellatio.

He becomes delirious as he suffers deliciously. This time she will administer a *ruined orgasm*. The sabotaged ejaculation will give her even greater pleasure. What he is about to experience will also preserve his ability to administer to her in the fashion she desires. She wants his incredibly thick dick inside her. She knows that she won't last long when he does her, because she has been on the verge of her own fulfillment the entire time she has been at him.

At precisely the right moment, she expels his erection from her mouth. While her hand continues to stroke him, she grips the gross head in her fist with her thumb blocking the urethral opening. The act will impede his cum-shot almost entirely. His sperm wail is cut short as he reacts violently to the blockage. In spite of her firm grip, a thin skein of ejaculate explodes from beneath her thumb to splatter onto her stomach muscles. The balance of his semen is forced backward into his bladder. The act denies him the full pleasure of ejaculation. He screams in agony, as though he has been mortally wounded. His erection does not wilt following his most glorious moment. Instead, he maintains his pig iron like erection.

She shrieks, "Hold your legs together!"

She stands astride his erection. She lowers her woman's-wound down onto his magnificent spike. As expected, entry is an arduous event. She has to bounce forcefully to commence the engorgement. Once she has gained initial penetration she has to fight her way down onto his undiminished thickness. She had not imagined she could cover such substantial size, but she manages with dynamic effort. The act causes several orgasmic events that leave her gasping.

She has never been stuffed this full of cock. His manhood feels the size of a milk bottle when she is fully seated on the glorious beast. Her first orgasm arrived at entry. During the spasms that followed, she was unable to prevent the slow glide of deeper penetration by his wonderfully thick horn.

Mongo is better armed for sex than anyone she has ever known. Amazingly, his erection had not ceased during the double ejaculations she had given him. His cock is firmly implanted. In the process, she has created a wrenching need in him that becomes engraved in his mind.

"That was extraordinary," he whimpers. "I've never had anything to equal this before."

"Neither have I," she sobs.

"Can I do you now? I should get a turn."

"What do you think you're doing?" she sobs. "I'm so full of cock I don't think I can move."

"I can hardly wait to hear you take flight again," he whispers. She unstraps his wrists, so that he is no longer restrained. His facial expression turns mischievous as his arms surround her. "Now, we shall see how much woman you really are."

He rolls them so that she lies full length beneath him. He moves her so that she is at an angle that will accommodate his body between her legs and still be on the bed. He rises up to stand on the floor looking down at her with his cock partially embedded in her. He holds her by her waist. She wraps her legs around him.

Her breasts are small, but firm with dime size pink nipples surrounded by modest areolas. Her waist seems only a double hand span wide above narrow hips. Her butt is small, but deliciously round. She has the most beautiful, longest legs he has ever seen. She has no pubic thatch. Her stomach is absolutely flat. She is muscular where other women are round and soft. Her very erect clit protrudes from the apex of her swollen petals. Her pubic bone is unusually prominent.

Marge is a woman who has been created for sexual pleasure. Only one of the housewives he has tagged had been anything like this. That one had been a long distance runner. He had gone back to her three times before he'd had his fill. He will never have his fill of this one. His erection hardens with such force that it makes him wince. Marge chuckles up at him, as she evaluates his fully re-starched cock.

"I hope you eat pussy?" she offers.

"I never have," he mutters.

"If you intend to satisfy a woman properly, then it's time you learned."

She unwraps her legs from around him as they uncouple. She elevates her bottom to slide a thick pillow beneath her hips. She spreads her legs wide. They are elevated above the bed with her toes pointed outward. She reaches down to stroke herself before she places her hands on either side of her delicate pussy. She parts the deliciously naked crease for him.

"Now, give me what every woman wants," she whispers. "I need your tongue before you stuff me full of cock again."

He kneels between her long lovely, elevated legs. His face is inches from her. This is the first time he has inspected a woman's wound. He can smell her. The scent arouses him. He slides his forearms along the outside of her hips so his hands can cup her breasts.

She continues to hold herself open with her fingers. Her lips are spread so that he can see the small oval orifice where his cock found warmth and comfort. She's so small. How can his out-sized cock possibly fit inside? He almost pities what he will do to her.

He lowers his mouth onto her. She tastes bruised. The taste of her turns him insane with need. He explores her with his tongue. When his tongue passes over her clit, she shudders all over.

"There, oh, God, there." She is turning her head from side to side in the false motions of denial. "Oh, God, oh, God, it's been so long."

His mouth fully covers her sex before he moves down so his tongue can caress the dimpled entrance into her vagina. His tongue enters her as far as it will go before he curls the tip upward to tickle the top of the muscular channel. He moves it in a circle before withdrawing to trace her vaginal slice upward. When he arrives at the base of her clit he strokes lightly from side to side. Her screams of pleasure are strangely rewarding. He wonders if the runner would enjoy him doing this.

Her toes remain pointed in their ballerina pose with her legs stretched as wide as they will go. Her leg muscles are flexed and fully prominent. He tickles the tip of her clit with tiny wispy strokes while he pinches her nipples between thumb and forefinger.

"Are you certain you've never done this before?" she moans, in faux agony. "What you are doing is something more than beginners luck."

"Never," he admonishes, as he palms her breasts.

As he tickles her clit, he begins to pinch her nipples and stretch them outward.

"Oh, God, don't stop," she squeals.

She enters into a massive seizure. Her hands fly from around her pubis to grip his head so that he can't withdraw his mouth from service. She bucks against him until she can no longer withstand the titillation. When she attempts to roll away, he holds her in position by cupping her buttocks while he continues to tickle her clit. Her screams fill the room as she claws his back. She hurls a multitude of meaningless words at the ceiling.

He grabs her hands in self-defense, while he tickles her pink pearl with his tongue. When she begs for mercy he raises up to place the head of his cock at her too small entrance. Although, he is certain it cannot possibly fit, he gives a firm thrust that buries nearly a third of his muscular man-meat in her.

Her scream does little to forestall his guilty pleasure. Three more thrusts and he bottoms in her with cock to spare. Her reaction is another enormous spasm that has her babbling in tongues. Her delightfully small ass moves in erratic circles while she vacillates between screams and giant whimpers.

She feels whorish, because she wants more of what he is giving her. He has awakened all of her appetites. In the middle of her latest cock induced, uncounted orgasm, he lowers his mouth to suckle her nipples. The tickling breast stimulation sets her off again.

This chance encounter caused by boredom has revealed to her the most erotic playmate of a lifetime. A few more strokes cause her to enter into a continuous orgasm that seems without pause. Her pleasure continues undiminished. She can't stop. The sensations turn her into a delirious, demented wild creature. Her nails shred his back while she bucks violently around him. Every motion is performed with her legs fully extended. While he is in her she has no control of any emotion or any part of her body.

His eventual ejaculation is of more than pleasing capacity. The ejaculate fills her with such velocity that the hydraulic action forces the excess out around his awesome thickness. When he withdraws, he is still erect.

"Bottoms up," he growls. "We might as well make you a three way girl."

"Oh, please, no," she whimpers. "Not that. It'll never fit."

He drags her out of bed and into the bathroom.

"Where's your hot water bottle with the enema attachment?"

"In the cupboard," she sobs, as she points toward a drawer and cabinet arrangement on a wall. "I need to douche, first," she mutters.

As he beds her again, he has her stand bent over with her spectacular upper torso lying face-first on the bed. Her pert butt is at the right elevation for penetration. He has her spread her butt cheeks for him with both hands. While she stands erotically exposed, he applies lube to her anal opening. When he is finished, he tosses the tube onto the bed. She sobs into the bed sheet. He listens to her counsel herself. The discussion is more than erotic.

"He's going to butt fuck you. If you are to survive this, then you must relax."

The sounds of her discomfort are music to his ears. He positions his cock against her anal opening. With a single mighty thrust, he enters her ass to mid shaft. She screams. The sound is of both pain and pleasure. Following entry, his hands move to grip her narrow waist so she does not fall forward. She begins to lean into him welcoming what is happening to her.

Her vocal offerings are the glorious prolonged wails of personal torment that he enjoys most. He has ejaculated three times, so what he wants now is for the woman to be properly tormented. He needs nothing more to satisfy him. In the past, what he has loved most is to listen to their terror when they first witness him. They have all been unaccustomed to being molested by a dick that appears to be too large for them to accept.

Entry into every orifice has been easier for the widow than he had imagined. He could hear lust rumbling in her throat during every occasion, even the butt fucking. The ease with which she accepted anal entry allows him to believe that she has been entertained in that fashion before.

He sinks his man meat to the hilt in her. The feeling of her warm entrails around him is wonderful beyond description. Her sphincter grips him while her ass wiggles with excitement. He fucks her vigorously and instructs her to play with her clit. Her hands move to obey. He strokes into her, while enjoying the sounds of her anguish. She writhes around the thick spike imbedded in her ass. Her hips never stop moving. He is fully buried in her at the end of every fore stroke.

The grip of a colon has always been one of his favorite sexual adventures. Butt fucking is second only to a well-trained mouth. The competence of this woman is a surprise capture in a surprising place at a surprising time.

He had found sexual aggression where he least expected it. This woman has not been astonished by anything that has happened to her. He had expected more of an outcry at the thought of being anal intercourse, but she enjoyed the act. All of the others had been mortally terrified when he unleashed his cock for that purpose.

While he pleasures himself with anal intercourse her legs stiffen. At the same time, her tummy begins to contract. Her back arches before she initiates an orgasmic wail that nearly shatters glass. Everything about her seems to convulse. She would have collapsed and fallen had he not held her up by her waist.

She remains firmly impaled on his cock. The pleasure she exhibits during this climax is more than she had displayed even during her prolonged vaginal orgasms. While everything about her is dramatic, her anal effort is the most stimulating event of the night. Not even the first time with the young sex slaves at the compound had aroused him this much.

Mongo spends the next hour reducing the sassiness quotient of the sheriff's trollop. The sight of him and his equipment provides the ultimate aphrodisiac for her. During the night, he has ravished her more thoroughly than any man before. She has never experienced such a mixture of male violence interspersed with the molten heat of sexual desire. Her voice finds every diatonic octave as he services her in a manner she has never known before.

Chapter Thirty-Nine

At daybreak, Harvey shows up at the Kraven shack. Clete follows him in a second patrol car. The two of them climb into a boat with Mongo for the run to the gator hole. Once there, they spend time studying Luke's boat, the bank above the pool and the gator hole itself. Nobody goes near water's edge at the bottom of the incline. Instead, they stand at the top of the bank where they study what can be seen from a safe distance. They see only what Mongo described. There is simply a muddy pool with a hank of white cotton rope floating among the dollar pads at the far side of the pool.

Clete rings the bell unexpectedly. Everyone nearly jumps out of his skin. The reed-line parts on the far side of the pool as Lucifer comes out of concealment.

"Luke's dead," Clete observes. "He ain't around or the boat wouldn't still be here. Nobody in their right mind would spend a night in the marsh with the skeeters if they didn't have to."

"You don't really think he's dead," Harvey offers. "Maybe the motor don't work and he's walking the girl back along the north shore."

"Motor's fine," Mongo mumbles. "I swapped boats yesterday so I'd know for sure."

"Might as well go tell everybody," Clete grumbles indifferently, as he swats at a cloud of skeeters hovering around his head. "If he shows up later, he'll have a good story to tell about what happened,"

Harvey offers, "In my heart, I know yer right. Luke's gone. I told him that gator'd get him if he kept fuckin' around with it."

"We oughta get a rifle and kill the bastard," Clete growls. "If we did that, then we could search the pool."

"No, we won't," Mongo comments with an air of authority. "The gator stays where he is. I might need him later. Everybody got that, nobody fucks with the gator." While he speaks, he glares at his accomplices until they all nod in agreement.

Mongo glances at the muddy pool again before he says, "Only one way to find out for sure. Anybody want to go wadin' in the gator hole?"

The men all shake their heads dramatically.

"Both bodies are probably stuck under that tree in the bottom, if ya wanna go check," Mongo stipulates.

Everybody stares at Mongo as though he's lost his mind. Nobody volunteers.

Clete finally offers, "If we found him, we'd just have ta bury 'im. Might as well leave 'im be."

Nobody disagrees.

"Christ, Harv," Clete offers, "he's our brother. We can't just leave him in there."

"You go look for him if you're that interested," Harvey offers. "I'll stand here and watch."

"Maybe we can get some of those long poles with hooks on 'em from the fire department," Clete considers aloud.

"Like I said," Harvey mutters, "you can go down there if you want and play tag with Lucifer while you stir up his hole. Not me, I got better sense than that. He can move faster in the water than you can on dry land. Besides, the water's muddy, so you can't see him comin'. After a couple passes with a pole, we'd be lookin' for more than just two bodies."

"Luke was a real mean son-of-a-bitch," Mongo mutters. "I ain't gonna miss him much, but we'll be short handed at the still until someone arrives from back home."

"Keep usin' Buddy for the time bein'," Clete murmurs.

"I'll call today and get somebody over here," Harvey volunteers in a thoughtful response. "The guy's like it here with the free pussy and all. We won't have any trouble findin' help fer the still. This place's better than back home any day."

Everybody nods in agreement. Mongo takes the extra boat in tow as they return to the shack. Harvey tells Luther that his brother was most likely killed by the gator. Luther shrugs and doesn't shed a tear, neither will Clyde or Harvey. They return to town as though nothing's happened.

Chapter Forty

Three o'clock Friday morning finds Axle and Toby in the canoe gliding over the inky-black waters of West Clear Creek. Humidity in the creek bottom is so heavy it's like swimming fully clothed. The skeeters aren't even flying.

An eerie three foot thick fog lies on the water surface like an evil frosting. The bow slices through the vapor leaving swirls behind them. Ahead, an occasional lightning flash illuminates the night-dark water.

As the storm approaches, a breeze begins to whip through the tree tops. With the movement comes an eerie effect that sounds like voices calling from the past. Somewhere ahead, an owl questions the night.

Toby mutters in the dark, "If we use this creek any more often somebody's gonna start chargin' us water rent."

"No talkin'," Axle commands. "And no bumpin' the canoe with a paddle either. Sound carries to well on water."

The boys paddle silently as they hug the west bank beneath a low tree overhang. The longest branches sag nearly to the water surface. The longest of those create a leafy black tunnel for them to travel through. Infrequently, the trees thin to expose the passage of the craft. A waning moon intermittently illuminates the sky.

When the narrow sliver of a moon is behind the clouds, the boys can see only about eight feet. Their two long cane fishing poles are tied to the thwarts. They are there to provide an obvious reason for them being on the water should they be discovered. A dozen crawfish in a minnow bucket serve as prospective bait. Eventually, they encounter the log-boom barrier they've seen before but never crossed. A single strand of inch thick steel cable spans the creek at that point. Long logs have been strapped lengthwise to the wire rope to form a barricade. Water passing beneath the timbers produces eddies that swirl in shallow crescents on the far side. Beyond the barrier, the dark void of the unknown beckons mystically.

While they set gripping the cable, the moon comes from behind a fast moving cloud to reveal a wooden sign atop the barrier. The sign bears an implied threat painted on a thinly-cut two foot cross-section of a log. The wafer thin sign stands facing upstream where it waits to serve those who can read. The faded poorly-lettered message marks the outer edge of the Kravens' domain. The sign reads *No Trespassing* in large white letters. The marker is meant to instill fear and discourage entry. The sign half works; the boys are scared.

They slide the canoe beneath the cable at the bank's edge where the strand elevates to loop around the base of an aged bank-bound willow tree. The cable encircles the trunk near the earth before it returns to be secured against itself by three metal U-clamps. A huge sycamore serves to anchor the cable on the far side.

There is a perceived danger from this point onward. The Kravens will shoot at intruders discovered anywhere within their territory. The boys recall the weapons they saw the Kravens carrying. They are always armed. It didn't matter whether they were taking out the trash or running the still, they always carried a firearm. Thinking about being shot makes their fondness for the night diminish more significantly with each paddle stroke.

They beat ahead with determination. Their souls are pointed inward as they journey ever deeper into the bowels of the unfamiliar.

Around them, the river is alive with the motion of feeding fish. Suddenly, every activity ceases. The creek becomes so silent you can hear bugs breathing. From somewhere downstream comes a sound that raises the hair on the nape of their necks. The vocal offering is that of a woman screaming in mortal terror. The sound is followed by a defining silence.

Somewhere in the darkness, a roosting water bird honks in anguish as though displeased at being aroused from slumber. A sullen airborne shadow arises in flight to admonish the night before it disappears ghostlike into the stifling blackness of the creek bottom. The creature's frightened calls and wing beats are made even louder by the ebony stillness. The cries of alarm gradually diminish as it flies away into the night.

Toby exclaims, "Jesus Christ."

Axle answers, "Yes my son."

The comment produces a muted giggle that quickly develops into something more. The mirth of the moment becomes obsessive. After nearly two minutes of semi-controlled hysteria, they are able to once again resume paddling.

The canoe rounds a bend where apparently the same bird flies once more. The creature is as angry and loud as before. Their heads swivel like owls as they peer in every direction. By now, they must be very close to their target. There is no giggling this time.

Endless trees and riffles glide past before they smell wood smoke mingled with the fog. The scent grows ever stronger as they move downstream. Their caution is sponsored by the ever increasing fear of discovery. Their pace is slowed.

They both flinch when a snake drops from an overhead tree limb to land with a meaty thud on the bottom of the canoe. Axle's skin crawls at the prospect of occupying the narrow craft with the unseen reptile. It can be either a harmless water snake or a deadly cottonmouth. Axle remembers the last time this happened. The last time was also in a fog.

The boys listen to the scales of the reptile rasp on the fiberglass hull somewhere between them. Axle's legs are pointed in the general direction of the alien mouth. He uses all his willpower to keep from jumping overboard.

Toby is about to get a whiplash on the bow seat as he wonders, which way the snake will scurry. Axle remembers his past fortune in such matters. With that in mind, he stands on his seat where he grabs a tree limb. Toby performs the same maneuver. They stand perched atop their respective seats where they are welded firmly into inaction by a mutually shared paralyzing fear of snakes.

The moon passes from behind a cloud. The light reveals the snake lying on the hull bottom facing aft. The reptile is coiling and uncoiling in fluid motions. The serpents tongue darts in and out as it tastes the air. The sight establishes new standards of nighttime terror.

"Jesus H. Christ," Toby whispers frantically. "This is the stuff nightmares are made of."

One of nature's more fearsome reptiles lies aimed in Axle's direction. The creature is nearly within striking distance. Three feet of poisonous cottonmouth water moccasin nearly as thick as a stout man's forearm winds and rewinds itself in and out of its fighting coil. The intensity of the snake indicates a willingness to inject anything within reach. For a short second the earth officially stands still for the two self-appointed rescuers.

Nothing to be afraid of. If I have to, I can pin its head like last time, pick it up and toss it over the side. And then some inner voice mutters in disbelief, *"Yeah, in the dark while balanced on the seat of a canoe? Get real."* This is no time to be afraid. *If I'm not afraid, then why do I want to stand up and yell for help?*

Very slowly, by the light of the intermittent moon, Axle eases the blade of his paddle beneath the coiled snake. When the animal is draped over the blade, he lifts and flips the creature over the side. The snake splashes loudly into the water as the boys begin breathing again. By now, both of them have enough adrenaline going to power a small village.

The snake surfaces in the dim light, its snout plowing the water as it heads toward the bank. The moon vanishes behind another cloud. Both boys marvel at the superb timing of the moonlight.

There is now a renewed sense of urgency. Before they begin traveling again, Axle whispers, "One snake's about my upper limit."

"Yo," Toby answers in agreement.

The boys allow themselves another 30 seconds for an attitude adjustment before returning quietly to the task at hand. They both feel that by now, they are very close to their objective. At long last, a swatch of firelight reveals their target. They can barely see the dim flickering light of the fire at the still. The light is defused by the fog but remains plainly evident. The glow reflects mutely downward from the underside of the dense tree canopy above the west bank. The smell of sour mash and wood smoke mingle with the fog that hovers on the water surface like some strange form of influenza.

They have nearly recovered from the mental and motivational hurdles of the snake when the side of the canoe scrubs against a limb protruding from the water. The scraping sound screeches in the darkness with an effectiveness that raises neck hairs. They set motionless as they await the report of a rifle or a scream of displeasure. Nothing happens.

The surest way to avoid getting shot still remains not being shot at. What the hell are we doing here? This is a job for someone who knows what he is doing.

The moon plunges into the clear again as it rides the summit of the night sky. Ahead in the near distance, the pipeline bridge hangs suspended above the creek.

To the right, the soft snap and stutter of a wood fire drifts on the night air. An aluminum John-boat with an outboard motor attached gently bumps against a small floating dock about 15 feet ahead. The boys freeze in mid-stroke. They are paralyzed by the revelation.

Beyond the bank to their right, someone hawks and spits in the darkness. Toby lifts a hand to grasp a tree branch above the canoe. They come to a halt as they sit stone-like for what seems a lifetime as they await certain doom from the spitter.

Toby turns to point up the bank toward the glow of the fire. He releases the branch before he quietly strokes the craft to the dock where he grabs the tilted outboard on the boat. The canoe becomes stationary as the moon disappears behind another cloud.

Curiosity nearly overwhelms them as they study the brush line. Conventional wisdom tells them to get the hell out of there, but once again they aren't listening.

They pull the canoe to the other side of the dock away from the aluminum boat. Toby grasps a plank as Axle slithers up onto the damp wooden surface. The boards are slimy from years of close association with water. Every rasp of cloth or air intake sounds like the clap of doom in the nighttime silence.

Axle navigates the short dock on his hands and knees. Another cough from atop the bank freezes him in mid-crawl.

A hard-packed earthen path climbs the bank, to vanish beyond towering weeds. Axle slithers up the trail on his belly. When the path veers sharply left away from the firelight, he hesitates momentarily before he enters the weeds in a more direct route toward the fire. Twenty feet into a face scraping crawl through vegetation finds him at the edge of a small clearing worn smooth by constant foot traffic. Scrub brush, weeds and stacked cord wood surround the bare earth. A canopy of 100-foot tall trees covers everything from above. The air is windless at this level. The smell of damp undergrowth is rank and stifling within the weed patch.

As he views the clearing from between two stacks of wood, an insect begins crawling upward inside his right pant leg. At knee height, he manages to crush it between folds of cloth by using his thumb and forefinger. The act is better than jumping up to perform a bug dance for whoever is at the still.

Following a long crawl, the light of a flickering wood fire reveals the moonshine still surrounded on three sides by stacked firewood and wooden kegs.

The contraption stands covered by a corrugated tin roof in the shape of an "L." The floor is elevated. It is either hard packed earth or perhaps concrete. A screen enclosed hooch sits about ten feet from the cooker. The apparatus is covered by the same roof. The hooch is a rectangular wooden frame affair that is covered on all sides with small gauge screen wire fine enough to thwart marauding insects.

Something moves beneath the roof at the edge of the firelight. Axle stares at the movement and sees nothing.

Night vision dummy, don't look directly at the target.

He looks to the side of the structure the way he has been taught. By using that tactic, a dark shape materializes. The shape is of a man lying atop a cot positioned along one screen wall. The man raises his hand to brush his face. He is lying on his back about 15 feet distant. He is looking upward at the underside of the tin roof. Axle shrinks closer to the earth with the knowledge of what lies before them. He wants to be as flat as a dead wet leaf.

On the floor near the bed rests another object of lesser bulk. The fire flares momentarily. The lower object moves. With movement, the curves of a woman develop in the firelight.

The man on the bed puts a leg over the side to jab the shape on the floor with a foot.

The shape protests in a female voice, "What you want?"

A guttural barely distinguishable male voice replies, "Get up 'n put wood on th' fire then come pleasure me."

She whines, "I don't want to do that again."

At that instant, Toby arrives beside Axle. His arrival nearly scares Axle out of his skin. Toby whispers, "Tied off the canoe."

The male voice from the cot mutters a little louder, "Girly, ye do what yer told or I'll put ye in the gator hole."

The woman sobs softly as she struggles up. A chain attached to her left ankle rattles against itself. The other end appears to be fastened to the cot frame.

The woman hobbles through the screen door toward the nearest wood pile. While she moves she clutches a mass of cloth around her body. The screen door slaps its door jam loudly as it closes. It traps the woman's chain so that she is brought up short. The woman gives the chain a jerk. Her effort provides enough slack for her to move forward. She pulls two billets of wood from a nearby stack. She holds them club like as she turns to look toward her captor. The movement makes the cloth fall away to reveal her nakedness.

"Don' even think about it," the man warns.

The woman shrugs in resignation as she pulls the cloth close around her. She squats beside the fire to poke wood beneath the boiler. A dollop of pitch flares on one of the shards of wood. The light increases so that the unidentified shape becomes the missing Melissa St. Clair. She is blond, beautiful and barely 16. She turns silently to hobble back to her sleeping pad.

The firelight revelation packs about the same wallop as an electrical shock.

So here we are. We've finally found what we've been looking for, for nearly a year. Now what? Mr. Black should send someone to deal with the problem. But what if there isn't time? A delay might spell death for Melissa. Now we've got a dancing chicken in every corner and no time to wait for help.

The certain knowledge of discovery causes a shiver along both spines lying in the weeds. They have come looking and found what they were looking for. Now they have to plan a rescue. With the dumbest luck possible, they've solved a ten year old mystery that has defeated everyone involved. Now they mutually wonder what to do with the knowledge.

What kind of drill is this? Two teenage boys assigned to ride herd over a formless blob of humanity living on an obscure creek bank in the middle of nowhere. Damn.

Axle immediately wants to be home safely tucked between the clean sheets of his own bed. His mouth feels as stale as an uncapped bottle of six-day-old beer.

The man on the cot stands abruptly. He stretches his arms above his head before he arches his back and then scratches himself. The thin light of the fire reveals Luther Kraven. With all that face hair, he resembles a Romanian Werewolf. The sight provides additional fuel for future nightmares.

Melissa quickly lies down on her right side facing away from him. She is looking toward the fire. She covers up as Luther jabs her in the back again with his foot.

"Din't you hear me? I want ye to pleasure me." Melissa begins to sob where she lies on the floor. He jabs her again. "Now," he commands.

She arises to a kneeling position, as she turns toward him.

Between sobs, she mutters, "You filthy old man. I hate you. My brother's will never stop looking for me until I'm found."

Her captor slaps her in mid-sentence. The impact sounds like the report of a small caliber pistol.

"As fer as they know, yer dead or run away. They stopped lookin' fer ye weeks ago. Yer mine now ta do with as I wish." Luther presents himself to the kneeling girl. "Now do my biddin."

Toby moves beside Axle as he starts to rise. Axle grabs him by the waist and holds on tight while Toby struggles to break free. Within the screened enclosure, Luther starts.

"What's that?"

He alerts to the sound within the weed patch. His hand finds his rifle on pegs above his bed. He stares alertly, as he jacks a round into the chamber. The harsh metallic snick of the cartridge into place returns sanity to the setting. The boys stop struggling. Luther moves outside the screened enclosure where he stands listening intently. Some 20 feet to the boys' right, a swamp rabbit surges from the weeds to race across the clearing toward the hillside.

"Damned varmint," Luther mutters, in the dark as he removes the cartridge from the chamber.

The sound of the rifle action causes a reaction in the weed patch. They understand that they dare not reveal themselves. They are not ready. One mental mistake at this point will mean the death of Melissa, themselves and their parents. They understand the threat from within the screened enclosure. They have no desire to enrich the soil beneath a nearby tree or feed the gator in a distant pool.

Luther turns back to the girl. He returns the rifle back on its pegs. Then in one smooth motion, he leans down to grab the hair atop Melissa's head. He pulls her to him as he twists her face upward.

"Do like I say girly, or yer gator bait by first light."

He positions himself before her. There is a rustle of cloth as his maleness arches outward in the dim firelight. She moves to grasp him before she proceeds with his demand. He slaps her roughly on the side of the head when she strokes him with her hand.

"Not like that fool, the way ye did it las' time."

Bile rises up in both voyeurs' throats as Melissa makes a final impassioned plea.

"Please, don't make me do that again."

He cuffs her on the side of the head a second time. When the infighting has subsided, she rises up to stand tall on her knees before she begins to obey his will. Toby trembles beneath his friend as they watch. Toby takes a deep breath that is nearly a sob. He shakes his head. The vision before them is revolting.

Axle rolls off his buddy, but holds onto his belt in case he decides to bolt again. Toby's face is demonic in the growing firelight. Axle has seen that look before. The look is a mask of resolve and promise. *When I am able, I'll put an end to this, forever.* The Kravens will pay with blood for this crime against humanity. The entire clan will be held accountable for what has become known on *this night.*

Luther makes a hoarse plaintive comment with his voice near the edge of ecstasy.

"Tha's it my lovely, yer almost there."

Melissa gives a muffled whimper. Four eyes watch from beyond the weeds as innocence is slaughtered. When the observers can no longer withstand the sight or the sound, Axle jabs his buddy. They crawl lamely away from the disquieting utterances of Luther in his rapture and the mewing sounds of abuse originating from Melissa. The sexual act being performed in the semi-light of a flickering wood fire scales sickening new heights for both young men.

Watching a sex slave perform is not like watching Leah Holmes service her husband in the privacy of their bedroom. Sexual abuse is a considerable distance from spousal pleasures. The emotion on the creek bank is stored for later recall. Two naive young men have peered into an addendum of hell. Axle is afraid for everyone, especially his family.

The fog begins to lift as they arrive on the bank above the dock. An overhead wind that rustles the trees could easily be the utterances of a lost soul.

The west bank is higher than the east bank so they can see across the creek in the pale silver light. The shack sets jammed up against the far edge of the clearing. A window glows dimly, the obvious product of lamplight. The shack is a disassociated clump of scabbed together boxes. A less elegant structure nearby appears to be a grain crib. The rusting hulks of several abandoned automobiles from other eras rest along the far edge of the clearing. Numerous cords of wood and a wheelbarrow stand near the pipeline bridge. An open topped steel drum adorns the center of the clearing. The barrel is heaped with trash. Refuse that missed the receptacle lies scattered in a heap around the base. The place appears to be the Albania of Texas.

The boys slide into the canoe and head back the way they came. The wisps of fog feel cool against their faces as they flee up stream. More stealth is involved now that they know the demons they face. The perilous knowledge turns them forever fearful.

As they again enter the dark tree tunnel, they hear footfalls on the pipe line bridge. The shift change at the still is apparently underway. A glance at a watch reveals 5:00. The Kravens are not your average moonshiners. Melissa is certainly a compensation for the fire stoker to enjoy while maintaining the blaze. Every subhuman in the clan is probably clamoring to work overtime. She will doubtless be required to service the new arrival before sleep finds her again.

The two teenagers are grim with apprehension as they paddle onward. *We need to tell the cops and let them handle this. Tell which cops? Hell, the Kravens are the cops. According to Sarah, the cops enjoy the captives as well as the proceeds of a substantial moonshine operation. Tell the Highway Patrol, tell the Rangers? Tell who? Trust who? As soon as anyone begins to investigate, the Kravens will kill the captive to destroy the evidence.*

From deep within, Axle something murmurs, "Don't reveal yourself. Tell nobody, you can handle this. I am with you."

Who the hell are you?

No answer.

Now I'm imagining things. I've developed the psychological delicacy of an eggshell.

We have to think this through. Above all, we must return to liberate Melissa. No doubt of that even for a second, but what do we do with her when we've got her?

I don't know.

Great come back. How about we paddle around out here in this frog choking humidity for the rest of our lives?

Axle steers the canoe to avoid a dark blob in the water.

When we've rescued her, we'll have two women we can't return to their parents. Their homes will be the first place the Kravens will look. Melissa will be a living witness for them to search for. Take them somewhere out of state?

Yeah, great idea. Beyond that we can't even let them talk to their parents. If we are stupid enough to allow that gem of lethal behavior, the next progression is predictable. All three of us, no make that every member of three families, would doubtless be used to over feed a very large reptile.

A spasm of logic anywhere in the future will result in at least one enormously over-fed gator in the marsh. There's also the thoroughly grim prospect of serving time on the end of a chain while servicing every member of the Kraven clan. So here we sit, locked in a state of perpetual consequence. We can't let this thing sleep and we can't tell anybody. If we screw this up, then we will incur the wrath of hundreds. Think it out. You can do it. Be brave and resourceful. Lives depend on what happens next.

While they paddle, the last of the clouds depart. The moon and stars come out to light the way. Dawn is forming a pink glow on the eastern horizon when they steer the canoe out of the tree tunnel. They are well beyond the Kraven outpost, so they arrow up the center of the channel. Transcendental paddling across a star sprinkled black mirror would be beautiful under different circumstances.

Chapter Forty-One

Axle is wild with anticipation when he calls the ad in the local paper. The advertisement reads: Wanted: Laborers, Lindsay Construction Company, for a Rural Electric Association installation project. A little further down the page is a short story stating that Marlene Dorian has disappeared from the small community of Bailey. The story indicates that the Amerada County sheriff's department is baffled by the disappearance. Anyone with any information is to contact the department immediately.

Axle calls Toby. Toby picks up the phone on the second ring.

"Hello," Axle says, "what you doin'?"

"Not a damned thing," Toby answers, "what you got in mind?"

"Did ya see the ad in the paper this morning?" Axle asks. "Lindsay Construction is looking for some apes to work labor for the local REA project. What say we give it a try?"

"What they payin'?" Toby asks.

"Didn't say, who cares." Axle answers. "Anything's more than we're makin' now. Get your lazy butt out of bed and let's go find out."

"Okay, see you in 20," Toby mutters. "You're drivin'."

Lindsay Construction is headquartered in a house trailer on blocks on a side street near the long abandoned town train depot. The boys find a gap in the other vehicles parked along the street. They parallel park at the curb a half block from the trailer.

As they approach the trailer, they notice a herd of men setting on the grass behind the structure. Some they recognize, others they don't. Toby waves in greeting to a school classmate lounging in the shade of a large pecan tree. More men are leaning against the north wall. Everybody looks as though they've already been hired and are ready for work. Everyone has a lunch bucket and a pair of gloves.

The boys file into the trailer through a door marked, *"Office."* Inside is an unsympathetic, older, bottle-blond secretary with a first sergeant mentality. She directs them to a tray on a table that contains job applications. They sit in desk chairs and fill out forms. The oak furniture is bleached-blond just like the secretary. The tables and chairs smell of ancient cigar smoke. A low murmur of voices from outside penetrates the thin walls of the trailer. The atmosphere inside is that of a high school mid-term exam class. Periodically, the phone rings. The blond mumbles into it dispassionately with a deep-south accent.

Following the determination that they can read and write, they are ushered one at a time into an office where a guy in khakis asks a few supplemental questions. By the time they depart through the back door, they are employees of Lindsay Construction at $4.25 an hour. The boys quickly return home, where they make up lunches in brown paper bags, find work gloves and report back for their first job outside the organization.

When they return, the men behind the trailer are gone. In their place is a barrel-chested tall guy hovering over six lesser individuals. The barrel-chested man is bare above the waist. He sits in the shade where he awaits their return. The guy greets them with an evil little grin.

"You guys are lucky, you get to work with me out here in the fresh air."

The boys don't particularly appreciate the tone of the statement. A little later, they like it even less. The guy will be their supervisor. His name is Merrill Marshall. Merrill does little more than point out the next utility pole to be moved. The initial job involves removing recently manufactured utility poles that are packed in open-topped, low-sided, coal cars on a rail siding behind the trailer. There are six cars on the track. The newly creosoted poles are jammed together within the confines of each car. The stacks barely rise past the top of the elderly black and rust colored cars. Summer seems to have arrived in earnest within the last five minutes. The weather is windless. The temperature is approximately 99 degrees in the shade with humidity near the top of the scale. The day has all the makings of a south Texas sun roast. The boys glance skyward hoping for rain or a wisp of a cloud but none appear to be anywhere in their immediate future. The heat inside the rail cars could be used to forge bronze castings.

Half an hour later, Toby mutters to Axle, "A day doing this will make death seem like a dramatic improvement."

Axle does little more than sweat and nod.

The creosote on the poles is pale green in color and flakes into the air like dandruff every time a pole is moved. The flakes bloom upward to form a thin iridescent cloud in the still air before they settle onto the sweat soaked skin of the immortal fools working in the cars. After the first pole is dislodged, everyone but Merrill is covered with the ember hot greenish flakes that burn human hide like the fires of hell. Merrill stands atop the poles in the next car and issues instructions. Within an hour, Axle whimpers, "I want to die of water intoxication administered by a fire hose."

"Same here, if I live that long," Toby groans.

About once an hour, the crew pauses long enough to wash down with a garden hose. The water sluices off most of the creosote. Ten minutes later, everybody groans before they return to the furnace like rail car. The creosote creates a narrow line of blisters around the top of their work gloves, their belt line, the edge of their arm pits and any other convenient crevice. As the top three poles are unloaded, the next layer has to be pried from their position in the stack. When the first pole moves, the stack shifts, causing everybody to jockey for position on the edge of the car to avoid having a leg crushed. When the shifting stops, individual poles are rolled up incline planks one at a time, toward the top edge of the railcar wall. Guys using logger's peaveys perform this act.

From the top of the planks, the poles roll across a metal ramp before they drop rock-like onto a 40-foot pipe trailer. The job is misery in its purest form. Both boys want to quit but don't have the courage to confront Merrill with the idea.

The second job of their lives is turning as one sided as the battle of the Little Bighorn. By the end of the first day, they both resemble unsuccessful alley cats. The boys have to force themselves to return for the second day. The third dawn is even worse. The men of the rail car detail unload poles for two days. After the creosote and the brutal labor have depleted the ranks a new batch of valueless idiots appears to unload the next string of cars. People are quitting on the rail car detail faster than a car with a blown clutch.

As new people are hired, the members of the previous crew are reassigned to dig utility power pole holes or drop poles from the pipe-trailer along a cross country stake line.

Mongo shows up for work the second day after the boys are hired. He works in one of the other rail cars. Their meeting is without acknowledgment. On occasion, the boys see him staring in their direction.

Every night after work, the boy's consider how to rescue Melissa without staging a full frontal assault. Their plans rarely advance before one of them scuttles the idea as being stupid. They are frantic for a plan but nothing they think of appears practical.

The morning of the third day dawns with Axle and Toby wondering how durable they are going to be. As they approach the construction trailer, the euphoria of having a job takes a sudden plunge.

"If they send me into them rail cars again," Toby offers, "they can have this job. I got blisters where no blisters ever been before. I didn't hire on to be barbecued."

"Right on," Axle comments. "After we quit we can go tell our parents that we can't handle man sized work."

"Guess we better stick it out," Toby mutters, following a moment of hesitation, "I ain't about to tell Dad I can't hack a simple labor's job."

Their dream of quitting dies with Toby's last statement. They are suddenly transferred to the brush crew. The transfer is as though a Genie has arrived to grant them a wish.

An hour later, Axle observes, "This is better duty but an unsettling thought occurs. In a couple days, we'll be working along side Mongo and he'll have an ax in his hand."

"The pays good though," Toby observes.

"I ain't especially thrilled by that prospect either." Axle concludes.

Brush from the right-of-way is stacked and burned in huge piles. Being on the brush crew involves working in close proximity to a raging wood fire. The brush crew is a tough call but nothing will ever be as bad as working in the rail cars. At one point, the hair on Toby's left arm flames and goes out. Following that, he has a slick left arm and a wild look in his eyes.

Midway through the first day on the brush crew, an old army weapons carrier with an air compressor bolted to the bed frame rumbles into view. The vehicle looks as though it survived the Anzio Beach Head, the Battle of North Africa and an overland trip through Mexico to Panama. The vehicle is completely devoid of glass. The condition of the truck makes any viewer wonder if it will make it beyond the city limits.

A shirtless guy wearing a straw hat and striped bib overalls approaches the foreman of the brush crew. Following a short conversation, the brush crew foreman yells to his sweating slaves, "Anyone want to work on the blasting crew?"

"Yo," Axle screams as he runs toward the prospect of a new job.

By now, Axle has developed isolated personal opinions about cutting brush. He has absorbed about as much of being roasted alive and swinging an ax as he can stand. When the crew boss extends the challenge, Axle nearly runs him down volunteering.

Within minutes, Axle is on the weapons carrier with Whitey the blast foreman. Axle looks back in time to see Toby give him the finger. Axle's departure from the brush crew is so fast it resembles a jail break.

Whitey drives for about ten minutes before turning off the highway along a line of unpainted wooden stakes stabbed into the ground. The stakes are spaced at pre-determined intervals in a straight line across rolling-hills in prairie country.

Whitey stops at every stake where Axle drills a ten foot deep hole using an air powered jack hammer with three drill stems of graduated lengths. The wooden stakes are driven into a thin layer of dirt atop a thick rift of red sandstone.

After Axle finishes the drilling, Whitey installs eight sticks of 60 percent dynamite in the hole. An electronic detonator cap is embedded in the forth stick. While Whitey tamps the charge, Axle strings 50 feet of two strand insulated Army field-phone wire from the hole to the truck.

Whitey plugs the top of the hole with red clay mud from a five gallon bucket before he tamps the clay with a long wooden posthole digger handle. He then attaches the phone wire to the red and yellow detonator wires. When he is finished, he crawls under the truck along side Axle. Whitey then produces a D-cell flashlight battery from a container attached to the truck frame. One bare wire end is applied to each end of the battery and the dynamite detonates. Rocks and dirt bloom more than 50 feet into the air. They then rain down on the grassland and the truck. Some of the rocks are the size of footballs. The resultant act of the detonation explains why the vehicle no longer has glass anywhere on its chassis. Axle speculates that when late fall arrives, the lack of a windshield will provide a cold airy ride to the first stake line of the day.

Death by hypothermia beats death by incineration or creosote blisters almost without exception.

After the fourth day of jack hammering and blowing holes in the ground, Whitey decides that Axle can handle blasting a stake line by himself. He then makes a recommendation to the superintendent. Following that, Axle is given his own truck, a raise and a helper.

Following work that day, Axle goes to the back door of the local beer joint where he haggles with Connie the bar keep. By the end of a five minute begging session, he has procured two six packs of Falstaff beer.

Axle tucks the beer into the rumble seat of his car before he drives to the pool hall. There he spends the next half hour alternately staring at a domino game and watching out the front window of the establishment. He reasons that in a little while, Whitey will come sauntering past on his way to the flea bag rooming house up the street where he lives.

John Wesley is an old man who lives near the railroad tracks in a tar paper shack. He is retired from the railroad and lives alone. Most of his daylight hours are spent at the pool hall playing dominoes, snooker and smoking Prince Albert cigarettes, which he rolls with one hand. On this day, he has a sling on his left arm and a large mouse beneath his left eye.

Axle asks, "What happened John, fall down on the way home from the beer joint?"

John answers, "Luke and Luther Kraven didn't like the way I crossed the street in front of them so they retrained me in the alley behind the hardware store."

"Did you call the cops?" Axle asks.

"What the hell for?" John answers. "Callin' them won't do any good. They're all Kravens. Them bastards has run roughshod over us for so long we've all become hopeless."

"Why doesn't someone go to the state cops for help?" Axle asks.

John makes a snorting sound. "Last time anyone tried that, he spent three days in the hospital."

"No kiddin'," Axle mutters. "Who was that?"

"Me first," John answers, "and then Marvin Hendrix tried complain' to the state cops again last year. The state idiots called Sheriff Kraven to ask him what was goin' on down here. By the end of the conversation, the state cops had supplied the name of the complainer."

Axle stands patiently waiting for John to continue. When he doesn't, Axle says, "What happened?"

John Wesley winces as though his mind has just returned from a long trip somewhere, before he continues. "That same night Marvin turned up unconscious outside the Shidler hospital. Since then, nobody's complained. Complaining's too painful."

Axle stares at John while he wonders what a solution to all the local brutality might be. From the corner of his eye, he sees Whitey ambling by on his way to his room. Axle raps on the window, flags him down and drives him to his back door.

Axle stops his car behind the rooming house where he uncaps the first beer with a church key. He hands it to Whitey. After they've both had a swig he enters into negotiations. Six beers later, Toby has become the logical selection as Axle's assistant. The application of malt spirits was apparently the deciding factor.

With the beer gone, Axle heads for Toby's house to give him the news. Axle stops in front of the Fitzpatrick dwelling, where Toby lounges in the porch swing drinking iced tea as he stares vacantly into the distance. He is without hair on his arms. One eyebrow is singed from working too close to countless brush fires.

"I got my own blasting crew today," Axle offers. "Whitey told me I could have a helper to do the scut work. When he mentioned, 'scut', I immediately thought of you."

A grin creases Toby's face before he responds, "It's me!" he shouts, "You and me on the blasting crew?"

Toby jumps up from the swing. Together they join hands to jump up and down in a circle like a couple of teenage girls. When the euphoria wears off, they carry the canoe to the creek and go fishing.

"Ten days ago we were only qualified to be speed bumps at the local drive-in movie. Now we are suddenly demolition experts," Axle mutters.

Between the two of them, there exists an explosives ordinance experience level of four days. That section of Texas is in eminent danger but no one yet knows to what extent.

Chapter Forty-Two

Being the senior member of the crew, Axle is in charge. With Axle at the wheel, the following morning they cruise out the highway, cross the creek and head north out of town. After they are out of sight of the headquarters trailer, Axle nods to Toby.

"You will be expected to lick my boots and call me *Sir* during the day. When we're off duty, I'll pretend I don't know you."

The right cross to Axle's shoulder is of sufficient velocity to numb his entire arm. After that, they drive in a state of continuous laughter. Ten miles out on the highway, they intercept the line of stakes to be drilled and blasted for the day.

They need to do at least 20 stakes a day to keep their jobs. They bust their buns to get 15 holes blown. When they have that many done, their pace slows while they consider Melissa, and complete another 10 before quitting time.

At mid-afternoon, they come upon a heavy-duty cattle guard in the fence that marks the western boundary of the Chatman-Burnhard ranch. The cattle guard is made of four-inch pipes spaced four inches apart with a three foot ditch beneath the span. A barbed wire fence joins the wings of the structure before it quickly disappears over the crest of a nearby hill.

When they discover that the ends of the horizontal pipes are open, a plan forms involving their approaching rescue attempt. They stow five sticks of dynamite in one pipe and five electric detonator caps in another before capping the open ends with damp earth. The nucleolus of a plan has begun to form in their minds.

The boys are averaging 30 stakes a day, which is more then anyone at Lindsay expected. Life is good, but in the back of their minds, they know that the rescue of Melissa must occur quickly before the Kravens tire of her.

Chapter Forty-Three

Toby and Axle work like fiends on Thursday. They manage to drill 45 holes. When they arrive home, the little Anderson boy is sitting on Toby's front steps crying. Howie Anderson is only nine years old. His father was killed during the invasion of Sipan. Because he is without a dad, Toby and Axle have taken him under their wing. When he has a problem, he always comes to them for help. Toby is climbing out of the car when he notices the kid running to meet them.

Toby asks, "What's the matter, Howie?"

Howie is rubbing tears from both eyes, as he announces, "Troy Kraven took my bike and won't give it back."

Toby asks, "Where is he?"

Howie points toward the center of town. "He rode off that way."

The boys jump into the car and head in the general direction of Main Street. About four blocks later, they see Troy Kraven rounding a corner ahead of them. They are near the police station. When they round the same corner, Troy is peddling the bike into the back lot behind the sheriff department administration building. Axle has been to the county complex enough times to pay traffic ticket fines that he knows what every building contains.

Behind the admin building is a CONEX container made of steel. The container is about 30 feet long, 10 feet tall and 10 feet wide. This type of container was used during the war to ship supplies by boat. The county purchased two of the containers at a government surplus auction. They installed them on concrete pads at various locations around town to act as storage for city supplies and equipment. This one is used to store recovered stolen property by the sheriff's department. The large double doors are secured with a padlock and hasp arrangement.

While the boys watch, Troy stops at the front of the container where he produces a key that unlocks the door. He then rolls the bike inside before he again locks the door. He looks around before he scoots into the Administration Building. The boys are close enough behind him to see where he goes, but not close enough to intercept him. Howie stays in the car while Axle and Toby walk to the CONEX and rattle the door. Of course it's locked. They then turn to see Troy watching them through a rear window of the Administration Building. Axle glances at the lock again before he announces, "We've got a lock just like this at home. Let's take a trip to Shidler. I know somebody who can show us how to pick a lock."

They return home where Axle removes a lock from the garage door with a key. Nearly an hour later, they park before a hardware store on the outskirts of Shidler. The place is a combination hardware store, lumber yard and locksmith shop.

The boys enter the building where they stroll nonchalantly to the locksmith department situated in a far, rear corner. The locksmith area rests beneath a multi-tube fluorescent light fixture suspended from the ceiling. The light hangs low above a work table. Willie Tyree, a high school classmate perches on a stool beneath the light. He is bent low over a cluttered work station. On the table are various locks, key blanks and parts of locks. Willie is working on a brass doorknob-lock that lies in pieces on a segment of white terry-cloth.

Willie looks up as the boys approach. Axle hands him the locked padlock and says, "Think you can open that?"

Willie looks at the keyhole in the base of the lock. He smiles as he places the lock in a small vice. He then selects a pair of homemade lock picks from an old porcelain coffee mug with the handle missing. The cup contains miniature screwdrivers and other small, slender, tool items. Willie grins at Axle as he mutters, "No sooner said than done."

Willie then makes a deft motion inside the keyhole with a pick made from a piece of thin spring steel. The lock snicks open almost immediately. He hands it back across the table to his admiring audience. He has opened the security device in about three seconds.

Willie hands Axle the lock and the lock-picks.

"We need a pair of those," Toby says. "Where can we get some?"

Willie selects two pieces of spring steel from a desk drawer. He then uses a vise and a three-corned file to produce a toothed pick on one end of the slender shard. The narrow tooth is similar to a tooth found on a cross cut saw. Another piece is bent at a 90 degree angle. The bent pick is used to turn the lock when the tumblers have been aligned.

Willie makes the picks while the boys watch in utter fascination. When the tools are finished, they all three play with the lock. Willie holds the lock in his hand, closes his eyes, and feels inside the lock with the pick. While he works he murmurs a description of what is happening inside the lock. After a dozen attempts, Axle can open the lock nearly as fast as Willie. The lock is of inferior quality and cheaply made, so when the first tumbler is aligned, the others generally fall in line of their own accord. The older and looser the lock, the easier it is to pick. Toby does not seem to have the same ability for burglary that Axle possesses. His brain seems to shut down after only a few attempts. The boys drive toward home with Axle practicing on the lock during the entire trip.

"I can pick that sucker tonight," Axle says, "and we'll get his bike back."

"No use goin' to the Administration Building and confronting Troy," Toby mutters. "His uncles would just deny everything and probably slap us around to boot.

We'll do it Troy's way," Axle mutters. "We'll do it sneaky."

That afternoon, the boys assure Howie that they'll get his bike back for him before they send him home.

They return to the Fitzpatrick house where Axle picks both locks on the canoe shed.

"I didn't think you'd remember how to do that, once we were out of sight of Willie," Toby marvels.

"My mind's like a steel trap," Axle replies. "Once I learn something, I never forget."

Axle does the first lock again and then Toby tries. In half an hour, they have picked every lock both families own, plus the ignition of two family cars.

At 1:00 in the morning, the boys jog to the police storage container carrying their lock pick tools and a penlight with the lens taped to a pin-point beam.

The lock yields to the pick in about five seconds. Toby shields the light and has a look inside the container. There are about ten bikes leaning on each other against the left wall. Howie's is a green and white Schwinn. It is nearest the door. Axle rolls it outside while Toby has a quick look around inside.

"Hey, what's this?" Toby whispers.

The light shines on a stack of trunk like chests that resemble narrow GI foot lockers. The trunks are stacked tall along both walls of the container. They are painted olive drab. They have a slot in the top and a set of two digit numbers stenciled on the visible end. The long side of the end row has a line of letters that reads Official Ballot Box, Amerada County. A five-digit control number shows beneath the title with everything stenciled in white.

Each box has a duplicate stacked along the opposing wall. A padlock secures each box. Axle picks the first lock on the top box of the stack against the left wall. The trunk is empty.

He picks the lock on an identical trunk against the right wall. Inside the trunk is a jumble of long narrow cards made of lightweight buff-colored card stock. Axle takes four or five of the cards from the trunk, lines them up in a neat bundle, folds them once and puts them in his hip pocket.

They lock the ballot box again before they leave the CONEX container. They have to dodge the lights of a couple cars as they roll Howie's bike to Axle's garage. They agree to keep the bike for a couple days before returning it to Howie. They decide to do this in the event Troy comes looking for his missing booty.

"Troy's got a bike theft scam going," Toby offers, "and it's condoned by the cops."

"When he's old enough," Axle theorizes, "he'll be a prime candidate to join the force."

"Boy, can't you just imagine him with a badge and a gun patrolling the county in the name of justice." Toby mutters as he envisions the event. "Makes me want to vomit."

After they stash the bike, they go inside Axle's house, where he produces a pair of glasses and a pitcher of limeade from the refrigerator. Big Mike comes out of the bedroom on his way to the bathroom. He pauses.

"Where have you guys been?"

"We had to retrieve Howie's bike for him," Axle answers. "Troy Kraven stole it. It's in the garage. We'll give it back to Howie in a couple days."

"Hmm," Mike replies, as he sails into the bathroom.

Axle removes the stack of cards from his pocket and riffles through them before he spreads them out on the tabletop. The boys sip limeade as they examine a card apiece. The cards are ballots for the forthcoming September special Amerada County election. Not only that, but they are already filled out. The entries are identical on all five cards.

The ballots are 10 inches long, 2 and a half inches wide, and printed on both sides. One side has a warning inscribed on it:

WARNING

Any person who, by use of force or other means, unduly influences an elector to vote in any particular manner or to refrain from voting, or who falsely makes, alters, forges, or counterfeits any ballot before or after it has been cast, or who destroys, defaces, mutilates, or tampers with a ballot is subject, upon conviction, to imprisonment, or to a fine, or both."

A 5-digit number is printed above the warning on a perforated tear-away stub. The tear-away tag reads: VOTER: DO NOT REMOVE THIS STUB. The rest of the document states that it is: *An Official Ballot Coordinated Election for Amerada County, Texas, September 12, 1950.*

The *A* side of the ballot has the Amerada County Clerk & Recorder's signature printed above his title. The name of the clerk is Clive Kraven. The *B* side contains the school district number, which is 66. A couple of referendums are listed in small print. At the bottom in large letters is the statement: VOTE BOTH SIDES.

Axle turns the ballot over. The *A* side is devoted to electing the sheriff plus the county clerk & recorder. The candidates for sheriff-at-large are Harvey Kraven and Eldon Hill. The candidates for clerk are Clive Kraven and somebody named Horace Winthrop. Imagine the boys' surprise when they discover that Harvey and Clive are the apparent winners on all five ballots in an election that is still four months away.

Toby mutters, "I don't know Eldon or Horace, but they're bound to be better than Harvey and Clive."

"Do you think? Do you suppose that Harvey and Clive have celebrated their victory yet?"

Toby wonders aloud. "Let's see now, how would this work? There are two sets of identical ballot boxes in the CONNEX. The empty set will be distributed to the precincts where the unsuspecting voters will cast their ballots."

Axle chimes in with, "The Kravens make out the ballots in advance for the candidates they want to win. They then stuff the second set of boxes ahead of time."

"The sheriff sends a police van to pickup the ballot boxes from the polling stations after the votes are cast," Toby says. "During the trip to the counting place they switch the boxes with the already stuffed fake-ballots and – bingo! The sheriff and the clerk both win a fourth consecutive, four year term."

"Who said hillbillies are dumb?" Axle growls. "What a sweet setup they have. Imagine employment forever with no possibility of failure."

"Old Harv would be unwilling or unable to clean up this mess," Toby mutters. "Wonder how many years he's been pullin' this scheme?"

"You can bet without fear of being too far wrong," Axle answers, "that he's probably the only person in the entire state who's figured out how to become sheriff for life."

"If he didn't," Toby reflects, "one of his relatives probably inspired the thought. At any rate, he's too busy serving his own interest to believe he can ever lose an election."

"There has to be a way we can use this," Axle offers. "The outcome of every election rests in a simple storage container behind the county offices."

"What we've discovered," Toby mutters, "is probably worth a bullet hole between the eyes. I don't think we'd better mention this to anyone, especially Mr. Black."

This latest discovery looms more important than air. Discovering the duplicate ballot boxes causes a crack to appear in the local political power foundation.

Big Mike emerges from the bathroom on his way back to bed. Axle has returned the ballots to his pocket before his father lumbers past.

"Do you realize," Axle announces in a hushed voice, "that we can defeat the sheriff if we can stuff the ballot boxes with our own ballots without him knowing it has happened?"

"We don't just have an opportunity," Toby mutters, "we have the world by the ass as long as nobody knows. All we have to do is figure out how to switch ballots without getting caught."

"They've probably been doin' this for several years," Axle speculates thoughtfully. "Let's hope they've developed industrial strength carelessness by now."

"Defeating this thing would be an incredible feat," Toby offers. "Especially if they have no idea what's happened until it's too late."

"We need help with this one," Toby mutters, "but who?"

"We can talk to dad about it tomorrow," Axle offers. "He'll probably figure out somethin'."

"Let's hope so," Toby growls, as he stands to head for home.

"If we don't tell him," Axle mutters, "then all we've gotta do is be resourceful and patient. If we think about this long enough then you know we'll eventually come up with a solution."

"Boy," Toby mutters, "you've gotta give a bit of grudging admiration to someone who's discovered a way to never losing an election."

Axle peers out the front window as he mutters, "Their method of operation means that they consider they are immune to discovery."

"In a couple years, they'll probably vote to change the name of the town to Kravenville," Toby growls. "I sure as hell hope I ain't around to see that one."

"Wanna bet on whether the ballot boxes would be stuffed that time." Axle mutters.

"Not me," Toby answers, "I only bet on sure things."

Chapter Forty-Four

Mongo has been working for the construction company for several days when he concludes that it's time to settle the score with Axle Mannheim. Since the guy doesn't have any brothers or sisters, the road to revenge lies through his parents. Big Mike seems the logical choice for a reprisal, but Big Mike is a powerful man who is naturally born to strength. This fact is not lost on Mongo. That consideration figures closely into his plan.

Mongo has Buddy watch Mike Mannheim for a week. He discovers that he stops at the post office every day on his way home from work. That Friday evening will be the best time for an ambush. Mongo talks with Clyde on Monday. Together, they decide on how to set the ambush.

"Maybe we oughta take somebody else along fer back-up insurance," Clyde offers.

"We'll bring Luther," Mongo agrees. "That way we're assured of success."

So the plan is formed to be at the post office before 5:00. They will hide behind the shrubbery so they can take him when he returns to his car.

Clyde suggests, "We'll bring along a ball bat and a couple pick ax handles. We don't wanna kill 'im, just cripple 'im up some. You can tell Luther tonight when ya relieve him so he'll be ready."

"Ya think Harvey'll give us any trouble over this?"

"Naw," Mongo responds. "He never did afore, why should he start now? I'll handle Harvey. You guys just worry about swingin' your clubs. I'll take care of the rest."

"Big Mike," Clyde snorts. "We'll see Friday evening just how big he really is?"

Chapter Forty-Five

Friday evening, Axle returns home to find his mother collapsed in hysterics on the living room couch. After several attempts, he finally gets the full story. Several men waylaid his father near the Post Office on his way home from work. They administered a beating of such magnitude that he's been taken to Shidler Hospital.

Maggie doesn't know specifically who did the deed, but Axle has a fair idea. He can always count on the Kravens for this sort of thing. As Axle heads out the door with his mother for the drive to the Shidler hospital, Toby arrives in his truck. Axle picks him up near the end of the driveway. By now, the boys are as close as the fingers of a clenched fist.

"Somebody beat hell out of my dad at the post office," Axle mutters, as he pops the clutch. "It just has to be the Kravens and it needed to be several of them 'cause Dad would have been more than a handful for one or two men."

Maggie sobs softly between the two young men. Toby glances at his buddy. There are tears streaming down his friend's face.

The hospital lies about 29 miles distant. Axle makes the trip in near record time. They leave the car double parked in front of the main entrance. They steer Maggie to the information desk. An elderly woman with blue hair indicates that Mike will be in Intensive Care on the third floor when he comes out of emergency surgery.

After an elevator ride, they install themselves in the waiting room outside Intensive Care. Maggie alternately wrings her hands and cries into a sodden handkerchief. While they wait for Mike to come out of the Operating Room, Axle pulls his mom to him and holds her.

"What happened, Mom?" he whispers.

When she is able to speak, she reveals that somebody attacked Mike when he came out of the Post Office. His known injuries are broken ribs, a collapsed lung, a broken nose, facial fractures, a broken forearm and probably a brain bruise.

"Does anybody know who did it?" Axle asks.

"No," Maggie answers in a wail. "He was unconscious when they transported him."

"What else do we know," Axle asks, as his voice assumes a shred of panic.

"The people at the hospital have said...have said that your father's heart stopped once in the Emergency Room but he came back. The next 24 hours will make the difference."

Toby and the two Mannheim's wait through the night. By noon the next day, Mike has pulled through the worst of what the doctors had anticipated. Now they must be alert for pneumonia.

Maggie remains at the hospital while Toby and Axle head home. When they exit through the hospital entrance, Sheriff Kraven is leaning against Axle's car. The car remains parked in a passenger loading zone. Harvey is his usual idiotic self. Every time Axle sees him, it makes his hands itch.

What is there about this guy? He is not beloved by anyone, nor is he respected. When Harvey Kraven speaks, it is as though fingernails are being screeched along a blackboard.

Harvey says, "I'm real sorry about your dad."

Axle acknowledges the comment, with a curt, "Thank you."

"Our initial investigation shows that he was set upon by an unknown assailant," the sheriff continues. "Nobody saw what happened. The sheriff's department will do everything within its power to bring the culprit to justice."

Axle doesn't want to talk with the sheriff but the conversation is a necessary evil.

"Thanks, sheriff, I appreciate your effort," Axle mumbles.

"I don't have any solutions, son," the sheriff continues. "We'll just have to keep lookin' and see what develops."

Don't worry, I'm willing to journey into the bowels of hell to find the answer.

The sheriff asks, "Ya'll have any leads we can pursue?"

"No, sheriff, we don't have any idea who did the deed," Axle answers. "Do whatever you think best."

The assault of Michael Mannheim is shrugged off as casually as a duck abandoning its old feathers. Axle walks around the sheriff to climb into his car. Down deep in a secret place where his soul resides, the boy knows that the vessel of justice will be served, but when it is Axle Mannheim and Toby Fitzpatrick will be at the helm.

Days pass before Big Mike is out of the hospital and back home where he is wrapped in the warmth and gentle affection of Maggie. His thinking is muddled. He is no longer interested in the investigation. The boys decide to keep future investigative activities to themselves. The night following, Axle files a report by short-wave transmission. He receives an encrypted communication:

RPTDE, RPTDE, NTOWL X

RPTDE HERE X

NTOWL SUGGEST MAG AND MIKE GO TO PROPERTY ON SABINE RIVER NEAR GRAND BLUFF TXS FOR RECUPERATION X CONTACT BURDOCK AT PETE'S BAIT SHOP IN GRAND BLUFF FOR DIRECTIONS TO PROPERTY X

NTOWL CLEAR X

RPTDE COPY X CLEAR.

Mr. Black wants Big Mike and his wife out of the area. The Amerada operatives decide that this will be the best thing for Mike and Maggie. That way they won't have to worry about him being sought out and attacked again. At 0300 hours the next morning, Mike and Maggie Mannheim depart Amerada with Maggie driving. The trip will take 10 hours.

Chapter Forty-Six

The police file their report of the Mannheim beating nearly a month after its occurrence. A copy is purchased for a dollar from the records division. In summary, the document merely states: *Victim found beaten in alley, off government property, behind U. S. Post Office building. Victim unconscious when transported by ambulance to the county hospital. Wife of victim transported to hospital by son. Victim's injuries described as 'bruises, broken bones and lacerations too numerous to count. Assailant unknown.*

When the boys read the last comment, they want to scream names they've learned from the rooftops. Three days after returning home from the hospital, Michael Mannheim tells his wife that three of the Kraven clan were waiting for him in the shrubbery behind the Post Office near the parking lot.

Mike is a substantial man so they brought along some equalizers. When he walked out of the building, they stepped from behind a pair of tall junipers and overwhelmed him. After he was down and no longer able to resist, the attackers then jointly kicked and used their clubs with dramatic effect. The deep cuts made by the blows required multiple internal stitches. He is not the first victim treated in this fashion, but if Axle and Toby have anything to do with future events, he will damned well be the last. This time, the Kravens' very existence has become a personal issue with Axle Mannheim. By their actions, the Kravens have created a pair of substantial, dedicated enemies.

After the attack, Maggie received three phone calls from anonymous callers. The callers informed her that Mike was injured and on the way to the hospital. All three callers identify the assailants as Mongo, Clyde and Luther. They spoke anonymously but with a significant degree of anxiety. They all refused to identify themselves.

The three suspects are well known to everybody who lives in Amerada. Any time the river dwelling Kravens come to town, senseless violence frequently occurs. Their arrival in town is worse then having a cadmium smelter move in next door.

The Kravens have waited a long time to retaliate for Mongo's public humiliation at the beginning of the previous school year. For Mongo, the bullying cure of the century had been administered in a parking lot by a teenage stranger with most of the student body watching. Since that event, Mongo no longer entertained his inclination to fight every day.

Axle has seen him agitated only once since the parking lot event. A senior class party in the school gym before the fire destroyed the school presented Mongo's only known indiscretion. He had demonstrated his legendary party style at the mid-point of the evening when he grabbed some guy by the throat. Axle didn't know the victim, but Mongo repeatedly slammed him against the wall until Coach Palmer intervened. Mongo left the party shortly thereafter. Every element of a hostile environment departed with him. Following that event, the party rolled along as smoothly as botulism at a picnic.

Axle had managed to stay as far from Mongo as was possible because he still views their fight from the prospective of being a survivor more than a winner. The boys jointly vow that the only way they can be deterred from securing revenge will be through illness, death or deportation.

Four days after the beating, Michael Mannheim mumbles the story of the attack to Sheriff Kraven. Kraven had stood at bedside where he attempted to appear concerned and official but not really managing either. The sheriff had worn his usual tan-colored linen suit that wrinkles dramatically if he does anything but stand upright, so he had stood at bedside to receive the report.

Sheriff Kraven ignores everyone in the room while he murmurs the obligatory questions. The inquiry consisted of too few questions. He seemed concerned mostly with where the Mannheim family came from and what Big Mike does for a living.

Axle is only 17, but he understands things that did not previously matter. The boy has only seen the sheriff a few times since his arrival in Amerada. Most of those times had been through the sheriff's bedroom window while Marge Barlow was servicing him.

Harvey Kraven is serving his third four-year term as sheriff. Fourth term, if they don't count the contents of the stuffed ballot boxes awaiting dispersal in the CONEX container. The Mannheim family can anticipate that any local investigation will result in insufficient evidence for prosecution.

With Big Mike's admission that he didn't see his attackers, the investigation is over before it begins. The sheriff offers his condolences and departs. Maggie remains with her husband the entire time he is in the hospital. Axle has kept her supplied with money and clothing.

From the first moment following the attack, Axle had begun moving to the cadence of general outrage. Revenge at this point is only a thought, but it has roots planted in a mental ritual solely for Axle's own pleasure.

When Axle is a little crazed by something Toby can generally clarify it for him. The evening of next day following the attack, Axle drives from the hospital directly to his buddy's house. Toby is on the front porch reclined in his favorite position in the porch swing. His feet are planted on the porch banister when Axle climbs out of the car. Toby makes room for him on the swing seat. He then takes a long look at his friend's face before he mutters, "We're in this together and we can handle it."

"I don't know what to do," Axle offers. "The Kravens have killed the soul of the man I have known as my dad and he's no longer recognizable to me."

"What do you plan do about it?" Toby asks.

"Get mad and get even," Axle answers. "I've already accomplished the first half of the equation."

"We've got to think this thing all the way through," Toby mutters, "before we do something that don't have an escape clause written into it."

"Like what?"

"I don't know," Toby answers, "but the solution better not involve dynamite," he observes as an afterthought.

Axle makes an immediate resolve that Mongo Baron and his entire tribe are in serious trouble. At the moment, Axle's mind is rambling in a circle with all the initial planning acumen of an eggplant.

First thought -- no need to daydream about using any extraordinary skills, we don't have any.

Second thought -- before we do anything, we would do well to look at the overall quality of our lives before entering into a revenge mode.

Third thought -- screw any thought of not doing anything. There is still the rescue of Melissa to deal with.

Axle's job, his father's injury, and subsequent hospitalization have occupied most of his time since it happened. There has been no time for dating or doing anything else but working and supporting his mother at the hospital. When he isn't working, he is either in Shidler lurking in the waiting room or sitting at his father's bedside.

Toby and Axle work their job with little conversation because neither feels talkative.

On Monday morning, July 31, 1950, Axle returns from spending a night at the hospital. He hasn't seen a newspaper for weeks. A long past Sunday edition is lying in the driveway along with several others. He gathers them all up and takes them into the house. He makes himself some breakfast before he opens a two week old Sunday edition. The front page of the damp newspaper brings Melissa roaring back into the immediate spotlight.

Axle reads and then it occurs to him: *the revenge for my father lies in rescuing Melissa and exposing the Kravens to the world.* The several-week-old small rag carries a front page story: Melissa St. Clair disappears. A search for the missing Amerada High School Homecoming queen covers the lower half of Texas. Local police are baffled.

The next day, Toby and Axle pick up their stake sheet, transfer their gear and climb aboard the weapons carrier. The stake line they need to pursue for the day lies south of town. During the drive to the highway, Toby mutters, "Now that we know who has been kidnapping women for the past ten years, what are we gonna do about it?"

"It's taken us a year to make this discovery," Axle offers. "One thing for certain, we're not going to turn this information over to

Black and his boy's to screw up. We're going get Melissa back and put the Kravens out of the moonshine business all at the same time."

"Discovered," Toby mutters. "Before now, all the evidence barely told us that there had even been a single disappearance."

"Now somebody's started working on the people we care about," Axle offers. "Christ, we gotta do somethin', even if it's wrong. By this evening, I'll have a plan we can use. We need to get Melissa by this weekend. Christ, I hope we're not too late."

"Saturday morning sounds about right?" Toby says, as a scattering of raindrops pelt the hood of the truck.

"Right as rain," Axle says.

A downpour drenches them before they turn around and head back to town. A full-fledged cloudburst develops. By the time they drop the truck at headquarters, they are soaked to the bone. Nearly two inches of rain falls in less than an hour.

"We ain't gonna be working for several days," Axle observes, as he gestures toward flooded bar ditches and storm drains. Maybe we ought to go sooner?"

"Deal," Toby responds. "My parents are gone, so you can stay at my place."

"Where'd they go?"

"They flew to Louisiana in the Cub this mornin'," Toby relates, in a low voice. "Grandma may have to go into a nursing home."

"What's the matter with her?" Axle asks. He knows that Toby has always been very close to his grandmother.

"Old age," Toby replies, without elaborating. "With no work to distract us, we can plot and scheme until they return."

"Mine will be tied up with medical problems indefinitely," Axle comments, with venom in his voice.

The motion is made and seconded by a quorum of two. The boys form a plan to act on this weekend. Their plan will be based on the three R's: *r*econnaissance, *r*age and *r*evenge.

Chapter Forty-Seven

Axle dreams a single sentence from his high school English class. The dream repeats over and over again: *The only thing necessary for the triumph of evil is for good men to do nothing.* Old Edmund Burke certainly knew how to identify a problem. The good men of this community have done nothing. Above all, they must save a friend or die trying.

They learn that the Lindsay Construction Company may have to work on Saturday, August 19, because of all the down time from rain. But thankfully, it rains again that night with such enthusiasm that there will be no work on Saturday. The rain allows their desire for revenge to fester with each passing second.

Sarah remains in the abandoned house by herself. She is a complete mental mess. They have to spend a lot of time with her. One of the boys remains with her over night every night.

Plans are formed and dismissed almost as quickly as they are spoken. Their stumbling thoughts falter, as though they haven't had an original thought in a lifetime. Their young minds continually return to the idea of using contemporary firearms to free Melissa. But that solution doesn't work from any aspect. People with guns always get caught. Even if they manage to live through the ensuing firefight, they would have identified themselves to the enemy. They would become either alligator food or candidates for doing time in Huntsville.

Axle imagines becoming part of somebody's fashionable alligator luggage when the plot fails. The memory of the alligator brings him back to reality. The memory of the monster reminds them both that they are laboring with about the same experience level as salami. A renewed since of urgency prods them with each passing second.

Time is not on our side. What if they tire of her or think someone has become aware of their crime? If that happens, they'll dump her in the gator hole to destroy the evidence.

"Those people have one universal character flaw. They are psychopaths. Psychopaths should be either dead or in an asylum."

"Their advisories vote for dead."

Finally it happens. If he had been a cartoon character, a light would have appeared above his head. He toys with the plan for most of the afternoon. Once voiced, they spend the remainder of the day refining their strategy. By 5:00 on Thursday, they are emotionally ready for what they must do. The physical side of preparation will take a little longer.

Chapter Forty-Eight

The image Axle acquires while eating a salami sandwich consists of a single mental picture: fire. He clings to the thought the way a drowning man grabs at anything within reach. The thought huddles in the back of his mind for several hours before it blossoms to life. The thought involves the 10 sticks of dynamite and 10 detonators they placed in the open ends of two horizontal cattle guard pipes.

"Remember, we said that any solution better not involve dynamite," Toby mutters.

"You're right, but I think that we can get away with using dynamite without anyone knowing that it's dynamite.

"Okay, pard, but for once I'd like to not feel like a target in an ax-throwing contest."

"Trust me on this," Axle mumbles, as he plunges ahead with the rest of his plan.

While they drive Toby asks, "Are you certain this'll work?

"I am if you are," Axle responds. "We're just a couple of six-pack guys with something less than champagne minds. It's time for the sheep to grow some teeth."

On Friday afternoon, they finalize their plan. The strategy is to deprive the Kravens of their livelihood while rescuing Melissa. The scheme involves less dynamite than they had thought. They devise a well-crafted scorched earth policy. The basic concept involves the Mannheim-do-it-yourself small-town arson kit.

Michael Marston had frequently told his son, "The road to success travels through the land of wisdom."

The Marston family has always saved newspapers. The newspapers reside in huge stacks in their basement. They are used for every conceivable thing from fire starter for the incinerator in the back yard to individually wrapping apples and pears for winter storage. Axle remembers a story from the pages of a newspaper near the beginning of the Korean War. The article had detailed explicitly how napalm was made.

They set about finding that particular newspaper from the hundreds standing in five tall stacks in the basement. An hour of dedicated search produces the desired results. When they look back on their fabrication, it seems to be a hound dog of a good idea. Once the framework is formed, concept is no longer the problem, and execution now becomes the goal.

The creek provides the perfect highway for a rescue mission, because it leaves no tracks. It strikes them that the canoe is the perfect method for any effort launched against the Kravens. If they go by land, they will leave tracks and tracks are trouble. Their plan requires perfect timing. They must execute everything with flawless precision. The plan becomes so elaborate that they must construct the sequences on paper. Their primary goal is to recover Melissa without being identified.

What would have happened in most communities has not happened in Amerada. Unfortunately, nobody has had the balls for a direct confrontation with the sheriff's department. The dubious distinction of ridding the town of the white-trash terror group has been placed in the hands of higher authority. Two teenage boys will handle the detail. Their plan seems molded from an idea that would probably be popular with fools. The imagined outcome consists of one giant question mark.

Chapter Forty-Nine

They set about being creative. First, they go to the dump where they gather five, one-gallon Clorox bottles by lantern light. These are dark brown glass with a metal screw cap and a glass finger hole molded near the top. With the acquisition of the bottles, they set about creating napalm bombs.

"All right, pard," Toby mutters, "we'll burn them suckers out. Then we'll need to act innocent while we await results. Or maybe we should just quit work and take up extortion."

"You do carry on," Axle murmurs. "We'll need five gallons of kerosene to complete the plan. There's not that much in the house next door."

"We better not buy any locally," Toby mulls aloud.

"That's a sure thing."

"Once the crooked cops determine that kerosene was used to rescue Melissa, then they'll begin to look for an excessive purchase of the stuff locally."

"Of course, they will," Axle agrees. "That's why we won't buy any more.

"If we buy kerosene at all, then they can trace it back to us," Toby concludes. "Our homes have gas and electricity, so we don't really have a use for kerosene except for the construction of bombs." Toby glances toward the street. "We're starting to run behind in this thing. Every gas station will be closed in a few minutes, but I know where we can get some really volatile gasoline for free." Axle looks at him with dread. Toby senses the alarm and that makes him smile. "I know where there's a drip we can run. We can mix drip gas with the kerosene from the old house next door. That'll make what we have go further."

Axle stares into space, and asks, "Okay, where and when?"

"Tonight, about 2:00."

"You sure you know how to do this? The last thing we need is to get caught doin' somethin' that will make the cops suspicious."

"Don't worry, we can hack it, but there is one slight problem," Toby offers. "They've started locking the drips around here. We've got to pick a lock before we can get the gas."

"Oh, hurrah," Axle mutters. "Just what we need: another fully functioning problem to resolve. We'd better load things us so we can head out right away."

Chapter Fifty

They chug through town at 2:00 Sunday morning in Toby's Model-A before they turn north on the Shidler highway. A few miles out of town they turn west on a low maintenance oil lease road. In the near distance, the sound of a one lung Superior 65 horse gas engine driving a well head booms and hisses its way through the night. Toby kills the lights before he parks his truck near the rig platform. Next, he removes a penlight from his shirt pocket while Axle pulls a five-gallon Jerry can from the truck bed.

Toby rummages behind the seat where he produces a spark-plug-insert-air-pump with 40 feet of air hose attached. There is a long handled two-prong gas-cock key made of sucker-rod along with a 20-foot section of black-rubber garden hose. Toby sweeps the area with the penlight until he locates an eight inch pipe protruding half a foot above the ground. The pipe has a slot with a section of flat milled steel slid through opposing slots near the top. Separate padlocks secure each end of the security bar. The slide through plate blocks most of the entrance into the pipe.

Ten seconds with a lock pick removes one of the locks. Another search with the light reveals a brass truck tire inner-tube air valve rising above the earth near the vertical pipe.

Next to the air valve stands a brass water cock valve. Toby attaches the garden hose to the water cock valve before he strings it along the ground running down hill. He lifts the truck hood where he removes a spark plug with a deep socket wrench. He then screws the air pump adapter into the spark plug hole. When the pump is ready, he attaches the end of the air hose to the inner-tube valve-stem protruding from the ground.

When all is ready he mutters, "Start the engine."

Axle hops into the truck as Toby inserts the gas-cock key downward into the throat of the standing pipe. He shines the light inside the pipe as he manipulates the double prongs of the long homemade valve key. Eventually, he fits the prongs between the spokes of the gate valve about five feet below the surface. He turns the valve off.

Toby shines the penlight at Axle as he rotates the light in a circular motion. Axle tromps on the starter and the engine comes to life. The normally smooth four cylinder runs with a slightly out of balance shake sponsored by the missing spark plug. Toby monitors the pressure gauge on the air pump hose until it registers 50 pounds. He then disconnects the air hose as Axle kills the engine.

Toby opens the water cock valve near the air valve. There is a hissing noise as rusty water gushes from a subterranean pressure vessel. He watches the stream closely until the rusty flow turns clear. When that happens he crimps the hose with his hand, inserts the hose end into the five gallon can and releases the crimp. Drip gas begins to flow into the Jerry can until the container is full. When the can is topped-off he turns off the gas-cock. He then moves the hose so he can fill the tank of his truck. With that finished, he disconnects everything and returns the equipment to the truck bed. Before he puts the locking steel plate back in place, he returns the subterranean gate valve to the on position.

The spark plug air pump is removed and the spark plug reinstalled. The tools are put away before they have a final look around to search for anything they might have left behind. Finally satisfied, they depart the well. The main ingredients for napalm are now secure in the truck bed.

They return home where they unload everything into Axle's garage. Toby cuts the top from an old five gallon gas can by using a can opener. The can will become their containment vessel for mixing napalm. Next, they spoon half a cup of LUX soap flakes into each Clorox bottle. They then turn their attention to the mixing container.

They add several cups of LUX to the drip-gas/kerosene mix and stir the liquid with a wooden paint stirrer. When the mixture begins to thicken, they quickly pour it through a metal funnel into the bottles where it begins to jell. When the bottles are three-quarters full, they swirl the liquid to place the additional soap flakes into solution. Finally, they fill the bottles to within an inch of the top with the rapidly jelling mixture. The recipe works exactly the way the article in the newspaper said it would.

Altogether, they fill five Clorox bottles with the solution. The longer the bottles sit, the thicker the mixture becomes. When the fuel has fully jelled, the bottle caps are screwed in place and punctured with an icepick.

One bottle is for the kegs at the still, one is for the still itself along with a half-stick of dynamite. One jug is for the Kraven pickup truck. A fourth is for the building that looks like a corncrib. The fifth bottle is for the area beneath the floor of the shack. They decide to leave the outhouse standing. They hope that the Kravens will move in there and the smell will kill them.

That night, they acquire a large quantity of insulated military field-phone wire from their job site and strip 300 feet of wire from reels in the demolition tool shed behind the construction trailer. The act requires picking yet another lock, because Whitey has the only key on a key ring in his pocket. One length of wire is for the house, pickup truck and out-building. The other is for the still area. There is a lingering doubt that causes them to wonder if either length of wire will be long enough.

Later, they use a keyhole saw, screwdriver and brass screws to construct two wooden wire holders. The holders resemble the metal spools that barbed wire is stored on. When they finish the project they have a pair of four-legged wooden spider spools with a hole in the center and a notch at the end of each leg. They rub damp bar soap along the center span of an 18-inch length of one-inch wooden dowel for lubrication. The dowel is thrust through the center hole of the first spider spool. The soaped wood rotates silently against itself as though it has been greased. They wind chalk line cord around the first apparatus for a test model. They find that the device works perfectly for stowing their wire. They assemble a second appliance for the other segment of wire.

Chapter Fifty-One

Sunday afternoon is spent fine-tuning the storage spools in the back yard. Cecil returns unexpectedly to find them using the spools.

"When did you get home?" Toby asks in disbelief.

"Flew in last night," Cecil mutters from his position in the car. "What are you guys up to?"

Axle fields the question before Toby can open his mouth.

"We're making storage spools for a couple trotlines, Mr. Fitzpatrick," Axle answers. "We plan to trotline the creek for catfish."

"Seems like you guys outta be about burned out on fishing by now," Cecil mutters as he shakes his head in disbelief.

"How's grandma?" Toby asks tentatively.

"Not good," Cecil growls. "She may have to go into a nursing home."

Toby nods as he studies the grass.

"Anything develop while I was gone?" Cecil asks.

"Nothin'," the boys answer in unison.

"Maybe we're lookin' in the wrong place," Axle suggests.

"I've thought of that," Cecil offers. "I've come home for a special tool I need for an engine I'm working on at the airport."

With that comment, he disappears into the garage. He returns shortly with the tool in hand and departs.

The boys stand in the yard where they watch an unsuspecting parent drive away. They both feel guilty. Here they are in the act of saving two women from certain death and they are being secretive with their own parents.

Both young men feel that if they tell Cecil what they have discovered, he will turn the project over to Mr. Black. They both feel that they don't have time for the overly cautious organization to formulate a scheme and move people into the area before they launch a mission.

After Cecil departs, the boys strip the chalk line from the reel.

They then wind the field phone wire around the notched ends of each spoke. The contraption looks clumsy but with the free end of the wire tied to something, they can unwind the double wire strands as fast as they can run. That providing the wire doesn't get caught on anything. They don't dare stop running though or the spool over-runs when they slow down and the wire balls up around the axle. They practice holding their hands more snugly against the spool hub to provide rotation resistance. The sides of their fists work well as a friction brake during their training sessions.

They half-hitch the wire end to a heavy duty rubber band. They then expand the band and stretch the loop over the next spoke of the spool. The package is neat enough to be used in the dark by feel alone. They strip the insulation from both ends of the wire segments. That final function renders the wire portion of their equipment ready for use. Axle places the wire strippers in his gas mask carrier with several other items of equipment.

They resolve to refer to each other as Number One and Number Two during the operation so they don't inadvertently mention their real names at the target site. Axle is #1 and Toby is #2. They practice all day referring to each other by their new names. Their effort occasionally results in a laughing fit when they utter their new names.

The WW-II gas mask carriers strap over a shoulder, across their back and around their rib-cage to end up riding on their chest with a right hand entry slot secured by a zipper. The carrying cases are made of olive drab-colored waterproof rubberized canvas. The gas mask holders become their equipment carriers for the mission. The other equipment involved consists of two half-rolls of two-inch wide duct tape, two five-foot lengths of heavy gauge copper wire with the insulation removed, a knife apiece, two D-cell flashlight batteries, two penlights with the lens taped to a pin hole, a half stick of dynamite, and one extra detonator from the company truck.

They take a set of large vice-grips from Cecil's toolbox in the garage. The vice-grips have a wire cutter near the jaw pivot. They try them and find that they cut through a 14-penny nail with little effort.

The ten detonators from the cattle guard are taped to the outside of the Clorox bottles, two to a bottle. Eventually they decide to add a small amount of dynamite to each detonator on each bottle. Dynamite is the approximate consistency of moist cookie dough, so they pack ten expended 16-gauge shotgun shells with dynamite. A single detonator is buried in the bottom of each shell casing. They then seal the open end with melted paraffin.

With the shot shell casings waterproofed, they make a shallow vertical cut along one side to create a shaped charge. They tape the shells to the bottles with the slit against the glass. When the charges are finally taped into position their fire bombs are complete.

Everything is redundant in case a detonator fails. Occasionally, a detonator has failed in the field. When that happens, they have to jackhammer the unfired charge out of the ground and that has proven to not be fun.

Toby makes a hole in the side of the half stick of dynamite with a wooden pencil. He places that item in his own pack. They place the detonator in Axle's chest pack. For safety, they stow the batteries in one pack and the detonator in another. No sense blowing themselves up on the way to the target.

Toby removes a fish-billy from his garage. The item is what commercial fishermen use to club large fish when they are brought into a boat. They need the bat because they anticipate having to overpower at least one of the Kravens at the still. Axle's mother's stocking drawer yields a pair of nylons to be used as face masks during the assault.

Using a cast iron pot and some fabric dye, they turn two pairs of Axle's father's khaki shirts and pants into black uniforms. They even paint the white soles of their tennis shoes black with shoe polish. They take brown cotton gloves for their hands from Mike's winter quail hunting gear.

Toby recalls that Melissa wasn't wearing much for clothing, so later that night they swipe a set of jeans and a man's flannel shirt from a clothesline across town. The clothes will be large, but better than nothing. They thread a piece of cotton rope though the belt loops to act as a belt. They decide to worry about shoes later.

Cecil is gone on an overnight pipeline survey in the Cub. He will be home the following day. Toby's mom remains in Louisiana. Axle's parents are still in the safe house on the Sabine River.

Last of all, they turn their attention to the canoe. They use a half pint can of olive drab paint to touch up the aluminum trim so it won't reflect light. They use flat-black paint on the paddles after they run out of olive drab.

While they work, they must guard against neglecting Sarah. Three times a day, they visit her with food and conversation. Their manner of entry into the old house is to crawl through the weed patch in a roundabout fashion. The trail they leave appears to be caused by stray animals living beneath the elderly house.

They paint the inside of the windows of the old house black and secure the curtains closed with a needle and thread. A night time look shows no lamp light filtering around the window edges. They use one of the in-residence kerosene lamps to light the place. One of the boys always spends the night with Sarah. She is as nervous as a cat, they all are. Sarah is more afraid of being found and returned than she is of dying.

The napalm jugs and other equipment are stowed in the abandoned house with Sarah while they await the mission.

The cops come to Axle's parent's house three days after Luke's disappearance. They sniff around with no apparent reason for being there. Nobody even glances at the house in the weed patch next door.

The Woodling household receives attention the same day when the cops roust Sarah's father and brother. They force their way into the house again later in the afternoon. Their arrival is without explanation.

The rescue team has no knowledge of the cops' thought process regarding the disappearance of Luke and Sarah. Toby remembers tossing the rope from Sarah's wrists into the pool. They decide that the cops are covering their ass by looking for both Luke and Sarah in case Sarah is only missing and not dead.

At 1100 hours Monday morning, the boys fish the creek. While they fish, they search for a hiding place for their napalm bottles. They fish absently as they study the trees along the bank. They travel as far as the log-boom. On the return trip, they locate a very large hollow cottonwood tree on the east bank big enough to hide all their equipment. The bank where the hollow tree is located is adjacent to a blow-down elm with its top in the creek. The boys decide that they can use the blow-down elm as a bridge so they won't leave tracks on the bank.

On Monday night, August 21, 1950, they transfer the napalm along with everything else into the hollow tree.

During the trip, the sky opens up to thoroughly dampen the country side. There will be no work again on Tuesday. Getting ready for the rescue has taken longer than either of them had expected.

They move the mission night to Saturday, August 26, 1950, at 0200 hours. In order to establish an alibi, a camping trip is planned for the benefit of the curious. The trip will provide a documented reason for being out of town. D-Day, as they have named their operation, will happen during the wee hours of Saturday morning.

They travel and time the canoe trip from town to the log boom, then double and then redouble the results. The trip to the target area is estimated at 35 minutes. They estimate the same time for the return trip. They allow an additional five minutes to stow the canoe in its enclosure at the house.

Friday, the 25th is another day too wet to work. About noon, Cecil returns from a pipeline survey before he leaves again in the Cub for Louisiana. The boys write a note telling him that they will be camping overnight and fishing at Greenleaf State Park. The note is placed in plain sight on the kitchen table beneath a salt shaker.

On Friday afternoon, they drive to the park where they sign up for a camping space and are given a written receipt. Greenleaf Lake is a long narrow body of water fed by a small stream. They drive Axle's car to the site, set up camp, and greet the Park Ranger when he comes by on his afternoon rounds. They spend the remaining hours before sleep pacing impatiently like caged leopards. Toby's truck has been installed in a live oak thicket near the entry road, but outside the park boundaries. If the need for an alibi surfaces in the future, their initial conversation with the park ranger is long enough to be remembered. Both the conversation and the receipt will verify their presence in the park.

At midnight, Saturday, August 26, 1950, they leave their gear set up in the park and jog to Toby's truck. With their usual form of luck, they figure the truck won't start, but it does. Cecil's car is parked at the airport so they head for Toby's garage.

Scattered raindrops fall as they enter town. The place seems even more dysfunctional than normal as they travel side streets. They put the truck in the garage, close the doors and sit on the tailgate in silence. The clouds drop heavy rain that causes scattered hand-wringing within both the garage and the abandoned house. Finally, Toby breaks the stillness.

"We're early. It's only 1:00, but let's do it."

Before they can change their minds, they pull the canoe from its storage locker, re-lock the compartment and head for the creek. They are about to engage in an act of vigilantism. For the next few hours, they will be citizens bent on retribution.

Their selected day of destiny has been peculiar from the onset. Friday's sky had turned dark by midday. The rain has stopped. The night sky is broken to overcast and without a breeze.

The creek lies hushed beneath them. No fish churn the water. No night birds call in the darkness. Even the riffles seem silent. The air on the water surface is segmented into warm and cool areas. Axle feels his heart beating through his father's shirt. He is all but consumed by an unspeakable fear.

When they fish successfully at night, the creek is always alive with motion. They don't fish when it's quiet like this. The fish are inactive and won't bite. On this night, the water around them is as smooth as velvet. Mother Nature lies quiet around them as though she is holding her breath.

The clock is ticking. In a nondescript house in a weed patch to the north. a young girl prays for their success. On a distant riverbank. Axle's parents sleep unaware of what their son has plotted. Cecil and Rebecca Fitzpatrick are installing her mother in a nursing home in Louisiana. Everybody is accounted for, but Axle knows in his heart of hearts that this adventure cannot be won, only survived.

Chapter Fifty-Two

The moon momentarily breaks through the overcast sky before it drops behind a serious looking cloud formation to the west. The top edges of the distant row of thunderclouds are luminescent towers that boil black and green.

The journey along the creek is like a trip to the dentist. It lasts about three breaths before the canoe bow nudges the blown down elm in the creek. Toby bumps the tree solidly with his foot twice. They hear several meaty splashes as reptiles leave their sanctuaries for the security of water.

The canoe is quickly tied by its thwarts to a pair of branches using short hanks of cotton rope. With the canoe secure, the boys climb onto the floating tree trunk where they move single file to their destination. The main log is large enough for stable footing, but the placement of several limbs along its top side makes movement treacherous. They conclude in hushed voices that if they both walk the tree in the darkness, they will surely lose something they need. With this in mind, Axle decides to remain on the log while Toby retrieves everything from the hollow tree.

Axle receives the gallon jugs of liquid death and stores them individually in the canoe. Toby makes five trips before everything is in the canoe. With everything stowed, Axle risks a pin light inspection to determine that they have everything and to discover which gas mask carrier is his. Once identified, they strap them on, free the canoe and resume paddling.

In the darkness, Axle whispers, "That took more time than we planned."

Toby doesn't answer but they both understand the truth of the statement. Thereafter, they paddle more firmly.

They pass around the log boom. Beyond the barrier lies *No Man's Land*. No time now for suspended cynicism or changing things dramatically. They are committed to winning or failing by what they have already planned. The next few minutes will be crucial.

Axle unzips his chest carrier. He pulls out a stocking before he loudly whispers in the dark stillness, *"Masks."*

He slides the stocking on over his head to find that he can't see a thing. He gropes for his pocket knife, opens a blade and slits the material before each eye. Now he can see about eight feet instead of one. On the forward seat, Toby follows his example.

The sky is moonless now. The cloud cover is absolute. In spite of the blackness in the unlit creek bottom, they are able to identify the pipeline suspension bridge in the distance. Suddenly, they are at the dock on the still-side of the creek. A thunderstorm rumbles overhead. The boomer gives off an occasional lightning flash.

As on the previous occasion, a subdued firelight gleams through the trees above them. The light is reflected downward by the under side of the leaf canopy.

Cautious hands keep the canoe from bumping the dock. The John-boat formerly tied to a cleat on the still side dock is now missing. Both boats are apparently on the shack side of the creek. The canoe is tied off with the bag of clothing destined for Melissa tied to a thwart where it functions as a bumper between the canoe and the dock to prevent noise.

Toby eases onto the dock whereupon Axle hands him two jugs and one roll of wire. Once out of the boat, they each pick up a bottle. After a two step false start, Axle returns to retrieve the fish-billy. He then leads the way as they move cautiously up the path toward the firelight. They travel single file, moving hesitantly with great stealth. After the near total blackness on the water, the glow of firelight seems almost as bright as daylight.

Overhead, a sudden wind surges through the tree tops. The rustle of leaves masks any sounds they might make. The upper wind moans through the night like ghosts riding a thermal.

The invaders move along the path to prevent the rustle of weeds when it rubs against their clothing. Near the clearing, Axle straightens up for a look in the direction of the screen enclosed hooch. A shapeless form lies on the cot outlined by the firelight. There is nobody on the floor. There is a sudden flash of panic when they discover there is no Melissa.

Axle has a surge of dread. He wonders if they are too late. He sets his jug on the ground at the edge of the clearing before he eases on quiet feet to the screen door. He tries the handle, there is no resistance. The hinges move silently. The blob on the cot snores on undisturbed. Axle creeps to bedside where he peers down from a foot away. The sleeper is Luther.

Axle punches him on the chest with the fish-billy, as he mutters, "Get up, girlie. Put some wood on the fire and come pleasure me."

Luther sits straight up on the cot. Axle hits him strongly with his club on the back of the head. Luther utters half a moan as he folds over onto the floor. His captors roll him onto his stomach where they pull his hands behind his back. His crossed wrists are bound together with duct tape. The tape makes ripping sounds as Toby strips it from its roll.

When Axle has finished the binding, Toby grabs a handful of Luther's greasy hair. He holds his head aloft as he makes wrapping turns around his face. He puts a double layer across his mouth and another over his eyes. Hopefully, someone will peel off his eyebrows and part of his beard when they unwrap the package later.

Axle stuffs the remaining duct tape roll in his carrier as Toby drags Luther by his legs out through the doorway. Outside the hooch, they each grasp an ankle before they drag him along the path toward the pipeline bridge. The wet dirt of the trail is slick from rain. That fact makes footing treacherous. Luther weighs like a double sack of cement. He also smells like a dead goat.

They tow him about a 100 feet along the path to a medium sized mulberry tree. The trunk is about eight inches thick. The vegetation beneath the tree has been flattened by foraging wildlife.

At the tree, they roll Luther face down before placing one of his legs on either side of the tree bole. Toby holds his ankles together while Axle tapes them. When they are finished, Luther is face down with his legs firmly taped in frog-fashion around the tree trunk.

Axle pulls the bat from within his belt and gives Luther two vicious whacks across his exposed forearms.

Luther gives a muffled cry of pain at the final blow. Axle can't be certain in the dark, but he figures that both Luther's arms are now broken.

Their business with the first Kraven is now concluded. They return to the hooch. Axle places his jug within a cluster of filled kegs near the end of the cooker coil. Toby sets his jug near a keg in the corner of the screened enclosure. They surround each jug with wooden kegs. Some are full, others empty. When they are finished, the napalm has been planted within a mass of alcohol soaked cured oak. The wooden kegs will provide the very best kindling available.

Toby inserts a detonator into the half stick of dynamite before he tapes the stick to the narrow top of the cooker at the junction of the coil.

While Toby works with the charge, Axle removes a hank of copper wire from his chest carrier. He makes a single turn around the dynamite and cooker housing before tying off with several twists. The wire is insurance in case the glue on the tape releases.

Axle pulls the end of the phone wire toward the napalm jugs until it is without slack. He then attaches the four detonator leads. Six wire ends twisted together make two individual bundles larger than a cigar. The distance between detonators leaves only about a foot of slack to play with. Axle peels off a short segment of tape before he folds each coupling back onto the wire insulation and separately tapes the connections.

Both operatives are now moving with the precision of a silent ballet team. There is an economy of movement as they work without comment. Axle takes the wire spool with both hands before he begins to back steadily toward the dock. To hell with the path, he decides that they will travel in a straight line. He has concluded that they will need all of the wire on the spool to get to where they need to go. The wire comes off the spool smoothly without even the slightest tug. The wire doesn't hang on the weed tops the way they had feared it might.

Toby joins him. They each take one side of the spool axle before they turn in the direction of the canoe and move rapidly. Axle glances at the illuminated dial of his watch. They have cleared the still in 16 minutes. They have more than made up the time squandered at the blown down tree.

They climb aboard the canoe where they paddle silently across the creek to the other boat dock. While the canoe moves, Toby aims the spool aft so the wire streams smoothly into the water behind them. Axle can feel the slickness of wet wire gliding along his lower rib cage.

The canoe slides easily between the John-boats tethered to the shack-side dock. Toby reaches into the nearest boat and unplugs the gas line to the fuel tank. He lifts the tank over the side where it sinks noiselessly beneath the surface. Axle does the same in the other boat.

Axle unloads their equipment into one of the John-boats while Toby moves it upward onto the dock. Once they are provisioned, they head up the path toward the Kraven hovel.

The shack stands further from the water than the still had been. Axle wonders once more if they have enough wire. They make an arc around the edge of the clearing so they approach the shack from its narrow end. As they move, a light rain begins to fall. A huge thunderstorm is nearly overhead by now. The sky is an eerie green black color.

Axle wiggles beneath what he assumes is the kitchen floor. There, he places a napalm jug between four upright posts holding that portion of the floor elevated above the ground. The building at this point is about three feet above the earth. He strings his detonator leads as far toward the truck as they will reach. While he arranges the leads, he is aware of Toby worming outward from under the truck. Once Toby is upright, he heads for the corn crib. The crib door stands ajar. A penlight inspection inside the structure reveals a metal cot without a mattress. Melissa is no where to be found. Following this latest revelation Axle begins dreading what he will find when he looks inside the house.

The corn crib sets flat on the ground without an apparent foundation. The structure is half full of bagged, shelled corn. Toby places his jug on the floor before he covers it with two sacks of corn. A rat scurries past as he uncoils the detonator leads through the open door.

Axle cuts the phone wire and strips the ends. No time for a mid-wire splice at this point. He strips and ties-in the wires from the crib jug to the ones from the pickup truck. He makes a cursory feel with his hand to be sure the wires are still in place before he folds them back against themselves and covers each splice separately with tape. Each boy grabs an end of the spool, as they scramble noiselessly across the clearing to disappear down the bank in a direct line to the dock.

Toby takes up the wire spool for the still. He strips a long segment of wire from the spool before he cuts it. The wire to the still is tied by an overhand knot around the aft thwart. When the knot is complete, the wire ends are put in the bottom of the canoe. He unties the canoe and together they move the craft so it is pointed upstream and tied to cleats at the end of the dock by a pair of slip knots.

Toby hoists himself onto the dock with his feet resting inside the canoe. From that position, he conducts the same preparations with the spool from the shack. Both sets of lead wires are segmented and arranged on the dock. The still wires are to his left, the shack wires are to his right.

Both wooden wire spools have been cut free. Those have been returned to the canoe. When Toby is ready, he turns to Axle and whispers, "Sixty count."

Axle scrambles up the slick bank where he sprints for the shack. While he moves in a shambling gate, he counts silently. His goal is to count 60-seconds without referring to his watch.

At the shack, he crawls beneath the floor where he waits. He begins to wonder if Toby has selected the proper wires for the still. If he hasn't, then he is about to become a cinder because the napalm jug beneath the house is about three feet to his left.

Axle lies beneath the shack on his stomach, while he looks toward the creek. At the end of his count, there is a loud boom across the creek followed by a flare of fire that roars up through the tree canopy like a miniature atomic explosion. Something large arches through the air to land with a splash and sizzle in the creek upstream. The fire slows initially, before it begins to burn with authority. Axle lies motionless beneath the house as he awaits a desired result.

Through the floor above, he hears a muffled oath followed by twin footfalls. The front door bangs open as two people run barefoot toward the bridge. From his vantage point, he can see their legs and the lower part of their bodies. They both carry rifles. Axle listens intently, but there is no other sound above him. The rumble of running feet on the bridge falls silent when they reach the far end.

Axle takes a hasty glance toward the still. He can see Toby highlighted by the fire as he drops to one knee behind the truck. He has the fish-billy clutched in his hand.

Axle takes a deep breath and slithers up the steps. He opens the screen door and enters the room on all fours. A kerosene lamp glows on a wooden table in the center of the room. The place smells like a high school locker room at low tide.

The trip becomes a near contact with the divine when Axle's eyes adjust in the dim light. Across the room Melissa St. Clair kneels on a sleeping pad, looking at the open door. The sight is more electrifying than a lightning strike.

Melissa is naked save for a chain attached to her left ankle. A padlock on the chair gleams in the lamplight. There is a look of apprehension about her even in the dim light. What she sees in the lamplight is someone crouched on the floor, dressed in black and wearing a face mask. She nearly screams before she is able to stifle the impulse.

The crouched figure says, "We're going home."

She puts the back of her hand to her mouth as she stifles a sob. The dark figure scuttles to the chain on her leg where he cuts the link nearest the band around her ankle. The shadow whispers, "We'll fine tune that later."

The gloved and hooded figure then grasps her hand and leads her toward the door. She jerks free before she turns back to her area of torment. At a cot against the wall she makes a snarling sound as she dives beneath the bed frame nearest her sleeping pad. In a flash, she is back with a cigar box and a 3-pound Butternut coffee can. The can has the original metal lid fitted snugly in place and held there by a wide rubber band. She hands the dark figure the can and darts across the room to retrieve two more cans from a cupboard.

"We don't need food," the shadowy figure rages.

She answers, in exasperation, "It's not food."

The shadow gives a muttered oath. "Can you walk as far as the creek?"

Her voice is forceful. "No, but I can run."

The two of them sprint through the open door into the brightness of the clearing outside the shack. As they run for the canoe, heavy rain begins to rage from a dark rolling sky. The black figure of her rescuer leads as he carries his assigned coffee can. Melissa runs close behind clutching two others and the cigar box against her naked chest. From behind the truck, another figure emerges to join their flight. The running figures keep the crown of the streamside gum tree above the dock lined up with the fire across the creek.

Something detonates across the stream, as they round the tree to drop down the bank toward the dock. Everything above the creek is bathed in bright firelight. Across the creek at the still, nothing is evident but fire and tree trunks. Sheets of rain blur visibility. An exploding keg rockets skyward. The blaze licks the treetops, where it extinguishes when it touches the wet leaves.

The rain intensifies. It turns into a cloudburst as they scramble across the dock into the canoe. Melissa kneels in the middle of the canoe as the two dark figures untie and push away from the mooring. Lightning rips the heavens as the canoe moves upstream. The forward figure makes a movement and the area above the creek bank explodes in a great burst of liquid energy. An incredible detonation ruptures the night as three jugs explode simultaneously. The sound is like a mallet stroke to the biggest base drum ever built. The pressure jars the pit of every stomach. A plume of orange flame rockets skyward followed by a shock wave that rattles fillings.

Beyond the creek bank, visibility has the quality of poor daylight as the rain subdues the setting. The depth of the creek channel and the trees lining it are something not previously considered. The canoe moves upstream concealed by the depth of the bank. Bankside trees cast the water surface in dark shadow.

The sky opens as a rainstorm develops that would have frightened Noah. The boys bend to their paddles without looking back as they head for home. In the torrent behind them, they hear the shouts of people in panic as their entire world burns brightly.

Axle glances back as they round the first bend in the stream. Every structure is gloriously aflame. Behind them, a figure scurries across the bridge toward the shack. Following the brief glimpse, the intensity of the rain reduces the fire to a dim glow surrounded by darkness. The sight of the running figure lingers in the subconscious like a first kiss.

Behind them, the dwindling resources of the Kravens flare as flames dance within wind whipped sheets of rain. Overhead, a lightning bolt precedes a clap of thunder that adds an exclamation point to the scene. As he stokes, Axle sighs with satisfaction.

"Well, we've left skid marks all over the Kravens. We've pocked their landscape with things for them to remember."

Chapter Fifty-Three

Mongo races off the end of the footbridge where he turns down the path to the still. He sees Luther writhing on the ground near the mulberry tree. He drops to his knees beside his uncle as Clyde staggers off the footbridge. Clyde is completely out of breath. The alcohol fed fire at the still has the intensity of a blast furnace. Mongo moves to the other side of Luther, so his back is to the flame. Luther's face is covered with silver tape. His hands are taped behind his back. Mongo feels for his knife.

"What the fuck happened?" he cries.

As Luther struggles to rise, Mongo notices that his uncle's legs are taped astride the tree. Mongo unfolds his pocketknife and cuts his uncle's legs free then he starts on his arms. Luther screams through the tape on his face. He screams anew as fast as he can draw breath. When the tape is cut free, both his arms fall limply to the earth.

"My arms!" Luther screams, as Clyde uncovers his mouth. "They broke my arms!"

Another gigantic detonation pierces the night. This time is comes from the shack across the creek. A gigantic fireball rolls skyward.

Mongo screams, "Melissa!"

He lunges upright and heads for the bridge. His rifle remains on the ground near Luther. Mongo covers the distance to the door of the shack with the speed of a running back.

The house is totally engulfed by the time he dives through the front door on his stomach. Smoke billows over him, but there is a narrow air space between the dense cloud and the floor. He slithers forward, as he feels for Melissa's sleeping pad. His hand finds the course ticking of her pallet as he gropes for the metal chain securing her ankle. He locates the bed and the chain bolted to the wall. The metal burns his fingers as his clothes begin to flame.

The heat sears his flesh while smoke stifles his breathing. As he gasps for air, his right hand finds the chain. He pulls it loosely through one hand with the other. The metal links move limply. He realizes that Melissa is not there. He crawls for the door gasping for air. Unconsciousness finds him about five feet from safety.

Chapter Fifty-Four

The field phone wire remains tied to the aft thwart as the canoe glides over the water. The slim black wires snake out of the weeds at the still and from across the house clearing. It glides in a duel fluid motion that is unimpeded by anything. The wires eventually trail in the water behind the graceful lines of the fleeing craft. Axle entangles his paddle in the wire.

He mutters, "Number two, ditch the wire."

The voice is commanding. The hooded figure in front lays his paddle aside as he pulls in the wire, hand over hand. When the wire-ends come into view, the red and yellow detonator leads are all still attached. The presence of the colored wires means that there will be few clues at the explosion sites. That fact will make it more difficult for an investigator to determine exactly what happened.

The dark shape in the bow turns and asks for the vise-grips. The rear occupant leans forward to hand them to him. While the rearmost man continues to paddle, the forward figure cuts the wires so that they stream over the side. Only then does the forward figure pull the wire free from around the thwart and discards that as well. The wire quickly disappears beneath the black surface.

The return trip is segmented into the remembered and the unremembered as the young men frantically stroke for home. Before they realize where they are, they are beyond the cable barrier and approaching the blown down tree in the water. As they near the tree, the forward occupant hurls the wooden wire spools one at a time, far beyond the weed-line on the bank. With everything disposed of, the dark figures resume paddling. The canoe seems to grow wings.

Melissa listens to everything, but remains hunched naked and shivering on the floor between the seats. The rear most figure taps her on the shoulder as he tosses her a rubberized canvas bag. Melissa feels for and unties the shoe lace from around the top. She finds and puts on the shirt. While she works on the pants, she alternates her gaze between the two dark shapes as they paddle. Finally, she speaks through chattering teeth, "Who are you?"

The question reminds her rescuers that they still wear the stocking face masks. Axle strips his off. With that action, a bolt of lightning pierces the darkness to reveal a welcome face. Melissa buries her face in her hands as she sobs, "I prayed someone would come for me. Every time I dreamed of rescue, you were the ones I knew would come for me."

"We nearly chickened out a couple of times," Axle mouths while he leans into his paddle, "but we were so intent on getting even with the Kravens for my father, it kept us going."

"What happened to your father?" Melissa asks.

"Three of the Kravens beat him with clubs," Axle answers. "He's spent time in the hospital and is now out of town somewhere recuperating. Don't talk anymore, our voices carry too well on water."

Melissa turns to face forward without further comment. Her hands grip the sides of the canoe while waves of relief shudder through her body. As they move, she feels for and retrieves the stocking masks. She crams them into her bag. She continues struggling with the clothing provided until the pants are on and pulled to her waist. They are miles too big for her so she rolls up the legs. She ties the rope that serves as a belt to form a crude knot. The act crumples the puckered excess close around her narrow waist.

Because the boys are fearful of what might await them on the bank behind Toby's house, the last fragment of the trip seems to take forever. They fully expect half the sheriff's department to be on the bank awaiting their arrival. A guilty conscience is apparently a sorry task maker.

When they beach the canoe, Toby fairly yanks Melissa overboard into the water. He does a jerk lift of the 120-pound canoe as he hoists it above his head. As he begins the lift, Axle goes over the side into the water to stand crotch deep alongside the rear seat. Toby immediately heads up the bank with the craft positioned above his head. The last few remaining items from inside the canoe splatter onto the bank. Axle tosses the coffee cans into the rubberized bag. He then hands the bag to Melissa while he gropes in the dark until he retrieves the paddles. Melissa clutches her cigar box to her chest with one hand while holding the bag with the other as she trails the procession.

By the time the laggards have everything in hand, Toby is at the canoe storage shelter attached to the house. Metal rattles as he undoes the locks and lifts the cover with the canoe resting atop his head. Axle arrives and together they arrow the craft onto its bunks. Axle tosses in the paddles as he closes the cover almost in a single action. The rain suddenly stops as though someone has thrown a switch.

With the canoe stowed, Toby takes Melissa's hand. He quickly begins to tow her toward the abandoned house. There are sand spurs everywhere in the grass, so Toby picks her up and carries her. Her gymnast's body probably doesn't weigh 100 pounds.

To their left on the highway, an emergency vehicle roars past headed toward the refinery. The cruiser has its lights on with its siren shrieking. The muscular engine throbs powerfully as it accelerates away into the night. A local hornet's nest has suddenly awakened.

Headlights turn a far street corner behind them. The refugees quickly dart behind a row of lilac bushes. The lights sweep the area as the car drives slowly past. The vehicle then turns a corner headed west. The single occupant is apparently on the way to work while studying the illumination on the clouds in the distance. Axle glances at his watch, the time is 3:45.

The fugitives approach the abandoned house in the usual round-about fashion. Toby unlocks the door. They enter to a dim flickering lamplight with shadows dancing on the walls. They stand in the faint light where they all begin coming down from an extended adrenaline high fueled entirely by fear.

Sarah peers around the bedroom door jam with the barrel of Toby's shotgun preceding her. When she sees who it is, the barrel drops to aim at the floor. She charges the new arrivals with her one unused arm outstretched. Everyone meets in the center of the room where four people stand sobbing as they hold each other.

Axle clutches Sarah to his chest while Toby gathers in Melissa. Outside the wind blows hard enough to peel the paint off a porch.

Suddenly, a double knuckle rap sounds on the door. Everybody separates as they crouch low to the floor. The noise has the timbre of a judge's gavel.

The boys are unprepared for the rigors of life in an abandoned house. They are equally unprepared for anyone knowing where they are. The scene freezes in stop-action as Toby grabs the shotgun from Sarah. He levels the weapon at the closed door. As he moves, Axle extinguishes the lamp. While their eyes adjust to absolute darkness, the knuckle rap sounds again. Axle gently slides aside the barrel-bolt on the door before he suddenly throws it open. His penlight illuminates face of Cecil Fitzpatrick. Cecil is crouched on the second tread of the old wooden steps.

Toby and Axle simultaneously ask, "What you doin' here?"

"Did you find anyone?" Cecil mutters as he shines the narrow beam of his own penlight into the room.

Sarah and Melissa peer around Toby's arm as Cecil mutters, "I'll be damned, you found both of them."

He stares in disbelief before he tosses his head toward the south, as he asks, "What's burnin'?"

"Douse the light," Axle mutters. "The Kravens had both of them. What's burning is a still, a house, a corncrib, a pickup truck; everything the Kravens own in that direction."

"I'll be damned," Cecil whispers, in total awe.

Cecil closes the door behind him. He slides the barrel-bolt into place as Toby strikes a match to fire the lamp. Obvious respect fills his voice.

"I'll be double damned you found both of them?" He studies the girls. "Everyone thought you were dead." His eyes are bright while he looks at the four young people before him. When he is satisfied that he is not dreaming, he addresses the boys. "I knew you two were up to something. I just wasn't sure what it was. Hell, I wasn't even certain I wanted to know." He stares hard at the two young men. "I'm damned proud of both of you." He turns away, but not before they see tears course down both his cheeks. He wipes his face with a shirt-sleeve. "You did what nobody else could do." His voice is clogged with emotion when he places a hand on each of the two young men standing before him. "You returned two of 'em to the world."

Chapter Fifty-Five

Cecil gets himself under control, then comments, "I saw your tracks in the wet grass and followed them."

"Big mistake; we never thought of that," Axle exclaims. "Who else knows you're here?"

"Nobody," Cecil answers. "It was just a hunch, 'cause I knew how the two of you have been since we arrived here. You always seem to be into something. Going down the river to search for a missing girl seemed about your style."

"Were the tracks very evident?" Axle asks.

"Not now," Cecil counsels. "It's raining again, that'll take care of the tracks."

Toby utters a low, "Wow."

Cecil says, "Tell me what you did."

And they tell about the watching, the first trip, the napalm, everything. When they've finished, Cecil's eyes are wide with the magnitude of what he's heard. He then studies a dark corner of the room as though he is deep in thought. Finally, he begins to talk, but he's talking mostly to himself.

"The Kravens were kidnapping girls as the mood struck them and then killing them when they tired of the victims." With a note of resignation, he says in an anguished voice, "And we all stood around for most of a year like idiots while it happened."

Cecil mutters, with a voice as hard as quenched steel, "This is a good place to hide them, but only for a short while. When the Kravens decide to search seriously, this place won't hold up. We need to get them to Louisiana. We have friends there who'll take them in and keep them safe."

Toby says, "Lou Boudreau?"

His dad nods, as he offers, "None better."

"Think he'll do it or will even want to?"

Cecil stares at his son with piercing eyes, before he answers.

"Those Cajuns are family people; once they've learned what this is all about, we won't be able to keep them out of it."

Toby agrees, "Yeah, that would be Lou and his boys."

"Where are you going with this?" Cecil asks as though he is speaking to a pair of much older people.

"We haven't thought any further than where we are right now," Axle answers. "Creative planning's a little beyond us at the moment."

The boys watch Cecil's features in the dim light as his survival instincts from the war click into gear. The father looks from his son to Axle, before he comments, "We have to move fast on this. When the fire is out and they decide there's nobody in the house, then they'll start exploring every possibility. By dawn, the cops will be looking everywhere; they're already stopping cars in town. They stopped me when I came home. If either of these girls gets to the right people..." he mummers, as his voice trails off in speculation. "Since the Lindbergh kidnapping, this sort of thing is a capital offense. Not to mention murder and all the other charges involved. If the Kravens are caught, they know that they will pay with their lives. Desperation will set in. The sheriff will try to keep this within his jurisdiction so the knowledge of it remains in Amerada."

"That's what we figured," Axle agrees. "That's why we didn't go to the state cops or Mr. Black. Our biggest problem is that we can't decide what to do from where we are right now."

Cecil turns away. He takes a short step before he turns back with a fresh idea. "We can fly them out," he announces, "but I'll need to borrow the WACO from Herb at the airport."

"The WACO is a cabin bi-plane that carries five," Toby explains to Axle. "It ain't fast but it'll carry what needs to be carried. The PA-18 won't 'cause it simply isn't big enough."

"I'll need tomorrow to set this up, "Cecil cautions. "We can fly them out of here the following morning at daylight."

"I figure it'll take the sheriff a while to figure out who did this," Axle critiques. "If we're lucky, they won't understand what's happened until everybody's safe."

"That's true only as long as they don't know who did the deed," Cecil murmurs. "Maybe you two can make the flight without being missed."

"If there's the slightest hint they know anything," Axle murmurs, "then we'll have to hide until we can fly away from here. They can determine what happened if they capture any one of us."

"What's at the still site they can use for evidence?" Cecil asks.

"Nothing," Axle answers. "We even retrieved the demolition wires. We went by canoe so there aren't any tracks."

"That's great," Cecil mutters, "but we have to stay on our toes. It would be awfully easy at this point to get sloppy."

"The sheriff doesn't know I can fly an airplane," Toby observes.

"Maybe," Cecil agrees. "If you go, you probably won't be missed, but if I go I'll be missed for certain. The company's got a compressor down that I have to work on." Cecil addresses Axle. "We can always say that both of you have gone to visit your parents."

"If the sheriff comes looking for either of us while we're gone," Axle murmurs, "you can let us know and we just won't return."

"That's the way it has to be," Cecil confides. "If that happens, then I'll have to disappear as well." Cecil looks at his son. "Think you can fly the WACO?"

"I can fly anything," Toby growls. "I had a good teacher."

Cecil grins. "That's my boy. Then here's what we'll do."

Cecil proceeds to map the strategy as though he's been thinking about it all his life. The boys begin to relax. Cecil is an obvious pro. His understanding of what to do next takes some of the pressure off them. Outside, they hear another police cruiser sprint along the highway. As the sound dissolves into the distance, five people in an old house wonder what the future holds for them.

Chapter Fifty-Six

Toby and Axle change into their camping clothes. They race through the rain to the Fitzpatrick garage where they climb aboard Toby's truck for the return trip to the campground. Cecil returns home. The girls remain alone, but together in the old house. Dawn brings a rosy tint to the eastern sky as the boys park the truck in the stand of scrub oak before they jog to their campsite.

The earth in the park is slightly damp. There has only been a light sprinkle of rain in the park. When they arrive at camp, they get a small fire going so they can make coffee. Half an hour later, the park ranger comes by on his morning rounds. He enjoys a cup of coffee with them.

"You guys are from Amerada, aren't you?"

"Yeah," they both answer.

"The law enforcement bands have been alive since last night," the ranger advises. "There's a fire raging somewhere over there. I think it's along the creek south of town. What's out there?"

"There's a gas line crossing the creek and then there's a refinery," Toby offers. "Other than that, there's not much else out there but trees."

"Must've been the pipeline or the refinery," the ranger continues. "I gather it's quite a fire. They mentioned something about a truck and a house. I think somebody's missing."

"Did they say who?" Axle asks.

"No names, but I think it's a man," the ranger answers.

Toby and Axle stare at each other. The ranger helps them break camp. They stow their gear in the rumble seat of the roadster. The edges of their sleeping bags are wet from the rain. The ranger accepts the last of their coffee as they initiate a sedate return drive to Amerada. The park ranger will remember them if the need should arise. He will remember that they stayed in the park overnight, and that they were there in the morning. He'll also remember what they were driving, because he admired Axle's car. Axle also has the receipt for the camping fee in his billfold.

He drops Toby outside the park near the oak thicket. He waits further along the road until the truck drives past, then heads home separately. Axle is parked in front of the Mannheim garage when Toby drives past 20 minutes later. Axle glances at his watch. The time is 5:00.

Chapter Fifty-Seven

The phone rings on the nightstand near Harvey Kraven's head. He turns toward the unwelcome sound, head throbbing as he picks up the receiver.

"Yeah," he growls.

"The still, the house and the truck all blew up a little while ago," Clete advises, through a radio/telephone patch. "I think you better come out here."

"Be right there," Harvey croaks, as his voice rises in panic.

Harvey rolls out of bed and climbs into jeans and a shirt. He clips his revolver to his belt as he heads for the door. To the south, he can see the glow of fire reflecting off the clouds. As he backs out of the driveway, rain begins to fall again.

A large number of both civilian and emergency vehicles are parked along the highway near the refinery road. Two deputies are posted on the refinery road where they are busy sorting traffic to keep the curious out of the area.

Harvey passes through the police barrier near the shack a short time later. He sees Jeb, Clete and several local volunteer firemen standing in the rain watching the pile of rubble that was once the shack turn to embers. Jeb and Clete meet Harvey at his car.

Harvey moves Clete to the side, where he asks, "Is that girl still in there?"

Clete offers, "Yeah, far as we know. You stand downwind of the fire and you can smell her cookin'. Mongo's missin' too. Luther claims that he ran back across the bridge after the house went up. Nobody's seen him since."

"What the hell happened?" Harvey croaks.

Clete mutters, "Clyde claims the still blew and while they was over there gettin' Luther untied from around a tree, the house, crib and truck went up."

"Did you see anybody while all this was happenin'?" Harvey asks.

"Nobody saw anything," Clete answers. "It was like a ghost caused the whole damned thing. Hell, Luther's got two broken arms and don't even know what day it is. It rained so damned hard out here earlier that we couldn't even find a track to tell us that anybody was here."

"That's really great," Harvey growls in disgust. He walks to where the firemen are standing. "How long before we know if anyone's in the house?"

"Couple of hours, sheriff," the fireman says. "Our pump broke on the tanker so we can't pull water from the creek. We'll have to wait until she burns herself out."

Harvey gives a snort of dissatisfaction.

Clete takes Harvey's arm as they return to the sheriff's car. "Clyde says the girl was chained to the wall when he and Mongo went to the still after the first explosion. While they were at the still, everything at the shack ignited. By the time they returned to the shack, it was fully involved. It smells like kerosene at the still and the house."

"Jesus Christ, Clete," Harvey mutters. "That don't mean anything. They used kerosene to cook with and for the lamps. There was probably ten gallons of the stuff in the shack, so no wonder it smells like kerosene."

"Yeah, maybe so," Clete agrees sarcastically. "But they normally don't cook at the still and there's the same smell over there."

"Use your head, brother," the sheriff growls. "They had a lamp didn't they? Got any idea who could have done this?" the sheriff asks hopefully.

"Name somebody," Clete responds. "It could be anyone in the county. We ain't got any friends around here, 'cause Mongo and Luke kept beatin' the crap out of everybody. Now they all hate us."

Harvey asks, "Where's Clyde?"

"He rode to the hospital with Luther," Clete answers. "Luther's really screwed up. Maybe we'll find some evidence we can use when it's daylight."

"Two broken arms," Harvey mumbles. "Do you suppose that Mannheim kid that beat hell out of Mongo could have something to do with this? Mongo, Clyde and Luther put his daddy in the hospital

Max Ibach

and he ain't recovered yet."

Clete contemplates the question. "Not a chance. Whoever did this knew what they was doin'. A teenage kid would never be able to pull this off."

"Who do we have in the county that's fresh outta the Army or the pen?" Harvey asks.

Clete answers "There's a couple of ex-cons in the county, but I don't remember exactly who they are. I'll look 'em up when I get back to the station. At least half of the male population was in military service during the war, so that thought won't help us much."

Harvey gives Clete a piercing stare. "We got the elections coming up in a couple months. We need to arrest somebody, so we can show some positive action."

Clete snickers. "Who's going to care about what happens out here? Wrappin' this one up ain't gonna influence an election, Harv."

"I ain't worried about winnin'," Harvey grumbles. "I'd just like for us to look good."

Clete walks toward his car. "I'm through here. Think I'll mosey back to the station and see who looks good for this thing." He hollers at the fire chief while he stands out of the mud on the doorsill of his cruiser. "Give me a call if you find any remains in the house, Burney."

The chief glances at Clete. "Sure thing, deputy."

Harvey and Clete head toward town in their respective vehicles. While Harvey drives, a bad thought forms in the back of his mind. *Who the hell could pull off something like this and not be seen or leave a clue?* He rubs the back of his neck as he considers the possibilities.

Chapter Fifty-Eight

On Friday Whitey indicates the company will work on Sunday, weather permitting. The long bout of rainy weather has slowed work to the point that they are falling behind on their contract. Sunday morning, Axle climbs out of bed. He is enormously sleepy, but his body is still running on adrenaline from the night before. Toby shows up five minutes later sporting a razor nick on his chin.

When they arrive at the Lindsay Construction trailer, Whitey tells them to go home for a couple more days. The ground is still too wet to work. Outside, the sky remains overcast with occasional showers. The boys cruise out on the south highway in Toby's truck. A line of vehicles sits along the shoulder of the road, where a deputy is directing traffic. Cars slow to a crawl as everyone looks along the road to the refinery.

"You suppose anyone made us?" Toby asks.

"Surely, you jest," Axle answers. "Two guys materializing out of the dark during a rain storm wearing masks and dark clothes, not a chance."

"Hope you're right," Toby mutters. "You whacked Luther in the head when he was half asleep. He probably has no idea what happened."

"If anyone saw the canoe they would have fired a couple shots in our direction," Axle concludes.

"Think the sheriff'll be around to find out where we were last night?" Toby asks.

"I'd bet it," Axle answers.

Toby swerves into a driveway on the east side of the highway. He turns around and heads back to town. Axle ponders what will happen next. What had seemed like such a swell strategy probably had major flaws. He can't figure out what they are, but the sheriff might. They anticipate being questioned concerning the night's events, so they begin to perfect their alibi.

"You suppose they'll search for the girls?" Toby asks.

"Undoubtedly, especially after they've determined that Melissa is not in the shack. That's when they'll start lookin' in earnest," Axle observes.

"The park ranger said that he thought there was a man killed in the fire," Toby offers. "Wonder who that could be?"

"Maybe nobody," Axle mumbles. "You know how rumors start."

They review the details as their heart rates gradually returned to normal. The story is recounted so many times they can tell it backward, forward and probably dream it in their sleep. All the facts are plausible, and besides they have the park receipt to back up their story. They struggle through a day that is almost without end. They wait through the morning and well into the afternoon, but still nothing happens.

"You got any idea why they haven't been here yet?" Axle asks.

"No, but I suppose you're gonna tell me," Toby complains.

"They've got so many enemies they don't know who to consider first," Axle offers.

"That might be true, but you can bet we'll be high on their list of possibilities."

Chapter Fifty-Nine

"The fire chief claims that Mongo died in the shack and there's no other body," Harvey growls, as he stares at Clete. "Where'd the girl go?"

"My thought is that she's runnin' around lose somewhere blabbin' to everybody," Clete comments, as his voice rises an octave. "If we don't do anything else, we've gotta find her."

"No kiddin', Sherlock, what was yer first clue," Harvey wails. "Now, I'm beginning to wonder about the one that was with Luke at the gator hole. Do you suppose someone killed Luke and took the girl?"

"Who the hell could kill Luke?" Clete mutters. "The bastard was a giant."

"Bullets don't care how big you are," Harvey replies.

"Hell," Clete wails, "we don't even know for sure that Luke's dead. The only thing we know fer certain is that the sun's comin' up tomorrow." Clete pauses. "But after last night, I ain't so sure about that."

"We got to look everywhere," Harvey wails. "We can start at the girls' homes. They ain't got anywhere else to go."

"The hell they don't," Clete replies. "This thing's been planned so well from beginning that we don't have a clue what we're lookin' for. Don't make another mistake by underestimating whoever did this. This thing can sink us in a heartbeat."

"The elections are just around the corner," Harvey complains. "We've got to start lookin' better on paper."

"Forget the fucking elections, Harv," Clete rages. "You're just too much of a politician fer your own good. If we don't find that girl, then we'll be ass wipe by tomorrow evening."

"That damned Luke got us into this," Harvey accuses. "Now, he ain't around to take the fall fer it. I ain't doin' time 'cause he couldn't keep his fly buttoned."

"I don't remember Luke taken yer pants down fer ye brother," Clete mutters.

Harvey stares hard at Clete. "Same fer you, brother. Now that we know who to blame for our predicament, what we gonna do?"

Clete shakes his head. "You damned well better hope I find something in the way of a clue when the sun comes up. I'm startin' to toy with the idea of goin' back home for an extended vacation."

"To hell with that," Harvey counters. "Get on the horn and call in all off duty kin. We're gonna need all the help we can get."

"You want me to start takin' notes, big brother?" Clete asks, while he grins at Harvey's discomfort.

"Start lookin' under every rock in town," Harvey continues. "She's gotta be somewhere. Our lives depend on findin' her."

Clete mutters, "Amen," as he heads for his office and a telephone.

Chapter Sixty

The age of sissies arrives Sunday morning about 10:00 when the boys are both scared nearly spitless. They have shown up for work and been sent home because the ground is too wet to work. Sitting around doing nothing results in nail biting tension.

The cops are everywhere in town. They are nearly as active as bees on a white clover patch. Search parties have descended on both the St. Clair and Woodling residences. Both houses have been searched three times at two-hour intervals. The cops appear to watch the houses from afar, in shifts. At 2:00, an employee of the gas company shows up at the Woodling residence with instructions to check for an alleged gas leak. Defective meter seals are the alleged problem. The gas meter is located in the basement. The gas company employee is a cousin of the Kravens. He checks the basement and the kitchen before he goes through all the rooms in the house. When he leaves, he reports to the sheriff. He tells him that not only are the girls not there, but their parents appear to have absolutely no idea what everyone is looking for. The search appears quite normal to everyone but Cecil, Axle and Toby.

Cecil is working at the airport so he can set up the WACO. The boys are toughing out the wait at home.

The weather from the night before has moved rapidly eastward. Clear skies prevail by mid-afternoon. The abandoned house looks even more abandoned than before the rain. The moisture has greened up the forest of weeds around the place. The damp roof appears to sag even more than usual.

Axle and Toby jog two miles Sunday afternoon. They eat lunch and wait. Following that, they sit and wait. They are in the garage lifting weights at 3:00 when the Lord High Sheriff arrives on an inspection tour. The garage door is open. The boys are plainly evident when the cruiser crunches to a halt on the gravel driveway. When the sheriff arrives, Toby is concentrating on bench pressing iron with

Axle tending the lift. As the cruiser rolls to a stop, Axle murmurs, "Here comes the sheriff, try not to look guilty of something."

Harvey Kraven is dressed in his khaki colored western styled wrinkle-suit with a light colored Stetson. When he saunters through the garage door, the barbell stops in mid-sequence before it finds a place on the bar rest. Toby sits up as he wipes down with a towel. When Axle sees the sheriff, he develops a bad feeling in the pit of his stomach. He begins to feel as though he is the center of gravity for the entire universe.

Toby stares at the sheriff, as he mutters, "Howdy."

"Hidy, boys," Harvey drawls, as he moves through the door. "Ya'll been keepin' outta mischief?"

"Don't have time for mischief," Toby answers, "what with work and all."

Harvey observes, "Why ain't you workin' then?"

"Because the ground's too wet to work," Axle answers, "maybe we can dig a few holes tomorrow."

Harvey glances around the garage before he moves to peer into the tool room.

"Is yer daddy home?"

"No, sir," the boy answers, "he's out of town, recuperating. My folks are with friends somewhere out of state."

The sheriff asks, "Did ya ever figure out who worked him over?"

Axle shakes his head, as he answers, "Nobody knows so we finally gave up tryin'."

The sheriff presses on. "Mind if I have a look around?"

"Not at all," Axle answers. "Help yourself. If you tell me what you're lookin' for, maybe I can help you find it."

The sheriff has a vacant look on his face, when he answers, "Not lookin' for anything in particular, just fightin' local crime."

"Crime?" Axle stammers. "What crime?"

"Ain't you heard, Mannheim," Harvey offers. "Big fire out south of town last night. Somebody burned my brother's place to the ground. We suspect foul play, so we're takin' every precaution to see that the situation don't multiply. Where were you kids last night?"

Such is life, Axle thinks. I've suffered through one demotion after another. I've gone from Mannheim to kid in three sentences. Big mistake, you think we're kids. Dad would love this.

"We were camping at Greenleaf State Park last night," Axle replies. "We got home early this morning and went to work. Lindsay Construction sent everybody home. We've been workin' on our glider. Before that, we went joggin' and now we're liftin' weights."

Harvey's face brightens as he mutters, "That sounds like bullshit, kid."

That's an alarmingly close description, sheriff.

"Ya got any proof ya was at the park?" the sheriff asks.

"Sure," Axle answers, as he produces his wallet and removes the receipt.

The sheriff takes the paper. He glances at it absently before he hands it back. Axle returns the paper to his wallet while he waits alertly, ready to field the next question. He looks toward the backyard clothesline where two shelter halves and two sleeping bags are busy trying to dry themselves in 98 percent humidity.

Harvey says, "Mind if I have a look in the house?"

"Sure," Axle says, "come on."

Axle picks up a towel and drapes it around his neck as he leads the way to the back door. The sheriff follows closely in his footsteps. Axle glances west along the street. He sees another cruiser parked almost out of sight.

They're looking for the girls but they don't have a clue where to search. That means that they're looking everywhere. They probably suspect everyone, because nearly everybody's been abused by them at one time or another. The fact the sheriff's here himself probably means we're high on their list of suspects.

Axle opens the door and enters the kitchen. The sheriff shoulders the boy aside as he proceeds to look in all the rooms, the closets and even under the beds. The Condor glider wing is plainly visible inside a closet where the airfoil stands on a wing tip against a rear wall. The fuselage sets astride the top of Axle's dresser. The sheriff gives the machine a tentative glance as though he expects to find one of the girls hiding in the cockpit. He looks behind the Hallicrafter's Radio. *Probably looking for evidence and doesn't know what some would* look like. He does the basement followed by the attic bedroom last. The sheriff exhibits great detail as though his life depends on what he does next. When he is satisfied, he gives the boys his tough cop stare.

"You two be where I can find you when I need to."

Toby asks, "Why? What are we supposed to have done?"

The sheriff growls, "Don't get smart with me sonny, or I'll club your head down between your knees."

Toby looks him in the eye before he says, "Yes, sir, you got it."

The sheriff walks through the back door where he takes a tour around the outside of the house. The boys stand on the back slab where they wait. The sheriff looks in the garage again before he glances at the weed choked lot next door.

"Whose house is that?" he mutters as he awaits an answer.

"I don't know," Axle answers. "Nobody lives there. The place has a lock on the door and no one ever comes around. It'll probably burn down one of these days. Some local kid will toss a firecracker into the weeds some Fourth of July, and the whole place'll go up. The fire might take our house with it when it does."

The sheriff listens to the explanation as he studies the silver gray wood of the eastern wall. He suddenly launches himself toward the edge of the weed patch. He stands shading his eyes with a hand while he surveys the back door from about 20 feet away. The rusty old padlock is plainly visible, even from the edge of the driveway. After a short pause, he decides to wade through the weeds to rattle the lock in its hasp.

When the lock doesn't open, he cups his hands on the glass of a window as he tries to look inside. Apparently, black spray paint in combination with curtains sewn across the opening works wonders for privacy. Axle suddenly realizes that he is holding his breath.

Sheriff Kraven rattles the lock one last time before he seems satisfied. He then strolls back through the weeds to his car. His suit is wet to the knees. He gives the boys another cop stare before he asks, "If you knew anything about the fire last night, would you tell me?"

"Sure," Toby says, "but we didn't even know there was a fire until you told us. Remember, we were out of town?"

Harvey Kraven climbs into his vehicle where he talks on the

radio for awhile. He then backs along the driveway. At the street, he takes one last look at the boys before he heads east on Birch Street.

He drives just far enough to turn into the Fitzpatrick's driveway. Toby and Axle glance at each other before Toby says, "Think he smelled fresh paint or kerosene when he tried to see through the window?"

Axle shrugs. "No way to tell. If he did though, I suspect the cop in the cruiser down the street would be here right now prying the hasp off the door."

"I think we'd better move them?" Toby growls, as he watches the sheriff knock on his front door.

"Yeah, I have the same feeling," Axle responds, "but where?"

"Have to think about that one for a spell," Toby comments, as he watches the sheriff.

The sheriff enters the Fitzpatrick house through the unlocked front door. He emerges some 15 minutes later. While the boys watch, Axle remembers something he heard one time on the radio during a Sky King episode.

"If you want to hide an apple, "Axle mumbles, "hide it in an apple tree."

"Say what?" Toby offers.

"Nothing," Axle mutters, "just thinkin' out loud."

"The sheriff just created an apple tree for us when he came here and looked around himself," Axle remarks. "When he did that, our house became our apple tree."

Toby looks at his buddy strangely as though his mind has suddenly slipped a gear. "You all right, pard, or did you hurt yourself thinkin'?"

"Perhaps," Axle replies. "We can hide the girls in our apple tree. We can put them in our attic. The sheriff has already searched the house. Chances are slim that either he or his deputies will waste time looking where they've already searched. He probably figures what happened to his brother's moonshine operation is beyond the realm of two 17-year-old kids."

Toby mutters, "Realm?"

"Yeah," Axle answers, "realm. I'm entitled to use big words like that. I made the outstanding student list two years ago during a moment of confusion by the teachers at my last school."

Axle recalls his Dad's final words as he departed for Grand Bluff with his mom. Now he understands what his father meant when he said, *"The joy of life is mostly about the journey."*

Chapter Sixty-One

When night falls, the boys move the girls into the Mannheim attic. The entry into the space is through a half-sized door in a closet of the upstairs bedroom. They have stored a lot of boxes from the move in the attic. What is there now is stuff that his mother maintains is too good to throw away. The boxes are stacked nearly to the steeply peaked ceiling atop loose planks spaced about an inch apart. The planks begin about eight feet from the entry door. They lie atop the downstairs ceiling rafters and extend to the far end of the attic space. The planks make a floor for storage that allows boxes to be stacked atop each other. Considerable effort was expended before the girls were brought into the house. The plank walkway now begins about eight feet from the entry door. The boxes have been rearranged to create a hollow space at the far end. In order to navigate to where the girls are, a person has to bend nearly double while taking 16-inch steps from one ceiling rafter to the next.

The storage area is directly above the kitchen ceiling. If the stepee misses the edge of a two by four ceiling joist, then he will fall through the ceiling into the kitchen. Bending nearly parallel to the ceiling joists while taking short steps and carrying something is a real bitch. The stepee needs to be fit and agile enough to perform the maneuver.

After dark, the boys spent more than an hour getting the girls installed in their new hiding place behind a triple row of boxes. Each girl has four pillows to use as a sleeping pad. Food and water is passed to them by means of a one by twelve that rests on the top of the row of boxes screening them from the outside world. They have a chamber pot along with a sheet and a blanket.

There are no lights within the attic. Following Harvey's rattle of the next door hasp the night before, the girls are terrified. They are as quiet in their new home as church mice. The boys figure they will need to hide the fugitives for only a portion of one more night.

Toby asks, "Are we over reacting?

"Perhaps," Axle replies. "I doubt that it's possible to over react in these circumstances."

With the girls securely hidden, Axle turns his attention to making something for supper.

The boys plot a show of openness. They open the drapes in the living room so that only the window sheers are in place. They then begin to play dominoes at the dining room table. They are plainly visible from the street. For supper, they eat peanut butter and jelly sandwiches. The dry sandwiches are chased with Kool-Aid. Upstairs, the girls dine on the same fair, but in the dark. The entire time Axle is at the dining room table, he has the distinct feeling that he is about to be shot in the head. He also believes that if he is, he won't know if it happens.

At 10:00, a pair of headlights sweeps across the window as a sheriff's cruiser enters the driveway. The vehicle stops near the garage where two of the town-Mounties climb out for a look around. They stand for a short moment in the light provided by an overhead fixture attached to the wall beneath the garage door's eave. The cops adjust their leather belts before they survey the area around them. One is fat and the other skinny. Together, they resemble a vaudeville act. Their marquee would read Fats and Slats.

The fat one scans the area with his five cell. They are both hatless when they head for the abandoned house in the weed patch. Fats carries a flashlight, while Slats carries a pinch bar. When they arrive at the back door of the abandoned building, Fats holds the light beam on the hasp while Slats pries it off. The aged maple door jam releases the screws grudgingly. Each screw makes a screeching noise as it is withdrawn from where it's been seated for probably more than 30 years.

The portly deputy stands on the second step with his hand on his gun butt while the other one enters to look around.

"These old lamps still got kerosene in 'em," Slats drawls. "The place is filthy," he adds in the next breath. He obviously can't see very well with Fats' flashlight sweeping the room from the doorway behind him.

After a ten second search, the thin deputy emerges. As he moves back through the door, he mutters, "About like I figured, another wild goose chase."

Fats runs the light beam around the room again before the search crew walks to where the boys stand watching them from the cement slab of the back porch.

The fat one is a Kraven the boys haven't seen before. He wears sergeant chevrons on his uniform sleeve. The other one is Jeb with his weak chin.

Fats commands, "We'd like to look in your house, please?"

"Sheriff Kraven already did," Axle mutters.

"He wants us to look again if you don't mind," the sergeant persists.

Axle leads the way inside. The deputies walk through the house as if they own it. They both stop to look at the Condor fuselage.

While they study the model, Fats asks skeptically, "Does this thing really fly?"

"Yeah," Toby mutters.

"Where'd ya get it?"

"We made it from a kit," Axle mumbles.

The deputy nods approvingly before they head for the back door. Jeb touches the door knob that leads to the upstairs bedroom before he asks, "Where does this go?"

"Unused, attic bedroom," Axle answers.

Fats opens the door, sweeps the stairwell with his flashlight beam before he locates the light switch. He turns on the overhead light before he heads upward. The boys' hearts stop beating.

At the top of the stairs, he has to move a box of books out of his way to enter. He looks around as he mutters, "This place got an attic?"

Axle gestures toward the closet door screened by numerous boxes. "Behind the boxes," Axle says. "The door is in the closet."

Fats steps aside, while Jeb moves enough boxes to bare the entry door. Fats is not into anything that might induce sweat. The boys are sweating enough for both of them and from places they didn't know had sweat glands.

When Jeb finishes shifting boxes, he stands aside. Fat's enters the closet where he turns a pair of butterfly fasteners on the attic door. Next, he grasps the small brass door knob to pull the door open. His flashlight sweeps the interior but all he can see are boxes stacked three high, four joists from the door. He ducks through the opening. When he stands up, he is panting. Bending nearly double with a beer belly apparently restricts his breathing capacity. He steps onto the first ceiling joist where he sweeps the space with his light beam.

Toby nods at Axle, then toward an open tool box on the floor. The tool box contains wood working tools from when the boys pulled the nails so they could remove the first few planks leading into the attic. The top layer contains a 30 inch crowbar and a claw hammer. Toby has decided to fight if the girls are found. He plans to use the crowbar.

Jeb stoops as he moves to enter the attic. His actions jostle his fat partner who immediately loses his balance. Fats falls astride the ceiling joist he was standing on. Both his feet plunge downward through the beaver-board ceiling into the kitchen.

The three-striper emits a loud wail as he tries to grab himself. The raw edges of the ceiling board have sprung back into place where they clamp around his legs. The edges now hold him rigidly in place. Cussing quickly gives way to whimpering as he screams for Jeb to help him up. Jeb has the approximate upper body strength of a lettuce leaf, so he is unable to lift his partner upward out of his position. After watching the comedy team for the better part of two minutes, Toby pushes Jeb aside to step through the door. Once inside, he braces himself before he lifts Fats upward. The beaver board breaks away as the fat man is pulled upward out of his resting place.

When he is back inside the closet, the three-striper stands knock-kneed as he holds his crotch in discomfort. From that position, he berates Jeb for causing him to fall.

"Pardon me," Axle says, as he interjects a note of anger. "Thanks for the ceiling fellows, who's gonna fix it?"

The three-striper answers, "The county'll send someone out. They'll make it as good as new." His comment comes from between clenched teeth. "I'll report the damage as soon as we get back to the station."

With one final withering comment to Jeb, Fats heads back down the stairs. Fats seems less spry than when he climbed the stairway. Jeb's face is screwed into a look of total mirth as he tries valiantly to stifle laughter. The girls haven't made a peep during the entire episode. Axle watches the departing deputies with a smile.

"I think that our apple tree is now safe," he muses. "We can begin looking forward to our departure in the WACO."

Chapter Sixty-Two

The night resumes its passage with all the speed of oak tree growth. At 11:30, Cecil arrives with the news that everything concerning the WACO has been arranged.

Over the next 45 minutes, he reveals his plan for getting the girls out of town in great detail. After that, he heads home to bed. The boys go back to their domino game. At midnight, Axle draws all the drapes before he sets up the short-wave radio. With the auxiliary equipment in place, he turns on the unit. The dials light up but the radio has no carrier wave. The boys check all the electrical connections, even to the extent that Toby climbs into the crawl space beneath the house to check the main unit. All fuses are intact but the unit is completely dead. They mutually decide that there must be an internal component failure.

An hour later after fruitlessly checking and rechecking the things they know about, they give up trying to inform headquarters of their proposed actions. Now they are on their own. The next few hours will detail their success or failure.

They return to the table where they play dominoes and discuss the latest development for nearly another hour. Finally Axle offers, "If I stay bent over this table all night, by morning I'll need a bumper-jack to get my head back up into position."

They finally adjourn for the night. Toby occupies the bottom bunk in Axle's room. Axle sets his alarm clock for 2:30 am before he lies down on his parent's bed in his clothes with the room lights off. About the time they drift into a restless slumber, the alarm goes off. They both spring upright as though they have received an electrical shock.

Toby goes outside where he checks the area by jogging the perimeter of the four adjacent blocks. There are no police vehicles or anyone loitering any place he can find. He returns to the house where Axle has just finished making everyone a cold cut sandwich composed of olive loaf and cheese.

At 3:00 in the morning, the boys hustle the girls into the rumble seat of Axle's hot rod before he closes and locks the lid.

Toby carries an old brown canvas valise that containing a 12-gauge, Winchester, Model 12, pump-action, shotgun. The weapon is broken down into two pieces. Also in the valise are ten rounds of high velocity goose loads, a canteen of water and three candy bars.

Melissa still carries the rubberized bag with the top drawn closed by the white shoe lace. The coffee cans rattle against each other as Axle stuffs the bag in the corner of the cab behind the front seat. They do not use the headlights when they pull slowly along the driveway.

From their vantage point, they watch Cecil depart in his car for the airport. When he is out of sight, they leave the neighborhood headed in a different direction. Axle drives slowly along side streets. While he drives, Toby assembles the shotgun. When the weapon is fully reassembled, he fills the magazine with shells.

Axle whispers in the dark, "If what we're doing don't work, try not to look astonished."

Toby's response is to point the gun barrel out the side window before he jacks a shell into the chamber. "Yo," he replies, as he rests the gun pointed muzzle first against the carpeted floor.

A sharp chill of reality slides along his spine as Axle mutters, "I've got a notion this trip is gonna turn scrapbook worthy before it's over with."

"You better hope not," Toby responds from his dark corner of the cab. "If this thing goes south and we get in a shoot out, don't think bandages for the cops, think tourniquets and a hearse."

In the darkness there is another metallic rustle as Toby slides another shell into the magazine before he places the butt of the stock into his left arm pit. The decision was made during the night that they will fight if they are about to be apprehended. There is no favorable percentage involved in being caught by the Kravens with two fugitive women in their car. As a result, they are both armed to the teeth.

They move along streets they seldom travel while they avoid well-lit areas. They are constantly moving toward the northeast edge of town and only see one cruiser during their drive. The vehicle crosses the street ahead of them. It is idling west as it sweeps the area along the street with a spotlight.

In response to the sighting, Axle turns south for a block along a north/south street. That effort allows them to see along the total length of Main Street. Cecil is parked on Main Street. A cruiser sits behind him with its bubble-gum light flashing. The cops are searching his vehicle.

Axle moves away from the area. Three blocks later, he is headed northeast toward the edge of town. They pass through a gate in a four-strand barbed-wire fence. Beyond the fence lies a large nearly barren, over-grazed pasture. The field parallels the creek as it bends around the town. When they are within the pasture, Toby turns toward the rear of the cab.

He says in a loud voice, "Can you gals hear me?"

A muffled voice answers, "Yeah, just barely."

"We're out of town. We're nearly to where we'll meet Cecil with the airplane."

"Thank God," is the muffled response.

Axle continues across the pasture of unknown dimension. Neither of the boys have been in this field before. The grass is short and the ground is nearly as hard and smooth as a pool table. They begin to angle toward the highway. About half a mile later, they reach the fence beneath the highway embankment where the highway elevates to cross the bridge. The wires of the fence here are very slack. Toby cuts the strands with the vise-grip wire cutter. After the car passes through, he wires the strands together with bailing wire he brought along for the occasion. The roadway bed at this point is elevated more than ten feet above the fence.

As Toby enters the car again, another vehicle passes on the highway above them. The vehicle is headed toward town. The lights of the vehicle illuminate the night sky well above the roof of the fugitive's car. Axle eases along the fence row paralleling the highway until he finds a place to cross the ditch at the bottom of the embankment.

The rear wheels spin on wet earth during the crossing but there is sufficient traction to make it up the bank onto the blacktop. Axle accelerates headed away from town toward safety. About five miles north of town, they turn east on a blacktop farm-to-market road.

Cecil's plan involves a crop-duster strip located on a long abandoned farm about ten miles northeast of town. Axle maintains a tranquil 50 miles an hour speed with the lights on. Halfway to the turn off, a sheriff's cruiser passes them headed in the opposite direction. Axle watches the tail lights of the vehicle in the rear view mirror. Not long after the car passes, its brake lights illuminate. The vehicle swerves to the road shoulder before the brake lights go off.

The cop continues on toward town. Axle rounds the next curve where he turns off his lights before he accelerates. He can see well enough by starlight to locate the entry road to the farm. At the entry, Axle slams on the brakes before turning onto a grass covered lane leading toward the long abandoned farmhouse. From the west, a pair of headlights can be seen traveling at high speed.

"Whatever you do, don't use the brakes again," Toby mutters. "The brake lights will give us away."

Axle slams the gearshift into second to slow for a low spot in the road. Behind them, headlights pass the entrance to the road and continue eastward. As the vehicle passes, Axle catches a reflection of chrome on the rooftop. They have just missed being spotted by a sheriff's deputy by 15 seconds.

Axle drives past the abandoned farmhouse plus several items of abandoned farm equipment before he enters a short grass pasture. Ahead in the dimness of starlight stands a barn with a sagging roof. The doors to the building are closed on the south side but are slightly ajar on the north side. He quickly turns the car, so as to back into the building while Toby opens one of the aged double doors. With a door finally open, he enters to check the floor with his penlight. He moves bailed hay to make space for the car before he returns to open the other door. He then guides the vehicle into a cavity between the bails.

When the car is situated in the dark barn, Toby closes both doors. Following much additional effort, he manages to secure the door with an elderly crossbar that hangs from a single bolt. The bar slides behind aged wood holders to secure the doors closed. With the entrance bared, he flicks on his penlight to have another look around.

Strewn about the floor are old gunnysacks and portions of broken moldy hay bales. The boys get the girls out of the rumble seat before they cover the car with feed sacks. The walls of the barn are fraught with cracks and missing boards. They set about subduing the reflection of chrome and a good paint job so their presence will not be noticed.

Stacked bails screen the car from three sides. They rearrange the hay until the vehicle is blocked from sight on all sides. They then toss the remaining sacks onto the car followed by armloads of loose hay to break up its outline. Following the camouflage session everyone climbs a ladder upward into the haymow. From the south end of the mow, they can observe the highway through a doorway that is missing both doors.

The trip thus far has consumed slightly over an hour. Axle glances at his watch as he calculates the time remaining until Cecil will make the scene. The floor creaks as Sarah settles in beside him in the hay. She wants to be held and patted, which he gladly does. They lay in the hay and hold each other. Following half an hour of close contact, Axle hears the beat of a car engine. He looks toward the highway where he finds headlights advancing along the weed choked lane near the farm house. The vehicle takes a turn around the old house before it heads toward the barn. Light reflects off chrome on the roof. The car is obviously a law enforcement vehicle.

A spotlight sweeps the pasture behind the barn before it settles on the barn itself. The cruiser idles around the building before it pauses to scan the structure carefully with the spotlight. The driver climbs out of the car to approach the east end of the structure. There is a screech of nails followed by the sound of a board being dropped on the ground. The beam of a flashlight illuminates the inside of the barn. The light beam sweeps the bailed hay. Seemingly satisfied, the cop returns to the cruiser. There is the bang of a car door before the cruiser heads back along the road to the highway.

The dirt airstrip lies beyond the curve of a hill on the back edge of the property. During summer, local crop-dusters use the sod strip when they work the area. The strip is not visible from the highway.

An hour before daylight, the fugitives dig the car out of the hay before they open the barn doors. When everything has been returned to its original condition they drive to the back fence line of the property.

A quarter of an hour passes. The stars begin to lose their fight with the orange-pink glow of another dawn before Cecil comes into view in the WACO. He is flying at tree top level when he banks sharply and lands. At the end of the roll out, he applies brakes and power as he spins the airplane to face back the way it had landed. The power returns to idle. He sets the parking brake before he climbs out of the cockpit. The engine remains running. The four kids scurry onboard and strap in. Cecil hands Toby a flight plan card along with fuel transfer instructions. He then smiles in the dark as he admonishes his son about ground looping on landing. Father and son give each other a hug before Cecil secures the door.

The sun is about to peek above the horizon when the airplane breaks ground. Navigation maps are attached to a pilot's clip board that lies atop the metal hood above the instrument panel. A note scrawled in black pen reads, "Good luck and Godspeed."

Toby flies with the navigation lights off. He makes one climbing turn before he assumes an easterly heading. Axle can see Cecil headed toward the highway in Axle's car. Toby levels off at 1,500 feet. Axle begins to pick up reference points on the map. The yellow biplane flies east bathed in the harsh orange glow of another sunrise.

The girls are at last out of Amerada and for the moment, out of harm's way. Toby's grin reflects so brightly in the sunrise that it could be used as a mirror.

"You and me babe," Toby growls at Axle. "You and me."

Chapter Sixty-Three

The fugitives fly for just over five hours. They make three refueling stops. The WACO isn't fast but it is reliable. The old radial engine burns fuel as though it is being fed through a fire hose. There is a hypnotic effect to the beat of the engine that makes the passengers drowsy. A thin film of oil collects on the windscreen as the flight progresses.

Near the heart of southern Louisiana, Toby waggles the wings as he searches for a sod strip along side an abandoned river channel. Both girls are asleep in the backseat. Toby weaves constantly as he searches for the landing site. Finally, he rolls wings level before he points downward. Axle elevates slightly so he can see out the left side of the cockpit. Below them, a landing strip is visible near an oxbow near a river channel.

He makes a pass down the landing area at a very low altitude. Several alligators can be seen as they slither into the water from the edge of a sod strip. Toby does a chandelle that places the bird downwind paralleling the runway. The landing that follows is as smooth as though he has been flying the WACO all his life.

The aircraft comes to a stop near three buildings adjacent to the middle of the sod strip. One structure is an old wooden hanger with an oval roof. The wood was originally painted orange with black trim in about 1920 and then never again. The hanger looks capable of sheltering three light planes if one has a wing missing. A Quonset hut serves as a combination country store, post office and flight operations building. The third structure is an outhouse with a half moon cut in the door.

A relatively new orange windsock hangs limply from the top of a utility pole near the store. Toby spins the bird on a wheel to stop near a fuel pump in front of the hut aimed back toward the sod strip. They all stand as stiff as boards as they watch an old geezer approach them. The man wears khaki pants below a pale blue work shirt. Toby tells him that they will remain over night and that he is to top off the tanks. As the man sets about servicing the bird, Toby climbs into the back of the cabin where he locates tie-down stakes.

Everybody combines to push the bird to a parking place where it is secured for the night. When the wheel chocks and tie-down anchors are in place, Toby checks the oil before he performs a walk around inspection. When he is satisfied, everyone enters the store. Toby's accent has gotten thicker since the aircraft crossed the Louisiana border. By now, he seems barely literate.

A blue tick hound lies in the sun across the threshold of the doorway. Everyone steps over him as they enter. The dog's tail thumps the floor in greeting as his head lifts to casually sniff every passing pant leg. He checks everyone as though he is fulfilling a contract for security. Following that effort, his head drops back to lie in the sunbeam. Toby approaches an elderly man behind a counter where he asks, "How ye be, Walter?"

Walter squint's his eyes nearly closed before he mutters, "Toby!" He stretches the name into something that sounds like Too-bee. While he is doing that, he is shaking Toby's hand and claps him on the shoulder. "Whar ye be, Too-bee? We miss you. We think we never see you again."

Toby offers, "Moved to Texas, Walt. We've just dropped in for an overnight visit. Does Lou Boudreau still live in the same place on Grassy Lake?"

"Yeah, since he was about 12 year old," Walter answers.

"Walt, I need a boat to go there," Toby growls. "It would be better if we had two. Anything around we can rent or borrow?"

"Yeah, take mine," Walter answers. "Ye can use Virgil's too, they just out back on the wharf. When ye be back?"

"In the morning," Toby answers. "That put you out much?"

"Naw, just wondering," Walter mutters. "What you want ol' Lou fer?"

"Personal business," Toby responds. "We need him to watch these two young women for a spell."

Walt's laugh exposes a gap in his front teeth, about three teeth wide. "Old Lou's first class at watchin' women," he observes. "He don't let his daughters outta his sight less they be goin' to the outhouse."

Toby asks, "Ya sure Virgil won't mind me takin' his boat?"

"Naw," Walter says, "I tell him not to."

The boys walk through the back door of the store where they find two 16-foot, well used Duracraft John-boats floating double-tied to a dock. They have relatively new 35 horse outboards bolted to their transoms.

The youngsters drop into the crafts, two to a boat. Toby hits a starter button and the engine instantly coughs to life. Toby idles past Axle whose boat is also running. He shouts above engine noise, "Follow exactly where I go and don't fall back."

Axle salutes as he begins to trail the now rapidly moving boat with Toby at the helm. Melissa clings perilously to the middle seat.

Sarah faces forward on the middle seat in the other boat as Axle gives the engine a small measure of throttle. The light boat shoots forward, instantly on plane. He chases Toby while staying exactly in his wake. The boats are light and amazingly fast. Axle estimates they are traveling nearly 50 miles an hour. Tree trunks whip past on either side of the boats with such velocity that they resemble a leafy green picket fence. Axle estimates that only the prop and about two feet of the hull remain in the water on the straightway, everything else is airborne.

Bugs strike Axle in the face as he guns along the narrow channel. The insects leave welts and residue in their wake. He wants to reassure Sarah, but he dare not open his mouth to speak. He wears sunglasses that quickly become frosted with bug juice. Sarah turns around in self-defense. Her hair blossoms around her face so that it totally hides her features. She white knuckles the seat with both hands while she sits hunched, her head bowed as though in prayer.

Toby follows the riverbed for about five wind stinging, bug streaked miles. Eventually, he beaches his boat at the bottom of a gently inclined clay bank. The boys unload all removable items from both boats. The portage requires the efforts of all four people to slide the boats one at a time, up the bank and over the top. The bank is the remnant of a very old river levy.

Behind the bank is a large lake. The lake is vaguely visible at the end of a short water trail lined by cypress trees. No earth is apparent on any shore. The only thing visible is cypress knees, Spanish moss, and tree trunks.

All loose equipment is loaded back onboard before Toby establishes another headlong flight across the middle of the lake. On the far side, he enters a winding cypress lined channel less than 30 feet wide. The boat speed never slackens as they drive deeper into the heart of the bayou.

Clouds have formed overhead that promise late day showers. Spanish moss hangs from tree limbs. The long gray tendrils give the place an eerie unreal appearance in the low light.

Toby reduces power as his boat glides around a left turn into a slack water cove. At the end of the cove, perched atop tall pilings stands a substantial Arcadian style house. The exterior has the silvery-gray gloss of aged unpainted cypress wood. Fully half the walls are devoted to window openings covered with new window screens that shine in the light. Storm shutters hang down against the outside walls of the house. The roof is corrugated tin with eaves that are fully six feet wide. A wooden deck circles the circumference of the house beneath the eaves.

The underpinnings exhibit the pale green sheen of pressure treated utility poles. There are perhaps 20 of them supporting the structure. Three John-boats float among the pilings beneath the house. A narrow wharf of rough cut planks bobs in various openings between the pilings. The wharf floats atop tar coated 55-gallon oil drums. Stairs lead from the wharf upward into the center of the house.

Axle follows Toby's example as he ties his borrowed boat to a piling mounted cleat before he walks the wharf toward the stairway. A medium height very muscular middle-aged man dressed in cut-off jeans and barefoot, bounds down the stairs to grab Toby in a bear hug. The man's enthusiasm is so spontaneous he lifts Toby up off the planks to shake him in mid-air.

"You've come home, my little friend!" he booms. "Damn, it's good to see you." He drops Toby and turns to survey the rest of the crew. He darts forward to kiss the hands of the two exhausted women.

After pumping Axle's paw, he turns back to the women. "You are traveling in bad company with these two, I fear. But now you are safe. Your Uncle Lou will take care of you." Melissa sobs and would have fallen had Lou not caught her. "What is wrong, my little one?" His face is clouded with concern. "Matilda!" he calls, in his distinctive voice. A black haired, tawny looking beautiful young woman glides barefoot down the stairs. She pauses to view the new arrivals. "My wife, Matilda," Lou offers, to his audience.

Matilda advances the rest of the way where she insinuates herself around Toby as though she is a second skin. Toby stands in quiet discomfort throughout the greeting process. None of the arrivals are oblivious to the warm welcome.

"I think these two need your attention," Lou says, as he nods to Sarah and Melissa.

Their escape, hideout and flight to what seems to be the end of the earth has caught up with them. They are both crying as they cling to each other. Axle feels as though he is about to join them.

"What is wrong my friend?" Lou turns to Toby, his face dark with concern.

"Before I tell you," Toby says, "can we sit down somewhere? I'm bushed."

Lou gestures to the stairs. Everyone climbs up into the center of the house. In the middle of the entry room stands a large table that resembles those found in roadside parks. This one is constructed of approximately three-inch thick unfinished cypress. The structure is of such massiveness it could probably support a corner of the house. The craftsmanship is superb.

Axle glances around the room. All the furniture is made in the same style, by the same hand. Matilda leads the two young women into the back of the house while the men climb aboard bench seats attached to the table.

Lou mutters, "You obviously need help, my friend, or you would not be here. What can I do for you and your companions?"

Axle senses that this man is sincere.

"This will be a long story, Uncle Lou," Toby mutters. "We have more than a slight problem."

Then he tells the story, all of it. Lou's eyes never leave Toby's face even while he rolls and lights a cigarette. His gaze remains intense, probing and thoughtful. When Toby finishes, Lou cocks his head as he looks away from the table. When he speaks it is in a lower than normal voice.

"You do need help. I will do what I can, and in most cases, that is considerable."

Lou summons his eldest son, Lou Jr. He sends the boy by boat to Lou's brother's home further along the bayou. In half an hour, the boy is back with the brother, Justin, who follows in another boat. While he watches the arrival of the two aluminum missiles, Axle marvels at the fact that the watercraft in this part of the world seem to have but two speeds. They are either at idle or at full throttle. Justin climbs the stairs and seats himself, after which Lou tells him the story. When he is finished, Lou growls.

"We need 20 volunteers to travel a modest distance to liberate a small town in southern Texas from corruption. Tell whoever asks that the corruption involves the kidnapping, rape and murder of young women. Tell those who volunteer to be here at first light."

His brother nods before he turns on a heel and leaves. Matilda enters to place two large platters on the table. For the next hour, the men peel and eat crawfish, drink beer and plot retribution. To the north, thunder rumbles as lightning streaks the sky. A breeze ruffles the Cyprus trees.

Axle has that same perception of voices from the past moaning their displeasure with what has happened to them. He is stricken with an extreme thought that they had better get this thing right, because a vengeful God is watching over everything that happens. Heavy bugs attracted by lamplight slam against window screens. By the time the men are finished eating, Lou has formulated a basic plan for the rescue of Amerada and its people.

Chapter Sixty-Four

The plotting session lasts deep into the night. The initial plan is composed of many questions with answers written on a long yellow lined legal pad. Each known action is covered by possible reactions. When they are nearly finished, Toby mentions the upcoming election. The subject becomes a focal point. Axle produces the ballots for everyone to examine. When the examination is completed, Lou again issues instructions. The boy has listened quietly during the planning session from his end of the table. Lou Jr., appears to be about 16.

Lou murmurs, "Louis, please take this card and note to Lyndon Bordelon and await his reply."

Lou scribbles a note on a piece of brown paper sack. He pronounces each word as he writes. The note reads: *We need 40,000 of these within 24 hours. The price must be negotiable. Is this possible?*

Lou Jr. places the ballot and the note in his shirt pocket. He buttons the flap and scampers down the stairs to the wharf. Lights come on that bathe the water near the house with high intensity lights. In seconds, Lou Jr. roars away into the night. He is aimed along the bayou with a tall white rooster-tail aloft behind his boat. Axle regards traveling at that speed to be a phenomenal feat when he considers that the boy is navigating at night along a narrow waterway.

From the doorway, Melissa says, "I overheard you say the price must be negotiable?"

Lou answers, "Yes, little one, that is correct."

Melissa leans against the doorjamb. She looks at Lou for a long moment.

"We have money, a lot of money, and part of it can be used to save our town."

Jaws sag at the revelation. *Money, where in hell would she get money?*

She turns away from the door. When she returns she carries the rubberized bag from the canoe. She places the bag on the end of the table where she unties the shoelace. She produces the three coffee cans from the shack she has been carrying for the last two days. She offers a can to Lou.

"Here is money. I don't know how much, but I suspect it's quite a lot. The Kravens divide the proceeds from their moonshine operation amongst themselves. They keep their money beneath their beds or elsewhere in the shack. There is more some other place, because Luke kept his separate, not in the house."

Melissa places the cans one at time on the table near Lou's elbow. Lou picks up the first can and removes the wide rubber band that secures the lid. Inside are rolls of paper bills. Each roll is tightly wound around itself. The rolls are stuffed within the can so tightly that when Lou inverts the container nothing escapes. After a couple of diminutive shakes, he pulls a roll loose with his fingers. He dumps the top layer onto the table. The cylinders are composed of $100 bills rolled and secured with a thin rubber band. The rolls waddle on the surface of the table. The onlookers catch the wayward bundles and return them to the pile.

The other two cans are emptied onto the pile. Lou picks up a roll and removes the band. He attempts to flatten the first roll against the table before he counts. The roll contains 30 $100 bills. Toby counts rolls. There are 45 in all, 15 rolls to a can.

Toby mutters, "If each roll has $3,000 in it, then we are looking at about $135,000."

Everyone gazes in amazement at more money than any of them have ever seen before.

"The money explains why it was so easy to corrupt the officials of an entire county," Lou comments. "Now we understand why the sheriff wants to keep his job so badly."

Axle was so sleepy he was nodding off. After seeing the money, however, he's no longer even tired, least of all bored. They all begin unfurling and counting money. When they're finished, there is $136,000 lying in unstable stacks on the table. The bills are arched from years of being compressed in tight rolls.

Toby mutters, "What now?"

"As soon as we get over the shock of this," Lou answers, "we will invent a solution." Lou gazes across the table with a look of amusement in his eyes. "I think we are about to see if what I learned as a small child really works."

"What's that?" Toby asks.

"It is something my father taught me," Lou answers. "The only way to defeat the treacherous is with treachery."

Sarah has joined Melissa at the table. "We know what we want to do with the money."

"And what is that, my lady?" Lou asks.

"We want to give some to each of the families who lost somebody," Sarah sobs. "What is left then will be placed a trust fund so those who would be unable to earn an education outside Amerada can find a life elsewhere."

"We must consider the men going on this mission," Axle offers. "I doubt that the men living here in this bayou can afford the extravagance of driving to Amerada and back."

"Just being able to do this will be enough for us," Lou offers. "We've had little to feel good about since the war. Being able to rescue a town will be enough for the volunteers."

Axle looks at the two women standing near the end of the table. Their eyes are very bright when he speaks to them. Melissa lowers her face so that when she speaks she is looking at the floor.

"When this is over, I want to tell the people of Amerada what happened. They deserve to know so it never happens again." Melissa speaks in a diminutive voice. "I would have been the valedictorian of my class. This will be my graduation speech."

"My little one," Lou volunteers, "perhaps it would be best if you speak to them before we begin the resurrection of a town. I have a plan for this. Let me think about it through what remains of the night. By morning, perhaps we will have a solution to place in motion." Lou says, in a loud voice, "Matilda, will you come here please?" When she enters the room, Lou says, "Please bring us two pillow cases." When she returns, he divides the mounds of money, placing them inside the pillow cases. He hands one to Axle and the other to Toby. "The heroes of Amerada will guard the money through the night," Lou instructs. "Tomorrow we will deliver it to a safe place."

Sarah, Melissa and Matilda leave the room. Once again, there is deep discussion. At some point during the discussion, a dark beauty sweeps into the room. She appears to be about 17, but as soon as she opens her mouth, Axle advances his assumption by 20 years. The young woman is an irrational love affair waiting to happen.

Her apparel is a thin shapeless cotton dress covered with printed flowers. She probably made the garment on the treadle type sewing machine that sits in the far corner of the room. Her hair is the color of a raven's wing with eyes as green as young watercress. She wears no shoes. Axle immediately speculates on what lies hidden beneath the cotton cloth.

Lou announces, "Meet my daughter Mariah. She is the teasing minx of the family, beware her beckoning manners. She will break your heart if you let her."

Mariah crawls onto a chair against a near wall. From there, she surveys the crowd at the table. She points her chin at Axle.

"He has followed me home, Papa, that one. May I keep him?"

"He is a stranger among us," Lou teases. "Please, allow him to live in peace for a few more years without the knowledge of you." Mariah gives Axle a smile that brightens the entire room. "Now that they have all seen you, you may run along and help your mother with whatever she is doing."

The girl leaves the chair reluctantly. She pauses at the door to cast a final smile toward Axle. For him, her presence closed out everything else in the room. When she is beyond the door and out of sight, the scent of her lingers in the air like spring rain. There had been a quality about her that created lust in everyone present but her father. There is an aroma of sexuality about her that compels attention. Lou looks squarely at Axle.

"Beware of that one my friend, she is not for you."

The men return to their discussion. Later, Lou shows the boys to bunk beds in another part of the house where they store the money between their pillow and the wall before they undress and lay down.

Bugs chirp outside the window. Several minutes pass before a clear feminine voice sings to the soft strum of a guitar. She plays and sings the way Axle has always wanted to be able to perform. He falls asleep with her song playing in his head.

It seems they have only just laid down when the deep rumble of outboard motors awakens them. The boys stagger out of their beds and onto the porch that rings the house. Dawn is breaking in the east. Lou, Axle, Toby and Lou Jr. stand on the wooden deck facing the channel where a cluster of boats is assembled on the water below the house. The motor noise ceases when Lou raises his voice to speak to the men on the water below him.

His voice resonates in the still of the morning when he says, "My friends, there is a small town in southern Texas about 15 hours drive from here. Corrupt policemen and politicians rule the town. We have had some experience with that situation, you and I. An evil group of people there has been kidnapping, raping and killing young women for their pleasure. This act has gone on far too long. These two men rescued two of the women and brought them to us for safekeeping. I intend to go there and do what I can to free this town from evil. The mission will be dangerous because I will be acting outside the law. I ask for 20 volunteers to go with me to Amerada. I intend to rid this place of depravity. Who goes with me?"

Below in the boats, every man stands and screams, *"Me!"* To their left, Justin counts the volunteers. When he is finished, he says to Lou, "There are 40 volunteers, my captain."

The men in the boat stand in silence as they wait expectantly.

Who is this man who asks for 20 volunteers and gets 40? Who are these people who would risk their lives to go with us?

Lou accepts the knowledge of the count with a nod before he speaks again, "It is as I imagined. There will be 44 of us and we are all patriots. I thank you for your help. We will leave within the week. Go home now and prepare yourselves for combat. I will send word when we are to depart. I ask Pierre Latrec, and Orland and Stilton Devereaux to remain with me. The rest of you may leave now, I will be in touch. Thank you, my friends."

Outboard motors burble to life below the porch as the men on the balcony reenter the house. Within seconds, the bayou screams to life. Axle turns to Lou as he asks, "Who are those people?"

Lou answers with quiet pride, "All combat veterans of World War II, every man. We enlisted together, went to jump school together. We were in the 82 Airborne. We were in Bastion when General Patton came to free us. We know the meaning of liberation."

"And who are you, that you would dare to go with us?" Axle asks, with a lump in his throat.

"You need only know that we are the soul of liberty and we will help you in any way we can," Lou Beaudreau answers. "Nothing else matters."

Seven men gather around the cypress table. They eat from bowls filled from a cast iron Dutch oven like the one at Axle's home in Amerada. Only this time, the kettle is full of crawfish and shards of fish in a spicy sauce with vegetables floating in the mixture. Pita bread is piled on platters that rest on lazy Susans near each end of the table. Both boys eat until they nearly founder themselves.

Following the meal, Toby and Axle remain at the table. Lou, his brother, and his three lieutenants move outside on the porch where they engage in low conversation for half an hour. Following that, everybody leaves but Lou, who returns to the dining area. All the women but Matilda remain in the other end of the house. All are apparently sleeping. At 7:00, Lou's son returns with a note from Bordelon. The note reads: I understand your problem. The work will be for free providing I can go with you." Now the participants number 45. Toby and Axle set out in search of the outhouse, which lies across a springy footbridge and up a slight rise on dry land.

As they walk, Axle asks his friend, "Exactly who is Lou Beaudreau?"

"My dad claims he is the bravest man he's ever known. He was a sergeant in a platoon with the 82nd airborne in World War II when they jumped ashore on D-day. The platoon leader was killed so the field commander gave Lou a battlefield commission. By the time the war was over, he had risen to the rank of captain. All these men fought behind him across Europe. Quite a few of them are highly decorated. Lou has nearly as many medals as Audy Murphy. He was wounded twice. I'm glad there are still such men."

The boys conclude their business in the outhouse and return

across the footbridge. Lou places the two pillowcases on the table. Their tops remain knotted. He calls for Melissa and Sarah before he speaks.

"I request $800 for expenses to get our vehicles to Amerada and back. Some will be for the printer who cannot afford to be so generous. He will do his work for nothing, but we will buy the materials. I will return to you the money we do not use." Melissa and Sarah open one of the pillowcases. Melissa counts out $800 before she hands it to Lou. "I suggest you take what money you think you will need for expenses and put the rest in our bank. It is an insured facility, but I suggest that you place most of it in a safety deposit box. That will belay suspicion. Let us put the money in shoe boxes and a briefcase so that it looks more like important papers and family jewelry."

The girls take $500 each from a pillowcase. The rest goes into an old black valise and several shoeboxes. A brown paper sack receives the balance. The boys say good-bye to Melissa and Sarah. The girls will remain with Lou and his family. They are comfortable staying with the Beaudreau's, but they cry when their rescuers are about to leave. Axle stands at the top of the stairway where he says good-bye to Sarah. He kisses her.

"I will see you again in a little while."

Eight o'clock finds three boats screaming along the waterway as they return to the airstrip. Walter meets them at the dock with a note in an envelope. The note contains two words: Shidler, Cecil.

"What's this?" Axle asks.

Toby mutters, "We land at Shidler instead of Amerada. Something has come up."

Lou borrows Walter's old tan pickup for a trip to the bank. The bank president is Lou's cousin. He is a portly gentleman with nearly the same facial features. Toby and Axle rent a jointly held safety deposit drawer. They use Lou's address, which is a post office box. They sign a contract for a year and pay cash for the receptacle. They then unload the valuables into the box.

A half hour later, they release the airplane from its moorings, taxi out and head for Shidler. In the back seat of the WACO are 40,000 election ballots, all made out in favor of the challengers for sheriff and county clerk. The people of Amerada are about to rain on Sheriff Kraven's election celebration.

In addition to the ballots, there are 500 flyers printed on a new type of florescent yellow paper that has just come onto the market. They will drop the leaflets at night before landing at Shidler. The date is August 29, 1950, 14 days before the election.

After the boys make their final refueling stop, they wait for the arrival of sunset. Mercifully, the skies remain clear. They lift-off just before dark, inbound to their final destination.

As they near Amerada, Toby turns off the clearance lights. He then makes a pass above and parallel to Amerada's Main Street. The WACO has a fuselage door that is similar to a car. There is both a door handle and a window. They are about 100 feet above the water tower as they approach town. Axle cracks the door and begins tossing out wads of flyers in 50 sheet quantities. They drop nearly a third of their leaflets before they turn back toward town. The leaflets can be seen filtering down in a wide path across the community. They make one more pass across the north edge of town with the same results. They visit the towns of Wolf and Brandon before they drop the last of their load on Shidler.

Toby lands the WACO in a blacked out condition at the Shidler airstrip. The strip is sod but with runway lights and a lighted Tetrahedron adjacent to the runway. Cecil is waiting for them in a large white Ford panel truck with *Holiday Produce* painted on the door in black letters on a white background.

Cecil gives both boys a hug, as he asks, "How are the girls?"

"We left them in the best hands in the universe," Toby responds. "They're a little rocky, but getting better. Lou has 40-something people coming with him as a fighting force. The number seems to increase almost daily. They'll be here on September 11th for back up. We just salted the county with leaflets proclaiming a town meeting on the twelfth at the new Amerada high school auditorium. We figure the meeting will be an inauguration for the new building. Two people returning from their graves to oust the local power structure will be more of a dedication ceremony than most buildings ever receive."

"I picked up one of the flyers on my way to the airport," Cecil offers, as he holds it in the overhead light while he reads it to himself.

-ATTENTION-

THERE WILL BE A TOWN MEETING ON SEPTEMBER 12th AT SIX O'CLOCK IN THE EVENING IN THE AMERADA HIGH SCHOOL AUDITORIUM. IN ATTENDANCE WILL BE SARAH WOODLING AND MELISSA ST. CLAIR. THESE TWO YOUNG WOMEN WERE KIDNAPPED AND RAPED BY MEMBERS OF THE AMERADA COUNTY SHERIFF'S DEPARTMENT, OTHER MEMBERS OF THE KRAVEN FAMILY AND VARIOUS POLITICIANS OF AMERADA COUNTY. THEY HAVE BEEN RESCUED.

THE INTENT OF THIS MEETING IS TO RID THE COMMUNITY OF CORRUPTION AND THE SERIAL KILLERS AMONG US. MELISSA ST. CLAIR WILL ADDRESS THE AUDIENCE. SHE WILL DIVULGE WHAT HAS HAPPENED TO ALL THE OTHER YOUNG WOMEN, AND ONE YOUNG MAN WHO HAVE VANISHED DURING THE LAST TEN YEARS. EVERYONE IS ADVISED TO BRING A GUN, A CLUB OR SOME OTHER WEAPON. THE TIME HAS ARRIVED TO TAKE BACK OUR COMMUNITY. BE THERE.

Cecil looks across the seat at his boys. "These flyers will ignite law enforcement like a road flare."

The boys place the ballots in their boxes into the truck. From there, they drive to the parking lot near the flight operations building.

Cecil says, "I had to tell Herb where the WACO went when he discovered that I didn't have it."

Toby says, "Jesus Christ, here we go."

"It couldn't be helped," Cecil mutters. "He came by the house to tell Rebecca there was work for me at the airport. When he knocked, I opened the door when I was supposed to be gone and was caught red handed. I told him only that you had the airplane and would be back in a couple of days. He was initially pretty mad, but then figured there had to be a good reason. When he asked me why, I told him to keep his mouth shut, that all will be revealed in less than a week. He looked at me for quite a while before he nodded and returned to his car. If he'd told anyone, the cops would have been to the house by now. He hates the Kravens about as much as anyone. His brother was nearly killed by Mongo who also probably raped his brother's wife. Cynthia would never say, but everyone was certain it happened. Herb has obviously kept our secret."

Axle watches a Shidler police patrol car round the corner of a hanger headed in their direction. The cruiser parks at the operations building. A single cop emerges and goes inside. Twenty minutes later, he comes back out, gets in the car and drives away without even a glance at the produce truck.

Toby asks, "How we gettin' home?"

"In this truck," Cecil answers. "The police have quit searching cars for the time being. They think Melissa might be around somewhere but haven't figured out where."

Axle asks, "What about Sarah?"

"Nobody's mentioned her," Cecil says, as he maneuvers the truck to the end of the operations building. "I overheard that at a bar when a couple deputies got schnockered and said more than they should have."

"Anybody lookin' for us?" Toby asks.

"No, not even a phone call," Cecil offers. "It rained the night you left, so the construction company couldn't work. Oh, and one other thing. Mongo's dead. They found his body in the shack."

"Mongo's dead?" Toby exclaims. "How the hell did that happen? There wasn't anyone else in the shack when we snatched Melissa."

"Killed by the fire some way or other," Cecil advises. "Don't worry about it guys, few will miss him."

The information gives them both a jolt. There is now a new hunger for them. They have an intense desire to witness the next sunrise.

We have killed another human being. He wasn't a very good person, but our actions killed him. Now he is all he will ever be, has done all he will ever do, dreamed every dream he will ever dream, loved all he will ever love and learned all he will ever learn. We took his life in exchange for the lives of two women. Viewed in that fashion, it doesn't feel all that bad.

"We can probably go to work tomorrow like we haven't been anywhere," Axle mutters. "What do you suppose that cop was doing out here this late at night?"

"I'll find out," Cecil answers, as he opens his door and walks toward the operations building.

Inside, he strolls into the flight planning room where he looks at a wall map for a while. On the other side of the main room, a gorgeous young woman is closing the snack bar for the night. Cecil remains in the planning room a while longer before he goes to the duty desk. Near the front door, a fuel truck driver sets leaned back in a swivel chair.

"Great night," Cecil comments. "Is there much traffic?"

"Naw," the driver replies, "just waitin' for the mail run to come through, then I'm headin' home to the old lady."

"I saw a cop come in here a while ago," Cecil says. "What gives?"

"Cop's got the hots for Cindy in the snack bar," the driver says. "He comes in about this time every evenin'."

"If you hear of any airplane work, give me a call," Cecil says, as he hands the guy a business card before he leaves. Cecil climbs back inside the truck. "The cop's chasin' a skirt working in the snack bar. The fuel truck driver says he comes in every night about this time."

The boy's heartbeats begin to return to normal. They were anticipating a frontal assault by a half dozen cop cars at any moment.

Toby asks, "Where'd you get the truck?"

"I borrowed it from a guy here in town. We flew combat together in Europe," Cecil answers. "We're expected to park it behind Karl's. We'll take the stuff out later tonight. My friend will pick up the truck in the morning."

They make the trip to Amerada without incident. Once there, they pull into the lot behind Karl's where Cecil parks the truck. At 0100 hours the morning of August 30th, they return to the truck for the ballots. They place the ballots in two gunnysacks and an old parachute bag of Cecil's.

The ballots are packaged in bricks held together with a paper band, much like stacks of money from a bank. Three spare gunnysacks are brought along to hold the original ballots. Axle and Toby carry the parachute bag between them while Cecil carries a gunnysack containing two other empty sacks. With Cecil in the lead, they move from one unlighted area to another.

They cross vacant lots and cut grass yards. They are always on the outlook for police prowl cars. They cross streets only when absolutely necessary. Eventually they arrive at the county administration compound without being seen by anyone. There is only one close call from a patrol car near the county offices. All the bags are dropped behind an oleander hedge growing three feet from and parallel to the foundation line of the county maintenance building. They are now less than 30 feet from the CONEX container.

There is a single light bulb burning above the door of the CONEX. The bulb protrudes from below a large porcelain reflector hood. Toby unscrews the bulb a single revolution. That action places them in near total darkness. The only light now originates from a street lamp about 100 feet distant in front of the Police Headquarters Building. The boxes are stacked one atop the other on one of the sacks

Axle picks all the locks while they crouch in the dark behind the bushes. When the boxes are open, they transfer old ballots into empty gunnysacks before they turn their attention to the new ballots. The paper bands around the ballots slow the transfer process but they make the ballots more compact and easier to handle. The bricks are held above an open ballot box where the bands are then stripped and the ballots dribbled into the box. When they are finished with the first set of three boxes, they return them and bring three more to the place behind the hedge. Every time they remove boxes, they lock the CONEX in case someone shows up for an unexplained visit. Altogether, they make five trips. They finally run out of ballots with two ballot boxes left untouched.

Cecil whispers, "Probably just as well. It will keep the voting from looking like a complete set up."

As an afterthought, they exchange about half the old ballots with the new ballots in the last two ballot boxes before closing the CONEX. When they are finished stuffing the boxes, Axle takes one new and one old ballot and slips them in his hip pocket. They jog back to the house where they ditch the bags containing the old ballots in the bed of Toby's pickup beneath four trashcans destined for a trip to the town dump.

The dump is unattended and always seems to have a fire going. At the dump, they douse the bags with kerosene. Cecil strikes a match and they all stand around until the ballots are completely consumed by fire. When the fire dies down, Toby stirs the pile with a stick to promote the final burn. By the end of the process, what remains is unidentifiable.

Three hours after they exchanged the ballots they are able to return home. When they are finally inside and basking in the after-glow of success, Axle takes out the two ballots he saved. They sit clustered around the dining room table while they study the finished product. The printer in Louisiana is apparently a master forger. They can't tell the difference one from the other.

Tuesday morning the boys return to work as though nothing has happened. They remain certain that the fake ballots will not be discovered. If they are, hopefully the sheriff won't have time to forge new ballots. The worst thing that can come from discovery is that the real ballots will be voted by the general population and counted the way they should be. Axle is hoping for a landslide of fakeness to take the sheriff down. Should Lou's prophecy come true, they will have used Kraven money to defeat a Kraven system. What a thrilling prospect.

Chapter Sixty-Five

Mr. Black makes an unexpected phone call to the Fitzpatrick residence the evening of August 31, 1950. During the conversation, he pretends to be Uncle Irwin who is a railroad water purification technician for the Rock Island Railroad. Uncle Irwin claims that he will be traveling through the state and would enjoy seeing his nephew. His comment is, "Aunt Lottie and I are in Oklahoma. We are traveling cross-country and would certainly enjoy seeing you when we are in your area. We'll be in Midland in a week or so for several days, I'll call when we get there. Maybe you can come visit us."

The code words in the message are: *Aunt Lottie*. That means it is important for one of the operatives to call the home office. The following day, Cecil flies a pipeline surveillance route. At the far end of the circuit, he calls an unlisted number in Rapid City, South Dakota from a pay phone. During the conversation, a meeting is arranged. The mysterious meeting is to occur at 1300 hours, Saturday, September 2, 1950, in room 216 of the Sea Mist Motel in Houston, Texas.

The meeting is to involve Mr. Black, Cecil Fitzpatrick and Axle Mannheim. Cecil and Axle fly to Houston in the Cub the morning of September 2nd. They arrive at the motel at 1255 hours.

Cecil knocks on the door. The blond woman with the peach-like complexion answers the knock. Within the room is Mr. Blue who peeks from around a connecting door to the next room. Blue is armed and obviously acting as security. The woman admits Cecil and Axle. When the door is once again secure, Jonathan Black emerges from the adjoining room. Everyone except Cecil, Axle and Black leave the room. The interconnecting door remains ajar, but the three are for all practical purposes alone. Mr. Black first shakes hands with his two agents.

While he holds Axle's hand, he says, "I have some bad news, son." Axle greets the comment without a change of expression. He has grown accustom to bad news. Black mutters, "Sit down," as he releases Axle's hand. Black alights on the edge of one of the two double beds in the room. Cecil and Axle sit on the other mattress facing him across the open space between the two beds. Mr. Black takes a deep breath. "I didn't want to tell you this by phone." There is a long pause. "I don't know how else to say this son, but your parents have both been killed."

Axle feels his heart die as the pain of understanding sweeps fresh and raw through his body.

"How in hell can that be?" the boy blurts out, as a pair of tears track down his face. "You put them in a safe house for their protection."

"Yes, I did," Black continues, in a declining voice. "There was also an armed agent living in the house with them. Unfortunately, someone came in during the night apparently with a silenced weapon and killed all three of them."

"When?" Axle asks, in a small voice as he turns his head away.

On the far wall is a framed print of a hunting scene. The print hangs above a table near the bathroom. Axle concentrates on dissecting the print as he attempts to control his emotions. Cecil Fitzpatrick puts his arm around Axle's shoulders and holds it there.

"In the early morning hours of August 31st," Black mutters.

"Dad had you guys pegged from the beginning," Axle growls. "He claimed you could lose an anvil in a locked room."

"This was a very unusual occurrence," Black offers. His voice is defensive and diminished in volume.

My parents died before they could tell me good-bye.

"Who did it?" Axle asks. The question hisses from between his lips like venom jetting from a fang.

"We don't know yet," Black responds, "but we will. I have six of our best men working the case. We will eventually discover who is responsible."

"Fuck eventually," Axle mutters. "I want to know what you know right now, at this very moment."

"We are compiling information," Black responds, in a guarded voice. "I wish there was something more I could tell you that would make this easier, but there isn't."

Axle gives Black a piercing stare, and asks, "Does their deaths have anything to do with our current assignment?"

"We don't believe so," Black answers. His voice slips from guarded to authoritative in a fraction of a second. "We see no connection between the two, whatsoever. We feel that whoever did this was a professional."

"Our radio's out," Cecil interjects. "You need to send someone to fix it."

"I'll arrange that," Black says, as though he is relieved to have a change of subject. Black returns his attention to Axle. There is a note of kindness in his voice. "You have done very well on this assignment. Frankly, you've done much better than any of us expected. Considering the circumstances, do you want to stay on this project or do you want to withdraw?"

"Stay," Axle answers. He refuses to trust his voice further.

"Very well," Black says. "You'll need to be very careful from this point forward. My initial inclination is to have you withdrawn. Your emotions will not be stable for a while and that will clearly be a detriment. You may stay for now, but you must have everything approved by Cecil before you act."

"I want them both cremated and their ashes delivered to me," Axle directs, as his voice breaks.

He hangs his head as sobs rack his body. He covers his face while his body convulses over and over again. Cecil turns to pull Axle against his chest as Black leaves the room. Several minutes later when the sobs have diminished to hiccups, Axle disengages from Cecil's embrace. He walks into the bathroom. In a while, the last member of the Mannheim family returns. His eyes remain red and teary.

"We better get back home," Axle mumbles. "I've had enough of this place."

Cecil raps his knuckles on the between-room door. The peach maiden opens the door slightly. A safety chain can be seen guarding entry into the room.

"Axle wants to return to Amerada," Cecil informs the brain trust in the next room. "I see no reason why we cannot leave immediately."

Black says, "Very well, you are free to go. Is there anything I can do for you before you leave, Axle?"

"How good are you at bringing my parents back?" When Black does not respond, Axle continues, "What do I do now, your honor? Exactly how do I get on with my life without my parents?"

"I'm sorry, son," Black responds. "I wish there was something I could say or do that would change things, but unfortunately there isn't."

"See you around," Axle growls, as he turns to leave by the door. With the doorknob in his hand, he turns to look back at Mr. Black. "If you don't remember anything else, remember this: I want to know anything and everything you have concerning my parents death as soon as it becomes available. My motive is revenge."

Cecil and Axle return to Amerada. They land, and Cecil drives them home. When Axle enters his home, he goes to his parents' bed where he lies down with his face buried in his mother's pillow. He remains there through the night. He refuses supper or conversation with anyone. *I need my mom and dad. They always made me believe in myself.*

Toby sleeps on the floor in Axle's parents' bedroom, but does not attempt conversation. Three times during the night, Toby checks on his friend. Axle sleeps fitfully. He is covered by the bedspread that Toby placed over him.

The night following the trip to Houston, two shadowy figures arrive at the back door of the Mannheim house and are admitted. They spend several hours repairing the short-wave radio. By the time they depart, contact with Night Owl has been reestablished.

For two days, Axle remains far removed from any activity. He ignores everyone, even his best friend. When he leaves the bedroom two days later, all three Fitzpatrick's beg him to become part of their family. On Friday, September 8, 1950, after giving the request consideration, Axle Marston/Mannheim agrees to become part of the Fitzpatrick household. At Axle's insistence, his intrusion into their lives will remain purely a living arrangement.

Cecil decides it would be best if they all move into the Mannheim house, because of the continuing requirement to use the short-wave radio. On Saturday, September 9, 1950, Toby's family moves into the

Mannheim dwelling. The previously used stock trailer is parked in the Mannheim driveway the morning of the ninth. All but a few of the household possessions are boxed and the trailer filled. As soon as the last item is loaded, Toby returns the trailer to the Oklahoma farm. Axle's furniture will be stored until a later date. While Axle is outside watching Toby disappear on his way north, Rebecca comments to her husband.

"Hopefully, the election will take his mind off of his parents."

"It would be nice to think so," Cecil answers, "but it will be years before he recovers from this tragedy, if he ever does."

The phone rings. It's Rebecca's brother in Louisiana. Rebecca's mother is dying. The following day, she boards a bus for the trip to Louisiana to see her mother for the last time.

Chapter Sixty-Six

Champagne and beer sits iced in three, square, galvanized washtubs on low tables assembled in the middle of the room. Harvey Kraven paces on the rostrum above a small admiring throng. Everyone awaits the outcome of the latest election. One of Harvey's cousins is at the county election board headquarters. He will relay the results of the election as it becomes known. In a few minutes, his next term as sheriff of Amerada County will be assured.

Harvey has a sly shallow smile on his face as he considers the fact that the stupid voters have absolutely no idea the election is rigged. The election plan has worked perfectly from the very first moment of its inception. Clete had originated the idea near the end of Harvey's first term.

Luke and Mongo had nearly killed somebody on at least four separate occasions during his first term. Harvey had taken them in hand and told them that they couldn't keep doing that or he would lose the next election. That's when Clete got Cousin Homer drunk one night and discovered a convenient way to rig the election. The idea was so masterful that the next two elections were cakewalks. After that first rigged election scheme, a tradition was established. The clan and their supporters would assemble in the town hall the night the election returns were posted. They would drink champagne, beer and moonshine while they celebrated the perfect scam. Only the three plotters knew the reason Harvey always won. He no longer had to campaign. All he had to do was show up at the celebration to accept conciliatory congratulation from his political opponent. Cousin Homer would call from where the votes were counted to give the glad tidings that Sheriff Harvey Kraven had once again survived an election by a landslide. This time would be Roman numeral number four.

The phone on the wall in the corner of the room rings. Harvey once again assumes a triumphant pose behind the podium where he stands ready to recite his victory speech in the traditional manner. Harvey watches his brother who is on the phone. His brother listens with a frown on his face. Harvey watches as Clete removes the phone from his ear. Clete turns to his brother with a look of complete bewilderment. He stabs the receiver back onto its cradle. He comes out of his trance long enough to wave both arms as though he's sending a semaphore message. Clete scuttles to where Harvey stands with both his arms raised above his head in the 'V' of victory. Harvey lowers his mouth toward the microphone.

He announces, in a booming voice, "I believe brother Clete had something for us. Let's hope we've been triumphant again."

The audience goes quiet as it looks expectantly toward Clete Kraven. Clete covers the microphone with a hand before he mutters to his brother in a barely audible voice.

"Ya lost, Harvey. Ya lost the election."

Harvey Kraven stands paralyzed behind the podium. "Brother Clete is funnin' us."

Clete doesn't like his older brother very much. There has always been a bit of jealousy between them. Clete removes his hand from the mic.

He says, in a strong voice, "No joke Harvey. Ya lost by a landslide."

Harvey screams, "How is it possible to lose a rig..."

The air goes out of him like a deflating balloon. Harvey Kraven is not a critical thinker. He had trusted his own scam too much to believe that it could possibly fail. He stands gripping the podium in silence as he descends into shock. Clete grabs Harvey's upper arm. He leads his brother to a corner of the room away from the mic.

"Lost?" Harvey mutters. "How is it possible to lose a rigged election?"

"Somebody out-rigged ya, Harv. Ya got only 10 percent of the vote."

"You were in charge of the ballot boxes. Didn't ya check what was in 'em?"

"Hell, Harv, you helped us mark the ballots and stood by while we stuffed 'em in the boxes. Of course we checked 'em."

"What the hell we gonna do?" Harvey whimpers, as he glances

back to the audience.

"I don't know about you," Clete offers, "but I think I'll head back to Arkansas afore the general population decides we ain't cops no more. I'm gonna find Clyde and Luther and get the fuck out of here."

"We gotta figure this out," Harvey pleads. "Somebody's after us, and we gotta know who!"

"You go figure," Clete offers. "I've already lost a brother and a nephew. That's enough for me. I knew this thing would fall apart someday. Those damned girls are out there somewhere waitin' to sink our ship. We ain't got time to find out who's behind anything. We need to get our asses out of town while we still can."

"Girl," Harvey says. "Only one girl, and we'll find her."

Clete reaches into his hip pocket where he produces a piece of bright yellow paper. He thrusts it at Harvey.

"Girls, as in two. These got dropped down Main Street last night by an airplane. The same thing happened at Shidler, and who knows where else. We didn't tell ya 'cause we was afraid you'd overreact."

Harvey reads the flyer. His face turns ashen.

"They've got both girls? Oh, shit. How the hell did that happen?"

"We tried findin' out who dropped 'em, but nobody's talkin'. A couple of the boys had a talk with Herb at the airport. After nearly puttin' him in the hospital, they decided that he didn't know anything."

Harvey says, "Did ya try anyone else?"

"We can't think of anyone else to question," Clete answers. "It's like nobody knows anything. Somebody has invaded us. We can't fight what we can't see."

"How many people in this town can fly an airplane?" Harvey asks.

"Eight or ten," Clete says. "Maybe more, who knows?"

Harvey says, "Round em all up and let's do some more questioning."

"It's a little late fer that. I'll see ya around, Harv. A lot of strange people came into town this morning. They started arrivin' early. All our kin are scared. A lot of armed people are camped out in town. They're sleepin' in pickup beds all over the place. Nobody at the station wants to go face down a bunch of armed rednecks carryin' baseball bats, axe handles and guns. There's too many for us ta roust."

In the background, the victory audience shifts as though they are embarrassed. They drift toward the door. Only a few look back as Harvey Kraven drops heavily on the edge of the rostrum. He stares again at the piece of bright yellow paper clutched in his right hand. Suddenly, he realizes something.

"I'm no longer sheriff. Hell, I'm nothing now. I'm just another criminal."

Chapter Sixty-Seven

Lou Boudreau Jr. arrives in Amerada the morning of September 9th. He drives to the Mannheim house by a round about route in a brown Desoto sedan with Louisiana plates. Lou is not a very big kid. He looks a lot younger than his years. He just turned 17 and looks 12. Axle provides Howie's bicycle for him to use. Lou Jr. rides all over town so he can observe what is happening.

The people that compose the gathering crowd in town have been set aflame by the flyers. Lou elects to hang out across the street from the county buildings. From his vantage point, he had watched as a police van picked up the duplicate ballot boxes on the morning of Election Day. Things are not always apparent to the untrained eye, but Lou Jr. is fairly certain that the ballot boxes were the ones that had been stuffed with the Louisiana ballots. They all appeared to be locked when the van hauled them away.

Toby, Cecil, and Axle wait at home. The uncertainty is agonizing. Lou Jr. returns in the early afternoon with the news that out-of-town vehicles are parked in great numbers throughout town. A lot of them are arriving in a continuous stream. Main Street is no longer a street. The main drag has become a parking lot.

Chapter Sixty-Eight

At 2000 hours the evening of September 12th, the Mannheim phone rings. The phone is on a party line, so everyone has a ring code. The Mannheim's code is two long rings. When Axle picks up the receiver, he hears several additional clicks on the line. When all the usual eavesdroppers are on line, Axle hands the phone to Lou Jr. who holds a conversation in Cajun French with his father. A convoy of 18 vehicles will be at the crop duster strip by 0400 hours, the morning of the 13th. That is the same place where Cecil gave the boys the WACO when they flew to Louisiana.

Butterflies stir in Axle's gut as he awaits arrest. When no cops arrive after two hours, the resident conspirators engage in eating breakfast. Tuesday is spent with Lou Jr. observing police movement, while the others peruse the accumulation of people flowing into town.

The center of town is so clogged with unattended vehicles that only foot traffic is possible. Only the main thoroughfare is open to any degree and that is filling up fast. No vehicles could leave town if anyone wanted too. The south highway in front of Karl's is lined on both sides with parked vehicles. Karl's remains open throughout the day.

When darkness arrives, large wood fires are kindled throughout the town. The fires continue to burn through the night. At midnight, Karl's closes. The restaurant is out of food. There are no prospects for more until the streets are cleared.

Chapter Sixty-Nine

At 0600 hours, Toby and Axle head for the duster strip in Lou Jr.'s Desoto with Axle driving. They drive across lawns and on the few streets that remain open on the outskirts of town. The county lot is full of parked and unattended sheriff vehicles. Large clusters of people are gathered on every street corner near the center of town. Every variety of hand held weapon is evident. People stare critically at the car as it passes. There is a distinct feeling of gratitude within the car that nobody inside is named Kraven or is in anyway related to the local power structure.

By 0700 hours, the Desoto has negotiated the pasture escape route and is headed east on the farm to market road toward the crop duster strip. Axle decides to stop on the road shoulder about half a mile from the turn off to the abandoned farm. Lou Jr. then climbs atop the car where he glasses the farm with binoculars.

Traffic on the highway is sparse but steady. Every passing vehicle is headed toward town. Axle turns onto the abandoned farm lane. After a short pause, he continues toward the back of the property. The earth in the tire track trail has been pulverized by traffic. At the barn, a pickup moves to block the roadway. Two men emerge from a weed patch on either side of the shallow ruts. A third man stands in the doorway of the barn with a lever-action rifle leveled at the cars driver. The men alertly watch every movement within the car. The men who approach the car carry shotguns. All are pointed through the cars open windows. One man looks through the driver's window at each face in turn. Lou Jr. mutters something in French to the man outside the driver's window. The man answers before he waves for the pickup to continue on. The guy at the passenger's window unscrews his 12-gauge pump from Toby's ear as the car pulls away. The men melt into obscurity again after the car passes.

Axle drives beyond the crest of the hill behind the barn before he stops. Ahead of them, the Louisiana contingent is parked in echelon formation. The vehicles are angled outward away from the fence bordering the landing strip. From that position, every vehicle could pull away at the same time, should the occasion dictate. Axle descends the hill to park near the lead vehicle where Lou Sr., Sarah and Melissa stand leaning against a truck bed.

"How's goes it, my friend," Lou asks, as the girls move to award their friends a kiss and a hug.

"Everything is quiet in town, Papa," Lou Jr. answers as he exits a back door "Lots of cars from out of town are parked everywhere. There are large groups of people assembled throughout the town. It won't be long before traffic will be backed up along the highway. The cops aren't traveling and their vehicles are parked in the lot at the county buildings."

Lou Sr. contemplates the information before he offers, "It might mean that they are fearful of travel around town. Or it might mean that they are getting ready for crowd control with riot guns, tear gas and night sticks."

"I think the majority of the Kraven family has either left town or is in the process of trying to leave," Lou Jr. offers. After a moments thought he continues, "I think some have already departed. If the general populous seems to be arming itself and you were the center of attention, wouldn't you want to be some other place?"

Lou Sr. nods and replies thoughtfully, "Oui. I think we have jabbed a rather large hornet's nest with a very short stick. Now we shall see what happens. What of the election?" Lou Sr. asks.

"The sheriff lost by a considerable margin," Toby replies. "His last day of duty will be the end of the month."

Lou looks at everyone before he mutters, "I think not. Perhaps his last day in office will be this day. We have a partial victory without firing a shot, my young friends. Let us proceed to town. If we can still get there, we will bivouac near your house. We can attend the meeting from there."

Lou stands in the bed of the lead pickup where he gives a wind up signal. Engines crash to life along the fence row as everyone starts their vehicle. A line of vehicles carrying armed men forms on the Desoto after Axle pulls to the head of the column. Lou Sr. has swapped vehicles so that he is now in the car with Toby and Axle.

Lou Jr. follows close behind in his father's pickup with the two girls. The procession streams onto the highway where it turns toward Amerada. The convoy passes over the old bridge north of town. Traffic beyond that point is at a standstill. Axle travels against traffic in the oncoming lane until he arrives on the embankment above the fence-cut they made a week ago en route to the landing strip. While Axle waits, Toby drops the wires again. The procession moves down the embankment to stream into the pasture that will lead them to the edge of town.

Near the fence gate at the end of Elm Street, Lou Sr. says, "Pull over."

Axle stops on the right side of the street where Lou Sr. climbs out. He stands in a pickup bed several vehicles back where he studies the line of traffic on the highway near the edge of town through binoculars. When he is finished he dismounts and walks to the third vehicle in line. He talks with the driver momentarily before he returns to the lead car. As he approaches his vehicle, three other vehicles detach themselves from the convoy. They travel a side street in the direction of the highway.

Axle stops on the side of the road near the Mannheim house where Lou gives instructions to his people. When he finishes talking, he climbs back into the vehicle. Axle pulls across the ditch-bridge into his driveway. In the back yard, he turns around and parks the car facing toward the street. He backs up until he is nearly touching the garage door with his rear bumper.

Lou Sr. and the Devereaux brothers park before they adjourn to the back porch where they sit on the edge of the slab and talk. The remainder of the convoy parallel parks on Birch and Elm Streets. The line of Louisiana vehicles is lost from view around the corner. While people survey the neighborhood, cooler lids are opened as people commence eating, smoking and talking in low voices. Lou Sr. goes to the street where he stands in the bed of a pickup truck. As he looks around with his binoculars, he calls to Axle.

"Do you have a ladder that I can use to climb on top of your house?"

Axle answers, "Sure thing," and disappears inside the garage.

He returns shortly with a wooden ladder tall enough for Lou to reach the roof of the house. Lou climbs to the tallest gable where he proceeds to look around. When he finishes scanning the distance, he comes down whereupon he talks to several men. Those men leave to talk with others. Soon, five individuals move single file at a trot toward town. Lou returns to the slab.

"Now we wait, my young friends."

In an hour, the vehicles dispatched from the caravan at the edge of town find their way to the Mannheim house. It seems a sheriff's cruiser with two officers in attendance had established a roadblock on the highway at the north edge of town. The officers are now handcuffed to the front bumper of their patrol cars. They have been stripped naked in case either of them had a spare cuff key on their person.

Melissa and Sarah had entered the house upon arrival. Melissa was carrying a brown paper grocery sack neatly folded closed at the top. The sack contains a stack of notebook paper and her cigar box. The boys have wondered what is in the cigar box, but have never asked.

The girls take a shower while the men lounge around the backyard. Every two hours, the guard detail at the approach and departure ends of the convoy changes with military precision. The people in the convoy remain alert even while they are engaged in other things. There are always four men looking in four different directions. Lou raises his head from a reclined position to look at Axle and Toby.

"What will you do when this is over?"

"Probably have to do a tour with the military," Axle offers. "We're both 1-A in the draft and the Korean War seems to be a threat. We'll most likely end up hup-twoing across Korea with the Army to the tune of gun fire."

"May I offer a measure of advice on that subject," Lou responds, as he puts his head down so that he is speaking toward the clouds. "Join the Air Force and remain out of the trenches. I have spent considerable time on the front lines and that is not a pleasant place.

Every day, I watched the airplanes flying high overhead and knew that the people in them would spend the approaching night beneath a roof, on clean sheets. I, on the other hand, would be sleeping in a foxhole hoping it didn't rain. During the night, we would experience incoming artillery fire. Sometimes we would go on patrol. If we were lucky we saw the next sunrise. We didn't sleep very often or very well. I was generally wet, always cold and dirty. Join the Air Force and live better than we did." The boys file the advice in the back of their minds. "Never serve with the ground troops," Lou advises.

When 5:30 arrives, everyone climbs into a vehicle and the column proceeds in the general direction of the school. After three blocks, they encounter abandoned vehicles that clog the street. At that point, the column parks at roadside before they head out on foot in two columns. They travel like a recon patrol with two armed point men followed by three armed back ups.

The girls are in the middle forward between the columns. Armed male bodies surround them. They are being protected as though they are fine China. The women's eyes are wide with apprehension. The closer the column comes to school, the more people they encounter moving toward the auditorium. The greatly manipulated society of Amerada County is on the move. The mass of people contains an odd assortment of weapons.

The refurbished high school comes into view. When the crowd becomes aware of Melissa and Sarah traveling toward the auditorium, a spontaneous applause erupts followed by a hum that resembles the sound of an angry beehive.

"This night is the culmination of ten years of not knowing," Lou mutters. "I think that this will be a bad day to be a criminal in this town."

The final minutes before the announced gathering have charged the crowd with the delicate agony of wondering and waiting. At the school, speakers have been installed atop tripods outside the building. The lawn is so packed with people that very little grass is evident. The Cajun's move slowly now as they clear a pathway for the two women. When they are inside Lou mounts the stage with the girls close behind. He stations himself before a microphone where he surveys the audience. No cops are evident. The room is standing room only. Everyone is standing in front of the installed seat. More people line the walls while others sit on the floor between the front row of seats and the raised stage. Melissa and Sarah stand close behind Lou. A murmur surges through the audience as the girls are recognized. The front row contains the parents of both girls who stand arm in arm with tears streaming down their faces. Everybody is holding onto someone for comfort.

Toby and Axle dropped out of the procession when they pass through the front door. Near the entrance, they find a place to stand with their backs to the wall. Lou lays his shotgun across the podium before he raises his hands for silence. The crowd stills as he begins to speak into a mic. There is a reverence in his voice.

"My friends, I am from Louisiana where these two young women sought refuge. You have several heroes among you this day. Melissa St. Clair will speak to you now. Following that, I suggest we go on a rodent hunt."

Lou picks up his weapon and steps back from the podium. His eyes are watchful; they never cease roaming the audience. The young women on the stage possess enough knowledge to erase all the uncertainty of past years. As Melissa steels herself to speak, a collective hum moves through the crowd. Melissa raises her chin as she looks out across the sea of faces. There are tears streaming down her face. The moment is numb with apprehension. The crowd is suddenly been struck mute. Silence rolls in as though from a far place.

The longsuffering victims of misery and violence of the past ten years fill the audience. They line the walls. They stand in front of seats. The room is breathless and yet there is a trembling sensation as though the atmosphere is about to explode. All that will be required is a detonator to spark ignition. Following her look around, the *detonator* steps to the microphone in the form of a 16 year old girl dressed in a blouse and skirt.

Melissa extracts her cigar box along with a sheaf of papers from the brown paper sack. She looks around for some place to put the sack. When no place materializes, she drops it on the floor. While she arranges the items before her on the podium, Sarah moves to stand near her left elbow. When Melissa is finally able to speak, her voice is so clotted with emotion it is difficult to understand her. She tries again.

"What I am about to say…will be very hard for me. I ask that you not interrupt…until I have finished. I speak for Sarah…myself and all the others not blessed to be here."

Emotion stills her voice. She turns with her head hanging as she hands the sheaf of papers to Sarah. Sarah moves forward.

"I will speak for Melissa, but it is her thoughts that you will hear." She lowers her eyes and reads from a page of notebook paper. "Last July 29th, I was kidnapped by Mongo Baron and Luther Kraven from the parking lot of the town hall." There is a gasp followed by a silence that grasps everybody's senses with the fullness of a near perfect vacuum. "I was struck on the head, rendered unconscious and then taken to their shack on West Clear Creek where I was raped and tortured for their pleasure. I was turned into a prostitute for them, their friends, and relatives. I remained a captive in that place, until two brave young men rescued me. I am 16 years old."

The crowd utters a sound that resembles the sullen growl of an angry dog.

"This town has watched while people were victimized and did nothing. The Kraven family has worked their delicate craft of death and deception upon us, and the final total is nothing short of stunning. When I faced the insecurity of coming here, to stand on this stage and tell you what happened to me, I wondered if I had the courage to follow through. And then my friend made me realize that unless you hear what I have to say, the killings might stop, but the perpetrators would escape and go unpunished.

"We have been swept here together in this time and place out of fate and necessity. Ten years ago last month, the first woman disappeared from this community. She would be the first of 13 people. Eleven died and two were rescued. At the time of her disappearance, the sheriff's department launched an investigation. Incredibly, they already knew exactly where the woman was. She was at the Kraven compound on West Clear Creek. Her name was Pam

Drabber. Anyone with the name Kraven and all their relatives were vested members of this conspiracy.

"The message I am about to convey will be chilling and likely overwhelm many of you. When they were finished with her, she was sacrificed, as were the others, to a beast living in the bowels of the marsh. A very large alligator provided their means of disposal."

Well back in the crowd, a woman wails, while a man screams, "No!"

A bellow of rage engulfs the audience. The sound vibrates to the very core of every soul. The crowd noise is much like the rumble of a large idling diesel engine. The rumble is the sound of power waiting to be unleashed. Sarah pulls Melissa's cigar box to her.

"This thing happened with the full knowledge of the police force of this county. In every instance, they participated in the abuse of the victims. I have this information from the mouths of my tormentors. Every Kraven on the force participated in the rape of the missing women. Only by the grace of God and two young men am I privileged to stand here and tell you what happened to the others who vanished."

Sarah drops her head, as though gathering strength. She then holds aloft the cigar box as though it is a flaming torch. She lowers it to the top of the podium. She removes a large rubber band from its circumference before she lifts the lid. From within she extracts a clear envelope. She mutters in a shaky sobbing voice.

"I give you trophy locks of hair and the names of the victims."

The crowd utters a cry of anguish. The envelopes are selected from the box at random before the names are recited in a muted voice that flows out over the address system. Sobs are heard in the audience as the names are spoken.

"Charlotte Cane, Mark Mayhew Jr., Pam Drabber, Kathy Fenton, Beverly Watson, Charlene Everhart, Charlotte Mayhew, Jeanne Dunn, Harriet Harris, Sugarloaf Hayes, and Marlene Dorian. A last envelope contains my name and a lock of my hair. Fortunately, they were denied the excitement of killing me."

By now, women are wailing. Grown men can be seen crying full out as Sarah continues.

"The sheriff and his kin committed other atrocities as well. They rigged the county election system so their relatives and cronies would always win. When they were finished with that, they organized the law enforcement system to suit themselves. The Kravens and their relatives were allowed to commit atrocities unmatched since the internment camps of World War II. We sat around and watched while our people disappeared. We did this out of ignorance or perhaps fear of bringing wrath down upon ourselves. We were their personal fools. We were victims at their mercy. This victim cannot forgive and will not forget."

Sarah takes a deep breath as she puts an arm around Melissa who is sobbing uncontrollably against her shoulder.

"I speak for those of us taken to the marsh and those who gave their lives, when I say that we want something from this community. Actually, we ask very little considering what has happened to us. First, I want every person with the name Kraven, their relatives, and all their elected politicians removed from this community. There is to be no place for them to hide. If they have fled, we want them returned to stand trial."

Somebody thumps the butt of a pick-axe handle on the floor. Others follow the lead. The room fills with the sound of hundreds of billets of wood and gun butts striking the auditorium floor. The building trembles beneath the impact. Sarah holds up her hand and the noise stops as though a fuse has failed.

"Second, I want every perpetrator of this atrocity caught and punished. We can no longer trust the laws of this land to do what is needed. We victims care only that justice is carried out, and we expect you to see to it. I leave the judgment of the criminals and their fate in your hands."

A crescendo of thumping again fills the room to stop again when Sarah continues.

"Third, I want the bell that's bolted to the tree above the gator hole in the marsh brought into town. A bell tower is to be erected near the entrance of this school. We want it made of native stone. A bronze plaque shall be embedded in the base of the tower. The plaque is to list the names of those who lost their lives and the names of the two men who put an end to it all. The tower will be called the Mannheim-Fitzpatrick bell tower. Every year on the 13th of September, the bell is to be tolled 11 times. The intent is to serve as a reminder to all who see it, and the message is this: There will always be those among us who do not treasure human life, but pray to God, there will always be a few who do." She hesitates for emphasis. "This has been a long and strenuous journey for us, but the rest will be up to you.

"We were rescued by two 18-year-old men. You know their names. I hesitated to tell anyone who they were, because it was their request that they not be identified. I find that I cannot honor their request, because they deserve recognition. I will tell you that their names and memory are etched on my heart for as long as it beats. When we were rescued, they hid us from our enemies and flew us to Louisiana where we stayed with an incredible family. Those people were also our saviors. They took us in when we had no other place to go. What our two young saviors did to this point would seem enough, but it was not. Next, they turned their attention to returning this town to some degree of normalcy.

"We could not tell our families we were alive, because the leaders of this community were too corrupt and the rest of you too afraid. We could tell nobody we had been found. Had we done so, our families would surely have vanished." She looks across the crowd. "I owe my heart and soul to two young men. The rest of this community looked the other way when the Kravens confronted them with hard choices. Everybody took the easy way out. They were an island of calm and intelligence in the middle of nowhere. They provided a cleansing breeze through hell. This moment is not about recognition, it is about devotion to another person and what is right. From this moment forward, my creed will be: Always do what is right.

"These young men were willing to participate in high crimes to clean the slate. Their names are Axle Mannheim and Toby Fitzpatrick. Were it not for them, I would not be standing here before you this night. God bless their courage in coming for us."

Axle looks left at Toby and jabs him with an elbow. They inch slowly out the door. The boys walk as briskly as they can through the crowd, along the sidewalk and away into the night. Behind them, the sound of a thunderous roar pierces the darkness of a September night. Sarah looks for a long instant at the faces before her. She sees faces in the crowd that she has known her entire lifetime. Outside, the boys jog away into the night with the realization that a 20-minute speech by a 16-year-old girl has become an anthem for a town. Within minutes, anyone who has been identified as a criminal will be as welcome as a case of Cholera. Toby speaks from two feet away in the darkness as their feet thud in cadence on the street.

"You remember when you told me you always wanted to write a song and be able to play it?"

"Yeah, still do."

"You stood up in Karl's when you were new in town, and defended a woman while everyone else stood around like potted plants."

"You'd have done the same thing," Axle offers.

"Wait 'till I'm finished," Toby urges. "This is hard for me to say. I've been listening to a song ever since I met up with you at Karl's. It was the sound of people applauding in a restaurant and just now in an auditorium. I still remember the sound of a backhanded slap to the face of a young hoodlum near a stolen car; the cry of night birds on a dark creek and the rattle of riffles as we paddled in the dark to find a missing woman. The words to all this were uttered by a great-horned owl callin' in the distance. It is the sound of a wind chime on your back porch. It was the base drum of napalm detonating in the night like the *William Tell Overture*. The melody was the red glare of a whiskey keg rocketing into the night sky followed by the sizzle when it landed. The body of the song was two women sobbing in relief at being saved. Tonight, I heard the drumroll of several hundred pick-ax handles and gun butts on a wooden floor. We listened while a young woman sung your praises to anyone who'd listen. The whole time I've been with you, I've been listening to a song, and the song is *you*.

"This thing may not be over yet, but this needs sayin'. During the whole time I've known you, I've loved you like I love myself and I've always love me more than anything. You are at your very best when things around you are at their worst. I don't know what the future holds for the two of us, but I wouldn't have missed these last

13 months for anything on earth. Maybe we just heard the end of the song, but it wasn't just a song. It was a hymn for a bunch of people who couldn't help themselves. What I've been listening to is a hymn for an entire town.

"If there was a song, we wrote it together," Axle mutters, "and neither of us can play a lick on anything."

"Naw," Toby answers. "This whole thing was yours. Sometimes, I was a little muscle when we needed it. It was your idea and you led the way. It's your song...it will always be *The Song of Mannheim*. That's the way I'll remember it. All I did was hum a few bars in the background."

The lump in Axle's throat is large and stifling as they slow to a walk beneath the soft glow of a streetlight. Both boys lean into each other while locked in an embrace. At the auditorium, Sarah takes a final deep breath. She bends her head to the microphone.

"Barbarians 11, Civilization 0.

The crowd that has been humming like a tuning fork since the name of the first victim washed over them goes silent. It takes a microsecond for the final chord of Sarah's voice to roll over the crowd. People stand riveted in place so shaken and indelibly stained by what they've heard, they seem unable to move. Suddenly, from the total silence arises a primal scream. The crowd turns and with a surge like a tidal wave, they burst through the open doors and into the night.

Chapter Seventy

The shrimp boat *Red Tide* passes through the southern most edge of Big Oliver Marsh into Discovery Bay. The diesel engines of the big boat rumble smoothly at cruise power as the craft heads south-southeast across the placid water into an early twilight. Overhead, a high overcast sky reflects the golden presence of the sun setting in the west. An hour distant lays a deep water shelf in the Gulf of Mexico that is the boat's destination. The water there is a constant 300 feet deep, before it drops away into a deep underwater trench. The shelf serves as a highway for most of the Gulf marine life.

Within the boat, five men stand secured to the inner walls of the main cabin. Their hands are cuffed behind their backs. Their legs are encased in round metal drums filled with cement that rises nearly to their waists. They are held against the wall by segments of rope that encircle their chests. The ropes are fastened to hastily installed boat-cleats mounted to the thick wood of the cabin walls.

All five of the bound men are ex-deputies of Amerada County. Their terms of employment were cut short during the night of September 12, 1950 when an angry mob of citizens bent on revenge had caught them within the city limits. Three of the prisoners still wear portions of their uniforms. Of those tied to the wall, one is dead. His body is held up right by the concrete in the metal drum and the rope that restrains his body. So the captors won't have to look at his mortal wound, a bloody brown paper sack covers the dead man's head. The bag is held in place by an encircling length of twine. The captain refers to a sonar unit mounted atop the instrument panel before him.

"There she is," he mutters, to his audience. "Let's start unloadin.'"

The captain throttles to near idle before he engages the auto pilot. The man at his elbow moves aft to a ladder that descends to the lower deck. The captain walks to the aft edge of the upper deck where he gives the thumbs up sign to the men waiting below. The boat's running lights are on but the captain constantly surveys the water around them for any approaching watercraft.

Overhead, a partial moon peers through a break in the clouds. The moon bathes the water in a golden light. Beneath the boat, gentle ground swells cause the bow to rise and fall as the shrimper plows slowly ahead.

Harlin Dunn is the other dark figure on the flying bridge. Harlin descends to the lower deck where he holds conference with three other men before they enter the enclosed main cabin. The four crewmen are Harlin Dunn, Mark Mayhew Sr., Keith Drabber and Morton Cane, all are fathers of missing teenagers. Mark Mayhew has lost both a son and a daughter to the men standing upright in the barrels.

Harlin produces a knife and cuts the rope freeing the dead body. Together, the four men skid the heavy drum holding the body of Harvey Kraven to the transom. The aft deck is dimly illuminated by flush-mounted gunnel lights that provide only enough light to prevent a misstep.

The men stand by the drum near the edge of the work platform. When all is in position, Morton Cane says, "Sorry you shot yourself in the head, Harvey. I would have loved to hear you beg before we hurry you along your path to hell."

Together, the men give the drum a shove. They all watch as it topples overboard to collide with the florescent wake of the boat. In the main cabin, the splash causes the remaining prisoners to scream at the top of their lungs. They all plead for mercy.

Sympathy for the captives is not in abundance among the fathers of the victim's who remain gathered on the aft deck.

Mark Mayhew faces the next man in a barrel nearest the door. Mark asks the man, "Is this the way my daughter screamed while you raped her? Did she make this same kind of plea for her life when you took her to the gator hole before you pushed her over the bank?"

Luther screams, "Didn't have nothin' to do with rapin' her, or keepin' her, or the gator hole! The others did it; kill them not me."

"It don't matter; you are guilty by association. You could have stopped it, but you didn't. We now condemn you to hell, you and the rest of your sorry lot."

While Luther screams and struggles, the men cut the rope securing him to the wall. When he is free, they trundle him to the sloped work deck near the transom where the nets come aboard. There they station the drum at the deck's edge. With Luther facing toward his accusers, babbling incoherently, Mark Mayhew reads from a sheet of paper. Keith Drabber holds a flashlight, illuminating the writing. Morton Cane holds a flashlight on the condemned man's face.

"Luther Kraven, it is the decision of the people of Amerada County, Texas," Mark reads, "that you be put to death for the crimes of kidnapping, rape and murder. Do you have any final words before the sentence is carried out?" Luther's eyes are open so wide that their whites can be seen encircling the irises. Luther stares, mouth agape as he wets his pants. "I think that just about says it for Brother Luther."

Together, everyone gives a shove. Luther's scream ends abruptly when he enters the water. Over the next half hour, the remaining criminals confess individually to their misdeeds before going into the Gulf. The last to face his accusers is Clete Kraven.

"Your turn, Clete," Keith Drabber growls. "If you want to live, you can tell us the rest of the story. If you tell us what we want to know, then we'll escort you out of town."

Clete is so overjoyed at being offered the possibility of saving himself that he begins to blab the awful truth from beginning to end. His words tumble out as an unintelligible jumble until Morton Cane has him stop. Clete starts over at the beginning. His story originates from June 3, 1943 when the first woman, Pam Drabber, was kidnapped.

Clete talks for a long time. The longer he talks, the more eloquent he becomes. In due course, a full account of what happened during his tour of duty with the sheriff's department is on paper. Several hours later, Morton Cane has nearly filled three steno pads with shorthand notes. He has asked a lot of questions.

Before Clete runs out of words, the story of agent Ralph Pine's demise and Sugarloaf Hayes' disappearance have also been documented. By then, the captain has brought the engines to idle.

The boat sits dead in the water. It rises and falls on the ground swells.

"Okay, that's all I can remember. How about gettin' me out of these concrete boots and take me back to shore."

"Untie his hands," Morton says, "so he can sign his statement."

Mark Mayhew frees Clete's bonds. The last note pad is attached to a clipboard so Clete can sign. When he is finished writing his name, Mark hands the clipboard to Morton who looks at the signature.

"Looks official to me."

"Okay, boys," Mark says, "let's send him to meet his maker."

"But you said I could go free if I told you everything," Clete rages, as he claws at the rope around his waist.

Mark Mayhew smiles. "We said we'd escort you out of town. This seems to be out of town to me and you sure as hell are being escorted. Now all you have to do is walk ashore and head back to where you came from."

Keith Drabber points north as he offers, "Shore's in that direction."

"If you're lucky, "Morton Cane adds, "we'll hit you on the head before we drop you over the side."

Clete Kraven makes a gagging sound as he takes a swing at his nearest tormentor. Unfortunately for him, Harlin Dunn is out of range. Keith Drabber steps forward, and punches Clete heavily on the forehead with the butt of a shotgun stock. Clete sags unconscious against his bindings while the men untie him from the wall.

Mark Mayhew cuffs Clete's arms behind him using his own handcuffs. The four fathers of the dead young women skid Clete to the edge of the deck. They stand him facing aft. The weight of the concrete and the depth of leg penetration hold him upright even though he is unconscious. Harlin Dunn produces a bucket of seawater that he throws into Clete's face.

On the upper deck, the captain places the boat in gear. The craft moves slowly forward as Clete comes groggily awake. He stares in dull comprehension at the florescence in the water behind the boat. The four men stand at his side and watch his face until they are certain he is fully awake. Clete begins to scream.

"Well, boys," Mark Mayhew comments. "I've heard enough. How about you?"

"Suits the hell out of me," Harlin Dunn responds. "This pecker-wood is long overdue for his reward."

The men put their hands in the middle of Clete's back and against the metal drum encasing his legs. As the drum moves, the men turn the victim around until he faces them. The drum teeters at the edge of the deck.

Mark mutters, "May God have mercy on your soul, Clete. Hopefully, it will be the same degree of mercy you've shown our children."

"Your past has carried you down the road to hell," Keith Drabber adds. "The wages of your sins are death."

Harlin Dunn steps alongside Keith to place his hand on the metal drum rim.

He adds, "I do this in the memory of my daughter and all the others you helped kill. May the crabs fight over your body."

"The substitute for satisfaction is patience," Morton Cane offers, "and I will only be satisfied when all the monsters like you are dead and gone."

"We desire most, that which we may not have," Mark Mayhew Sr., observes. "Since I cannot have my son and daughter back, I accept your life as payment."

All the men apply a slight pressure, and Clete topples screaming over the side into the water. The captain watches from the upper deck until the outlaw disappears beneath the surface. Then he returns to the helm. Captain Cory Forest disengages the autopilot, and spins the wheel. The *Red Tide* makes a sweeping arc as it retraces its path back to the marsh.

Chapter Seventy-One

Axle Marston-Mannheim stands before the desk of Jonathan Black after giving in detail his written and verbal report concerning the Amerada Operation. Toby slumps in an armchair beside him where he wonders what will happen to them now.

"Is everyone satisfied with our performance on this mission?" Axle asks.

"Our client is more than satisfied with the results," Mr. Black offers. "Little else matters. On the whole, you did everything we asked of you. Would you care to continue working for the Ironstone Group?"

"Yes, sir," Axle answers, "we would. As you know, I no longer have a family, which brings me to the final item of this visit. I want to know what you have determined concerning the death of my parents."

"We have concluded our investigation," Black announces. "The case has been moved to our Cold Case Unit, because our investigation was inconclusive. The senior investigator will brief you on the evidence we have. Our investigation has provided us with a theory concerning what we believe happened. Please have a seat while the briefing officer is summoned."

Axle drops into a chair beside Toby where they both await the briefing officer. In a few seconds, a man who is vaguely familiar enters the room. The man is Morgan Farnsworth, alias Mr. Brown. Morgan shakes hands with the two young agents.

"I am very sorry to have to tell you this," Farnsworth mutters, "but we were unable to determine who killed your parents. There are several things that will perhaps allow you to place this tragedy to rest." Morgan refers to a small notebook for an instant. "The family who previously owned the safe house your parents were living in was Mr. and Mrs. Jordan Pardo. Together, they accumulated a gambling debt in Nevada in excess of $200,000. The debt was a year old when

452   *Max Ibach*

the Pardo's placed their house on the market. One of our agents informed headquarters that the house would make an excellent safe house because of its location. The dwelling is well off the beaten path and so would not normally be subject to casual visitation by anyone. The fact that it sits isolated on a large tract of land made the property ideal for our purposes. Additionally, the black walnut trees on the property, if harvested, would more than pay the asking price of the owners. Mr. Black gave his approval and the Ironstone Group purchased the property."

Farnsworth turns a page where he checks additional facts before continuing.

"Nobody," he continues, "either at headquarters, or the agent in Texas was aware of the gambling debt incurred by the Pardos before the sale. We have reached a conclusion based on certain facts uncovered, but the conclusion results only in a supposition.

"Thirty-one days after the Pardo family sold their property and disappeared, they were found dead in their new house in a Chicago suburb. Their manner of death was by gunshot. Both bodies had a single small caliber bullet to the forehead and another in the throat. These are the same wounds suffered by your parents and the resident agent living with them in Texas. The rifling marks on the slugs were different, but the ejector marks on the casings were identical. We conclude from this information that the barrel of the weapon had been changed between killings. We further believe that a contract was issued to a professional hit man who was detailed to collect the gambling debt. We believe that the assassin went to the last known address of the Pardos and killed the people living there. Those unfortunate people happened to be your parents. When the mistake was discovered by the killer, the Pardos were traced to their new residence where the contract was fulfilled."

Mr. Black observes, "We have concluded from what we know that your parents were in the wrong place at the wrong time. They were killed in a case of mistaken identity."

Farnsworth continues, "All of the agents involved in this investigation agree on this premise as the motive for their deaths."

Perhaps there is no perfect ending except in great poetry, Axel thinks to himself. He looks at the floor for a long time as he digests what he has heard.

"Does anybody have any idea how professional hit men are hired?" Axle asks. His eyes are very bright when he looks up.

"Not yet," Mr. Black says. "Perhaps there will be a time in the future when we will discover additional information that will lead us to a person of interest, but for now the case has gone cold."

"When will you have another assignment for us?" Axle asks. "Toby and I will work only as a team from this point forward. We plan to make our permanent home in southern Texas along the Gulf coast. When you have further work for us, please call this number."

Axle hands Mr. Black a cream-colored business card with the name Axle Mannheim engraved in mahogany-colored ink. There is a phone number and nothing more.

EPILOGUE

Neal Mannheim has not read the entire contents of the chest, only scattered portions of the first manuscript before he attempts to find the place where his mother wanted her ashes scattered. After several months of research, the location of the site remains a mystery. He has researched road maps, aerial charts, and Geodetic Survey Maps, but Amerada is not located on any of them. The last entry in her journal describes a large red oak tree on a hill near a place identified as Big Oliver Marsh, but neither the marsh, the town, nor the hill are on any map they can find. The only reference he can locate is a town named Shidler.

After several weeks of consideration, he decides to go there. Surely someone in Shidler will be able to provide the desired information. This will be no unemotional effort, so he brings the M & M's with him. His new wife Megan and her sister Margo will provide sterling company for the estimated three-day drive to Shidler.

And so, on September 25, 1996, they point their vehicle southeast towards Texas. The middle of the third day finds them nosing into a parking spot before a store on the outskirts of Shidler. New gravel pops beneath their tires as the front wheels of the truck nudge against a white-painted horizontal utility pole, which functions as a curb near the building.

A sign above the door reads *Shidler General Mercantile*. The building looks like something from an old western movie. The square architecture is constructed of redwood-stained, rough-sawed wood. A long thin vertical sign near the door bears a thermometer that registers 93 degrees in the shade beneath an extended roof overhang. Neal speculates humorously to the women before he climbs out of the truck.

"This place will be owned by a 70-year old man named Zeek who'll sell you anything from a dozen Black Minorca pullets to a

Caterpillar tractor. Zeek's wife will be named Maude. She will be able to supply all the local gossip in circulation for the past three years."

The two women grin as they await the findings inside the store.

A low porch surrounds the front of the building. A wooden bench fashioned from rough-sawed planks sits old and resplendent in the shade beneath an impressively long roof overhang. The bench seat has been polished to a dull luster by the application of 10,000 butts or more. On the bench sits a skinny southern-fried character study in faded-blue overalls and half-laced work-boots. His presence is made conspicuous by the mere absence of anyone else. He sits leaned back with his legs extended before him, ankles crossed. His hands are clasped behind his head. A well-used straw hat with sweat stains lies on the bench near at hand. His eyes are mere slits peering from a face slightly bloated by past indiscretions. The oldster's manner is so laid back that Neal wonders if he has a pulse. About a week's worth of weathered gray stubble patterns a face that appears as stubborn as a borrowed mule.

Neal's truck is the only vehicle parked at the front of the store. A rust-accented white Chevy pickup sits in the shade on the north side of the building. Neal steps out of the air-conditioned truck into 90-degree-plus heat as he heads for the front door of the place. The slight salty-tang of the nearby Gulf rides a gentle southern breeze.

Since his path carries him near the man on the bench, Neal nods, and mumbles, "Howdy."

The oldster squints at him, but does not respond. The lack of a response makes Neal feel ignored. Perhaps it's the Washington state license plate on the truck or the guy has a thing about strangers. Neal is nearly as stubborn as the old man looks, so he pauses near the doorway where he turns back.

"Pardon me old-timer, are you from around here?"

The old man fully opens his eyes then. He looks at Neal in a fashion that implies, *who the hell wants to know?* Some internal engine tells Neal that the man is not to keen on the term, old-timer. The oldster appears to engage in creative thinking as they warily survey each other. Finally he nods, as though Neal has passed some crucial test.

He exhales a low, "Yep."

"Maybe you can help me," Neal offers expectantly. "I'm looking for information about an old town that's no longer on any map I can find."

The old man gazes at Neal suspiciously. After a substantial pause, he mumbles in a sigh, "Amerada?" Neal nods in appreciation. The old man turns his head to look westward. After an extended deliberation, he asks in a sorrow-strained voice, "Why you want to know fer?"

"My people were from there," Neal stammers, as he tries not to seem too eager. "I want to see where they lived."

The man still peers into the distance, when he asks, "What's your name?"

"Neal Mannheim."

"And your mother's maiden name?"

"Sarah Woodling."

The old man's head snaps around so that his gaze meets Neal's. A strange expression slices across his face as he stands abruptly.

"Wait right there, sonny, while I get somethin'," he says, over a shoulder as he heads for the rusty white truck.

He returns with a short cylindrical cardboard tube. The old man detaches a red plastic end cap and shoves it in a pocket. When everything is stowed and he has again installed himself on the bench, he removes a rolled up map from the tube. The map is the type Army artillery uses for coordinates.

Neal drops onto the bench across the map from the old man where he holds-down one side of the curled chart. A glance at the document reveals a well-used map in a scale of 1:250,000. The chart glares upward in muted, yellow, green, and off-white tones. With one gnarled finger, the old man points to a section near an area depicted as swamp.

He says, "The place you want is right here near this hill. That's a special place for the people who once lived there. A few of us still go there every September to remember how it was in them days. Had you been here a couple weeks ago you could have gone with us." The man makes the trip sound like a religious event. "You'll need a 4 X 4 to get in there," the man continues, as he taps his finger on the paper at a place that indicates a streambed. "You have to cross the creek 'bout here to get t' other side. The site of the town is north of that hill. You'll find it between two sets of old bridge pilings in the creek. Both bridges are gone now. Highway's abandoned too. All that's there now is a bell tower, the walls of a couple of native stone houses, and a bunch of foundations."

His voice quality changes during the last comment as though he and the stranger are separated by something more than merely years. There is a sort of anguish in his voice. It is perhaps the sound of what must have been. Neal senses a slight chill in the heat as though someone has just presented him with a frag order for an air raid over Baghdad.

"Is that swampy area Oliver Marsh?" Neal asks.

The old man nods, answering, "Yeah, the one and only."

"And would that elevation on the map be The-Hundred-&-Forty-Foot-Hill?"

"Yep, that's it, the highest hill around there."

"What happened to the town?"

The old man studies Neal for several seconds before he makes another decision.

He offers, "Let's sit here fer a spell and then I'll tell ye what I remember."

Neal beckons to Megan and Margo. They get out of the truck to sit on the end of the bench. Both lean eagerly forward like kids awaiting a kindergarten story.

The old man absently rolls the map and returns it to the tube while considering what he is about to say. When he finishes with the map he lays the tube on the seat between them. He continues to ponder in silence for short time. Finally, he gazes past the roofline as though he is homed in on a distant satellite. Eventually, he clears his throat, squints toward the eave of the porch and begins. He speaks in clipped differential tones while looking away from his audience as though what he is about to say is hard to remember or repeat. He speaks as though reciting an old documentary from memory.

"'Twas 1950 when it happened," he begins. "A little oil town with a small refinery and near 1,800 people livin' thereabouts. Kind of a temporary place with most everything made of wood. You need to understand how it was back then. People makin' sort of a scab livin' off the oil field while fightin' with the sheriff and his riff-raff kin most of the time. Nest of bullies and criminals is mostly what the cops was; beatin' up on somebody every time the mood struck 'em. 'Twas the county seat back then. The place came complete with a corrupt sheriff's department and a gang of hillbilly's name of Kraven from out of state somewhere. Place turned into a complete sewer. As the years passed, 'twas like the souls got sucked out of the people.

"Finally, these two teenage kids came to town with their parents. Big muscular boys they was. The kind you look at and remember. Went to school there fer one year and graduated. Did real well in athletics and sort of stuck to themselves. After school, they stayed around and worked for a construction company puttin' in the REA lines. The whole time they lived in Amerada, they was havin' run-in's with the cops and the other riff-raff. Whipped hell out of the local bully and sort of got that problem under control."

The old man pauses while he seems to deliberate. He then smiles and continues.

"Afore it was over with, them two boys had slipped through local history like a greased eel, an' we never even got to say good-bye to 'em. The Kravens waited about a year after the boys arrived before they made their first big mistake. They beat one of the kid's fathers nearly to death with clubs. Hurt him bad enough to put him in the hospital. They didn't seem to know it then, but they'd just jabbed a big wasp nest with a crooked short stick. By then, that kid and his buddy were as close as a clenched fist. Before the kid could react to his father's injury, both his parents were killed upstate somewhere. When that happened, them two boys turned into the sheriff's worst nightmare. Hate broke out in the two of 'em. When that happened, they turned their attention to revenge.

"Times were hard here after the war. After more than 10 years of bad cops and no justice, the town was no longer building character in its young 'uns. I guess after all that time of bein' beat down, none of the grown ups had much character left. The county had a bigger problem than character though and that problem kept everybody in an unspeakable panic. Girls kept disappearin' from there and near 'bouts, one a them my second cousin. As I recall, the total was about a dozen women and one boy missin' in just shy of 10 years. By then, the whole town was as skittery as a school of mullet when the red fish start feedin'.

"The sheriff investigated and always came up with the same conclusion. Run-a-ways was what he called 'em, but none ever came back or wrote home from wherever they went. Everybody thought that sort of strange, but let it slip by unchallenged 'cause they were all scared of the sheriff and his kin.

"One night after the last girl disappeared, there was this big fire out by the marsh. The fire was on land posted by the sheriff's kin with nobody allowed to go there. A shack and moonshine still owned by some of the sheriff's kinfolk burned to the ground. Fire burned all night. By the time the smoke had settled, one of the sheriff's brothers and his nephew was missin'; worst bullies of the lot they were. The nephew turned up dead in the ruins of the shack. The brother was never heard from again. It was like the earth had swallered him up.

"Sheriff's department got all excited and did a lot of lookin' fer somethin'. They spent near a week ransackin' houses in town, even lookin' in houses that had been closed up fer a long time. People didn't know what the cops was lookin' fer and the cops wouldn't say. Cops couldn't seem to find anything that mattered. Afore long, the searchin' stopped and things got back to normal with the town folks intimidated all to hell, but even more 'n before.

"About then, a county election fer sheriff came along. By then, the sheriff had been in office more 'n 10 years. He had hired most all his relatives as deputies. Not many people was votin' by then 'cause the sheriff always won and it didn't seem likely he should. Sheriff didn't win this time, though; lost by a landslide. Turned out later that the sheriff's kin rigged all the passed elections so he'd win. This time them two boys re-rigged it so the incumbent lost."

The old man gives a subdued chuckle as he recalls the way it happened.

"There was a big town meetin' the very next night. Meetin' called for by circulars dropped on a dark night by an airplane. The flyers claimed that two of the missin' girls had been found alive. Time ran out on the sheriff right then. The next thing anybody knew he'd stuck a gun in his mouth and pulled the trigger.

"People came from everywhere. Biggest town meetin' anybody ever heard of. All the streets blocked by jammed traffic. Cars parked on lawns and all over the town square, even backed-up way out on the highway. By then, the sheriff's deputies was scared near half to death. Most of 'em disappeared. Them as stayed, was hidin' in their houses. Most seemed ta have fled back to wherever they came from, and the place was in complete chaos.

"'Bout that time, these two kids showed up again with two of the girls who'd disappeared, name of Melissa St. Clair and Sarah Woodling. The Woodling girl spoke at the town meeting fer 20 minutes. When she finished, everybody started burning the houses of the sheriff, his kin, and his deputies. Seems the sheriff's kin was kidnapping girls fer their own pleasure. When they was through with 'em, they fed 'em to this big old alligator way back in the marsh. The entire sheriff's department was involved. The gator was a pet of the moonshiners. They'd call him by clanging an old school bell bolted to a tree near his hidey-hole. The gator's why the victims always disappeared without a trace."

My God, my people were right in the middle of all this.

"While the sheriff and the deputy's houses were burnin', a big wind came up and the fire hot and angry like a blacksmith's forge started jumpin' from one house t' other. By the time 'twas over with, the whole town was burned to the ground. Th' story goes that some of the deputies died that night when they didn't get out of town fast enough and got caught by either the people or the fire. Nobody knows how many bodies were never recovered. Place was a cinder by the time the fire finished with it."

The town meeting apparently turned into the modern version of a biblical stoning.

"There was a big investigation by the state attorney general's office. They tried to learn somethin' about the fire and the cops, but not much came of it. Hell, they couldn't even figure out how many cops had disappeared much less where they went. Every kind of town record had been lost in the fire. Most everybody had left the town site by the time the attorney general's people got there. Nobody seemed to know where the people had gone. Those two boys hung around fer a spell. They built a tower outta rock and put the gator-bell from the marsh in the top of it to make a memorial to the people who'd died. Sometimes when the wind blows hard enough out there, you can hear that bell ringin' from a distance. It's as though the spirits of the departed are pullin' the chain.

"The refinery was mostly destroyed by the riot too. After the smoke had settled, the oil company decided that it weren't worth rebuilding with oil production down the way it was. It was cheaper to lay a pipeline to somewhere else. The people as was left didn't have much to say to the state investigators about what had happened. Nobody ever arrested or prosecuted."

Holy mother Jesus, I've got all this in that chest. I've got the entire story.

"A few locals stayed around the old town site tryin' to rebuild their houses and what was left of their miserable lives. Place was peaceful then, everybody certain they was shed of the sheriff and his kin. The county seat moved to Shidler with a new sheriff's department. The new one is a lot smaller 'n it used to be.

"The next summer a big hurricane came right across what was left of the town. It was the biggest hurricane anyone could remember. The storm hovered above the old town with tornadoes workin' in there like a nest of snakes. When it was finished, nothing was left by then but the bell tower and the stone walls of a couple houses.

"Bell tower's still standin' out there, mostly all by itself amongst the old foundations. Hurricane made the marsh a lot bigger 'n it was before. 'Twas like a modern day Sodom and Gomorrah. It was as though some giant hand came down and purified the place. An artesian well sprang up atop The-Hundred-&-Forty-Foot-Hill where one never was afore. Best water ye ever tasted. Every year on September 12th, a couple hundred people go out there, ring the bell a dozen times, say a prayer and leave. Not as many now, everybody's gettin' old. Hardly find anyone anymore who claims to be from Amerada. They're mostly all dead I guess."

Thank you, old man; you've given me the beginning of my life.

The oldster continues, "Not much out there, but the tower. If you're goin' there have a look at it afore you leave, it's worth seein'." He hands Neal the map in its tube. "Take this with you, it might come in handy."

"I wouldn't want to take your map," Neal says. "You might need it later on."

"Son, I been going out there every year since this all happened," the old man mutters in a strong voice. "I think I can still remember how ta get there. Ya'll take the map, you'll need it."

"What happened to those two boys you mentioned?" Neal asks.

"Nobody knows. They just sort of disappeared like smoke in a high wind." He glances at the three young people. "If your daddy was Axle Mannheim, you can be proud of him. He was one a them two boys that showed up when the town needed help. You got any idea whatever happened to him?"

"No, sir, maybe I'll find out some day," Neal mumbles, in a voice clogged with emotion. "You've already solved a great mystery for me, though."

Neal, Megan and Margo all say, "Good-bye," before the three of them stand to walk toward the truck. Neal realizes that he doesn't know who they've been talking with, so he turns back to the old man sitting on the bench. There is a washed out look about him now. His hands are clasped in front of him with his elbows resting on his knees.

"Thanks again for your hospitality, mister," Neal says. "By the way, what's your name?"

"Sheldon Woodling," he answers, as he arises to head for his truck.

Neal watches the man climb into his vehicle, and close the door with a bang before he drives away. He doesn't look back, only waves one time with a casual hand out the driver's window. Neal speaks to no one in particular.

"Probably a distant relative, maybe a cousin."

Megan's green eyes dance, as she offers, "I have a feeling we can probably count on that."

The approximate 51 seconds of crazed initial introduction at the bench has turned into good breathless stuff like some shimmering fairy tale. Neal fires up the diesel and heads south out of town toward Amerada and the place of the unknown. The trio finds the creek. They ford the watercourse at a riffle with the truck in four-wheel drive. They climb a steep incline on the far bank. Beyond the bank is a two-wheel tire-track trail. The narrow trail leads them across a grass-covered countryside.

In the middle distance stands the bell tower. Further to the southeast the walls of two native stone houses stand like solitary sentinels. Neal stops at the tower where they read the inscriptions on two bronze plaques. The tower is about 20-feet tall with a small alcove at the top, open to the elements on four sides.

As they prepare to leave, a forceful gust of wind buffets the truck. The bell peals three strong tones, before falling silent. The sound is like a welcome before the velocity of the wind reduces to what it had been.

Neal drives west on the trail. Eventually, they come to a sagging barbed-wire fence near a hill. By then, the trail has reduced to two faint indentations in a grass-covered surface. Sheldon had indicated that the rise in the distance is The-Hundred-&-Forty-Foot-Hill. Neal stops the truck as near the hill as possible. He stands beside the truck and removes a bronze canister from behind his seat.

Together, the young people cross the dilapidated fence. They walk through knee-deep wild grass, scattered brush, and small cactus plants toward the rise in the distance. The top of the hill towers above everything. Its summit is densely covered by a grove of trees. The grass along the way is thickly saturated by clusters of small white fall flowers with yellow centers.

Neal walks looking down, lost in thought as he carries what is left of his mother in a bronze urn. A covey of bobwhite quail returns everyone to reality when they explode into the air. They glide from view to become lost in the distant trees. Megan turns to her sister.

"Feel like singing when we get there?"

"Yeah," Margo answers, "maybe something special for the occasion."

According to his mother's letter, the site will be at the brow of the hill on the marsh side. The searchers top the crest where they stand looking down at a special elegance that can only be created by nature.

Big Oliver Marsh lies below them. Its startling loveliness is radiant in a warm autumn day. To the southeast stands an endless sea of tall waving grass traversed by potholes and narrow channels. Waterfowl arise from the marsh to vanish in the distance like thin bands of smoke. A quail calls from the tree line behind them. Other members of the flock answer the call.

The newcomers begin to move along the crest of the hill. Finally, they hear it before they see anything. The haunting fluted music of a wind chime falls softly on the listening land.

They move toward the sound until they come to an area where the brush has been hooked back from beneath a tree. The old stubs are still visible above the earth. They enter the clearing that surrounds a place that is almost too beautiful for words. Neal recognizes it immediately for what it is. This is a place where memories lie tucked away like private treasures.

A massive red oak tree towers above the summi, its branches flung wide. Some actually touch the ground. The tree's roots grip the top of a layered rock ledge. An artesian well bubbles to the surface at the base of a limestone shelf. Spring water streams down the hill toward the marsh. The narrow waterbed has been lined by someone with fist-sized river-washed rocks. A solitary circular pool forms at the crest. The circumference of the pool is encrusted with watercress. The soft earth near the pool is densely embedded with deer tracks.

Sunshine dapples through the tree canopy to cascade down on ancient humus. Thin short grass and a rectangular slab of polished, gleaming silver-white stone lie in the mottled-shade of the large tree. The stone cap lies in quiet repose. The memorial is constructed of a swirling mass of Silver Cloud granite. The massive horizontal ledger is about six inches thick. The perimeter of the stone has been smoothed and rounded so that the honed edges curve into the polished top. The spherical edge is ornately carved with a wide raised band of oak leaves. Each leaf clings to the next in an endless pattern.

The design is finely sculptured by a master hand. The craftsmanship is exquisite.

The oakleaf band completes the circumference of the stone to conclude at the base of a deeply carved gnarled outline of a tree. The upper branches of the carving enshroud the bottom of an inscription. The far end of the slab is impressed with four names carved into the polish, one above the other:

Axle Reed Mannheim
Tobias Graham Fitzpatrick
Melissa Grace St. Clair
Sarah Dawn Woodling
Etched in the polished stone beneath the names is a verse:
Immortality
Do not stand at my grave and weep.
I am not there. I do not sleep.
I am a thousand winds that blow.
I am the diamond glints on snow.
I am the sunlight on ripening grain.
I am the gentle autumn rain.
When you awake in the mornings hush
I am the swift unflinging rush of quiet birds in circling flight.
I am the soft star shine at night.
Do not stand at my grave and cry.
I am not there, I did not die.

The slab lies by itself, isolated from everything by a sizable band of succulent ground cover. The foliage is blue-green with thick cabbage-like leaves. Near the giant oak tree stands a tall Japanese lantern in the shape of a pagoda. The edifice sets sentinel like on four short legs. The object is nearly five feet tall and made of dark volcanic rock.

Vertical stone grills near the top are pierced by numerous square holes. Through the grills of the upper chamber can be seen a small metal wind chime. The chime tinkles melodically in the breeze. Inlaid into the base of the grill is a small bronze plaque turned green by the patina of time. The inscription reads:

    I mark the time until you return again to me

    A song by every breeze

    That sings of once upon a time

    The Song of Mannheim

    Below the inscription is carved a single word: *Eventyre.*

Neal studies the word as he tries desperately to recall its meaning. The bottom legs of the pagoda rest on four small granite pads nestled flush with the earth. Between two of the legs rests a canister similar to the one Neal holds.

Neal stands on the hill overlooking the place where his father's story began and ended more than a generation ago. Behind him, the chime sings to itself. A breeze breathes against his body. It touches his face and rustles his hair.

The breeze caresses the backs of his hands as it swirls around him in cool autumn shards. A sound accompanies the breeze. The tone is but a murmuring whisper that bends the thin grass beneath the tree. As the leaves of the giant oak rustle, he remembers the meaning of the word. The sound of the leaves soothes him like nothing has since the small distant sound of his mother's voice. From all those years ago, he remembers her murmuring endearment, "Eventyre, my little one, Eventyre."

When he was very small and she had nearly vanished from the depths of his memory, he could still hear the sound of her voice filled with affection. Years later, he learned the meaning. The word is Gaelic and means, "Once Upon a Time."

With the memory comes an indescribable emotion. Neal stands on the land where his family once trod in time gone by. Nothing shines brighter in his mind than his mother's writing of this place. She told of the people who lived here and shaped her life.

In the background, the two sisters' sing a harmony sweet enough to make the angels cry. When the last note has been whipped away by the breeze, Neal stands silently for a while. He is so deeply moved by being here it is hard to endure.

He has heard *America the Beautiful* sung 1,000 times without really understanding what the words meant, but now during an autumn day, on a high hill in a very special place he understands it all at last. *"Freedom purchased by the lives of others is priceless."*

There is a solace in knowing this place will always be here, its beauty holding the memory of his parents forever young, the earth never yielding to time or the endless seasons that pass.

Neal turns toward the crest of the hill as he removes the top of the urn. He holds it at arms length as he inverts the canister. The ashes drift with the wind as they curl out over Oliver Marsh to cascade down into the green leaves of Nature's bosom. The words come tumbling out as the ashes vanish, "Once upon a time, my mother, once upon a time."

When the last small particle has found its final resting place, Neal strides to the pagoda where he stoops and pushes the reassembled container between two of the legs. Two cells remain empty, perhaps to be filled later by some other visitor like himself. Neal closes his eyes as he listens to the call of the wildness around him. The sound is the ancient voice of time walking the land.

In memory of Max R. Ibach

Made in the USA
Columbia, SC
22 May 2019